The

By

For my friend Gerald Griffin, who sadly died in
December 2020.
We spent many happy hours with him and his wife
Jenny cruising on and around the River Dart.
Much missed, fondly remembered.

This story was inspired by a casual remark from
George Baker, good friend, and former
navy engineer.
I hope it lives up to expectations.

*To gary
with very best wishes*

The Grey Zone

Find Ed Lane on Facebook:
https://www.facebook.com/ed.lane.31

Visit his website for the latest news:
www.edtheauthor.wixsite.com/the-books-of-ed-lane

Email:
edtheauthor@gmail.com

Bowman Publishing

First Published 2021 by Bowman Publishing,
Hundleby, England.
Printed by Amazon.

Full-length Novels by Ed Lane.

(All the following titles are available in all ebook formats from Amazon).

The 'Going Dark' Series

(featuring Gill Keane nee Somers)

A Circling of Vultures

Terrible Beauty

The Lunatic Game

A Circling of Hawks

The 'Fields of Fire' Trilogy

(featuring David Troy aka Rick Lacey)

Blood Debt

Dragonfire

Dust to Dust

Chris Lennox Stories

To Fight Another Day

To Serve Another Day

To Live Another Day

To Dare Another Day

The following titles are available in paperback and ebook formats:

To Brave Another Day

To Win Another Day

a western novella

Bannerman:

Blood Runs Thicker Than Water

Acknowledgements

I would especially like to thank my beta reader, Veronica Stonehouse, for suggesting improvements and finding and correcting my errors.

My thanks also go to the Royal Navy for supplying details of their maritime interdiction methods and tactics as outlined in this book.

I would usually dedicate my books to a worthwhile military charity. In this instance I have decided to support The Royal British Legion.
So far my book sales have raised many hundreds of pounds for worthy military causes and I would like to say a big thank you to everyone who contributed by buying them.
The cost of donations is not part of the cover price but come from my own funds.

The Grey Zone
Related to hybrid warfare, the term commonly refers to power being employed to achieve national objectives in a way that falls short of physical conflict. Such warfare is conducted in
"the grey zone".

April 2023

It was a high spring tide pushed by a strong westerly gale that raised the water level in the River Dart above normal and sucked the body from the bank. It floated upstream just below surface level until the tide turned and it floated back towards the sea, bouncing off the hulls of moored small craft until it became entangled in a mooring line. Putrefying gasses in the body caused it to rise to the surface where it bobbed free and went on the ebb tide towards the lower ferry and the Kingswear Marina. There it lodged between a pontoon and the hull of a yacht until the weather moderated and the yacht owner's wife, thinking it was discarded clothing poked at it with a boat hook and screamed as the body turned and the ravaged face broke surface.

Marina workers hauled the water-logged body onto the pontoon and waited, shuffling their feet and fielding questions from passing boat owners until the police arrived an hour later, having come from their headquarters in Exeter, closely followed by the Scenes of Crime Officer and the duty medical officer who pronounced the man dead from multiple gunshot wounds.

It was the beginning of a mystery which was to have far-reaching, complex and dangerous repercussions.

1

Chichester

The official looking Jaguar pulled up and the driver climbed out, hesitating as he glanced around as if unsure of his surroundings. His head came up and he gave a brief smile as the wide front door of the house opened and a man stepped out into the hazy morning sunlight.

"Colonel Lacey is it, sir?" The driver called.

The man nodded. He had a look on his face that was between concern and puzzlement. "Who's asking?"

The driver scurried around the car's bonnet to reach the nearside rear door and put his fingers on the handle. "I've been driving around for ages looking for this place, sir, it's a bugger to find."

"Uh, huh," Lacey said. "Place is new. Even the mailman has problems." *And that's the way I like it,* he didn't bother to add. "What is it you want?" He had a slight accent, somewhere on the eastern seaboard of America.

The driver opened the door and a tall spare figure climbed out.

"Thank you, Jack," he said to the driver.

"Yessir, General. Thought we'd never get here."

Major-general Mark Sparrow nodded in an absent-minded way, his eyes fixed on Lacey. The offside rear door opened and another man came out, shorter, stockier and darker, he moved like an athlete, his face neutral and his eyes narrowed against the sun.

"That you, Ben?" Lacey called. His voice was quiet but it carried over the twenty metres between them.

"Morning, Rick. Nice to see you again," Brigadier Ben Reid replied. "Can we come in?"

"I guess this isn't a social call but, yeah, come on in. I'll get the coffee on."

Lacey showed them into the kitchen which had open bi-fold doors and a distant view of the waters of Chichester Harbour.

Reid walked to the doors and nodded. "Nice house. Good place to retire to."

Lacey showed Sparrow to a stool and turned on the percolator before answering. "Suits us."

"Oh, yes," Reid said. "How is the good Doctor Andee?"

"Médicin sans Frontières," Lacey said. He didn't elaborate, he didn't need to.

"Therefore you're at a bit of a loose end," Sparrow spoke for the first time.

Lacey gave him an arch look. "Not that you'd notice, Mark. Plenty to do around here and there's the boat to look after."

"Oh, yes, the boat," Sparrow said as if remembering it for the first time.

"How do you like it?" Lacey said.

"I haven't seen it," Sparrow replied.

Lacey pointed to the cups. "The coffee."

"Oh, yes. Black, no sugar."

"White and two," Reid said. He walked over to the breakfast bar and perched on a stool. "You're looking fit, Rick. Keeping in shape I see."

"Apart from the leg. Still gives me gyp on occasion, when the weather's cold."

"Yes, bad that, but you recovered well."

"I had a good doctor."

"Plus points all round," Reid said and grinned.

Lacey looked from one to the other. "Good as it is to see you, as I said, this can't be a social call. What's up?"

Reid's face became business-like. "You're still on the reserve list."

Lacey gave him a slow nod. "At my discretion. It was written into my contract."

Sparrow held up a hand. "We're not here to force an issue. We need your help. Purely voluntarily of course."

Lacey pulled a face, his grey eyes narrowing. "My currency has lapsed. Despite what Ben said I'm not in any condition to take to the field. What use could I possibly be to the Sharp End?"

"You're doing yourself an injustice," Sparrow said and put down his untasted coffee. "You are one of the finest operatives that ever served with the ISPA."

Lacey smiled but there was no humour in it. "The International Special Projects Arm. I thought it had been disbanded after I retired."

"That's what we want the world to think," Reid said. "We're still operational but it's all much deeper undercover now. The politicians prefer it that way; they don't want to be seen to get their hands dirty. Nothing in the papers, everything swept nicely under the carpet."

"You sound bitter, Ben."

Reid grimaced. "It's been a fight all the way. Even more difficult now that we've left the EU; cooperation is harder to get. Podzimski's gone back to GSG-9 in Berlin, your American president isn't keen on our methods and has withdrawn the American contingent and the French ... well you know the French, always want to go their own way and get kicked in the balls for it. However, all governments want to appear squeaky clean but like their problems to disappear. It's a hard line to walk. One mistake on our part and the axe will fall."

Lacey smiled again but this time he meant it. "I'm beginning to see the light. Is this where you don't want the ISPA to get its hands dirty?"

"There is a small problem that perhaps you could help us with," Sparrow said. A hank of hair had fallen across his forehead and he brushed it away, giving himself time to think.

Lacey watched him with a sudden spurt of affection. Sparrow had been his commanding officer throughout his time with the organisation and he had a great deal of time for him. Reid had taken over when Sparrow had retired and Lacey knew that Sparrow had been drawn back in an attempt to influence his decision on whatever it was that was about to come.

"Spit it out, Mark," he said. "I'm listening."

Sparrow gave a sober nod. "That's encouraging."

"I'm not making any promises but I'll hear what you have to say."

"I'll leave it to Ben to give you the basic details," Sparrow said.

Reid swigged his coffee and put the cup down. He took a breath and began. "About two months ago a body was fished out of the River Dart. It was a man who had been shot three times. Twice in the chest and once in the head. The head shot was what you Americans call a through and through and so was one of the chest shots. The third shot didn't pass through, it hit a bone and the bullet was deflected down and ended lodged in the pelvic girdle. The forensic people retrieved it and found a match. It was an odd calibre, 5.8mm. The same calibre as used in the QSW-06 silenced pistol. The pistol now in service with Chinese Special Forces. You can begin to see the problem."

2

"China!" Lacey said.

Reid nodded. "China. That's not the worst of it. The man whose body was fished out of the Dart was an American. A navy commander to be exact. He'd been working at the Britannia Naval College as a lecturer in anti-submarine warfare, at least, that was his cover but we think he could have been navy intelligence. The Yanks, pardon the expression, are jumping up and down at the lack of progress in the investigation, the Devon and Cornwall Police are a bit out of their depth, and the US Navy are threatening to send over an NCIS investigator."

"Where do I come in to all this?" Lacey asked. "I'm no cop, I'm a soldier."

Sparrow coughed and raised a hand to butt in. "You're American. If the NCIS think we have appointed one of their own to the problem they may agree to let us get on with it. You won't be alone of course, we shall give you all the help you need."

"I'm sorry, Mark, but I still don't get it. What is it I'm supposed to accomplish that the police can't?"

"There's something going on down in darkest Devon that is beyond the experience of a regional police service. We have ways and means that they do not have access to … and methods they cannot employ. It's not the murder that we are concerned with as much as the reason for it. Why kill an American serviceman? What could it possibly achieve except to bring the Americans' attention to the matter as it has done? What is so important that whoever killed the commander saw no alternative but to resort to murder?"

Lacey shook his head. "I can see some gaping holes in the logic there. You may be jumping to conclusions. There's a big market in weapons, most seeping in from Eastern Europe where the gangs have connections with the Chinese black market weapons trade. Anyone could have picked up a silenced pistol for a couple of thou. Maybe the commander ... what was his name ...?"

"I didn't say," Reid said, "but it was Forrestal, Commander Adam Forrestal."

Lacey sucked in his cheeks. "The same as the aircraft carrier, USS Forrestal. Named after a former Secretary of the US Navy."

"I believe the family are distant cousins, but you can see why NCIS is concerned," Sparrow said.

"I was about to say that maybe Commander Forrestal was killed for whatever real reason he was here," Lacey continued, "nothing to do with a Chinese handgun."

"You might have had a point," Reid said, "except that the QSW-06 model is new. If it had been the old Type 67, which is 7.62mm, which it replaced, there might be some credence to your supposition but the Chinese aren't letting their new covert pistol onto the black market, not yet anyway."

13

"We'd like you to stir things up a little, try to find out how the land lies and what is really going on down there," Sparrow said. "Stir the waters and who knows what will rise to the surface."

"It could get messy," Lacey said.

"We're aware of that."

"Which is why you want me. None of the stirred up mud sticking to the ISPA, not directly. Retired American, living a quiet life with no traceable connection to an undercover dirty tricks, anti-terrorist unit that doesn't exist." Lacey gave a small grunt of bitter amusement. "I thought that all the deep cover precautions when I left was for my benefit but it seems it was a two-way street. There's no way anyone can connect me to the ISPA no matter how deep they dig."

"It *was* for your benefit," Sparrow said. "It's the same for every ISPA operative who could be subject to reprisals."

"But you're happy for me to stick my head above the parapet again, Mark."

"No, not happy. I have strong reservations about many things, including the impracticality of it but not least any threat to your own safety. However, I have been reluctantly convinced that you are the best man for this particular assignment. Your experience uniquely qualifies you."

Lacey gave him a long hard look before he nodded. "Okay, Mark, if it was anyone other than you I'd treat that as a load of bullshit. I know you wouldn't feed me a line, you're too straight-up for that. What's the plan?"

Reid grinned. "Are you in, or what?"

"I'll decide once I've heard what you have in mind … and what this help is you talked about."

"We had two scenarios in mind," Reid said. "The first was a straight replacement for the commander, insert you into the college as a lecturer."

Lacey shook his head. "Wouldn't work. I know squat about anti-submarine warfare."

"No, we thought you could lecture on marine insertion operations but then we had a better idea."

"Which is …?"

"You take your own boat as a visiting American and use it as a base working from the Kingswear Marina. Much lower profile but in the heart of things."

Lacey gave a reluctant nod. "Could work as a basic premise but it's a little thin on content."

Reid grinned. "That's where the help comes in. Look, if you're in I need to know now, I have a call to make."

"I'm in," Lacey said. "I'll probably regret it but I have to admit to becoming intrigued."

Reid grinned and took his smart phone from his pocket. He headed for the door. "Give me ten minutes."

Lacey frowned and turned to Sparrow. "Where's he off to?"

"He'll explain when he returns. Listen … David, I'm sorry to drag you into this. If it wasn't so important …"

Lacey pulled a face. "It's a long time since anyone called me that. David Troy is dead and buried. It's something that's keeping me alive."

"I just can't bring myself to call you Rick," Sparrow said with a slight smile.

Lacey tilted his head. "I much prefer Rick these days but I know what you mean. I take it that Ben doesn't know."

"Apart from Andee, and Gunn Podzimski, I'm the only other living person that knows David Troy survived the assassination attempts. None of us would ever breathe a word."

"I know that," Lacey said. "One thing bothers me though. Troy was a combat specialist. Rick Lacey spent the last five years with the ISPA mainly driving a desk and planning ops. I'm not sure I'll be up for any rough stuff."

"You still have your PDWs?"

Lacey put a hand behind his back and eased out a Sig P228 pistol from its holster hidden under his loose-fitting shirt. "Never without a personal defence weapon."

Sparrow pursed his lips. "And I daresay you have kept in practice."

"When I can."

"I have no worries on that score. You were always far too good for the competition."

"There will be a price to pay, Mark. One big favour deserves another."

"Which is?"

"I haven't heard from Andee for a while. I need to know where she is and that she's okay."

16

Sparrow nodded. "I'll do my best."

There was a clatter from the door and Reid came back in, a smile on his face. "Come outside, Rick, there's someone I want you to meet."

Lacey put the pistol back in its place. "Who?"

"Your wife."

Surprise flashed across Lacey's face and he pushed past Reid. Outside in the sun, leaning on the wing of a Mercedes saloon, was a woman he did not know. The sight gave him an unexpected jolt of pain. She was tall and willowy with a streak of grey in her auburn hair, a woman who might once have been very beautiful, but with the weight of untold cares and unforgiving years was now just very attractive. She stood and held out her hand.

"Hello, Colonel, my name's Gill, as in fish, Gill Keane."

3

Camberley
One week earlier

Gill stood at her office window that overlooked the Sandhurst Military Academy and ran a hand through her hair. She could see a slight reflection of herself in the glass and did not like the hazy image that seemed a ghostly presence. She wondered if it was a presentiment.

She was not given to depression but this particular day the past lay heavily on her shoulders as memories bubbled up, brought to the surface by the phone call of yesterday and the visitor she was expecting at any moment to press the security alarm buzzer at the front door; another ghost from the past which had come back to haunt her.

Her old friend and colleague, Stu Dalgleish, tapped on the doorframe to attract her attention. "Penny for 'em, boss."

She turned and gave him a weak smile. "Not worth that much. Have you finished?"

Stu shook his head, the former SAS man's normally lugubrious face even more solemn than usual. "Not yet but almost. The end of an era. We still have two teams out in Iraq but their contracts are coming to an end. The pandemic put paid to a lot of people travelling and needing protection. We never really recovered from 2020 and it's been hard going ever since."

18

Gill shrugged. "We had a good run for our money but the writing was on the wall when Colonel Tim caught the virus and died; the heart went out of us then."

"Yeah, sad time for all of us but that's the business; knuckle down and crack on couldn't stand a knock like that. Bill Cowley retired, Tonka and Mo have taken up sheep farming in Wales, may the gods of farming help them, and most of the other boys have found themselves little sinecures. Just you and me and what's left of Achilles' Shield to wrap up."

"Will you be all right, Stu?"

"Me? I've got no problems. Missus Dalgleish Q.C. makes more money per day than I'd earn in a month. Her chambers are going great guns, she has more business than she can handle."

"How is the beautiful Ann? Give her my love."

Stu grinned and it lit up his face. "She's never better. Marrying her was the best thing I ever did. What about you, boss? What will you do?"

Gill shrugged. "Not really thought about it yet. I put enough by in the good times not to worry about keeping the wolf from the door. I thought maybe I'd visit my father in Spain now that all the travel restrictions have been lifted. I haven't seen him or Aunt Matilde for three years. Kept in touch via Zoom but that's not the same."

"It's been tough all round," Stu said. "Anyway I'm off now, gotta pick the kids up from school. Will you lock up?"

19

Gill pointed to her desk. "Just leave the keys there. There's something I have to do before I go."

Stu raised his eyebrows. "Oh! Anything I need to worry about?"

"Probably not but I'll keep you in the loop if necessary."

Stu grinned. "Sounds suitably need to know. See you tomorrow, boss."

"Night, Stu. Take good care of those lovely girls of yours."

Stu stopped in the doorway and gave her a mock salute. "I intend to. Same goes for you. Be good."

"And if you can't be good be careful," Gill whispered the response as Stu whistled his way down the stairs. She heard the latch click behind him and sat with a sigh behind her desk.

It really was the end of an era. The security and close protection company she had set up with her late husband Ricky, Colonel Tim Bailey, Stu's wife Ann and several ex-SAS soldiers who had fallen foul of the government, was being wound up while it could still pay its debts. Work, as Stu had said, had all but dried up and there was no option but to shut up shop. It had been a good ten years but all good things had to come to an end sometime. She tried to comfort herself with the platitude but it didn't work. She realised she had not felt this down since Ricky died of an accidental morphine overdose back in 2013. Had she really been a widow that long? And maybe there was something in the old chestnut about thirteen being an unlucky number.

The door buzzer sounded loud and she jumped as it brought her out of her reverie. She pressed the intercom button. "Yes?"

"It's Blake."

She did not reply but pressed the latch release. There were soft footfalls on the stairs. For such a tall man, Blake was light on his feet.

He rapped lightly on her door. Light feet, light touch. It brought back memories, not all of them pleasant.

"Come in, Blake."

He had the look of an aging public schoolmaster, affable but stern with the boys when it was needed. "Good evening, Gill. I hope I find you well."

"Stu and I were talking about pennies earlier and now you turn up, the proverbial bad one."

Blake threw his raincoat over the back of a visitor's chair and sat. "That's a little harsh, especially after all I did for you back in the day."

"And what would MI6 want with a failed businesswoman. I suspect it's payback time."

"I did hear that you were having some difficulties and wondered if I might be of some help."

"What's it going to cost me?"

"Your cynical streak hasn't mellowed over the intervening years."

"I know you of old, Blake. There's always a price to pay for your largesse."

"You and I made a good team once."

"That was when I had a lot to lose ... that's not the case now."

"I am so pleased to hear it, except you are not being entirely honest with me. You have your company to lose."

Gill gave him a hard look. "You're too late with that line, Blake. The company's lost already. I'm winding it up."

"It's not like you to give up so easily. That's not the Gill Keane I knew of old."

"Times change, time changes people. Now, enough of the fencing. What are you here for?"

"I have a job for you ... if you're up for it."

4

Chichester

Lacey reached out and took the woman's hand. It was cool and firm, almost masculine in the strength of the grip. "You can drop the colonel, ma'am, call me Rick."

She flinched as if stung and blinked. "Oh!"

He kept hold of her fingers although her grip had slackened. "Something wrong, ma'am?"

She forced a smile. "No, no, nothing. Pleased to meet you … and *you* can drop the ma'am, it's Gill."

Lacey gave her a searching look before he nodded and released her hand. "Okay, Gill." He sized her up. She was almost as tall as he was with their eyes on the same level. A green-eyed redhead which made him think the hair colour was natural and not out of a Stacey Dooley bottle. Late thirties or early forties he guessed, with an expensive taste in clothes; maybe five years younger than he was. He sensed the steel beneath the attractive façade and he liked what he saw. "I guess I made a good choice of wife."

She blushed then. "They've told you?"

The blush pleased him; she couldn't fake that. "A few minutes ago. Kind of a surprise."

"They thought it might be better for your cover. A couple raises less suspicion than a man alone."

"Maybe," Lacey said and his eyes misted for a brief second as a flashback occurred of the couple of East German assassins who had nearly killed him. He hadn't suspected them until almost too late. He carried the scars of that mistake together with several metal pins in his leg.

Reid called to them. "Come inside. We can make a start on the detail. We've been working on legends for you both."

Lacey grinned. "Could be interesting."

He made more coffee and handed the cups round before settling on a bar stool where he could see everyone without turning his head. Gill had found a seat around the kitchen diner and Sparrow sat at his place with an elbow resting on the breakfast bar. Reid stood by the open doors and Lacey noticed he had a briefcase that the driver must have given him when he and Gill were getting acquainted.

Reid opened the case and took out a sheaf of papers and a laptop which he placed on the table alongside Gill with an apologetic bob of the head. "Firstly I'd like to introduce Gill to the team. Rick Lacey you've met, I'm Ben Reid and the gentleman at the counter is Major-general Mark Sparrow.

"Major-general retired," Sparrow said.

Reid nodded a confirmation and turned to Lacey. "For your information, Rick, Gill is with MI6."

Gill shook her head. "Uh huh, Ben. I'm not with MI6, I'm just what is quaintly and colloquially known as a 'K', a paid contractor who can be disowned if the shit hits the fan."

Lacey couldn't quite hide a grin. "Sounds about right."

Reid was too old a hand to let it faze him. "Happy to be corrected. Anyway, Gill has impeccable credentials," he pointed at the file, "worked undercover in Spain and Northern Ireland, firstly with 14 Independent Company, the Det, and then attached to the SAS with MI6 oversight. She speaks Spanish and Basque like a native."

"That's going to help in Dartmouth," Lacey said.

Gill beamed a smile at him. "You never know, sweetheart, when it may come in useful."

Lacey laughed. "Touché, Señora ..."

"Arnold," Reid said. "That's your cover name. Rick and Gill Arnold. You're originally from Maine, Rick."

"Okay, let's get something straight right off," Lacey said. "I spent a deal of time in Vermont and I know more about that place than Maine which I only visited twice and know as much about it as you could write on the back of a beer mat."

Reid bowed. "I stand corrected again. But while we're on you as a subject I'd best let Gill know what she's in for working with you." He grinned at Gill, "Rick has worked with counter-terrorist organisations such as GSG-9 and GIGN across Europe and the Caribbean. He's a former Green Beret and knows his way around most of the weaponry you're ever likely to encounter. A safe pair of hands. He's also a skilled sailor with his own motor cruiser which will be your base of operations."

Lacey nodded. "It's got the latest digital communication systems. I had it fixed up when we sailed around the Med and the Caribbean after we retired."

Gill cocked an eye at him. "*We?*"

"My wife, Andee."

She gave him a tight smile. "What does she think about your proposed bigamy?"

"I haven't told her. She's somewhere in Africa with Médicin sans Frontières. Been out of touch for a while, sat phone's down; battery's gone I guess."

"Aren't you worried?"

Lacey shrugged. "Of course but she can take care of herself."

Sparrow stirred in his seat. "Missus Lacey worked with us for over five years, she's military trained and one of the finest gunshot-wound surgeons in the world. We were sorry to lose her."

Gill frowned. "Big shoes to fill."

Reid coughed. "Can we get back to the subject in hand?"

"My apologies, Brigadier," Sparrow said. "Yes, please continue your briefing."

"*Major-general, Brigadier,*" Gill whispered to herself. "*Exalted company. Just what have I got myself into?*"

As if Reid could hear her he said, "I don't know what MI6 have told you about this op, Gill. We've given an outline to Rick and I'll leave all the data that we have in these files and on this laptop for you both. In essence we are not quite sure what we are dealing with and we're looking to you to dredge up anything you can to throw some light on the happenings in Devon. All we know, or suspect, is that the Chinese are involved and that is bringing our masters out in cold sweats. There is too much riding on our continuing good relations with countries that we trade with, especially now that the focus has moved away from Europe and is now fully international in scope. Losing a trading partner as large as China would put a massive dent in the economy and whatever else you do you must tread carefully."

"No pressure then," Gill said.

"The government cannot be seen to be involved," Sparrow said, "hence dealing with this enigma at third hand. It is not something I am comfortable with but … and it is a big but … there is no other way that we can either contain or remove any threat that Chinese involvement would pose. If they are found to be running clandestine ops on our soil and it comes out, all hell would break loose. Pre-emptive action is sanctioned should it be necessary but confidentiality and deniability are key."

Sparrow rose to his feet and checked his watch. "Ben and I must be going. We will leave you two good people to get to know each other and get on top of your brief." He paused and looked from one to the other. "It will not be easy and it could prove to be extremely dangerous. Good luck and god speed."

5

Lacey poured some more coffee and handed the cup to Gill. "Well, Missus Arnold, what do you make of that?"

Gill pursed her lips and then took a sip of the lukewarm fluid. She crinkled her nose. "Coffee could do with freshening."

Lacey smiled and took the cup from her hand. "Maybe you'd prefer tea."

"I'd prefer an industrial sized gin and tonic but I still have to drive."

Lacey shrugged. "You could stay here. There's plenty of room and we need time to get our stories straight."

She looked at him from under her lashes. "No funny business."

He smiled again. "As if this business wasn't funny enough. No, you're safe. There's a key in the bedroom door if you're feeling nervous."

She gave him a cool appraisal. "You don't look like a lothario."

"I'm not sure that's a compliment."

"Take it whichever way you like."

"It's a gin and tonic then?"

"If you'll join me, I hate drinking alone."

"Sure, why not. I'll rustle up some lunch too, can't drink or think on an empty stomach."

"Fine. While you're doing that I have to make a call."

"You can make it outside on the patio and close the doors if it's private. Is Mister Keane expecting you home?"

She stopped, her hand half in her bag reaching for her smart phone, and turned. "Ricky's dead."

His eyebrows went up and then he nodded. "Ricky … yes, now I understand your momentary shock when I introduced myself."

"You seemed a bit pale around the gills too when you came out."

"You don't miss much, do you? It was when I saw you leaning on the wing of the Merc. My first wife died in one of those and just for a second it took me back. You looked a little like her."

"Your first wife? How many have you had?"

"Just the two."

"And you've mislaid the second."

His grey eyes narrowed and turned glacial. "That's kind of unfair."

Gill felt a shudder zip up her spine. It was as if the man had changed character in an instant, his mask of civility gone. "Yes, you're right, I'm sorry." She saw the tension leave him as quickly as it came. It was a warning sign as sharp and swift as an arrow and it reminded her of a killer she had known in Spain.

"I guess I'm sorry too," he was saying and it brought her mind back from the past. "About your husband. Sorry for your loss."

"It was a long time ago, I'm almost over it, almost but not quite."

"You want to talk about it?"

29

She shook her head. "No. I have this call to make." She pulled the phone from her bag and walked onto the terrace. She didn't bother to close the doors and Lacey could hear her side of the conversation.

"Hi, Stu."

"Yes, sorry about that, I should have left you a note."

"Yes ... look ... I'm going to be away for a while ... can you manage?"

"No it's not a holiday it's a job."

"Could be for a week or two ... you're sure you are okay with that?"

"I can't say over the phone ..."

"Yes, I'll be careful ... stop honking, you're a bloody old woman ..."

"All right ... look, another reason I'm calling. There should be a payment of ten grand coming into the account. It'll keep us going until I get back. It's part payment, they'll be another ten at the end of the job ... call me if the first ten isn't in the account by tomorrow."

"No, I can't say who it's from and you shouldn't try to find out."

"It's clean ... you don't have to worry about that."

"Yes, I'll call if I need you, don't worry."

"Okay ... love to Ann. Ciao."

She wandered back in and showed the phone to Lacey. "My office manager."

Lacey pushed a plate of sandwiches at her. "I didn't know you had an office. Eat before they go cold."

She picked up the bread. "They *are* cold."

He grinned and the man she first met was back. "Then before they go stale. Just eat, I'll fix the drinks."

She stuffed a triangle of bread in her mouth and picked up Reid's file. "Mmm, we need to get going with this," she said around a mouthful of crumbs which sprayed out. She put a hand to her mouth. "Ooh! Sorry."

He laughed. "Nothing a dustpan and brush won't cure."

"It's because you make me nervous."

He tilted his head and raised his eyebrows. "Me? Why?"

She noticed a pale patch on his left cheek as the light caught it. Plastic surgery? "I'm not the nervous type, not normally. I'm not sure why … yet."

He placed her drink on the breakfast bar. "Industrial strength. Maybe it'll straighten you out a little."

She gave him a disgruntled stare and plopped the file down alongside the glass. "Is this our first married tiff?"

"Not on my part; you can tiff away all you want."

That made her laugh. "I have my doubts but maybe we can get along."

"Maybe," he said. "Early days. Just so you know I don't suffer fools and if you're under instructions to keep MI6 in the loop I want to see your reports before they get them."

It was Gill's turn to narrow her eyes but he did not seem to notice ... or care. "My, my, you are the paranoid one."

"Been screwed over too often I don't want it to happen again."

She nodded. "I can identify with that. Same goes for me. Look, speaking of being paranoid, I don't know who you people are. My control at MI6 was cagey about it. I don't like mysteries not when there's danger to life and limb ... my life and limb ... but we can work together on this. I'll have your back if you have mine. Deal?"

"How's the drink?"

She took a sip and grimaced. "Bloody hell, that's almost neat."

He grinned and held out the tonic bottle. "Maybe your idea of industrial and mine don't yet gel."

She grimaced again and it wasn't from the taste of gin.

6

They worked through the afternoon using the legends Reid had supplied as a basis covering all the usual questions they were likely to encounter; how long have you been married, where did you meet, where do you live, what does your husband/wife do for a living, any children etc.?

Lacey was beginning to get the measure of the woman. It was obvious she was a professional and knew what she was doing, adding some pertinent suggestions to the mix that he hadn't thought of. He was always a little wary of attractive women before he got to know them as he'd had his fingers badly burnt at one time. He usually got a feeling early on if he could trust them in the dangerous business they were engaged in but not always and he trod carefully.

It was a warm evening by the time they had completed their first run through and Lacey tossed his notes onto the breakfast bar and checked his watch. "You want to come and meet Andrea Two?"

Gill looked bemused. "Who's Andrea? What does she have to do with this?"

Lacey grinned. "A lot. C'mon, it's a nice evening for a walk."

"Okay give me a minute." She went to her car and took a small overnight bag from the boot. She held it up. "Always carry a change of clothes and shoes, wellies too. Never know when you might need them. I can't walk in these heels."

"I bet you have a flashlight and a pair of binoculars in the glove box," Lacey said.

She smiled and it softened her face. "There's no fooling you."

"Maybe because I'm the same. Spare boots, waterproofs, flashlight and binos, if you want to check my car."

She shook her head. "Uh huh, I'll take your word for it." She opened the bag and pulled out a pair of sturdy flat shoes. "Here, lend me your arm." She gripped his forearm as she slipped off her heels, balancing on one shapely leg at a time as she pulled on the walking shoes and bent down to lace them. "Where are we going?"

"Not far."

He walked her along a pleasant country lane that led away from the house for about half a mile before he turned through a gate at the side of a marina.

"How the rich live," Gill said as she looked over the packed moorings filled with pleasure craft of all shapes and sizes.

He pulled a wry face. "Someone once told me that when you buy a boat it's like emptying your wallet over the can and flushing the money away. Not too far off the mark, I'd say."

She gazed around. "Which one's yours?"

He didn't reply but gestured for her to follow him along the side of a car park and onto a pontoon.

She stopped. "Oh no, don't tell me." She pointed to a dilapidated Princess with dirt streaking its hull and green weed floating gently along its waterline.

He grinned. "Close but no cigar."

She threw her hands wide. "What then?"

"Follow me." He walked ahead along the finger towards the end.

She stopped again, her eyes wide. "That? It's a floating block of flats."

"Fairline Squadron 64. The *Andrea Two*. Bought it second-hand when the bottom fell out of the market a few years back."

"It's huge."

"Sleeps six in style and has room for ten at a pinch. C'mon aboard, let me show you around. You'll need to be familiar with it once we get to Devon."

"Look, I've been thinking about that. I'd rather drive down. We'll need wheels when we get there."

"Not seasick, are you?"

"It just makes sense."

He nodded. "It does. Even so you need to seem at home aboard. Have you sailed?"

"No. Flying was our thing. We have an aging Piper Seneca; it was Ricky's when he was alive. I have my pilot's licence and so do all the company directors."

"Speaking of how the rich live," Lacey said with a grin.

Gill grimaced and nodded at the Fairline. "Yes but nowhere near as expensive as that beauty."

He hunched his shoulders and dropped them. "Family money. I don't have much else I want to do with it."

He held out a hand to help her aboard. She gripped his fingers and stopped for a third time.

"Why do you do it?"

"What?"

"The anti-terrorist business. You don't need to."

"Just something I have to do."

"Because it's there?"

"You could put it like that. I guess I was just born to be a soldier." He pulled on her hand. "C'mon get aboard."

She smiled. "A soldier, a sailor and a pilot went to Devon. There must be a joke in there somewhere."

Lacey felt a sharp twinge of bitterness. "Yeah! And it's usually on me."

Gill followed him through the transom door onto the aft deck. "That was said with feeling."

"Sorry. Don't mean to put a damper on things before they get off the ground."

"Don't worry, I've been shat on from a great height in my time; I know that feeling."

He led them into the sumptuous saloon. "Cabins are down the companionway there are two with en-suite. You can have the master cabin. I'll take the other."

"Separate beds, Mister Arnold?"

"Didn't think you'd want it any other way. I'll keep some clothes in the locker in case anyone gets nosy.

"The stairs lead up to the flybridge which has a duplicate set of controls and instruments with some seating for when the weather's good. I tend to con from there as visibility's better. Full set of navigation instruments, satnav, auto pilot, digital radio, radar, echo-sounder, fish-finder, weather station, the works. Damn thing all but sails itself."

"You run this all by yourself?"

"When I have to. I get the marina staff to help cast off but once we're underway it's easy enough for one to manage."

"Well, I take my hat off to you."

"No big deal. Look, we can have dinner at the yacht club or I can call for a takeaway."

She sat on one of the leather seats. "It's such a lovely evening, why don't we have a takeaway here?"

"Why not. There are glasses and a bottle of Veuve Cliquot in the fridge. This may be our last chance to relax in a long time. Might as well enjoy it while we can."

7

A motorcycle courier arrived at the house the next morning as they were sitting down to breakfast. He brought a large package which Lacey signed for and took into the kitchen.

Gill was downing the last of her coffee and looking at her watch at the same time. "Gotta go. There's a myriad things I need to do before I leave for Devon."

Lacey slit open the wrappings and emptied the contents onto the breakfast bar. "You may want to take some of this with you."

Gill squinted at him. "What is it?"

"Your new life, Missus Arnold. Passport, credit cards, birth certificate, marriage lines, you name it."

"Courtesy of MI6." She stood and prodded the items into a rough circle. "Pretty thorough job. Your stuff's there too."

He grunted. "Wonder what the credit limit is on those cards. American Express Platinum, must be at least ten grand."

Gill gave him a sideways look. "Don't get your hopes up. The bean counters at Riverside will want every penny accounted for."

He grinned. "I'll remember to keep the receipts."

"When are you leaving," she asked.

"Like you I have things to do. Probably tomorrow morning at free-flow through the lock, that's at high tide. The boat just about fits through the gates on the beam width so I like to get a gentle run at it without messing with queueing and mooring lines. The trip will take around ten hours providing the weather holds fair, which it promises to do. It's around a hundred and sixty-five nautical miles at an average of twenty knots plus the hour it'll take to reach and cross the Chichester Bar before I get into the Solent and any messing at the Kingswear end. With luck I should be moored up by early evening tomorrow."

She leaned forward and gave him a peck on the cheek. "I'll see you there then, darling." She picked up her bag and turned. "Adiós."

She climbed into her Merc and put her head back against the restraint. This was all going a little too fast for her liking. She did not know who she was jumping into bed with, metaphorically speaking, and she did not entirely trust Blake. She was going into unknown territory with a partner who was an enigma who was hard to read and cool, almost distant. He tried hard enough to be civil but the effort was palpable. Maybe it was indifference to her position as his partner which was not a good thought to have. She wanted to know that if the proverbial hit the fan he had her back covered and that was far from certain. Was there another agenda that she knew nothing about? Was her head being slowly sucked into the lion's mouth? She didn't know and it worried her.

She pulled out her phone and hit speed dial for her office.

Stu answered. "Achilles' Shield."

"It's me. Sky Bar in two hours."

"Wilko."

Stu knew her too well to ask questions, especially not on the phone. "Code one."

"Roger." He broke the connection.

She pulled out of Lacey's drive and headed for the Aviator Hotel in Farnborough. They occasionally kept their plane at the private airfield there and used the hotel for its convenience. The Seneca was usually kept at Blackbushe but Farnborough was closer to the office when they had to get from A to B quickly.

The drive took an hour and a half in the late rush hour traffic and she was sitting in one of the black leather rocket chairs in the Sky Bar when Stu came in. He gave a casual look round the almost empty room before nodding and coming to sit opposite.

"One bloke looks out of place."

"Directional mike?"

"Probably."

"Can't trust anyone these days," Gill said.

Stu took an MP3 player from his pocket, connected it to his phone and put it on loudspeaker. "This will make their day. Best of ABBA."

'*Mama mia*' burst out, just loud enough to cover their conversation without causing undue annoyance, except to the spook sitting at the bar with a newspaper covering his mike.

"Is it this new job?" Stu asked.

40

Gill nodded. "Came from Blake."

Stu pulled a face. "Blast from the past. Thought we'd seen the last of him."

"I still owe him but he did agree to pay for my professional services."

"Hence the ten grand. Came from the Cayman Islands; very fishy. Why the hell does Her Majesty's Secret Intelligence Service have bank accounts in the Caymans?"

"Use your imagination."

"Okay, boss, what's the problem?"

"I don't know if I'm getting out of my depth."

"Tell all to your Uncle Stu."

Gill spent ten minutes bringing Stu up to date while ABBA went through the '*The Name of the Game*' through '*Fernando*' to '*Take a Chance on Me*'. Gill hooked a thumb at the MP3. "Seems apposite given my circumstances."

"Do you trust this Lacey?"

Gill sighed. "I don't know, Stu. I'm usually good at reading people but I keep getting mixed signals from the man. If I'd met him in the street I'd pass by with just a casual glance at an averagely attractive man who I'd forget in ten minutes. Having met him and spent a day with him I get an entirely different impression of something that's really deep … and troubling. The guy has an aura. He seems up front but I can't get a handle on what he's really thinking, who he really is and who the bloody hell he's working for."

"I can make some enquiries."

"Okay but be careful. Cover your tracks. Use untraceable phones just the once; you know the drill better than I do."

"Roger that, boss."

"Get me two burner phones. Have them delivered to my local post office for collection by tomorrow lunchtime. I'll be driving down to Devon soon after that."

Stu took a breath and held it for long seconds before he said. "Should I contact our man in Spain?"

Gill narrowed her eyes and thought. "I don't like doing it but I may need him. Put him on standby. And the plane too, you might have to fly over to pick him up in a hurry. He may not like it." .

Stu grinned. "He'd jump through flaming hoops for you, Gill. You only have to ask."

She smiled at a memory. "I know but I never like taking undue advantage of someone's good nature."

"I wouldn't worry on that score. He'll be an insurance policy. From what you've told me you may need one."

8

In a perverse way Lacey was looking forward to the cruise. He'd made it sound a formality to Gill but there was more to it than just jumping on a ferry. The auto pilot would handle the leg work once they were out of the busy waters of the Solent but he would still need to be on watch for the whole cruise, keeping an eye on the radar and checking his position on the chart with the satnav that was working the helm. But he liked being alone at sea. It was a place where he could feel at peace.

He made some sandwiches and a flask of tea for the trip and called up the marina office for a departure time. It was an early high spring tide and the lock gates had been opened at 07.50 to allow free flow. He got the green light at 08.35 and eased the big cruiser through the narrow lock walls and into the harbour proper. He kept below the eight-knot speed limit, trying not to rock the short-tempered yotties sitting on their sterns having breakfast. Chichester Harbour was always busy and he had to keep alert to avoid tacking yachts and much smaller craft that tended to ignore the rules of the road.

He crossed the Chichester Bar with six metres under his keel and turned west into the equally busy Solent, past Portsmouth with the Isle of Wight off his port beam. He called the Solent Coastguard with his details and likely ETA then opened up the twin inboard Caterpillar diesels. The powerful boat surged up to fifteen knots and onto the plane. He adjusted the trim and sat on the open flybridge with the wind playfully slicking back his hair. He had once been blonde but now he was more ash in colour as age and stress had turned him a premature grey. At least he still had hair, he thought and it amused him. He looked at his right hand where the tip of his little finger was missing, torn off by a Kalashnikov bullet, the one thing the plastic surgeons could not fix when they changed his looks to hide his battle scars. In one way he preferred his previous persona but he knew that his old face could eventually get him killed. The 'Fatwa' would be resurrected if any of the organisations he had damaged learned he was still alive.

It was one of the things that really worried him about Andee's silence. The last he'd heard from her she was heading to Mozambique as the Islamic rebels there were causing serious injuries to the local mainly Christian population and her skills as a gunshot surgeon were greatly in demand. The rebels had allied themselves to Daesh and that did not bode well for anyone, especially a woman, in their clutches. He hoped she was safe but there were never any guarantees. He had made light of it to Gill, he did not want her to think his mind was elsewhere.

Gill had been paid the money to keep her company afloat but the price for his involvement was the promise from Sparrow they would try to find Andee, get her out if it was necessary and if she would allow it. She could be stubborn where her medical skills were concerned and she would not run out on patients.

After they had returned from cruising the western world he wanted to settle down but Andee had the taste for adventure and could not remain unchallenged for long. She had been an Olympic standard skier and loved the thrill of competition … and the danger. He had introduced her to the ISPA which fed her continued need for excitement. At the end of her five year contract with the ISPA she could not settle and despite his misgivings had joined Médicin sans Frontières. If it made her happy he wasn't going to argue.

It had been over a year now and in that time she had been home for just four weeks, working in various Middle-Eastern countries and in the more dangerous parts of Africa. He hoped that her thirst for adventure and her need to succour the wounded would burn itself out but so far the hope had been forlorn. She was changing, he could see that from her brief visit home; the stress taking its toll, but her determination to continue was as strong as ever. He hadn't tried to dissuade her, he knew it was useless and he did not want their last night together to be ruined by arguing. As it was they had coupled repeatedly, her love-making tinged with something approaching desperation that had left them both sweat-soaked and exhausted. The next morning, when she left, it was as if he was saying goodbye to a stranger, as if her mind was already back in some primitive operating theatre trying to save the life of a seriously wounded child.

The radar pinged and broke his chain of thought. He eased back the twin throttles as the Cowes Ferry crossed his bow and the boat rocked in its wake. He tutted to himself, he would have to stay more alert until he passed the Needles and into the English Channel proper.

He was just passing Sconce Point off Yarmouth when the satellite phone warbled. He snatched it off its cradle. "Yes?"

It was Sparrow. "I have some news."

"Good or bad, fire away."

"Médicin sans Frontières have Andee located. It's outside Nova Mambone but in rough country. The rebels have been known to raid into the area so it's unstable. Their communications are shot. They think the power is out in the region with no fuel for the generators until they can get a re-supp in."

"Nothing else known?"

"Not yet," Sparrow admitted.

"Satellite surveillance?"

"Not a priority. We cannot task a bird without an exceptional strategic need."

"That's it?"

"Operatives are on the way from the South East Africa Team. They'll extract if necessary, if the situation warrants."

"How soon?"

"It's over six-hundred miles from Pretoria. We can chopper as far as the Mozambique border but then it's by sea to Nova on the re-supp boat. A couple of days at least."

"Okay, thanks, Mark. I know you're doing all you can."

"Don't thank me, I'm merely the messenger. She's one of our own; that's how I sold it to Ben and it's he who pulls the strings now. I'm just a retired has-been."

Despite his worry Lacey couldn't stop a smile of amusement. "With as much clout as an ICBM."

"I'll be in touch when I know more." Sparrow rang off.

Lacey replaced the handset and turned his mind to navigating the boat between the Needles and the Shingles, the three mile long drifting bank of sand and pebbles that had brought many a ship to grief. Once clear and in quieter waters he turned on the autopilot and increased speed to twenty knots. The wind had freshened to Force 3 and was kicking up a slight swell. He went below to the lower helm position with its greater degree of comfort to get out of the spray that occasionally swept over the bow.

The news from Sparrow had not been entirely unexpected, it gelled with what he imagined but it was still worrying. He would rather be on a plane heading east to Africa than a boat churning its way west to Devon but he would have to leave it in Sparrow and Reid's hands. The call had done little to allay his fears and he had a gut feeling that something bad was in the wind.

9

Gill hadn't been joking when she had told Lacey she had a myriad things to do. If she was supposed to be the wife of a millionaire she would need to look the part. She took the train to London for a mammoth shopping spree using the platinum card that MI6 had so thoughtfully provided. Her Basque cousins had helped to instil supreme dress sense in her. It was a lesson well-learned and a habit she had maintained in all the intervening years since those heady days working undercover with the SAS as bodyguards. It was there she had met and fallen for Ricky who commanded the SAS detail but it wasn't until much later, after she, Stu and Ann, had helped him get out of a spurious court martial, that they had married. That shenanigan had upset the government and MI5 who had done its best to load the dice against Ricky and which eventually led to the final assassination attempt on all their lives that ended in Ricky's death.

She shuddered at the flashback and nearly dropped the Jimmy Choo sandals she was about to buy. It was long in the past but still seemed like yesterday; the memory so real.

The supercilious saleswoman asked if 'madame' was all right and 'madame' said she was. She handed over the shoes to be wrapped and offered the card for payment. She had been sensible and gone for lower heels bearing in mind she wasn't that much shorter than Lacey and did not want to tower over him in six-inch stilts. She hoped he would notice and appreciate the gesture but expected he would not.

She visited a salon, had her hair cut into a stylish bob and dyed honey blonde, had her nails done too. She went to Harrods to buy designer casual clothes and two stunning evening gowns; one never knew the parties one might be invited to. The thought made her grin; she hadn't enjoyed herself so much in months. Her adrenalin was beginning to pump at the thought of working undercover again; she had been behind a desk for too long. Working undercover was where her true forte lay although she excelled at planning ops too.

As she rode a taxi back to Waterloo Station loaded with bags she had a slight twinge of conscience over the money she had blown. She looked at the receipts, over £4,000. The bean-counters would go ape. Well, let them. She needed to get in character. With that thought she upgraded her return ticket to first class and paid a sweating porter to carry the bags to the train. Missus Arnold would only ever travel first class.

The next morning she went to pick up the two burner phones from the post office and found Stu waiting for her.

He raised his eyebrows. "Wow! Like the hair, hardly recognised you. Takes five years off you."

She gave him a peck on the cheek. "Keep talking, you smooth bastard."

He held out a hand. "Thought it better if I delivered these in person."

She took the two small mobiles and slid them in her handbag. She cocked an eye inviting an explanation.

"Office phone has been bugged. I did the sweep early this morning. I expect your car has been too."

"Any idea who?" Gill asked.

Stu shrugged. "Could be Six, or Five, or even your new playmates."

"Anything on them?"

Stu turned around in a casual manner but his eyes probed nearby vehicles. I had a tail but I've lost it. How about you?"

Gill grimaced. "Learned to spot one long ago. I think I'm clean."

"Best be careful, eh."

"Always. Now what do we know?"

"Not a lot. Nobody knows much, or, if they do, they're not saying. Rumours only about a high impact unit that works under the radar. Pre-emptive action people; bit like Bond's licence to kill. Another rumour says they were disbanded a few years ago when the politicians got cold feet. There were some high-profile hits back then against Al Qaeda, a dissident IRA unit and some Russian mobsters but that was put down to the Regiment. If it's the same people, and if the rumours are true, they are too hot to handle. You could get your fingers burned."

"I'm a big girl now, Stu."

"You sure are but not too big to get taken."

"Taken in or taken down? My eyes are wide open, I know the risks."

"I've been watching you get more and more restless these past months, since the business began to slide. You're itching to get back in the field to take your mind off your problems but you might just be adding to them."

"My choice, Stu."

"Well you know where I am. Use the burners."

She patted her bag. "Noted."

"Here." He opened his jacket and showed the butt of a small automatic pistol in his belt. "Just in case."

"Where'd you get that?"

"No names, no pack drill. Take it. H&K P7. Small but packs a punch. Squeeze the pistol grip to cock."

She stood close and slid the pistol into her own belt. "Thanks."

"Don't mention it. If you use it, lose it."

"Roger that. I'm leaving for Devon now; going dark."

"You just take care."

She smiled and kissed his cheek again. "I've said this before and I'll say it again for the record, you're a bloody old woman."

"Let's hope you live to become one," Stu said under his breath as she walked away with the stride of a woman who seemed sure of her own destiny.

Gill punched the Kingswear Marina address into her satnav and began the journey. She decided to ignore the satnav guidance and take the M3, A303, A30 route to Exeter rather than the longer but quicker M4, M5. The scenery was better crossing the Wiltshire plains and through the rolling countryside of Dorset away from the manic motorway traffic. She got clogged up in a tailback passing Stonehenge but was in no hurry and it gave her time to think.

She had brushed off Stu's concerns but the hard lump of the pistol pressing against her side put the matter in perspective. Where she was headed was into danger and there was no arguing with it. She did not know what to expect other than there could be Chinese Special Forces involvement. She did not know for sure who she could rely on for support and she did not know why her office was being bugged and surveillance in place on her and Stu. What she did, and where, was of of interest to someone … but who? That was the million dollar question, closely followed by the 'why', for an extra million bucks. She decided the odds were too long; the cost too high, she needed some insurance. She pulled into a layby, climbed out of the car and used one of the burners to call Stu.

10

The voyage was uneventful. Once he passed the tip of Portland Bill, showing bright on the radar screen, and entered the huge sweep of Lyme Bay he rarely saw another pleasure craft. He aimed the bow to the north of Exmouth as he wanted to familiarise himself with the coastline from there down to Dartmouth. It added an hour to the journey but he was okay with that.

He had pre-booked a berth for a month at the Kingswear Marina by phone before leaving. A boat of his size was not easily accommodated and it was coming up for high holiday season. The marinas were getting busier and would not accept casual arrivals. At £2.50 per metre per night, his 19.5 metre length was good money for them and they had promised mooring space at the end of a finger pontoon.

He picked up the mouth of the Exe on the radar and swung the bow to starboard nudging closer to the coast past Torquay and into the deep waters of Torbay. There were several large ships riding at anchor, two were tankers, one a container ship, two cruise liners and another was a new navy strike cruiser. He knew that tankers would often anchor up while waiting for the price of oil to rise before sailing on to a refinery to offload and increase their profit margins. The navy men were probably due some shore leave and Torquay was a good place to enjoy it.

He passed the ships between them and the shore line where many small craft plied the waters and he could see the bright colours of holidaymakers' parasols on the beaches.

He passed Brixham and rounded Berry Head for the final leg down to the Mew Stone and the entrance to the Dart. He called up Brixham Coastguard to notify them of his safe arrival and eased the throttles back to six knots. He jumped down to throw the fenders over on both sides then climbed back to his helm seat for crossing the bar into the mouth of the river.

It was busy, it always was in summer, and he slid the big boat slowly past the yacht club jetty where members could get a good look as they sipped their drinks on the terrace. The yacht club figured largely in his plans to catch the local gossip.

He had to hold water for a few minutes to allow the two lower car ferries to traverse across his bow with their loads of tourists. He called the marina on Channel 80 and two men were waiting to take his mooring lines as he edged up to the pontoon.

Gill was waiting on the boards with her arms folded and her foot tapping.

"You're late," she called.

He leaned over the flybridge side, blinked in surprise at her new appearance, and then bowed. "So sorry, darlin', a bit of rough weather slowed me down."

He could see but she couldn't the grins on the two men's faces. Off to a good start.

"Come and help me with my luggage."

"Sorry, honey, I'm bushed. If you ask nicely I'm sure these two guys will lend a hand."

The two marina hands turned and their mouths dropped open in unison.

"Well don't just stand there like guppies. Follow me," Gill said, turned on her heel and marched along the pontoon.

One of the men turned and looked up at Lacey and pursed his lips in a silent whistle.

Lacey grinned. "There'll be a few bucks in it, boys. Go give the lady a hand like she says."

They came back a few minutes later, Gill marching ahead with a Harrods bag swinging from one shoulder followed by the two men each pushing a loaded trolley.

Lacey had a glass of Champagne in his hand as he stood on the rear deck and watched. He tilted the glass at Gill. "Harrods, honey? You musta bought that place by now." He stepped down to the boarding ladder and gave her his hand. Welcome aboard, Champagne's cookin'."

He gave her his glass as she passed giving him an air kiss. "Your accent has moved Midwest," she whispered.

"Aw, geez, I thought it was closer to Texas," he whispered back.

He smiled as the two men dropped the suitcases on the deck and gave each man a ten pound note. Over-tipping would be expected and he wasn't going to disappoint. "Okay, boys, that's all for now. Thanks for your help. If I need anythin' I'll sure know who to ask."

Once they were out of earshot he said. "You look …"

She grimaced. "I know, five years younger."

"No, I was about to say …"

"I look different. That's the whole point."

"Uh huh, no again. I was about to say before I was interrupted that you look … good. Maybe on balance I prefer the real you but you sure look like a millionaire's doll."

She closed one eye and squinted at him. "Is that a compliment?"

He grinned. "Drink your Champagne before it gets warm."

"You joining me?"

"Maybe later. We'll check out the yacht club and have dinner there. I've heard they have a great restaurant."

She grinned. "Will they let you in?"

"I'm a member of the Royal London Yacht Club. They'll welcome me here."

"As Mister Arnold?"

"All taken care of. You should check out the small print in the briefing notes."

"It's a little late for that. Read, inwardly digested and destroyed. The Royal *London*?"

"It's based in Cowes. Maybe I'll take you there when we get back. It's an experience." He picked up two suitcases and puffed at the weight. "You planning on moving in permanently?"

"Just a few things a millionaire's wife would need. Exotic jewellery, a few gold ingots, half a gallon of Yves St Laurent, you know."

"If you say so." He carried the cases to the master cabin and came back for two more. Gill was leaning on the starboard side with the untasted wine in hand. "It's pretty here. I could get to like this way of life."

"Live the dream while you can. The hard work starts tonight. By the way, I think we got off to a good start. First impressions count and word will spread. Wealthy guy, trophy wife, the kind some people would want to get to know pretty fast."

"Hence the yacht club?"

"A place to start."

"Am I all right like this or do I need to change?"

He put down the cases and eyed her. "I think you'd look pretty good in just about anything but maybe a smart cocktail dress and heels will set the right note ... if you have them."

She glanced at the suitcases. "You can take your pick."

"I'll leave the haute couture to you. I have some things I need to check on the computer. Ben Reid promised us he'd hack the Devon and Cornwall Police files for their reports on the murder. May be something useful there we should know about."

"Okay. I'll shower and get changed. You can fill me in later."

He nodded and carried the cases to the cabin with Gill following with the remainder. He squeezed past her on the way out and got a whiff of her expensive perfume. She looked the part and played the part. He was beginning to think this long-shot operation might not be a waste of time after all.

11

Dartmouth

Gill was sitting on the kingsize bed in her underwear when one of the burner phones burred into life. She picked it up quickly, made sure the cabin door was closed and answered.

"Yes, Stu?"

"All set. Flight plan's posted to Vitoria airport. I leave tomorrow."

"How is Aftershave?"

"He was never easy to read but I got the feeling that he was pleased to be asked."

"When are you due back?"

"Give us a day's break to get organised. I should be wheels down at Exeter Airport in two days' time."

"Okay. Ask him to use his Colombian passport for this trip. Put him in a taxi when you get to Exeter and send him to the Dart Marina Hotel in Dartmouth. Not cheap but good. I'm glad Six is picking up the tab, although they don't know it yet."

"You're sailing close to the wind there, boss. They'll know right away. "

"Okay, enough of the nautical talk and let me worry about explaining the bills."

Stu chuckled. "Wondered if you'd pick up on that but I mean it, you have to be careful. Blake won't stick his gold-plated pension on the line to save your neck."

"Point taken. I'll steer a safer course from now on."

"Well heave-ho me hearty. I'll call once Aftershave's in the taxi and on his way. After this conversation dump the sim in that phone. I'll call on the other line."

Gill put on a figure hugging dress that came halfway down her thighs and showed off her good legs. She put on the Jimmy Choo sandals, eased the creases down over her slim hips and nodded at her image in the mirror. She was never one to use much makeup but she put on a dab of red lipstick to add a touch of colour to her face and liked the result. "Knock-'em dead, honey," she whispered.

She dropped the small pistol into a shoulder bag and made her way up to the saloon where Lacey was hunched over a laptop. She put a hand on his shoulder and felt his muscles bunch under her fingers. He was tense.

"How's it going, Rick?"

He turned his head and pointed at the screen. "Take a look." He shuffled over to make room for her on the white leather seat. She sat and she peered at the screen.

"Is this the police report?"

"It's the report on Forrestal's murder. Not much there that we don't already know. Their enquiries have drawn a blank. No known motive, no suspect, no time of death, although he was known to be alive two days before his body was found. The salt water washed away any forensic evidence there might have been. No other injuries apart from those which occurred due to being in a tidal river for nigh on two days. His rental car was found outside the college walls with two parking tickets on the windshield. He had a parking space inside and no one knows why it was left there.

"They questioned students and staff at the naval academy where he worked but no one was able to shed any light on the matter. Seems he was well-liked, good at his job and a valued member of the faculty. In short, there's nothing there that we can work with."

Gill turned her head to look at him and saw he had changed into a blazer with a London Yacht Club badge on its breast pocket and a white open-necked Ralph Lauren shirt. Their thighs were touching and she felt the warmth spread along her bare leg. She shuffled away an inch. He didn't appear to notice.

"Is this all they have?"

He waved a hand at the screen. "There's some other stuff that Reid attached on local problems, more in hope than any expectation it might give a lead. Drugs are a problem, especially in the high season. Mainly cocaine but heroin is growing in popularity in places where the wealthier holidaymakers congregate. Here in Dartmouth, Totnes and in Salcombe particularly. There's no suggestion there's any connection to Forrestal's death."

"Do we know anything more about Forrestal? There *was* a suggestion he might have been Naval Intelligence."

"If he was, the Department of the Navy hasn't admitted it. He was a submarine warfare expert, that much we know is true and that is what he lectured on. Just here for the one semester though, kind of a quid pro quo with the American Naval War College based at Newport Rhode Island who are hosting a Brit navy commander who's an expert in amphibious assault techniques."

"Not much there to get our teeth into."

"Maybe not but we can check to see if there has been any drug problems at the college. It's an off-chance but there might be something to it. Reid must have included those reports for a reason."

"You think Forrestal might have stumbled on some dealing?"

Lacey shrugged. "Who knows. I'll call Reid on the secure Iridium sat phone to see if we can get an in to the college. Maybe it's a question the police didn't get around to asking.

"Speaking of making a call, I've booked a table at the yacht club for eight-o-clock. You hungry?"

"Me? Ravenous. I could eat the proverbial."

Lacey closed down the laptop. "Let's go. It's a short walk, glad you had the nous to wear sensible heels."

She smiled. "You noticed."

He stood and held out his hand to help her but she ignored it and stood under her own steam, wriggling the tight dress down over her thighs.

He grinned. "Those spray-on dresses sure take some adjusting."

63

"You don't approve," she said. It was a statement not a question but she found herself hoping for the right answer. She got it and it unaccountably pleased her.

He turned his head on one side and eyed her. "Not for everyone, maybe, but it sure looks good on you."

She didn't show how pleased she was with the compliment but took his arm. "Then I'll let you take me to dinner. Are we liking each other tonight or are we in a spat?"

He grinned. "Let's be friends. There's time for the playacting when we get to see the lie of the land."

It was a short but circuitous walk from the marina to the yacht club in Priory Street. They stopped on the road and took in the view across the Dart to Dartmouth itself. The water traffic was still busy but the river was in shadow as the sun set behind the hills to the west. Lights were already coming on in the bars and restaurants and they were reflecting in the calm water. There was barely a cloud in the pale blue sky and it was warm. Gill slid her hand into the crook of Lacey's arm.

"I know it's not professional but can we, just for tonight, forget why we're here. It's so lovely I don't want to think bad thoughts; I've had enough of those to last a lifetime."

She felt the fingers of his left hand close over hers. He gently squeezed and released his hold.

"I guess you've earned some respite. No business talk over dinner, I promise."

The way he said it convinced her he'd read her files. Just for a second she felt irritated. He knew all about her but she knew next to nothing about him. For all she knew she could be cosying up to another cold-hearted assassin. What did Stu say? Like 007, a licence to kill. She wondered if his licence had been revoked but even as she thought it she hoped it hadn't.

12

Lacey meant what he said; there was to be no business talk over dinner but that did not stop him from taking stock of the club, its members and visitors and it didn't cover the period after the meal was over. They were shown to their table after signing in by an attentive young waiter and given menus. Lacey noticed that they created quite a stir amongst the busy crowd with several long calculating looks being cast in their direction. He knew Gill had noticed it too and played on it by acting on the sexual allure she undoubtedly possessed.

She leaned towards him over the white linen tablecloth. "We seem to have attracted some attention."

He smiled and made a point of taking her hand. "Mainly the women. They're just jealous."

She smiled, tilted her head and rested her chin in the palm of her free hand. "Oh, Rick, you say the loveliest things." She simpered and he had to choke back a laugh.

"You're good," he mouthed.

She raised her eyebrows. "I know."

"You learn that in Spain?"

She took her hand away. "I'd like some wine."

"We haven't ordered the food yet."

"That's okay. I only drink white, red gives me a hangover. Besides, I've decided, as we're in Devon, to have fish. I'll start with the mussels and go on to the freshly caught Whiting."

Lacey waved the waiter over. "Good choice, honey." He repeated the order then added. "I'll have the melon to start and the sole. Keep it on the bone, I like to do the filleting myself. Bring a spare plate for the bones. We'll have a bottle of Sancerre too, you can bring that first."

The waiter finished scribbling, nodded and hurried away.

"You're not bad yourself," Gill said. "Very positive, right in character."

"I've done that before, no big deal."

"Tell me about yourself, your real self"

Lacey eyed her thoughtfully. They had to talk about something unrelated to the job they were on. It wasn't something he was comfortable with, he didn't like giving too much away, but whatever subject they settled on had its drawbacks.

"Not much to tell. I spent some time in Vermont, that's where I learned how to drive a boat on Lake Champlain. Had a good friend called Kingly, a rancher, he taught me, but he's dead now, died a while back, natural causes. Also spent some time in Maryland, DC and North Carolina."

"Fort Bragg?"

He exaggerated a look around. "Sssh! Not so loud. Yeah, Fort Bragg."

"Where were you born?"

"Would it surprise you if I said I was born in London, England?"

She sat a little more upright. "Yes it would. Is that true?"

"Would I lie to you?"

"Probably."

He grinned. "Oh ye of little faith."

"Really?"

He gave her another grin. "Believe what you want. That's enough about me. What about you?"

"You mean you haven't read all about it already?"

"Just the big picture. I'd like to hear some of the fine detail."

She imitated his habit of cocking his head to one side. "How long have we got?"

"Until the first course comes. Give it five minutes."

"I was joking."

He gave her a serious look. "I'm not."

She was about to reply when the waiter interrupted them with the wine.

"Would you like to try it, sir?"

"No thanks. Just leave it." He poured them both a full measure and raised his glass. "Here's to us."

She clinked her glass against his. "To calm seas and a safe passage." She took a sip. "Hmm, good."

Lacey tilted his glass at her. "Well, go on." He wanted to know more about her, about the woman not the undercover soldier. Records were bland, dehumanised, lacking in emotion. He wanted to know how much of herself she was prepared to reveal. He wanted to know her weaknesses … and her strengths. He was about to kick over the can of worms and he wanted an insight on how she would react.

She was eyeing him warily as if she was assessing the implications and his reasons. She was bright, he gave her that.

She took another sip of wine and put her glass on the table. She looked at her wristwatch, a gold Rolex, and nodded. "Five minutes? That's all, or less if the starter arrives early.

"I was born in the Basque region of Spain. My dad was a British engineer and my mother a local woman from a wealthy family. We moved to Kent on around my eighth birthday. I grew up there, went to London Uni and got a degree in chemical engineering. I met my first real boyfriend there but dumped him when I joined the army as I thought he was too dull for me. We're still friends, I see him occasionally but no romance. I met Ricky … my husband, when he was commanding the close protection team I worked with. We set up our company, Achilles Shield, together but he was injured and died. I've lived alone ever since. Never found anyone to match him. The company has been my life for the past few years. Satisfied?"

He pursed his lips. "I think that's the most potted of potted biographies I've ever heard."

"You're a fine one to talk."

"Chemical Engineering?"

"Yes, don't sound so surprised, Rick. It's had its uses in the past."

He had her strengths tagged. She was intelligent, unafraid of a challenge, determined and single-minded in pursuit of her goals. Any weaknesses weren't showing, not yet, maybe she wasn't allowing them to show, but time would tell.

13

They finished the meal and two thirds of the bottle of wine between them. Making small talk had been difficult as neither of them wanted to give any more of themselves away. Gill thought this as she sipped the now warm dregs of wine in her glass.

He lifted the bottle from the cooler with an unspoken offer to top up her glass. She shook her head. She could take her drink but she needed to keep sharp as she noticed a couple of other guests were working up the courage to come over; at least that's what it seemed like to her. Glances in their direction and whispered asides.

"We may have company soon," she said to Lacey.

"Yeah, I noticed. Time for business, holiday's over."

The couple seemed to pluck up enough courage and came across to their table. The man leaned over and held out his hand. "Hello, I'm the chair of the welcoming committee and this is my wife Lilian. I hope you enjoyed your meal."

Lacey part rose and took the hand. "Yes, thanks, it was great."

"My name's Alan Drew."

"Well, Alan, nice to meet you. This here is Gill, as in fish, she always says."

Gill smiled bright and brittle. "And he's Rick, rhymes with ..."

Drew coughed. "You're American, Rick."

"Not so's you'd notice, yeah."

"He has a sweet American way with words, don't you, darling?"

"Are you planning on staying long?" Lilian asked trying to diffuse the sudden air of veiled hostility."

"About a month, I've been told," Gill said. "I'd have preferred San Trop but the master has spoken."

"We'll have the pleasure of your company for a whole four weeks then," Drew said and tried to make it sound as if he welcomed the idea.

"Yeah. I got a message from a friend of my father. Said his boy had been killed down here. Name of Forrestal. He was a navy commander. Seems your limey police don't have much clue and I was asked to come on down and rattle some cages. The family want to know who, how and why. So far they have diddly squat."

Lilian put a hand to her cheek. "Oh, I remember that. It was some time ago. One of our members found the body floating in the marina. She was in a terrible state for weeks afterwards."

"Not such a state as Commander Forrestal," Gill said.

Lilian turned pink. "No, no, obviously not but it was still a shock."

"Well I intend to get to the bottom of it," Lacey said. "You can put the word out if anyone has any gen. I'll pay good money for the right information. We're in the *Andrea Two*, you can't miss it."

Lilian looked from one to the other. "*Andrea* Two?"

Gill pulled a tight smile. "His other wife. I'm just the new fixture. Can't get him to scrape the name off the bow. He says it's unlucky to change the name of a boat."

Drew's face brightened. "Oh, yes, that's quite right. It comes from the days of sailing ships when the name of a craft was often carved into the mainmast. Planing it off and adding a new name weakened the mast and it was seen as unlucky."

Gill gave him a cool look. "Thank you for that, Alan. Just what I needed to know."

"Pull up a chair and take the weight off," Lacey said. He waved at the hovering waiter. "Get these two people a drink. What'll you have, folks?"

"I really don't think we need intrude any longer," Drew said.

Lacey grinned. "Nonsense. Hell'll freeze over the day Rick Arnold can't buy his friends a drink."

"It's very kind of you ... but ..." Sylvia said.

Gill put a resigned expression on her face. "He won't take no for an answer, he'll be miserable for the rest of the night if you don't have at least one."

"Oh, in that case I'll have a gin and tonic."

"Me too," Drew said.

"Make them large ones," Lacey said.

Drew pulled up two chairs and waited while Lilian sat before seating himself.

Gill pursed her lips. "You see, sweetheart, that's the way a gentleman does it."

Lacey grunted. "I spend too much time makin' money; there ain't no gentlemen in that game. Maybe you could find yourself one with a Harrods account."

Lilian shifted uncomfortably in her seat. "Have you two been married long?"

"Two years," Gill said. "Seems like ten."

"That's what it seems like in my bank account," Lacey grumbled. "Never seen anyone blow through dough so fast."

Gill simpered. "Blow and dough. You do have some poetry in your soul."

"Okay, can we call a truce, honey? These good people are getting' caught in the crossfire. Don't mind us, folks, this is what passes for small talk with us."

Gill added what sounded like a genuine twinge of anger. "You promised you wouldn't talk business tonight."

"No, I said I wouldn't talk business over dinner. Dinner's done. Now I need some answers." He turned to Drew just as the drinks turned up and waited while he took a sip. "I need to get things moving, Alan; give the authorities a kick up the ass. Anyone around here who can help? Anyone in the know? Any names?"

"I can tell you the name of the investigating officer, if that's any help," Drew said. "Otherwise I'm at a loss. I'm sure no club members would be involved."

"The body was found in the marina, wasn't it?"

"Yes but the police said it had floated down from upstream. From a place called Noss Mayo. There's a creek opposite the boatyard there; Old Mill Creek it's called," Drew said.

"It's a start. Give me the cop's name, I'll check it out with him."

"I don't have it to hand, it's on a card on my yacht with a phone number. Tell you what, I'll radio over the details tomorrow. Leave your VHF radio on channel seventy-two, that's the one the fishermen use, not as busy as channel eighty."

"I'd appreciate that, Alan. Gives me a place to start."

Drew pointed at Lacey's badge. "It's the Royal London isn't it?"

"That's right."

"Do you live in the U.K.?"

"I do now."

"That's how we met," Gill said. "A party at the club. Love at first sight, a whirlwind romance, isn't it romantic? We still have quite a lot to learn about each other." She looked at Lacey as she said it and realised there was more than a grain of truth in the words. It was beginning to bother her.

The Drews left after finishing their drinks and Gill sat back and sighed. "That's ruined my good mood."

"We're on duty twenty-four seven, we have to make a start; we need some leads. I've just cast some bread upon the waters and now we'll see who or what rises to the bait."

Gill wrinkled her nose. "Let's hope whatever it is doesn't leap out and bite your head off."

14

It was obvious to Lacey that Gill was in a poor mood when they returned to the boat and she went straight to her cabin. As far as he was concerned the evening had gone well and he had achieved his first objective to get the mission on its feet. They had to take every opportunity when it arose but he was sorry to burst her bubble of contentment earlier than she would have liked. That in itself was a strange feeling. It really shouldn't have bothered him.

He shook it off and went to check the mooring lines were tight and the shore power was properly connected, all the myriad things a boat owner needed to do. He took down the red ensign and laid the flagstaff on the rear seats ready for the morning. Inside the saloon he sent a secure email to Reid and copied it to Sparrow, outlining the day's work and what he planned to do with the information he got from Drew when he received it.

The story that his father was a friend of the Forrestals had been included in any false records that had been posted. It paid to cover all angles; you never knew who would be poking around in them.

He set the VHF radio to channel seven-two. It was quiet at this time of night and all he got was a hiss of static. He turned the squelch down so that he could not hear it. Channel seven-two was a ship-to-ship channel and anyone could tune in.

That was okay, maybe the word would be spread more quickly that he was here to follow up on the murder. He wanted a reaction, the sooner the better.

Gill came up from below dressed for bed. Her hair was mussed and she was wearing a flowered silk dressing gown that did little to disguise her curves. She yawned and flopped down opposite him, tucking her legs beneath her.

"I've come to apologise," she said.

"For what?"

"We were going to do the friends thing tonight and I messed it up. I'm annoyed with myself, it was very unprofessional. I don't know what made me do it."

He shrugged. "That's okay. It gives us another avenue. If people think you're discontented with your lot, with me, they may open up."

Gill yawned again and covered her mouth. "Who knows? The blue touch paper has been lit we'll just have to wait for the fireworks to start."

"Would you like a nightcap?"

"Hmm, what have you ... we ... got?"

"Not much. Boy's stuff mainly. Scotch, cognac ...?"

"I'll take a stiff malt."

"That's something we do have in common." He poured two large measures and handed one over. "Slangevar."

She tilted her glass at him. "Slange." She took a sip. "Boy's stuff? Are you that much of a dinosaur?"

"Probably. I don't have much time for that PC crap. I guess I'm not used to women drinking hard liquor. Sorry if you're offended."

"No you're not. You don't give a damn."

He raised his glass in mock salute. "You catch on quick."

"You're testing me ... all the time."

"And so far you've passed."

"Should I be grateful?"

Lacey put down his glass and turned to face her. "Listen, Missus Arnold, I don't know you, other than what I've read. In my day we spent months getting to know our men so that we all thought as one, acted as one, knew what each of us would do in any given situation. We had to trust that our backs would be covered.

"We don't know what we've let ourselves in for on this operation but I have to know that when the chips are down you won't roll over on me. So far I've liked what I've seen but there's been no real pressure. You've been tested but not tried."

Gill snorted into her scotch. "I could say the same. I don't know you either. You said in *your* day. When was *your day*? Are you over the hill? Can you still hack it?"

He smiled and his face softened as it reached his eyes. "I guess that's a good question that only time will answer."

She snorted again. "That's not very encouraging."

"Maybe but it's all I got," he said, then, as an afterthought, added, "you don't like me much do you?"

Gill eyed him for several long seconds before replying. "Whether I like you or not has got nothing to do with it. I just want my skin intact at the end of this. I'll make a decision then.

"Anyway, if you'll forgive the pun, we're both in the same boat. You can't trust me and I can't trust you, not until we know each other better, after things have got *trying*."

The laptop pinged. He reached over, read the email and turned the laptop so that she could see the screen. "Speaking of which, we have an appointment to see the commanding officer at the naval college tomorrow. Reid set it up. Not sure where it'll get us but we may have an insight on what Forrestal had been doing over the past weeks."

Gill looked at her Rolex. "What time?"

"Eleven-hundred hours. Why, do you have someplace else to be?"

She gave him a tight smile. It had a touch of mischief in it. "Oh, I need to do some more shopping; girl's stuff, you know. But it can wait."

The dig wasn't lost on him but he didn't react. He deserved that. "Good. We'll take the tender over at ten-thirty. It'll avoid queueing for the ferry."

"It's getting late." She stood, swallowed the last of the malt and handed the glass to him. "Must get my beauty sleep. What time's reveille?"

"I don't sleep much. I'll be up early and give a tap on your door at around seven-thirty."

"No chance of breakfast in bed, I suppose."

He grinned. "You suppose right. It'll be ready up here at eight."

She shrugged. "Worth a try."

Gill waved a languid hand as she disappeared down the companionway. Despite himself, he appreciated the view as the silk dressing gown clung to her back and buttocks.

"See you in the morning," her voice floated up just as her cabin door closed. He heard the latch snap locked and grinned.

He went below to the crew cabin behind the engine compartment and dragged out the rubber dinghy that doubled as a tender. He carried it up to the open deck then went back for the outboard engine and the foot pump to inflate it. The tender fitted onto snap davits bolted to the swim platform. Once lowered onto the water it rose and fell with the boat making boarding and disembarking easy.

With the tender prepared he took his Sig pistol back to the crew cabin to clean it. It was where he kept its cleaning equipment and spare ammunition in a locked box beneath one of the bunks. Beneath the other bunk was a small armoury of special operations weapons. His fighting suit made of Kevlar and ceramics, with a helmet also made of Kevlar, was in an upright case in a floor to ceiling locker. It had a shaped visor of gold-tinted bullet-resistant Pilkington armour plate glass. He checked that the batteries that powered the state-of-the art helmet were fully charged. The suit and helmet were attack mode; he hoped he wouldn't need them. What he had said to Gill had been the truth. He did not know how well he'd perform after five years driving a desk. Was he really over the hill? That had hit home and it was a thought that genuinely concerned him.

15

True to his word Lacey rapped on Gill's cabin door the next morning. She stretched and yawned. "What time is it?"

"Time to get going," the reply came through the door. "There's a cup of coffee on the deck if you want it."

Gill mumbled her thanks and slipped out from under the duvet. Coffee wasn't exactly breakfast in bed but it would be welcome. She opened the door a crack and peered through. Lacey had gone, she could hear him moving on the deck above accompanied by the clink of cutlery on crockery and the smell of grilling bacon. She picked up the coffee mug and took a gulp. He'd remembered how she liked it, black and strong. It was clearing the cobwebs rapidly. She shrugged on the silk dressing gown and climbed the steps into the main saloon. Lacey turned his head and the grin was back.

"You always look that good in the mornings?" He turned back to move the bacon rashers around on the grill pan.

"The words jolted her back several years to Spain and her jaw clenched shut. "Are you being sarcastic?"

He didn't turn this time. "Take it whatever way you want."

She took a deep breath and exhaled. "I'm sorry. I didn't mean to snap. I just had a flashback. A friend who died."

He laid down the spatula he was using and wiped his hands on a towel. "You wanna talk about it?"

"No … no … thanks. I got over it years ago but flashbacks can be painful when they hit you so suddenly."

"Yeah. I know. Sit down and you can have breakfast. Bacon, eggs over easy, toast and English marmalade, if that's okay with you."

Gill ran a hand through her hair. "I must look a fright and I haven't showered yet."

"You look fine. I wasn't being sarcastic. Anyway, now that you've brought up the subject of showering and using the heads, I'd prefer it if you used the shore facilities. The showers are pretty good here, the blocks are just the other side of the railroad tracks."

She noticed his hair was damp. "I see you've sampled them."

He smiled. "I did the recce. Door codes are written down on the pad by the laptop. Now what'll you have?"

"Everything. Just hit me with what you've got."

"Not on a diet then?"

She giggled. "I burn off more calories than I put in. I'm lucky, I've always been that way. My problem is keeping meat on my bones." She slid onto the long seat behind a table as he piled eggs

84

and bacon on a plate and handed it over. "You not eating?"

"I've already had mine, I tend to eat early."

"Did you sleep last night?"

"Some. I get dreams. I try to stay awake until I get really tired; tired enough to drop off for a couple of hours."

He was letting more of himself out and Gill digested the thought with her food as he sat opposite sipping coffee and gazing out over the Dart towards the naval college on a rise to the west. She wasn't sure why he had opened up a crack. Maybe he was being genuine but maybe he was doing it for some other purpose. The man never seemed to do anything without an ulterior motive; each action taken to gauge a reaction.

She finished her bacon and eggs and started on the toast as he poured her another cup of coffee. She decided to push him a little to see how far he was prepared to go.

"Those dreams. Are they nightmares?"

"Some could be called that. Some are like your waking flashbacks. There's always a price to pay for past sins."

She nodded and echoed his words. "Do you wanna talk about it?"

He screwed shut one eye and bit his lower lip. "About time you were getting cleaned up. I'll take care of the dishes today. You're on KP tomorrow."

Door slammed shut, Gill thought. Need to know or playing mind games? She was no nearer finding out. She wiped her mouth on a paper napkin, went to her cabin, dressed in jeans and sweatshirt, collected her towel and washbag and walked to the shower block alongside the marina office. It was relatively quiet with just one other cubicle in use.

Lacey was right the shower was good and as hot as she wanted. She finished towelling off and heard the main door open and a couple of women come in chatting to each other. Small talk. The same the world over. Clothes, makeup, slagging off husbands. She smiled as she pulled on her clothes. Then the conversation changed, the voices lowered as a third woman joined them, coming out of the other occupied shower.

"Did you see that pair at the club last night?" One voice asked.

"Yes, reeking of money and that boat, oh my god."

"Well he is an American," another voice chipped in. "Overpaid and over here."

Someone laughed at the old quip. "And the woman, she's British. She looked a bit tarty to me. Wouldn't mind betting she's his bit on the side."

"Hate to disappoint you, darling," the first woman said, "she is his wife but you're missing the real goss."

The second woman sounded unconvinced. "Oh, what's that?"

"Well, you remember the body that Angela found floating in the river …?"

"Yesss! Vaguely. What about it?"

"Apparently the American has come to find out who did it. He's a family friend or something. He's put the word out he'll pay for information."

"I wish him luck with that," the third woman said. "As long as he doesn't stick his nose in where it's not wanted."

"Oooh! Do you have something to hide, Shell?"

It was said with a hint of malice and Gill, listening with her ear to the door, couldn't help smiling at the veiled bitchiness."

The third woman got huffy and Gill could hear her packing her things away. "We don't want any Tom, Dick or Harry poking around in our business. It's all right for you two, your husbands are both retired. My Derek has a business to run."

With that the door slammed.

"Did we touch a nerve or what," the first woman said. "I'm not sure what business *her Derek* is in but I've heard rumours that it's not that savoury. I was against him joining the club but I was pooh-poohed for being snobbish. I wasn't being snobbish, I just don't like him."

"Not our usual type of member, I grant you," the second woman said, "but it takes all sorts even though he does tend to make my skin crawl too."

Gill had heard enough. She unlocked the cubicle door and stepped out to see the flustered looks on both women's faces. "Morning, ladies. Such a lovely day." She smiled, slung her towel over her shoulder and sauntered out.

Was it something or nothing? A lead or barking up the wrong tree? Why would Derek, whoever he was, be worried about having his business under scrutiny? Was the wife just being protective or paranoid? It was something she could follow up alone. She was sure Lacey would dismiss it as just woman talk. It was too vague and airy. But it made her stomach tighten and the hair on her neck rise. It was a hunch and from past experience, she knew better than to ignore it.

16

Whilst Gill was out Lacey dressed in a white open neck shirt, slacks and blazer. He wanted to appear the archetypal rich New England preppy. He thought about a cravat but dismissed the idea as being too over-the-top.

He climbed up to the main saloon and made himself some tea. He had just sat down to drink it when the VHF radio burst into life.

"*Andrea Two, Andrea Two, Andrea Two, this is Agamemnon, over.*"

Lacey sighed and reached across for the microphone. "This is Andrea Two, go ahead, over."

"*Oh, morning Rick, Alan here, over.*"

Lacey pressed the send switch. "Hi, Alan, what have you got for me, over?"

"*Here are the details you asked for. It's a Detective Inspector Craddock, Exeter CID. It's an Exeter number.*" He read out the digits slowly and repeated them.

Lacey dropped the mike and scrabbled for a pen and notepad that was on the chart table. "Can you repeat those last three digits, I missed them, over?"

"*Certainly. You got Craddock I assume. Here are the figures, all of them again.*"

He repeated the phone number as Lacey scribbled it down. "Got that, Alan, thanks, over."

"*I hope it's of some help. We would all like to know how that poor chap came to be floating in the Dart. Perhaps you chasing the police will do some good, over.*"

"Let's hope so. Andrea Two, out."

As he tore out the sheet and folded it Gill came back. She dumped her towel and toilet bag on a seat and pointed at Lacey's cup. "Is that tea? Any more in the pot?"

"No pot. It's just a teabag in a cup."

"You Americans. One day we'll teach you how to make a decent pot of British tea."

Lacey gave her a knowing smile. "Do tell. Water's still hot. How'd you take it?"

"Like my coffee, black but not so strong."

Lacey re-boiled the kettle put a teabag in a cup and splashed water on top. As he worked he watched her out of the corner of his eye. "How'd the shower go?"

"Interesting."

"Caught some gossip?"

Gill put her hands on her hips and gave him an exasperated stare. "What is it with you? Do you think most women are airheads?"

"Some maybe. Not all, though I doubt you overheard any high finance going on."

Gill pulled the mug from his fingers and glared. "As it happens I did hear something."

"Oh, what was that?"

"That you're overpaid and over here ... and I'm a bit tarty."

Lacey pulled a face, made a claw with his fingers and miaowed."

It was out of character and Gill laughed, nearly spilling her tea.

He steadied her hand and their fingers touched. "Mind you don't scald yourself," Lacey said.

She took a pace back and sucked in a breath. "Right. Did I hear the VHF as I came aboard?"

"Yes, it was Alan Drew with the gen on the police inspector running the case. I'll call to see if we can get a meet set up."

Gill nodded. He could see there was something on her mind but she was tight lipped.

"Fine, I'll get changed." She walked to the companionway, stopped and held up the mug. "Thanks for the tea."

"You're welcome."

She disappeared and he picked up a mobile phone to call Inspector Craddock. The line was engaged. He went to his own cabin and picked up the Sig. It was in an Inside Waistband Holster and his jackets had been tailored to hide the slight bulge it made. He positioned it carefully over his right hip and checked it was invisible. "Loaded for bear," he whispered and grinned. It was a precaution he always took, although he admitted to himself that after the intervening years it was probably a redundant one but he could not relax his guard. He checked his watch. It was time to get the tender lowered and the outboard fitted.

Gill came out right on time and he took them across the river to the Dartmouth side, mooring at a jetty and walking the short distance to the gate of the naval college.

Their IDs were checked and they were allowed inside the grounds as the sentry called ahead. The commander, a navy captain in shirtsleeves, was on the terrace to meet them. He held out his hand.

"Mister Arnold? Captain Portman."

Lacey took the firm grip. "Thanks for seeing us, Captain." He hooked a thumb. "This is my wife Gill."

Portman held out his hand with a wide sailor's smile. "A pleasure, Missus Arnold."

"Gill … please," Gill said and allowed Portman to hold her fingers for a little longer than politeness required.

Portman's smile broadened. "Come this way, we can talk in my office."

The office was cramped but had a superb view over the river. Portman indicated seats.

"What's this about, Mister Arnold? I must admit my curiosity was piqued when I had a phone call from a Brigadier to arrange this meeting. More of a polite order than a request."

A rating knocked and came in with a tray of cups and a cafetiere. Lacey waited until the door had closed behind the man before starting.

"It's about Commander Forrestal. His family would like to know more about his death but facts are in short supply. Maybe you could fill in some of the blanks."

Portman paused in pouring the coffee and pursed his lips. "It was a shock to us all. I'm not sure what I can add to the details. The commander was well liked, good at his job and an excellent ambassador for the US navy."

"Yeah, that's the diplomat's answer if you don't mind me saying. What exactly was he doing here? Did he have a run in with any of the students or faculty?"

"Did he have a girlfriend?" Gill asked, her finger to her chin and her eyes wide.

Portman gave her a benevolent smile. "Well for that you'd have to ask the police as they were here asking similar questions but I've no idea as to the response they got. As to the first part of your question, Mister Arnold, I'll leave that to Rear Admiral Chichester who is our Flag Officer Sea Training. For the second part, Chief Petty Officer Spicer would be the one to ask. He has an ear to the ground that often comes in useful in such matters."

"Will we be able to speak with the admiral and the chief?" Lacey asked.

Portman frowned. "The chief, yes, but I believe the admiral is at sea."

"Will he be back soon?"

"Oh, yes. He's only out in Torbay. He'll be back this evening."

"On the cruiser there?"

Portman raised his eyebrows. "Yes. *HMS Norfolk* out of Devonport. You know your ships, Mister Arnold."

"Another Duke Class, yeah, I know a little. Based on the type 45s but new, bigger and more powerful."

Portman smiled, relaxed and steepled his fingers. "Seems to me, for an American, you know your onions."

"Guess it runs in the family," Lacey said. It wouldn't hurt to let Portman think he came from a naval background; he would be less likely to begrudge any help as his feathers had apparently been ruffled by Reid's call. "Can we speak with the chief now?"

Portman picked up a phone. "Ask Mister Spicer to come to my office right away. Thanks." He put the receiver down. "He's on his way, he'll be a few minutes. In the meantime you can tell me just who the hell you are, Mister Arnold."

17

Gill was watching Lacey as the barbed statement zipped across Portman's desk. Lacey didn't blink. His eyebrows went up a fraction, the right one higher than the left as if the muscles there were damaged. It gave him a mildly quizzical look.

"I'm sorry?"

Portman sat back in his seat and gave an exasperated snort. "It's not every day I have a high ranking officer on the phone asking in no uncertain terms to give you any help I can. What are you? NCIS, FBI, CIA?"

Lacey tilted his head slightly to one side. "Sounds like alphabet soup. No, none of those things."

"Look, sir," the way Portman said it, it sounded like an insult. "This is my college, I need to know what is going on, or more exactly, what has gone on under my nose for the past six months."

Gill was watching both men now. Portman was getting hot under the collar, this must have been brewing up for some time with him and had finally built up a head of steam. Lacey was cool, as if he did not have a clue what Portman was talking about, the quizzical look now reaching his mouth as his lips went up at one corner.

"I'm merely a family friend. I've been asked to try to get some answers for Commander Forrestal's nearest. I can guess the name of Forrestal carries some weight this side of the pond."

Gill raised her hand as if asking permission to speak.

"Yes, Gill?" Portman said.

"It's quite true, Captain. Until four days ago we knew nothing about this murder. We were contacted and asked if we could come down here to try to shed some light on proceedings and perhaps give the police a nudge. The Brigadier who called is my Uncle Ben, I do hope he wasn't too overbearing; he can be sometimes, you know. It's all those years shouting at soldiers and things. I'm sorry but we didn't know how else to get to speak with you. I'm so glad you agreed to see us."

Portman exhaled slowly but Gill could see she had drawn the sting. "I had little choice in the matter," he said. "What do you hope to achieve? If the police haven't been able to solve the case, what makes you think your presence will make any difference?"

Lacey shifted in his seat. "We do not expect to achieve anything, Captain, it's going through the motions for the sake of family friends. We'll gather together what we can and email it to the States. I guess it's all we can do. Getting to speak with you will show that the college is doing its best to be helpful and that will mean a lot."

"Well if you put it like that ..." Portman said but was interrupted by a loud knock on the door. "Ah, that's the chief ... come in Mister Spicer."

A tall barrel-chested man stepped smartly into the room and saluted. He was wearing a white shirt with navy blue slacks and had a wristband on his right wrist bearing a laurel wreath with a crown and anchor in its centre. "You sent for me, skipper?"

"Yes, Chief. These two people have some questions about Commander Forrestal that you may be able to answer. Give them whatever help you can." Portman glanced at his watch. "Eight bells. Time for my rounds." He rose and held out his hand to Gill and then to Lacey. "I'll leave you in the chief's capables. He'll see you out when you're finished."

Portman left and the chief relaxed from his stiff posture. "How can I help you?"

Gill smiled. "Gossip, Chief. We've heard all the official stuff from the captain."

Spicer took off his cap and scratched his head, looking from one to the other. "Why'd you want to know?"

Lacey stood and offered Spicer his seat. "Take the weight off, Chief." He walked around the desk and sat in Portman's chair, resting his elbows on the desk.

Spicer frowned. "Who are you people?"

"We're friends of Commander Forrestal's family and we're looking for any answers that the police haven't dug up. Did he have any run-ins with anyone recently?"

Spicer shook his head. "Not heard anything. The commander got on with everyone, students, staff, no one had a bad word to say about him."

"Nothing in the weeks prior to his murder, you're sure?"

"Nothing I've heard, sir. I'd know if there had been any bust ups."

"What about his sex life?" Gill asked. She leant towards Spicer and rested her chin on her palm.

Spicer straightened his back. "Nothing like that, miss. Straight as a die was the commander."

Gill smiled. "No, I wasn't inferring anything. I just wondered if he had a girlfriend."

"Again, not that I've heard, but sometimes the young gentlemen meet up in the pubs with young ladies and nature takes its course, you know how it is, miss."

"Of course, Chief. By the way it's missus but you can call me Gill, everyone does." She thought it was worth a try to get him to relax more but Spicer had the look of a man who had sailed the world too many times to be a soft touch.

Spicer narrowed his eyes. "Yes, miss, thank you. If it's the commander's personal life you're interested in you could try Lieutenant Tarrant. He and the commander used to go out together on occasion. They were both keen on birdwatching, the feathered kind. Often on the terrace watching the gulls was Commander Forrestal. Lieutenant Tarrant would know more than me on any other score."

"Where can we find the lieutenant?" Lacey asked.

"He's at sea with the admiral. Back tonight though. I'll be sending a tender to pick them up at eight bells, that's around sixteen-hundred hours.

They should be back here by mid-watch, eighteen-hundred hours, er, that's six-o-clock this evening."

Lacey tore a page from a pad on Portman's desk and scribbled a note. He held it out for Spicer to take. "If you would be so kind as to put that in Mister Tarrant's pigeon hole, Chief, I'd be grateful. The family would like to learn as much as they can of the commander's last days, you understand."

Spicer nodded and took the note. "Right sir," he stood, "if that's all ...?"

As they passed back through the gates Gill took Lacey's arm. "You were cool back there."

Lacey couldn't suppress a grin. "Uncle Ben?"

Gill laughed. "Spur of the moment. I had the feeling that the skipper was feeling put upon so I had to give him a good reason why Reid would ring; put the blame on myself and he would be less likely to investigate further. He already had suspicions that this was a security investigation and it may just have given him pause for thought."

"I doubt he completely swallowed it," Lacey said. "He's too astute for that but perhaps he'll take the hint and leave it lie. Spicer too was pretty reticent. I think he knows something but is probably frightened it will bring the college into disrepute if it gets out."

Gill wasn't sure about that, not sure that Spicer knew anything for certain, just that he wasn't about to conjecture on scuttlebutt when there was no solid basis to rely on. He had passed the buck to

Tarrant and maybe that was where they needed to go for answers.

It was as if Lacey read her mind. "I'll deal with Tarrant when he gets back. How soon he calls will be an indicator of how keen he is to help. I hope I don't have to chase him up."

"What about the admiral?"

Lacey shrugged. "He'll keep. Depends what I get from Tarrant whether it will be worthwhile bothering him."

They reached the quayside and Gill hesitated. "Look, Rick, I have some things to do. I'll get the ferry across later."

"Girl stuff … right?" He waved and walked to the pontoon.

She watched him as he untied the tender and began the short crossing to Kingswear. She had picked out the tail early on, she had half-expected one, and now Lacey was out of the way she was determined to find out who was so interested in her.

18

Lacey always kept spare clothing in a waterproof bag under the thwart of the tender in case of bad weather. He idled the outboard alongside a buoy, tied the painter to a cable and shook out the bag's contents. A black hoodie and a baseball cap were there together with a waterproof sailing jacket and overalls. He quickly stripped off his blazer and put on the hoodie and cap.

He let the tide drift him away from the buoy and then gunned the engine in a fast turn back towards Dartmouth. He had picked up the tail too and decided he couldn't leave Gill in the lurch. She could probably take care of herself but he wasn't sure if she was capable enough to deal with a three-man tail.

It took a few seconds to nudge back to the pontoon and tie up. He leaped up the ramp to the embankment where a kiosk shielded him. He saw the tails first; two on his side of the road and the third on the pavement twenty metres behind Gill who was window shopping at the corner of Raleigh Street. She had not moved very far and seemed in no hurry. The tails were hanging back, studying postcards and tourist souvenirs but watching Gill with their peripheral vision. The place was busy with tourists and they had plenty of cover to conceal them.

It wasn't the individuals who had alerted him but the pattern they made in the swirling tide of humanity that coursed along the pavements. It was as if an eddy had occurred in a smooth stretch of water, swirling around a hidden rock, or made by the fins of a browsing fish. It was distinct and he was trained to spot it.

Gill seemed oblivious. She turned back on herself which gave the closest tail a fright as he stepped quickly into an open doorway and turned his back to her. She appeared not to notice the sudden flurry of movement and continued on casually towards the small pool known as the boat float where she turned left and walked through the parked cars to the corner of Duke Street. She stopped to peer in the window of a jewellers. There were fewer people here but it was still busy. The tails had swapped over and the two who had been on Lacey's side of the road, one man and one woman wearing bland clothing now loitering nearby, and the third man further back on the opposite side of the road having taken his hat off and stuffed it in a pocket. From where he was standing, leaning on the wing of a parked car as if he owned it, Lacey could see a fine silver wire trail from the man's left ear and disappear under his collar. None of the watchers seemed to be aware they were being watched in turn. Lacey hoped that the *Andrea Two* wasn't staked out as the news of his non-return would have been reported by any watchers there. It was a risk that they might think he had turned back but a small one.

He wondered why they had a tail and what their motives were. These people were good at their jobs, if a little slack, therefore professionals. That narrowed the field but not enough to provide a definitive answer.

Gill had walked on, turning up a narrow street full of small boutiques and coffee shops where a few women in the main were chatting and eyeing the clothes in the windows. Gill walked into one shop and ran a hand along a clothes rail, taking the odd blouse and holding it up. The female tail stood outside the door looking in through the window while her partner stood opposite using the window of a men's shop as a mirror.

Lacey stayed back around the corner where he could see their reflections but they could not see him. The third man had passed further along the lane where he too was pretending to study the goods in a tourist trap. He could see they were becoming uncomfortable in the thinner cover provided, their body language edgy.

Gill appeared in the doorway holding a yellow shirt up to the light with the shopkeeper behind her. She smiled at the tail and said something to the surprised woman, probably *'what do you think of this … would it suit me?'* The tail made a noncommittal wave of the hand and walked away, her usefulness blown. Clever Gill, she knew she was being followed and was thinning out the opposition.

Gill bought the shirt and came out with a colourful carrier bag over her shoulder, turning left again and further into the lane which had several dark narrow alleyways running between the buildings. She abruptly stopped near one of these and kicked off a shoe. The second tail was so close to her that he had to swerve around her as she toppled towards him. She pushed out an arm to save herself and gripped his wrist.

"Damn stones," Lacey heard her say. "Could I just hold on to you for a second?"

She pulled the shoe back on, then suddenly hopped sideways into the alley and pulled the man in with her.

Lacey saw the front tail's head swing round and he turned back, his left hand to his ear, his right reaching under his jacket.

Lacey moved too at a fast walk, he was right behind the man as he rushed into the alley.

"Drop the weapon," he heard. He turned into the alley, pulled his Sig and pointed it at the back of the man's head. "That goes for you too, pal," he said. He craned his neck to see that Gill had the first man up against the wall with a small automatic pressed under his chin. "Busy day shopping, honey?" he said then spoke to the man with the gun. "Nice and easy, mister. Drop the shooter and raise your hands."

The man was crouched in the isosceles stance with his arms stretched out in front holding his Glock with both hands. Lacey clicked back the hammer on the Sig. "Last time of asking."

The man straightened, separated his hands and dropped the pistol.

"Thanks, now turn and face the wall, keep both hands on it and step back."

Gill had done the same with the other man. She ran a hand down the man's back and pulled the wires from the radio.

Lacey followed suit then cocked an enquiring eye at Gill.

She shrugged. "Don't know."

"Let's assume we have a couple of minutes before the cavalry arrives," Lacey said. "Must be back-up somewhere close."

"I need to know who these dorks are and why they're following me," Gill said.

Lacey pulled a face. "Just you?"

"Yes, I think so. My phones were bugged before I left."

"Nice company you keep," Lacey said and grinned. He nudged the man next to him with the barrel of the Sig. "Well?"

"Piss off."

A mobile rang in the man's pocket. Lacey patted until he found it and brought it out. He pressed the green button. "Yes?" He listened and held the phone up. "It's for you," he said to Gill, "someone called Blake. Ring any bells?"

19

Gill gave a resigned shake of the head. "I should have guessed." She stepped back towards Lacey until she was between the two men. "Right, you two, down on your bellies and clasp your hands behind your necks, fingers entwined. Do it now."

Both men looked sheepishly at each other before complying slowly.

"Keep these two covered," she said to Lacey, took the phone from his hand and spoke into it. "Yes, Colonel? … I don't need nurse-maiding … right … keep them out of my way in future … and the same to you." She cut the call.

"Friend of yours?" Lacey asked.

Gill grimaced. "Not that you'd notice. We have a history." She kicked the sole of the nearest man's shoe. "Okay, you two, you can get up now. Party's over, your boss will be giving you a bollocking for getting caught when you reconnect your PRRs so you can piss off and don't let me see you again." Both men climbed to their feet as Lacey picked up the dropped Glock, ejected the magazine and the round in the breech and gave the three items to its owner. "Better get the sights checked," he said.

The man glared at him pushed the pistol into its holster and dropped the mag and round into his pocket. He shuffled out with his companion and turned back towards the river.

"Think that's the last we'll see of them?" Lacey asked.

Gill shrugged. Blake had said it was for her own good, that he was keeping an eye on her and she only partly believed him. There was more to this than the man was letting on and it was beginning to nag at her more and more as the operation unfolded. She turned to Lacey. "Fancy a coffee?"

They found a small café and sat outside in the sun where they would not be overheard. "Why'd you come back?" Gill asked in a low whisper.

Lacey matched her tone. "I picked up the tail, same as you. Thought it better to take myself out of the equation, or seem to."

"And you didn't say anything to me."

Lacey smiled a lazy smile. "That cuts both ways, honey."

Gill grunted in annoyance. "Even so. You should have said something."

Lacey nodded, his face now serious. "I get what you're saying."

"Dammit, we're supposed to be partners in this and you're treating me as if I was a player not an operator. Don't keep me in the dark, Ricky." The Ricky slipped out with temper and she immediately regretted the stab of pain the memory brought.

Lacey seemed to notice and he slipped a hand across the table to grip her fingers. The touch jolted her and she pulled her hand away. "Don't."

He settled back in his seat leaving a hand on the table top. "Fine. I guess I do play my cards close. Been burned once too often. I'll try to do better."

She let her breath out in a long sigh. "Look, I'm sorry too. I suppose I didn't want to get you entangled in my mess. Blake doesn't trust me to play straight with him and I'm beginning to think there's more at stake here than either of us has been told. I get that the Chinese may be involved and the fact that Forrestal has been killed makes it a dangerous connection but beyond that there's something more that our masters suspect and either don't trust us to know or they don't yet have a clue themselves what's going on."

The coffee arrived and Lacey stayed silent as it was served. Then he nodded. "I think you're right. We're a catalyst thrown into the mix to get a reaction. My people are pretty straight, if they knew they'd say. I can't speak for MI6 but I guess they're past-masters at keeping left hands and right hands in ignorance of what each is doing. Speaking of which, why is Six in this and not MI5?

Gill twitched her lips, it was almost a snarl. "I wouldn't work with Five if they were the last hope for mankind. I wouldn't trust them as far as I could spit, not after what they did to Ricky. They worked with a government dirty tricks department to get him court-martialled and then one of their top operatives tried to kill him when he was in his hospital bed. No time for any of them, not now or ever."

"But Six is okay," Lacey said, "although it's unusual for their agents to go routinely armed." He arched his lazy eyebrow at Gill.

She gave him a taut grin in return. "I think those guys were Special Reconnaissance Regiment. The isosceles stance. The army is still teaching it. I prefer the Weaver. It's more adaptable."

"The army are concerned about seam weaknesses in body armour if you stand three-quarters on to an enemy as you do with the Weaver." He paused, as if he was about to add something, then nodded and pursed his lips before continuing. "It's early days and we've barely made a dent. Maybe once we speak with Tarrant and the police we'll get an idea but at the moment we're shooting in the dark."

Gill raised one eyebrow. "Shooting? Is that why you're here?"

"It's my job."

"What exactly is your job, Mister Arnold? Who exactly do you work for? And don't say if you told me you'd have to kill me."

Lacey grinned. "As true as that may be. All you need to know is that we're on the side of the angels. That's all I can tell you."

Gill grimaced. "The new order of honesty and openness didn't last long then."

"Not as far as my organisation is concerned but I will share everything else. I now know I can trust you to work with me and you don't have a hidden agenda. You handle yourself well but, having said that, you took a risk dragging that guy into the alley. The front tail was on it immediately."

Gill raised her eyebrow again. "Risk? I don't think so."

109

"The guy got the drop on you."

"And *you* got one on *him*. I saw you lurking on the corner when I came out with the shirt to get rid of the woman. I just knew you'd have my six."

Lacey chuckled at the terminology. "You must watch too much T.V. You're right though. I'll always have your back covered."

Gill looked him straight in his colour-flecked gunmetal grey eyes for a few long seconds then nodded. "I do believe you will. You'll have to forgive me about the television though; what else does a lonely old maid have to entertain herself?"

Lacey pointed at the brightly coloured carrier bag on the seat next to her. "There's always a little retail therapy. If you're done shopping, shall we get back to the boat? I'll try to call Inspector Craddock again."

When they arrived back on the *Andrea Two* there was a note taped to the sliding glass doors. Gill peeled it off as Lacey removed the outboard and raised the dinghy out of the water. She waved the note.

"Shall I open it?"

He picked up the outboard engine and waved his free hand in return. "Go ahead. I'll need to stow this below."

He brushed past her and she used a thumbnail to prise open the envelope. "It's an invitation," she called. "To cocktails at the yacht club. Tonight, seven for seven-thirty, dress optional."

Lacey reappeared wiping his hands on a rag. "Who's it from?"

"Obviously from someone who wants to get to know us better." She turned over the heavy paste card and bit her lip. "From a Derek and Shelley Pierce."

Was this the Derek she had heard about in the shower room whose wife was concerned about people nosing into their business? If so, they were damn fast movers; so fast that it was suspicious. Guilty consciences? Underhand dealings? Or something more? It would be interesting to find out and the invitation had saved her the bother of putting out feelers of her own. She had a little guilty twinge about not telling Lacey but decided her decision was the right one. This evening would tell if her instinct was sound.

20

Lacey took the invitation from Gill's hand and flipped it over. "No RSVP. They must be confident we'll turn up."

"We should go," Gill said. "It may be interesting."

Lacey nodded. "No problem, making friends and interrogating people is what we're here for." He went back into the saloon and picked up the satellite phone, punching in a pre-set number with a stiff forefinger. "Ben? It's Rick. Can you do a quick search on a Derek and Shelley Pierce who live in the Torbay area? I need to know soonest … by eighteen-hundred latest. Thanks." He put the phone back in its cradle and looked at Gill. "At least we'll know just what we're getting into here."

"Forewarned is forearmed," Gill said.

Lacey grinned. "Very philosophical. I suppose that's why you carry the P7."

"Can't be too careful these days. What about you and that 226?"

Lacey grinned. "Old habits … but I wasn't complaining. Now I need to call Inspector Craddock." He picked up his mobile and hit the redial button. This time he was lucky and the call was answered on the first ring.

"What?"

"Detective Inspector Craddock?"

"This is she. Look, I'm busy. What do you want?"

Lacey decided to cut the formalities. "To know what progress you've made on the Forrestal killing."

"What?"

"The Forrestal killing. You are investigating it?"

"Jesus, that was weeks ago."

"It's still an ongoing case."

"Yes, we never close a murder file. Anyway, just who the hell are you?"

"My name's Rick Arnold, a friend of the Forrestal family. They need some answers."

Craddock snorted. "Well I don't have any. The trail is cold and stuffed like last year's turkey."

"Is that what I tell the commander's family?"

"Look, Mister Arnold, I'm in the middle of a crime scene. I have SOCOs all around me and I'm knee deep in blood and guts. I don't have time for this right now."

"When will you have time?" Lacey waited for a reply as Craddock shouted instructions to a subordinate.

"What was that?" she said when her attention was back on the call.

"I'd like to get something solid to work with, Inspector. When can we meet?"

"Whereabouts are you?"

"Kingswear."

"Can you get to Exeter?"

"Yes, we have transport, Inspector."

"We?"

"My wife and me."

113

"Oh, okay. Can you get to headquarters for ten-thirty tomorrow? I can give you ten minutes."

Lacey indicated to Gill for a pen and pad and she quickly found both on the chart table and handed them over.

"Fine," Lacey said. "We can make that. Give me the details."

"We're at Middlemoor." She gave the postcode. "Punch that into your satnav. I'll leave word at reception to expect you." She cut the call.

Lacey threw the pen down and arched his lazy eyebrow at Gill. "Detective Inspector Craddock is a woman and by the sound of things way overworked. We have an audience at ten-thirty hours tomorrow in Exeter."

"One step forward," Gill said. "Did it sound promising?"

Lacey shook his head. "Ten minutes of her valuable time. It seems that Forrestal's murder has been put on the back burner for lack of clues. Craddock has moved on to new adventures and she doesn't seem to be enjoying the experience."

"Can we give her a nudge back onto our case?"

Now Lacey smiled and it reached his eyes. "My thoughts exactly. Let's give Inspector Craddock a reason to dust off her Forrestal files."

Gill returned the smile. "Leave it to me. I'm sure Colonel Blake will be only too happy to lend a hand." She pulled out her mobile and stepped out onto the rear deck. Lacey could part hear her conversation and approved. Craddock would be getting a call from the Chief Constable in the next hour. She wouldn't like it but she would have to learn to live with it.

Lacey had just finished swabbing the superstructure on the foredeck when his mobile vibrated. He dropped the mop and sat on the raised sunbed to take the call. "Yes, Ben?"

"You certainly pick 'em, Rick."

"Our friends the Pierces?"

"They have quite a reputation between them. He started out in petty crime, cautioned twice but never convicted. The police suspected him of minor drug dealing but could never pin anything on him. Seems he decided crime didn't pay, at least not enough, and moved into business. He part owns a new casino in Torquay together with a business registered in the Virgin Islands. My sources say it could be linked to organised crime but again there's no proof. The casino is a money pit and he makes a small fortune out of it according to the accounts. He also has part ownership of two fishing trawlers and a tipper truck company which runs loads from a quarry they own on the edge of Dartmoor. All above board as far as we can make out."

"A shining example of bad boy made good, it would seem," Lacey said.

Reid grunted a laugh. "I'd not put too much money on him being clean. There's something not right there and it's probably money laundering through that Virgin Islands connection. Nobody goes from petty crime to part owning a casino in a few years unless he's hooky. Just be aware he may have some serious partners behind him."

"Point taken. What about Missus Pierce?"

"A couple of charges for soliciting when she was a teenager; slap on the wrist jobs." Reid said with unconscious humour. "She helps run the casino as floor manager, hiring and firing the croupiers who are mostly young women. She appears to have cleaned up her act on a personal basis but she's in neck deep with her husband's businesses and listed as a director of all four companies. That's all I have for now. How's it going down there?"

"Early days, Ben, but this info may help, thanks."

Lacey cut the call and juggled the phone in his hand as he thought. He could see no obvious connection between the quarry, the tipper company and the fishing enterprise. Fishing was more profitable now that their catch limits had increased. It was probably a good investment and that was likely the reason Pierce was involved with it. Stone, aggregate and gravel were always needed for construction and that would be a good solid business to be involved with too. Maybe Pierce was hedging his bets and hoping to hide behind their legitimacy.

Why were the Pierces so keen on making their acquaintance? Perhaps Derek saw him as a soft touch for the casino; someone who could afford to lose a few thou and not miss it. There was just a possibility that it was as a result of the enquiries into Forrestal's murder and they were about to dip their toes into murky waters.

21

Gill came into the saloon dressed to kill. She was wearing her new yellow shirt unbuttoned to show the swell of her breasts in the V, white slacks and yellow snakeskin sandals. She noticed Lacey's irises expand when he saw her.

"I thought the invitation read dress optional," he said.

She tilted her head. "You want me to go naked?"

"I just figured an old jacket, slacks and deck shoes. "You look a million bucks."

Gill grinned. She was pleased with the compliment but did not want to let it show. "You can thank uplift bras and Blake. This lot has gone on his platinum card."

Lacey sucked his teeth. "Worth every penny. Let's hope he sees it that way."

Gill waved a hand. "I'll worry about that later." She looked at her Rolex. "Time to go. Are you ready?"

Lacey pointed to the Rolex. "I hope that didn't go on the card."

Gill shook her head. "It was a present from my dad and step mum. When they got married I was their maid of honour. This doesn't owe anything to Blake."

Lacey gave a nod of approval, picked his mobile off the table and slid it into his pocket. "I'd hoped to have heard from Tarrant by now." He tapped the pocket. "Just in case."

Gill pulled her Louis Vuitton shoulder bag round to her front and tapped that. "Just in case."

Lacey nodded. "Looks heavy."

"All the usual stuff a girl needs. Compact, lipstick, nail file, comb, perfume ..."

"P7," Lacey said.

"Well ... maybe the odd unusual thing," Gill replied. Lacey had briefed her on the Pierces and she did not think she was being paranoid. It was insurance pure and simple and she felt more comfortable with its weight in her bag.

They were a few minutes late and the Pierces and one other couple were waiting when they entered the bar. Pierce stepped forward with a wide smile and a hand out to greet them. He took Gill's hand first and kissed it, eyeing her over her knuckles. "Missus Arnold, what a pleasure. I'm Derek Pierce"

Gill narrowly avoided a shudder but gave him a return smile. "How gallant. Gill, please."

"I'm Rick," Lacey said and waited while Pierce dropped Gill's hand with obvious reluctance.

"Rick. Nice to meet you. Let me introduce my wife Shelley. Shell, this is Gill and Rick." Shelley turned and held out her hand. "Charmed."

"These other two are Kate and Bill. Bill is a colleague." Pierce waved a vague hand in the other couple's direction and they both raised their glasses in salute.

"Sure," Lacey said. "Hi folks."

"What can I get you?" Pierce asked.

"If we're talking cocktails, I'll have a Singapore Sling," Gill said and moved so that Pierce could no longer peer down her cleavage.

"Manhattan for me," Lacey said. He moved to stand closer to the other couple and Gill could see him sizing the man up. He was in his sixties, tall and thickset with fingers like salami sausages making the cocktail glass he was holding look even more fragile.

"What do you do, Bill?" Lacey asked.

It was his wife who answered. "Bill's in aggregates, Rick. He supplies all the roadworks in the area."

Lacey nodded but still looked at Bill. "Quarry your own?"

It was Kate again. "Oh yes, we have a quarry near Buckfastleigh on the edge of the moors."

"Always thought I might like to get into aggregates," Lacey said. "Always a market for it."

Pierce materialised at Lacey's elbow with a glass in his hand. "Here you go, Rick." He handed the glass over. "What is it *you* do then?"

Lacey blinked slowly and turned his head. "Nothing. Not now. Retired a few years back. What about you, Derek?"

"This an' that. Partners with Bill, and I have a part share in two trawlers that moor up at the fish quay here."

"Derek owns a casino," Kate said.

Gill had placed herself alongside Shelley. She felt that the woman had taken an instant dislike to her, probably because of her husband's ogling and wanted her as a buffer. She heard Kate's remark and saw Lacey rise to it as if it was a surprise. She tilted her glass at Shelley. "A casino, how exciting."

Shelley gave her a cold smile that didn't reach her eyes. "Not if you worked there."

Gill pretended to be amazed. "Really? I'd have thought … you'd meet so many interesting people … all that glamour … and all that money won or lost on the turn of a card or the spin of a wheel. Makes me quiver just to think about it."

Shelley sniffed. "There's a lot more to running a casino than that. You don't know the things we have to do and the problems we have. Just getting decent croupiers is a nightmare. The good ones all want to work in London or Monte Carlo. Most of the ones we have are off the cruise ships that got mothballed during that pandemic a year or two back and they're a flighty lot."

Derek had been listening with half an ear and turned. "It's not all bad news. The place is called the Golden Nugget. We took over an old hotel that had gone bust and converted it. Great views over Torbay. We have rooms and plenty of parking. Why don't you pay us a visit? Stay for a night or two. Might suit you better than sleeping on a boat."

Gill gave him an amused smile. "Golden Nugget? Very original."

Derek gave an exaggerated shrug. "Okay, we might have borrowed the name from the Yanks in Las Vegas, oh, sorry, Rick, but there's a good reason for calling it that, as you'll see when you visit."

Gill made a pointed correction. "*If,* we visit,"

"Yes, don't go twisting the poor woman's arm, Derek," Shelley said. "She may not like gambling."

"Oh, I don't mind a flutter as long as the odds are good," Gill said. "I just don't like losing."

Derek gave her a leer. "Well maybe we could make special arrangements for you."

Gill raised her chin towards Lacey. "What do you think, Rick?"

Lacey grunted. "I only bet on certainties but you go if you want." His mobile jingled in his pocket. He pulled it out, peered at the display and waved it. "Gotta take this." He moved to the window that overlooked the river out of earshot but was back in a few seconds. He took Gill's arm. "Sorry, honey, it's the call I've been waiting for. The navy are gonna cough up some info on Commander Forrestal and I have a meet with them now." He kissed her cheek. I'll see you back on the boat." He turned to Pierce. "Thanks for the drink, I owe you one." He waved at the other couple and left.

Kate put her glass on the table. "I think we ought to be going too. Bill has an early start tomorrow. Nice meeting you, Gill."

Pierce made a show of asking them to stay but Gill could see he was pleased to see the back of them. He waved a hand at Shelley. "Can you see them out, Shell?"

Shelley shot him a barbed look but did not argue as she ushered the pair quickly towards the door.

Pierce sidled up to Gill's elbow and put a hand around her waist. "Well what do you say for a visit to the Nugget? How about tomorrow? We could have a few drinks and I'll give you a personal tour of the place."

Gill eased herself free of his arm. "Sounds wonderful but I'll need to think about it."

He took a card out of his wallet and slipped it between her breasts. "Give me a call, let me know what you decide. It'll be something to remember, I'll make sure of that."

22

Lacey had seen a flash of something cross Pierce's face when he mentioned the navy. Surprise, maybe, or concern, he wasn't sure but he filed it for future reference. He took the lower passenger ferry across to Dartmouth and walked the short distance to the Royal Dart Hotel opposite the boat float. The Harbour Bar, Tarrant had said and he turned right into a narrow room with low beams and small booths along one wall. Two men sat in the window seats and one half rose when he entered and waved a hand.

Lacey eyed them. One was young, late twenties, and the other was older, thick-set with an air of command about him. Lacey walked over.

"Mister Tarrant?"

The young man nodded and turned to his companion. "This is Admiral Chichester."

Chichester waved a hand. "Pull up a chair, Mister Arnold, and explain what this is about. Tarrant, get us some drinks."

Tarrant left for the bar without a word. Lacey sat and gave the admiral a level stare. "Didn't Captain Portman bring you up to speed, Admiral?"

Chichester grimaced. "What little he knew. I got more from the Admiralty. It appears we have to be nice to you."

Tarrant returned with three neat malt whiskies cupped in his fingers. "Malt all right, Mister Arnold?"

Lacey took a glass. "Sure, thanks." He set the glass down on the table and waited for Tarrant to hand a glass to Chichester and sit. "I understand that you and Commander Forrestal were buddies, Mister Tarrant."

Tarrant took a sip which gave him time to frame his reply. "We were on friendly terms, yes. He was a good bloke and we got on well; he was a keen ornithologist like me and into owls in a big way. He always had a pair of binoculars in his hands. We went to a couple of bashes together, had a few drinks, that sort of thing but we didn't live in each other's pockets."

Lacey nodded. "So you'd have no idea if he was seeing a woman, someone particular?"

Tarrant shot a sideways glance at Chichester who gave an almost imperceptible nod.

"Look, I'm not sure but there may have been someone. He was prone to disappearing off by himself in the latter days. Not sure where he went but it may have been Torquay. Couldn't swear to it but he did seem to have something on his mind and it may have been girl trouble. He did get a bit awkward at times, which was unlike him."

"Did you tell this to the police?"

"I might have mentioned it but it was all conjecture and they didn't seem to think it had any bearing on the case."

"Do you … think it has a bearing?"

Tarrant shot another look at Chichester and got the same response. "There was something else … something we couldn't tell the police about."

125

"Why not?"

"Navy business, Mister Arnold," Chichester said. "And it was not judged to be relevant to the police's enquiries."

"So, why are you telling me?"

Chichester poked a finger towards the ceiling. "Orders from on high. It appears that the US Navy holds some sway with their Lordships at the Admiralty. You will of course appreciate that whatever we tell you will remain confidential."

"I don't have a problem with that."

"In that case … tell him Tarrant."

"Well … you know that Commander Forrestal was an anti-submarine warfare expert …?"

Lacey nodded and Tarrant continued. "… we had a group of cadets aboard the new cruiser, *HMS Norfolk*, in Torbay, making them au fait with the new more sophisticated anti-submarine warfare systems they have aboard, when the commander suddenly went quiet. He'd picked up something on the screen. I don't know what but I thought it might be a basking shark, we do get them in this area, but he wouldn't confirm it. He just scribbled a note and put it in his pocket. I asked him about it but he just shook his head and muttered about something not being possible. He went back aboard the *Norfolk* a couple of times to speak with the sonar men but I'm sure nothing came of it. The sonar's switched off most of the time while the ship's at anchor and there's no need for it. Its mid-frequency range can affect cetaceans, whales and dolphins and the like, so we have to be considerate."

Lacey turned to Chichester. "Do you think this may have a bearing on Forrestal's death, Admiral?"

Chichester narrowed his eyes. "We don't know what it is that the commander saw, or what he thought he saw, and cannot say if it has a bearing or not. It was something that obviously disturbed him but why is an enigma. The ship's chief electrical engineer regularly checks the equipment to ensure there are no faults with the kit and he has found nothing untoward. On balance, I believe it is more likely that the commander fell foul of someone unconnected with the navy."

"And I should look elsewhere for answers," Lacey said. It was natural for the admiral to want to protect his service and he wondered if they had been told of the significance of the weapon's calibre in Forrestal's death; it appeared not or they would be more concerned about security.

"I think we've helped you all we can, Mister Arnold. I am so sorry that this matter cannot be concluded satisfactorily. We would dearly like to see the murderer brought to justice but, as I said, there is little more that we can do."

"Do you still have the commander's possessions?"

Chichester shook his head. "No. The police made a thorough search of his cabin looking for clues but found nothing of significance. They released it to us and we packaged up the commander's personal belongings and sent them back to the States. Why would that be of interest?"

Lacey shrugged. "I just thought there may be something, letters maybe, anything that could shed some light."

"Unfortunately not."

Lacey grimaced. "Worth asking I guess. Well, thanks for the drink and your time. Seems we're no further forward; I've nothing more to tell the commander's family."

He left and walked back to the ferry where he stood in the queue waiting for it to return to the Dartmouth side. The information the admiral had given him could be something or nothing. He was willing to bet that the admiral was downplaying it to protect the navy, and maybe to hide the capabilities of their new sonar array. He had heard that not only was it more sophisticated it was far more sensitive than previous versions. Type 23 frigates were the main anti-submarine warfare screens for capital ships like the two new aircraft carriers, the *Queen Elizabeth* and the *Prince of Wales* but they were aging. *HMS Norfolk* was the latest cruiser in the navy, specifically commissioned to join the *Prince of Wales* battle group with its cutting edge weapons technology. Whatever it was that had spooked Forrestal could have ramifications for the safety of the big ships. Maybe the Chinese were testing the *Norfolk's* capabilities and Forrestal had discovered it. Maybe that was what got him killed. But why had he not mentioned it? Why keep that sort of knowledge to himself?

Maybe he didn't. Maybe he sent a report further up the food chain and that was why the powers-that-be were looking into it. If that was the case why wasn't he and Gill fully briefed? Something didn't add up.

23

"Pierce is a creep and a lech," Gill said as she nosed her Mercedes out of the marina car park and up the hill towards the A379 on the way to Exeter the next morning.

Lacey looked across from the front passenger seat. "Did he give you a hard time after I left?"

Gill snapped a look at him. "He tried. Had the fuckin' cheek to push his grimy business card down my bra. If Shelley hadn't come back I'd have clocked him then and there." She was still fuming from the insult. She had gone straight to the showers and washed herself before dropping into bed. It was as if she had been molested and no one should have to suffer that in this day and age. She still had steam coming out of her ears. "The man should be locked up."

"Maybe he will be when this is finished," Lacey said.

Gill exhaled loudly. "I know I shouldn't react to it but it damn well gets my goat that men like him think they can get away with it." She knew she was being precious. She was a highly trained undercover specialist and should be able to cope with sexual predators but somehow this was different; she wanted Lacey to know … and maybe to care. It was a rogue thought and it jolted her.

Lacey saw the flash of shock that crossed her face. "What led up to that point," he asked.

Gill grimaced and relaxed a little. "It was that invitation to visit his casino. I said I'd think about it and that was when he pushed his card down my shirt and leered about showing me a good time. Bloody thing scratched too." She rubbed her chest with her knuckles.

"Leaving that aside what did you make of the whole scenario?"

Gill shot him another glance. He was changing the subject in a subtle way, getting her back on track. She couldn't help a stab of disappointment.

"Odd. That's what I thought. That other couple, Kate and Bill, I reckon the cat got his tongue, or maybe he was a dummy and she was the ventriloquist. He looked more like a nightclub bouncer than a company director and she was a bit overweight and mousey on the outside but hard as nails underneath that frilly exterior. They couldn't wait to leave once you went and I got the impression they were only there as a makeweight; to try and make us feel more comfortable. Pierce soon spoiled that though."

"What do you make of Shelley?"

"Hard-boiled bottle blonde. She's had some work done to her face, botox and a lift here and there. Breast enlargements too; they were far too perky for her age."

Lacey gave a wry smile. "I meant technically."

Gill blinked. "Oh, yes. Well I think she actually runs things, certainly the casino. She's scared of Pierce, that's why he can get away with his leching but I reckon she's a tough nut in her own right."

Lacy nodded. "I agree. Do you think they have anything to do with why we're here?"

"God, I hope not. I'd hate to have to spend more time trying to suss out the connection with randy Derek."

"Seriously."

"I get the feeling there's something not right there," Gill said. "But I don't know what it is."

"We'll let it simmer for a while. I had an interesting conversation with the navy last night which might be more pertinent." He recounted the story and waited while Gill digested the information. "That could be why we're here," he said finally.

"The Chinese spying on our military secrets?" Gill said. She shrugged. "It could be possible. I read a newspaper report that the *Prince of Wales* battle group is headed for the South China Sea soon. It makes sense for the Chinese to find out what they're up against."

"Yes, but what was it that Forrestal picked up on? Frogmen? They would have had to come from nearby."

Gill grunted. "Take your pick. The area is alive with tourists, snorklers, pleasure boaters, kayakers, the works. Nobody would blink twice on seeing a bloke pull on an aqualung and head out into the briny bay. Then again there wouldn't be much for a diver to see, I think that sonar gear is retractable and only lowered when in use. They usually have a towed array strung out behind them too."

Lacey's eyes opened wider and he turned his head to look at her. "My, my, you do know a lot."

"It's my job to keep pace with developments. I get all sorts of technical magazines sent to me. I need to know what I'm sending my boys into when a contract is mooted."

"Attractive and caring. A heady combination."

"Oh shut up, Mister Arnold," she said with a laugh. She made a joke of it but she was unaccountably pleased with the remark. He might not have meant it to be taken seriously but she liked the sentiment just the same. She was moved and she didn't understand why.

"Which gets us no further with knowing what piqued the commander's interest and what got him killed," Lacey said. "Maybe the police will have something we can work with but it's a long shot."

"I get the feeling the emphasis is correct," Gill said. "We're not here to find the who but the why. We already know how."

"I reckon that's a fair assessment, knowing what we think we know now. The police are the people who should be chasing down the killer and they won't be particularly interested in the why, only in as much as it supports their case."

"Whereas the why has much more significance for us." Gill finished Lacey's train of thought for him.

They pulled off the M5 motorway and followed the satnav directions to the police headquarters off a large roundabout. The building was late sixties red brick in parts but had been extended over the years with some 21st century additions. Gill found a visitor's car parking space and pulled in.

"Gird up your loins, Mister Arnold, it seems, from what you've told me, your Inspector Craddock is a bit of a battle-axe."

"Tetchy and overworked I guess."

They waited at reception where they were handed lanyards with VISITOR, printed on the attached card in large block capitals. They were told to put them on and keep them on for the duration of their visit.

Gill had just sunk into a low chair when heels clip-clopped on the hard floor and a connecting door opened.

It was a young woman with brown hair tied into a ponytail that swung behind her as she turned. She was tall and slender, mid thirties, with sharp brown eyes and a nose that looked as if it had been broken at some time. Gill noticed she had a smoker's brown stains between the first and second fingers of her right hand.

"Mister and Missus Arnold, please come this way."

She held the door for them then led them along a corridor and up a flight of stairs to a door which was marked 'Interview Room 2'.

The woman, who had not introduced herself, opened the door with a swipe card and gestured them inside. "Take a seat."

She left them for a minute but came back with a thick folder in her arms. She sat opposite them and dropped the folder on the table with a thwack.

"Right, I'm Fiona Craddock and I don't like my Chief Constable breathing down my neck so let's get this over with as I've got a lot on my plate right now."

24

Lacey looked across the table at the feisty inspector and nodded. "We appreciate your time, ma'am. We can only guess at how busy you are. Whatever you can share with us will be welcome for the commander's family back home in the States."

Craddock blew through her nostrils, looked up at the ceiling and then slowly closed and opened her eyes as if she was assessing Lacey's attitude as patronising or he was merely being an American. She seemed to come to a decision and sat forward in her seat, hands reaching for the file. She flipped open the cover.

"This is all we've got. You're welcome to read through the reports but you can't take anything away."

Gill gave her a thank you smile. "Could you give us a brief overview?"

Craddock looked at her watch, a Fitbit on a black rubber strap. "Okay, I have a few minutes."

"We know Commander Forrestal was murdered but that's about the size of it, ma'am," Lacey said.

Craddock exhaled again but this time through her mouth. "I can tell you that he was shot three times, once in the head and twice in the chest at close range. Any one of which could have killed him. It looks very much like a professional hit. His body was found floating in the Dart by a woman unconnected with the murder; bit of a shock for her. The post mortem did not throw up anything of interest, although we did recover a bullet. So far we have not been able to match it to any known firearm other than we know it was fired from a pistol. After some time in the water we could find no DNA evidence to help our enquiries. The victim wasn't robbed, he still had his wallet and wristwatch which was an expensive Raymond Weil, so robbery has been ruled out."

"Do you have any theories at all," Lacey asked.

Craddock shrugged. "This appears to be a motiveless crime. Everybody liked him, he had no problems at the college that we know of, we couldn't trace a girlfriend … these things usually come down to sex or money. It appears motiveless but we know that can't be the case; there has to be a reason, it's just that we've had bugger-all success in finding one. If it was a professional hit, which seems most likely, it's probable we'll never know who did it or on whose orders. We had uniform from the Kingsbridge and Dartmouth Basic Command Unit doing house to house but you'll appreciate, if you've come up from Kingswear, that the houses are widespread and not ideally placed.

They found his car parked on the street outside the college but it had been wiped clean and gave us nothing to work with. Due to the number of tourists and yotties who come and go it becomes almost impossible to find anyone who saw anything, heard anything or admitted knowing anything. We have no crime scene, no weapon, no suspects, no nothing."

"You say no one heard anything. Three shots didn't draw any attention?" Lacey said.

"We think the pistol was muffled, something which adds to the idea that it was a professional hit."

Craddock looked at her Fitbit again. "Look. I'm sorry I have to go. I have a meeting with my chief over all the drugs flooding into this area … maybe I shouldn't have told you that … but it's what's taking up most of my time right now. Yesterday's murder was one slime ball drug dealer carving up another over territory. Look, stay as long as you like, read through the files if it will help. I can say that Commander Forrestal would not have suffered, he would have died almost instantly. Maybe that will help his family come to terms with it.

"If you press the button beside the door a constable will come and let you out. Just remember, don't take anything from the files."

Craddock left with a swirl of ponytail and the door clicked shut behind her.

Lacey reached across and dragged the file towards them. "What do you think, Gill?"

Gill pursed her lips. "No further forward, I'd say. It seems a bit odd that the calibre of the pistol that killed Forrestal didn't ring any bells with them."

Lacey grunted. "Not in their usual ambit. It's unlikely they would have come across such a weapon in the normal course of events. It may be they will link it to the drugs trade. Guns are being smuggled in from Eastern Europe and finding their way into the hands of gangs. I don't think Craddock's slip of the tongue over drug dealing in this area was an accident. She wanted us to know."

"She suspects Forrestal's death was gang related," Gill said.

"Which puts an entirely different complexion on the case; nothing to do with secret sonar and Chinese spying," Lacey said.

Gill grimaced. "My brain's beginning to hurt. I can't imagine Forrestal was involved in the drugs trade but who knows. Let's thumb through the file to see if the Brigadier missed anything or something might jump out at a second look."

"Maybe the odd moth," Lacey grumbled. "What gets me is that this must be related to China somehow. We know that the pistol is only used by Chinese Special Forces and hasn't been sold on the black market. There must be a connection somewhere."

"I wonder how certain our people are about that. It's possible a Chinese soldier somewhere decided to make some cash for himself by flogging some pistols on the side. It's happened before."

"You could be right," Lacey said and shrugged. "It's a slim connection at best." He took half the papers from the file and handed them to Gill. "Here's your pile. I'll wade through the other half."

They sat for half an hour turning pages like metronomes. Lacey wondered if it was worth the time as all he had found just corroborated Craddock's verbal report. The stomach contents revealed nothing other than Forrestal had eaten a two course dinner from the college kitchens and he had no alcohol in his system, neither was there any trace of recreational drugs, even his hair where it tended to lodge for many months. Anything under his nails had been washed out by his immersion and replaced by river mud. In fact there was nothing that would help. He turned over another sheet when Gill grunted and held out a plastic evidence bag.

"What do you make of this?"

Lacey took it from her hand and held it up to the light. A sheet torn from a notebook."

Gill nodded. "It says here that it was found in his wallet and was drenched. They peeled it apart and dried it out. There's some writing on one side which was made with some kind of wax pencil and wasn't washed off completely."

"I see it." Lacey squinted at the vague squiggles. "Doesn't make any sense."

"Do you think it might be the note Tarrant told you about that Forrestal made when he was working with the sonar?"

"Could be. I can make some of it out. *Nar S,* question mark. *10m,* comma, *H. NNE. 5ks. Disa.* As I said, doesn't make any sense."

Gill pulled out her mobile. "Lay it on the table, Rick. If we can't take the actual item I can take a pic of it. Give us time to work it out at leisure. Maybe it's the clue we need."

Lacey did as he was asked and smoothed the plastic flat so that it didn't reflect the light. He had a feeling that Gill was right, this piece of paper somehow held the key to the mystery but just what did it mean? He was no Sherlock Holmes and not much of one for deciphering strange messages but some of the characters were ringing distant bells. All he needed to do was make sense of the discordant jangle.

25

"Don't go straight back to Kingswear," Lacey said. "Take the A38 not the A380."

Gill glanced across at him slumped in the passenger seat with a thoughtful look on his face.

"What are you thinking, Rick?" He had been quiet ever since they had left Middlemoor and it was the first words he had spoken.

"I just need somewhere quiet for a while. Take a turning off to Bovey Tracey and we 'll find a place to park up."

"You want to commune with nature?" She was seeing another side to him, a quiet reflective side that puzzled her. Ever since she had first met him he had been sharp, tense almost. Here, with her in the car, that edge had left him. She saw his eyes flick across to her and felt the need to say something.

"I was wondering what's on your mind, Rick. It might be too busy there for a necking session." She didn't know why she said it and she regretted it as soon as the words were out of her mouth.

He didn't reply but his lips drew taut and she wondered if he was offended. Tough if he was; she didn't feel like apologising.

He grunted. She looked across and he was trying to stifle a laugh. "Another time perhaps," he said but she could tell he didn't mean it. At least he saw the funny side which was a relief.

"I just want to clear my head, try to make sense of everything. There's something about that cipher that's bugging me and maybe some fresh air will help."

Gill turned off the dual carriageway onto the A382 towards Bovey Tracey. Lacey stayed quiet until they reached a roundabout signposted to Widecombe in the Moor.

"Lacey jerked a thumb. "Turn left here."

"Towards Widecombe?"

"Yes. There a place a couple of miles further on called Haytor. We can stop there at the third car park on the left."

Gill's mouth dropped open. Lacey seemed to know a lot about the area which surprised her but she did as she was asked and stopped in a rough car park opposite a stack of rocks on a tor.

Lacey unclipped his seatbelt, opened the glove box took out his Sig and Gill's small binoculars. "Fancy a walk?"

Gill glanced from him to the long rise up to the rocks where one or two tourists were sitting. "My walking shoes are in the boot, give me a minute."

Lacey came and stood beside her as she opened the boot, sat on the rim and changed her shoes.

"Haytor Rocks," he said and nodded towards the stack of grey megacrystic granite. He waited as she tied her laces then crossed the road and headed up the close-cropped grassy slope at a fast walk.

Gill caught up to his elbow by jogging. "Where are we going?"

He pointed upwards. "There."

143

"To the top?"

"Yeah. There's a way up around the other side. I've climbed it a few times."

"When?"

He didn't reply but lengthened his stride to circle the base of the rocks. He began to climb and Gill followed with the agility of a mountain goat. They reached the top together but she pulled herself up first and offered him a hand. He grinned and took it.

"I need all the help I can get. I have three titanium pins holding my left leg together," he said.

That surprised her too. He was letting a lot of himself out. "I wouldn't have known."

He grimaced. "It gets a little sticky in the cold but otherwise it's okay."

She turned away and gazed at the view. "It's beautiful up here."

"Yeah, take a seat."

She sat on the rock and he sat beside her. She looked sideways at him. "You want to tell me?"

He nodded but his eyes were fixed on the distance as if remembering. "You recall I told you I was born in London?" He waited for her to nod before continuing. "Well, I wasn't kidding. Born in London and went to school a few miles from here. Boarding school, good place, closed now though. I was in the school cadet force. We used to have exercises on the moor, camping out and doing the Ten Tors Expeditions. I was here for five years and I know this place well. Sometimes, if I wanted to get away for some me time, I'd climb up here and pretend I was king of all I surveyed."

He turned his face to her now. "D'you know what struck me about the moors the first time I laid eyes on them?"

"Gill shook her head but said nothing, not wanting to break the spell of the moment.

"No trees. That's the thing that struck me. A kid out from a leafy London suburb and it made an impression. I loved the place right away, still do, with all its moods. I like wide open spaces where you can breathe. Today she looks benign in the sun, like a lady in her best summer dress, but she can change in an instant into a howling banshee."

He stopped speaking and Gill felt the mood pass. "That begs more questions than it answers, Rick."

He wrinkled his nose. "Maybe we can talk about it another time but right now I've just realised what it is about those characters on Forrestal's note that bothered me. Pull up the picture on your phone."

Gill pulled out her mobile and located the picture. She handed it to him and he shuffled closer so that they could both see the screen.

"At first I thought it was a code but it's not, it's a shorthand notation. See here these characters, *H, NNE*. That's heading, north, north, east. Then these following characters start to make sense. *K5* is probably five knots. Forrestal was tracking something, something headed towards the ship. Maybe the *10m* is a length, ten metres."

Gill put her finger and thumb on the screen and enlarged it. "Yes, I see your point but what does *Nar S?* and *Disa* mean?"

He shook his head. "I've no idea. Email that to your Colonel Blake, see if he can make head or tail of it."

"It seems we're back on the Chinese spy theory, doesn't it?"

Lacey didn't reply. He had stiffened and was looking down towards the distant car park. He pulled the binoculars from his pocket and stared through them.

She touched his arm. "What is it?"

He handed the glasses to her. "We're being watched and it's not idle curiosity. The black Range Rover there, rear window wound down. A camera or binoculars, I saw light flash on a lens."

Gill decided not to ask him how he was so sure it wasn't just a tourist taking pictures and peered at the distant vehicle in turn. "The rest of the windows are smoked, I can't see the driver," she said. "We weren't followed, so how did they find us?"

Lacey stood. "Let's go and ask them." He spun to his feet and began a rapid descent with Gill hard on his heels. They rounded the rock and half jogged down the slope towards the car park. Just as they reached the edge of the road the Range Rover's rear window wound up and the car roared off towards Widecombe.

Gill watched it leave with her hands on her hips. Another can of worms opened. She wondered if

146

Blake had put another tail on them but thought it unlikely and the question remained; how had they been located?

Lacey continued his walk back to her Mercedes and began to check under the wheel arches. He came out with a black box at the third attempt. He held it up and waved it. At least one question answered; a tracker which could have been attached to her car at any time in the past couple of days. They were now the objects of acute attention and the odds against them had just been raised.

26

Gill parked on a grass verge beside a cattle grid. Lacey dropped the small box between its bars. "Let them think we're still here. Hopefully, if they get curious and come back to look for it, they'll assume it came off as we drove over the grid. They'll be suspicious but won't know for sure that their little toy was found. It's short term but it'll keep them guessing while we lose them for the rest of the day."

Gill watched him, she was leaning on the front wing, her arms folded across her breasts. "What now, Rick?"

He gave her a long sideways look. "It seems we've successfully stirred up the mud."

"Or a hornet's nest," she replied.

He wondered if the situation was getting her nervy but she appeared calm; maybe it was another one of her lame jokes. "Who knows but as you so wisely said recently, forewarned ..."

"You said the rest of the day. Where are we going now?"

"Seeing as we're so close, I thought we should take a look at this quarry Pierce owns. Just curiosity but I haven't ruled him out of anything yet. Kate said it was near Buckfastleigh so it shouldn't be too hard to find."

"We're just going to roll up, are we?"

Lacey shrugged. "Why not? I told them I was interested in the business. It's only natural I'd want to take a look around."

"To what end? I can't see it would have anything to do with our mission."

"I want to tick it off the list. There are too many variables and we need to start narrowing down possibilities."

"I thought we were back on the Chinese spy angle."

Lacey joined her leaning on the wing. He rubbed his cheek where the scar tissue sometimes still itched. The plastic surgeon had done a reasonable job of covering it but the skin was slightly shiny in strong light and he did his best to camouflage it. It was that and the missing tip of his little finger that brought bad memories flooding back. The beating he'd taken from a terrorist that scarred his face and the subsequent gunfight at the National Exhibition Centre where his finger had been hit by an AK47 bullet. He shuddered at the flashback.

He felt Gill's hand on his arm. "You okay, Rick?"

He reached up and touched her hand and she moved it away. "Yeah. Sorry. Miles away. Where were we?"

"Chinese spy ring."

"Oh, yeah. Chinese spies, drug dealers, professional hit men; nothing concrete. All we can do is make a few more waves and hope something tangible surfaces. The quarry's a start."

149

"What about our chums in the Range Rover? I doubt we've seen the last of them."

Lacey grinned. "Could have been worse. Could have been a sniper scope. They were being nosy for now but you're right, they're not going away any time soon. They want to know where we go, who we see and what we do. Someone somewhere has got the wind up over our cage rattling."

Gill nodded, her lips a tight line of determination. "Right, then let's go rattle another one."

She turned but Lacey stopped her with a hand on her wrist. "It could get dangerous from now on, Gill."

She looked down at his fingers but did not try to shake them off. "I know. It's a place I've been before. I can handle it."

He looked at her face and knew she was ready for whatever was coming their way. He nodded and released her arm. "I guess you can. Let's go."

It was only a few miles to Buckfastleigh and it didn't take them long to get there. Gill complained of feeling hungry and they stopped at the Kings Arms for lunch in the beer garden. Lacey paid on Blake's credit card and carried the sandwiches out with a couple of soft drinks. He put them down on the table and Gill pushed her Gucci sunglasses up onto her hair. She looked like a fashion model and was drawing some admiring glances. He sat and cocked his head to one side. "How the hell did you ever work undercover?"

She smiled. "I'll take that as a compliment."

"I'd never forget a face like yours."

She sobered and he knew he had struck a nerve. "Sorry."

She shook her head. "Don't be. Spectres from the past; I have to live with them."

"I know that feeling."

"I know. I saw that earlier, you went into yourself for a brief moment."

"I was feeling sorry for myself."

"It's allowed," Gill said and picked up a well-filled tuna sandwich.

"And you?"

She took a bite and chewed slowly as she eyed him. "First time I killed a man close to was after he recognised me from my surveillance days with the Det. It was self-defence. It wasn't fun."

"It never is."

She chewed again for a few seconds. "Is it any easier the second time?"

He picked up a sandwich. He didn't know quite how to answer that and copied her by taking a bite giving him time to think of a suitable reply. "Depends on the situation, I guess, and the person. Some guys get a taste for it."

She mimicked his words. "And you?"

"Physically, it's the training kicking in, action-reaction, muscle memory, get the job done, stay alive, keep your men alive as well as you can. I'm not an assassin and only kill when it's kill or be killed. Morally it can raise a few questions if you believe there will be a reckoning on judgement day. Emotionally it can sap you if you let it. I have some regrets but not many."

She smiled. *"Regrets I have a few but then again too few to mention."*

"You a Sinatra fan?"

She shook her head and started on a second sandwich. "No, never did like his style of crooning but those words rang a bell."

"What kind of music do you like?" It was small talk, getting away from the realities of his life but he now found he really wanted to know.

"Eclectic," she said. "I like all sorts from classical to heavy metal. What about you?"

"I have a thing for Debussy. I can listen to his stuff any time. Not sure I like much of the modern era, anything from the turn of the century. It all sounds too whiney."

"Maybe I should educate you."

He gave her a half smile. "Maybe you should."

They finished lunch and Lacey asked around for directions to the quarry. Most people looked at him blankly but an old boy propping up the bar gave him a pointer in return for a pint of Guinness.

The quarry was up a narrow lane barely wide enough to get a tipper truck down but it had passing places every couple of hundred yards. They followed the track for over a mile until it reached the side of a hill. There it branched off upwards and widened to a well-used double width as it led up to a steel fence and a wide metal gate around a bend.

Lacey had Gill stop short and keep the car out of sight while they went forward on foot keeping to the thick shrubbery that formed a barrier between a fast-flowing stream and the track. He wanted to take a look before driving up and announcing themselves. He wasn't one for leaping before he looked.

Gill had brought her pair of palm-sized binoculars and she handed them to Lacey. He knelt down in the dust and peered through some branches. He said nothing but handed them to Gill. She looked in turn and her mouth drew into a tight line.

"Black Range Rover. Well, well."

"Check out the two standing by the Portacabins," Lacey said. Both were standing idly but had an alert air about them.

"Guards?" Gill whispered. "And one of them is Chinese."

27

Gill put the binoculars back to her eyes and refocused them. "Have you seen what's behind the two men? Looks like a tunnel."

She handed the glasses back to Lacey who studied the hole in the hillside that Gill had found. "Not just a quarry. That looks like a mine entrance."

Gill gave him a cool look. "Still set on going in for a visit?"

"Yes, but not right now. I think I'll postpone it till later. Let's get out of here before we get seen."

On the drive back to Kingswear Lacey was quiet again but not as relaxed as before. Gill kept giving him sideways glances in the hope that he would respond but if he saw them he chose to ignore the unspoken invitation to talk. Eventually she lost patience.

"Penny for 'em."

His head turned towards her but he stayed silent.

"What's passing through that grey matter of yours?" She gave him a few more minutes then pulled the car into a layby. She switched off the engine and waited. Two could play at that game.

"Why have we stopped?"

She angled her body towards him. "I know you're a colonel ..."

"Retired colonel," he interrupted.

"… retired colonel, I stand corrected, and I'm merely the hired help but I thought we'd agreed we're a team."

"Up to a point."

Gill could feel her temper rise. Normally able to control her instinct to react she found Lacey was getting under her skin. Part of the problem was she didn't understand why and it irked her. "Look, you can play the strong silent type all you want but it won't wash with me. I've worked face to face against Irish terrorists and Basque separatists, any of whom would have slit my throat in an instant if they'd known who I really was. I think I've earned some respect and some cooperation. I don't know who you are, I don't know which organisation you work for or even why I'm sitting here taking this silent shit from you. I'm either all the way in or I'm out and bugger the money they're paying me."

She was just getting into her stride when her mobile rang. She heard Lacey whisper, 'saved by the bell'. She gave an exasperated grunt and snatched it off its cradle. "It's Blake." She put the phone on speaker. "Yes, Colonel?"

"Ah, Gill," Blake's voice sounded distant. "I have some news."

"Fire away."

"That scrap of paper that you photographed and emailed."

"Yes?"

"We've had the Q Branch look it over. They've been able to make out a few more characters that were washed off. The first words should read '*narco sub*' question mark and the last word is probably '*disappe*', which we take to read disappeared.

"It's interesting to note that Commander Forrestal was previously an anti-submarine warfare expert seconded to the American Coastguard patrolling the waters of the Gulf of Mexico where he was able to locate and track Colombian Narco Submarines."

"What the hell is a Narco Submarine, Colonel?" Gill asked.

"Ah, well, it has come to the attention of the American Drug Enforcement Agency that large quantities of cocaine were arriving in the States outside the normal routes. They found that the shipments were being delivered by sophisticated underwater craft, specially built for the job. The Colombian cartels have financed several of these Narco Subs. With a crew of two or three they could transport several hundred kilos of the drug completely unseen, which makes them, consequently, difficult to detect and to stop."

"Colonel Blake, Lacey here."

"Ah, good afternoon, Colonel."

"That's happening over in the States. Why do you think Forrestal was sure it was happening here?"

"The commander knew his business. The length, about ten metres, the speed, etc., the equipment he was using on the *Norfolk* is sophisticated enough to give a simulated outline of any craft. He must have had some reservation as he put the query after the words and its disappearance seems to have baffled him."

Lacey grimaced. "Thanks, Colonel, but I'm not sure how useful it'll be."

"Best we can do for now. Oh, there was one other thing, personal submarines are a new fad with the billionaire set and the Tao Chin Company in China has moved into the market to construct them."

"Is that it?" Gill said.

"Yes for now. By the way, take it easy on Colonel Lacey, Gill." He rang off before Gill could ask him what he meant.

She hooked the phone back on its cradle as Lacey spoke. It was as if he could read her mind.

"He either knows you of old or he's got your car bugged."

She let out the breath she did not realise she was holding and sank back in the seat. "Probably the latter." She paused for a second then yelled, "bugger off."

"Feel better?" Lacey said.

She scowled at him. "No!"

"I've been thinking ..." Lacey began.

"Go figure," Gill snorted.

"I don't mean to hold out on you but I've been trying to get a handle on things in my mind before I decide what to do next." He opened the door to climb out and indicated that Gill should do likewise. She joined him leaning against the grille.

"It seems the spy theory has top spot now with this info from Blake," she said.

Lacey grimaced. "Maybe, I can see the attraction of that scenario, with a Chinese built mini-sub nosing around which got Forrestal hooked on an idea which got him killed. What bugs me is the connection with the quarry and the Range Rover which tailed us with the tracker under this car. It was a sophisticated method and not one that a tin-pot quarry owner or a casino boss would use. I'd still like to take a look at the quarry tonight."

"I can take you."

"Uh huh, I need you to take Derek up on his offer of a guided tour of the casino. Find out if he just wants to get inside your pants or whether there's more to it."

Gill pulled a face at him. "And what if all he wants is to get his leg over?"

"You'll deal with it; you dealt with the PIRA and ETA Militar so Derek will be a pushover by comparison."

He was throwing her words back at her but with additional detail that told her he'd read the file that should have been buried deep in MI6's vaults. She bit down on her annoyance. "Thanks for the vote of confidence."

"You're welcome."

"Anyone ever tell you you're an irritating dick?"

"Many times. I got used to it."

"What now?"

"To the boat eventually. We'll need to prepare for tonight. Tomorrow we'll take her out into Torbay for a nose around. You never know what we might find. In the meantime head back to Exeter, I need to rent a car."

28

Lacey hired a Discovery 4x4 from Europcar in Marsh Barton and it was getting on for evening when they both arrived back at Kingswear in convoy. As they walked down the finger pontoon to the boat Lacey suddenly put a hand on Gill's arm and stopped her.

"There's someone moving on board."

"You're sure?"

"Yes. Wait here."

Before she could reply he ran forward and vaulted the side to land silently on the rear deck. He padded to the glass doors which were open a crack. He knew that he had locked them on leaving. He slid open the door and pulled the Sig from its holster. Whoever it was had gone below; there was no sign in the main saloon and nothing appeared to have been touched. He inched forward to the companionway and listened. A noise came from the third cabin, the one that wasn't in use. Again the door was ajar and he pushed it open with the barrel of the Sig. He set foot inside and a dark shape launched itself from across the cabin, hitting him hard on the chest. The pistol was twisted from his grip and flung onto the bunk as an elbow sank into his midriff with explosive force.

His breath whistled out and he doubled over. The chin jab was fast and expert but he knew it would come and twisted his face away so that it just grazed his cheek. He gripped the man's wrist and thrust upward and outward creating an opening for a punch of his own into his attacker's kidneys. He heard a grunt of pain but the man was strong and very fast, he twisted back, stabbed upward with a knee that hit Lacey's thigh and yanked hard breaking the grip on his wrist, turning the movement smoothly into a forearm blow to the throat which Lacey blocked, turned and smashed the man's head against the wall. It didn't slow him, he spun away and gripped Lacey's arm to put it in a lock against the elbow. He hooked a leg away and they both fell onto the bunk, Lacey face down with the man pushing a knee into his back, his thumbs rammed into the small bones on the back of Lacey's hand.

"Keep still will yers," the man said, "Or I'll break your fingers."

The lights went on and Gill elbowed the door open. "You'd better do as he says, Rick."

Lacey had his face pushed into a pillow but he had his left hand on the Sig. His voice was muffled. "Okay."

The grip on his hand was released and the knee removed from his back. He spun fast and rammed the Sig under the man's chin.

"Whoa! Hold it," Gill yelled. "He's one of us."

"Could have fooled me," Lacey said with undisguised venom.

The man was short with tightly curled blonde hair and of mixed race as far as Lacey could tell. He was muscle-packed and the best bare hand fighter he had come across since his time at the ISPA training centre at Firwood, where only the instructor, Jimmy Ferguson, had beaten him.

Gill was grinning. "This is Aftershave Murphy, Rick. I knew it was him as soon as I got aboard. You can't mistake that scent."

Murphy had his hands up but he too was grinning. He spoke without turning his head, the pistol still pushing against his chin. "Hello Petal. Got tired of waitin' at the hotel so I thought I'd pay yer a call."

Lacey dropped the Sig and gave Gill a questioning look.

"My insurance policy," she said. "We're old mates. Aftershave was the best jap-slapper in the Regiment; he taught me a thing or two."

Lacey nodded and rubbed his ribs. The little man was certainly an expert in that field. "Come on up to the saloon, we can get better acquainted."

Gill made some tea for them as they sat around the table. Lacey was coming to terms with Aftershave's presence. After the first shock he was growing to like the little Liverpudlian who had an obvious deep respect for Gill.

"Former Reg man?" Lacey asked.

"Aftershave pulled a face. "Not somethin' I'd usually admit but yeah, a ways back. B Squadron for a while then on the staff teachin', y'know."

Gill slid onto the seat beside him and put a cup in front of him. "We met in Spain. Aftershave was one of the CP team sent to cover my back. Did a great job. How are things going by the way?"

Aftershave picked up the cup and sipped noisily, then he shrugged. "Not that great right now. The pandemic did fer a lot o' me business, had to close a few o' the bars. I only have the one now an' that's runnin' on borrowed time. Loxl got herself arrested by Ertzaintza …"

"That's the Basque police," Gill said to Lacey.

" … yeah, well, she's inside now doing a three stretch for incitement to riot. They got her in the end. Since she's bin gone her cuadrilla buddies 'ave faded away an' taken a lot of my trade with 'em."

Gill turned to Lacey. "Loxl is Aftershave's girlfriend. She was a member of Herri Batasuna, the political wing of ETA Militar, and she was always involved in organising the street riots."

Lacey nodded. He had read the files.

"Aye, she never found out that I was a Brit soldier. She still thinks I'm from Colombia," Aftershave said with an apologetic smile. "Not sumpn' I'm happy with but …"

"We all have our secrets," Lacey said.

"Yeah, she'd probably kill me if she knew."

"What were you doing below deck?"

Aftershave gave another apologetic smile. "I was lookin' fer the heads. I didn't have the code to get into the toilet block. Age an' all that."

"You okay now?" Gill asked with a grin.

"Oh yeah. I was on me way out when I was caught by …?"

"Rick Lacey," he held his hand out. "I wish I could say I was pleased to meet you but you pack a helluva punch."

163

"Yeah, sorry 'bout that. I was tryin' to take it easy but you pack a wallop too." He took Lacey's hand and pumped it.

"It's retired Colonel Lacey," Gill said with a sly wink.

Aftershave raised his eyebrows. "Oh! Brass. I'll haveta watch me Ps and Qs."

"It's just Rick. Round here we're known as Mister and Missus Arnold."

Aftershave gave a small leer. "Oh yeah!"

Gill elbowed him. "It's not like that. It's just the cover legend."

"If you say so, Petal."

Lacey changed the subject. "I'm glad you're here. You can shadow Gill tonight. She's got a hot date at the casino in Torquay and she might need a chaperone."

"I can fill you in on the way," Gill said. "Things are hotting up but we don't yet know who is turning up the gas or why. This is going to be a recce of a possible suspect."

"We also have to invent a legend for you. We can't call you Aftershave," Lacey said.

"Me name's Tristan St. John," Aftershave said and grimaced. "Me ma had delusions of grandeur and thought I'd make somethin' of meself if I had the right moniker."

"Tristan's good," Lacey said. "You're a business acquaintance from Spain dropped in for a break. You and Gill can flesh out the details and let me know by tomorrow what you've decided."

"I'll text you," Gill said. "We already have the bones of a story with Aftershave's ... sorry, ... Tristan's background in the bar business, it just needs a little tweaking."

Lacey nodded, it was best to stay as close to the truth as possible, less chance of a slip-up if someone got nosey and asked questions. "I'll leave it in your hands." He rose and picked the satellite phone from its cradle. "I have some calls to make." He went below. This night might prove dangerous and he wanted to brief Mark Sparrow on all that had occurred so far and to find out if he had any news about Andee. It was playing on his mind and he needed to clear his head for the dark hours to come.

29

"Rick? Tha's a bit of a coincidence," Aftershave said when Lacey had gone.

Gill shrugged. "Is it?"

"I'd say, yeah. Maybe too much o' one. Who's he with?"

Gill shrugged again, she was uncomfortable admitting she knew little about Lacey. It struck her with a jolt that maybe Rick wasn't his real name, something it needed Aftershave to put his finger on. "I'm not sure who he works for. Some sort of shadowy outfit but they're pretty high-powered, all colonels, brigadiers and major-generals."

Aftershave smacked his forehead. "All soddin' brass, they'll be lookin' after their own skins, you can bet on it. An' Rick's a Yank too. Funny though, he reminds me a bit of a Rupert who was with B Squadron back in the Gulf War. Can't remember his name. He got RTUd for some reason. All very hush, hush."

"Well it can't be Lacey," Gill said.

"You're right, it's just a vague resemblance. My problem is I never forget a face and it drives me nuts if I can't place it."

"It's not your only problem," Gill said and grinned. "Make yourself useful while I'm getting dolled up for tonight. I think my car is bugged. Go find where it's hidden and disconnect it, just for now. MI6 don't know you're here and I'd like to keep it that way for as long as possible. The keys are on the chart table."

"MI6?"

"Yes, Blake, I don't think you know him but he ran interference for us out in Pakistan. I trust him up to a point but I like to play my cards close to my chest."

"Point taken. Never trust the buggers. They 'ave so many axes to grind they could be in the lumberjack business. Speakin' o' which, do you 'ave any tools?"

Gill frowned. "I think Lacey keeps stuff like that in the crew cabin behind the engines."

She went to her cabin to change. Aftershave had given her more food for thought. It was beginning to look as if this was an MI6 operation. Lacey knew about her record which could only have been released by them, the tails were ordered by Blake and her car was bugged too. She couldn't see the point of them giving Lacey the name of Rick unless it was to give him a more sympathetic persona. If that was the case her strings were being pulled and she did not like it. She hated being manipulated. MI6 had tried it before and had come off second best. She resolved to tackle Lacey about it. She thought she could trust him but she wasn't a hundred percent certain and that troubled her too. In fact it troubled her the most.

There was a light tap on the door and she went to open it. Aftershave stood there with his finger to his lips. He crooked a finger and she followed him along the passageway to the rear cabin. He opened the door and pointed.

"What is it?"

"You wanna see this for yourself."

She brushed past him and looked round. The cabin seemed normal. She spread her hands. "What?"

"Under the bunks."

She got on her knees to peer under the bedframes. The long metal boxes had digital keypads and could not be mistaken for anything other than gun cabinets.

"There are ammo boxes in the wardrobes. They've got keypads on 'em too. This bloke's set up for war if you ask me."

"The cabin's also alarmed," Lacey said from the passageway.

"I came for some tools," Aftershave said. "And I found this lot."

"This looks like an armoury," Gill said. "Care to explain?"

"The tools are in a box in the engine room," Lacey said. "Come topside once you've found what you're looking for."

Gill followed Lacy as Aftershave turned to rummage in the engine compartment. She waited as Lacey settled himself. "Well?"

"Sit down, Gill."

"What's all that kit for?"

"That's in case the worst happens. It's a precaution."

Aftershave came rattling up the companionway holding a set of pliers and a screwdriver. He saw the looks on both their faces and kept going out through the sliding glass doors and onto the pontoon.

"I've checked him out, Lacey said. "He's solid."

Gill felt her temper rise and she snorted. "Don't change the subject, Rick, if that's your real name."

He let out a long breath. "Look, sit down. I have something to say and it'll take a while."

She sat with bad grace and stared at him, challenging him with the look. "It had better be good or I'm ... we're out of here."

"Okay. What I'm about to tell you is highly classified and should go no further. I'm with an organisation called the International Special Projects Arm. We do the dirty jobs that governments don't want to be involved with. You won't have heard of what we do, it's always played down or covered up, never appears in the papers unless the special forces of one country or another is credited with the results.

"The weapons below are mainly for my personal protection, although there are some additional items should any of our units need them. Al Qaeda put a price on my head a few years back and an assassin nearly collected, that was how my leg got broken. You're right, Rick isn't my real name, my name was changed to Richard Lacey under a CIA protection programme as it was let out that I was dead, that the assassin had succeeded. I can't tell you my real name as that was buried with my original persona. I'm afraid that should the remnants of Al Qaeda find out I'm still alive the fatwa will be re-issued.

"I'm here to take out whatever threat has been posed by Commander Forrestal's assassination. It's a worst case scenario but it may only be solved by extreme prejudice."

Gill's mouth had dropped slightly open. She should have guessed there was something about Lacey's involvement that was different but this went beyond her imagination. She was pleased that his new name was just a coincidence and not a ploy to engage her sympathies but was having a hard time coming to terms with the rest.

"So you're ... what? A one man hit squad?"

He grinned, a wry twist of his lips. "That's a colourful way of putting it."

"But not far off the truth."

"I do what needs to be done but I'm no loose cannon. As I said an insurance policy for the government, just like Aftershave is yours. The powers-that-be need to know what's going on down here and to have it neutralised, if necessary, in the quietest and most efficient way possible. No headlines, no names, no comebacks."

"Why wasn't I told?"

The grin again but less wide. "Need to know."

Gill felt her anger of before replaced by exasperation. "What's my part in this supposed to be? Am I merely decoration, a smokescreen for you to hide behind while you go around capping the opposition?"

"No, it's not like that, never was. We needed someone with your expertise to get inside and dig out what we need to know to succeed where the police have failed. Besides, a couple is always less suspicious than one person alone, you told me that. You've worked with MI6, you know the score."

"Since you've brought that up *you* need to know I was used by them and I didn't take kindly to it, no more than I'm taking kindly to this. I'm not a bloody mushroom and I hate being manipulated. No more secrets, Rick."

"Deal," he said leant forward and offered his hand. "If it's any consolation I was for being upfront right from the start but your boss, Blake, thought it best to keep you in the dark until it became necessary to let you in on the real mission objective."

She felt his strong fingers wrap round her hand. A new beginning, things had changed, the balance of the relationship altered, now on a footing she could manage. A whole new game plan had been set out but right that moment she did not know if she wanted to play.

30

Lacey saw Gill and Aftershave off on their visit to the casino. They knew what they had to do and he had no qualms that they would not do an excellent job. He set about preparing for his own jaunt to the quarry cum mine. It baffled him why a small-time gravel business should need guards during daylight hours. He could understand them having a night watchman to keep an eye on expensive equipment that could stick to someone's trailer but during the day there were enough workers around to keep equipment from falling into the wrong hands. The mine too was a mystery. Had they found a workable seam of tin? A workable seam had been discovered at the Hemerdon Mine in the 1980s, which he had learned about whilst still at school. It had finally borne results in 2015. A tin mine was a possibility but it hardly required a guard to keep it safe.

He parked the Discovery a mile away and walked in along the narrow track until he reached the bend where he could see the high metal gates. They were padlocked and chained. There was a light in one of the Portacabins. He walked to the fence and could hear a low hum. He clipped down his night vision goggles and studied the wire. Every few yards there were porcelain insulators. The fence ran around a square compound and was electrified. Highly illegal but effective at keeping the unwanted out. Again overkill. What were they so desperate to protect?

He walked the fence line into a copse of stunted trees. They had been cut back from the fence so there was no chance of using them to climb over but they hadn't allowed for nature. Roots had twisted up from the ground and animals, badgers or foxes, had taken advantage of the natural dip created to burrow under the wire. It was a shallow depression partially hidden in clumps of thick weed. He used his hands to dig out some of the disturbed earth until he had enough room to snake his way under the wire. It was slow work and he was perspiring in his black combat overalls by the time his body had inched its way clear enough for him to stand upright. He used one of the cut down branches that were left lying around inside the fence to prop up the lowest strand of wire in case he needed to exit quicker than he'd got in.

The moon had not yet risen but it was a fine night with the Milky Way visible as a faint blur of light from its myriad stars. The only other light came from the single bulb burning above the Portacabin which threw a narrow beam just a few yards towards the mouth of the mine which was in darkness.

Lacey jogged towards the building, clipped up his goggles and put his head to the thin cabin wall. He could hear voices inside and muted music, either from a television or radio, the volume was too low to be sure. At least two men and wide awake. He knew he should wait to time any security patrols, if they were that way inclined, but this far out in the cuds they would not be expecting any determined callers bold enough to tackle the electrified fence. A siege mentality would soon take hold and foot patrols would seem redundant. At least, he hoped so.

No sooner had the thought crossed his mind than the door swung open spilling light further across the open space. Lacey flattened himself against the cabin wall in shadow and held his breath. The man looked neither left nor right but marched across to a portaloo swinging a torch on the end of a strap. He went inside and closed the door. Lacey could hear him humming an unfamiliar tune as he peed. He would almost certainly be seen when the man made his way back and the only cover was inside the mouth of the mine itself. He levered himself to his feet. If his biology lessons were right he had eighteen seconds to cover the fifty metres before the man finished. It would be touch and go, he'd already wasted five of them. He ran doubled over for the black mouth flinging himself in just as the portaloo door swung open and a torch beam flicked across in his direction.

The man called out and Lacey froze.

The man called again in sing-song Cantonese as Lacey held his breath. There was an answering shout from inside the cabin and the man laughed. He called again and flashed his torch around before sauntering back inside.

Lacey puffed out his cheeks in relief. The mine was pitch black, the total darkness of caves. Starlight could not filter far into the entrance. Lacey powered up his goggles and waited as they whined and a green image began to form. He looked around. From what he could make out the mine had been roughly hewn from the granite but was wide enough and high enough for two tall men to stand side by side without ducking their heads. Black cables ran along one wall and he could hear the distant sound of running water and the hum of a generator. He knew from his history lessons that Dartmoor mines were infamous for needing to be pumped out below certain depths with adits dug to de-water the shafts so it wasn't surprising if water was a problem.

He followed the shaft down a slope to a gallery that widened out to three times the width of the passage. The roof was supported by old thick wooden posts placed every few metres along the walls which held modern metal RSJs acting as crossbeams. A rickety wooden trough ran down the centre, it was lined with zinc and water flowed along it at a steady rate. The hum of the generator was louder here but was coming from behind a metal door. The black cables disappeared through a hole above the door and were obviously the source of power in the mine. He looked around further and found a pile of circular sieves in one corner with fine nylon mesh in place of wire. Lacey furrowed his brow; this was beginning to ring bells.

He turned to retrace his steps but a noise echoed down the tunnel and lights snapped on. The sudden glare flared out his night goggles and seared his eyes. He grunted and clicked them up, rubbing his eyes to clear his vision. The vague shape of a man came out of the tunnel and he stepped back behind a post as a flat thud sounded and a bullet thwacked into the gallery wall. A second bullet chewed splinters from the post he was standing behind and an excited voice mouthed a stream of Cantonese.

The guards weren't intent on taking prisoners.

The man advanced into the gallery still shouting in a high-pitched voice. Lacey didn't understand the words but the meaning was clear enough. He popped his head out for a quick look and the man fired again, the muffler on the end of his pistol making a quiet thud. Lacey dodged back as the bullet fanned his cheek then he darted forward and leapt over the wooden trough. He landed on his feet then forward rolled so that he popped up opposite the guard. The man swung towards him, pistol stretched out. Lacey jumped, one foot on the trough and launched himself into the man. He pushed the pistol arm aside and rammed his shoulder under the man's chin snapping his mouth shut and sending them both staggering into the wall.

Lacey still had hold of the gun arm but the man hit him hard with his free hand making his ears ring. He pulled away and broke the guard's nose with a head butt.

176

The second guard ran out of the tunnel and aimed at Lacey's back. He heard him, spun the first guard around and ducked. The bullet caught the man high up on the spine, the over-penetration spewing blood on Lacey's shoulder as the bullet cracked past his head. The man grunted and sagged in Lacey's arms. He threw the body at the second guard and followed it keeping low. He hit the man in the stomach and they both fell to the stone floor. The guard was strong and well-trained in Qigong. He rolled Lacey over and jumped to his feet, swinging the pistol in a smooth arc towards Lacey's head. He kicked out catching the man on the kneecap and buckling his leg throwing the pistol off aim. The guard spun and leapt back twisting in a full circle to bring the pistol to bear again. He was fast but Lacey was faster. He snapped his Sig from its holster and double-tapped two rounds into the guard's chest. He fell as if his strings had been cut.

Lacey climbed to his feet and exhaled. He kicked the pistol away from the man's hand and checked that both men were dead. When he stood he noticed the small infra-red camera in one corner up near the roof, its power cables running into the generator room. That was how they'd discovered him.

Two Chinese meant problems, two Chinese armed with special ops pistols meant even bigger problems. He arranged the bodies so it would appear as if the men killed each other, pushing the pistols back in their dead fingers. It wouldn't fool a

SOCO but he doubted whether anyone in this business would want the police involved and it just might keep them guessing. He looked around to find his two ejected cartridge cases and put them in his pocket. He knew of old to police his brass.

He walked back to the Portacabin and found the video recorder. He erased the tape but put it back into the recorder and left it switched off. He nosed further and found a big safe built into one of the cupboards. It had both a keyhole and a tumbler dial, heavy duty and no way he could open it. A big safe, armed guards, an electrified fence, infra-red cameras; they weren't mining tin, they were panning for gold. It had to be a rich seam to make sense of all the precautions.

He left the way he had come, kicking the stick away as he squirmed under the fence. He left no trace of his presence. Maybe he had solved the riddle of Forrestal's killers but why were Chinese Special Forces involved? He had a lot of thinking to do.

31

The Golden Nugget Casino was perched on a rise overlooking Torbay. Once a hotel, the foyer had been turned into a hall full of flashing lights and slot machines all whirring, ringing and pinging, with a handful of punters busily pushing coins into slots in the hope of winning the £20,000 jackpot that was flashing in mesmeric fashion on a central column.

Towards the back of the room were a few blackjack tables with bored dealers standing idle and a lift shaft guarded by a muscular security guard who was popping out of his garish blue dinner jacket. Gill made straight for him with Aftershave following a pace behind. The man eyed her with suspicion and an 'I've heard it all before' look on his face.

"I've come to see Mister Pierce, is he in?"

The man's top lip quivered and his gaze slid to Aftershave who was looking around with his hands in his pockets.

"Who wants to know?"

"Missus Gill Arnold. I have an open invitation."

The guard's lips twisted into a faint sneer but his eyes never left Aftershave. "You two together?"

"Yes."

The guard pulled a radio from his belt and called in Gill's name. He was wearing a black ear plug and Gill couldn't hear the reply but the man grunted and stood aside. "When you get in, press the button for the mezzanine. Someone'll meet you there."

Gill gave him an icy smile and pressed the call button. Aftershave went to stand beside her but the guard caught him by the arm. "Not you, mate, just the lady."

Gill turned. "Either he goes with me or I don't go, make your mind up."

Aftershave had a lazy grin on his face and he looked up at the guard who stood a good ten inches taller. "Take your hand off me arm, pal, don't want to wrinkle the threads." He pushed his thumb into the small bones on the back of the guard's beefy hand and pulled back on his middle fingers until they cracked. The man squawked and pulled his hand away.

"Tha's better, ennit," Aftershave said and smoothed down his sleeve.

The man had turned red and his lips into a thin menacing line. He took a pace forward and then stopped and put a hand to his ear, pressing against the ear plug as though he couldn't make out the words ... or didn't want to. He took a deep breath and dropped his hand away. "All right, you can go up." He wagged his finger. "But I'll remember you."

Aftershave's grin broadened. "Sure you will, pal."

The lift doors were agape and Gill was inside holding them open until Aftershave joined her. She let go of the hold button and nodded her head at the ceiling. "Security cam. They're all over the place."

"Yeah, I know. Maybe they don't trust the punters."

Gill grimaced. "Or the staff. With goons like that one you never can be too careful."

"Just muscle," Aftershave said as the doors slid open. "No brains."

They were met by an attractive Chinese woman who was nearly as tall as Gill. She had sleek black expensively cut shoulder length hair and a slender figure under a tight-fitting black business suit.

She clasped her hands in front of her chest and nodded a bow. "Mister Pierce will not keep you long. My name is Ling-Ling." She waved an arm over the wide room behind her. "Please take the time to look around."

This place was much more expensively furnished with poker tables and a roulette wheel formed into a circle around a central glass display pedestal that was lit from above. The croupiers were all women, much better dressed and more attractive than the people on the ground floor. No flashing lights, no loud music and pinging one-arm bandits. The lighting was low and discreet. Two of the tables were fully occupied with wealthy-looking gamblers all dressed in evening wear playing Texas Hold-em.

"Would you like a drink?" Ling-Ling asked. She waved a hand without waiting for a reply and a scantily dressed waitress hurried across with a tray balanced on her palm.

"I'm driving, I'll just have a Perrier," Gill said.

Ling-Ling angled her head. "Oh, I understood you would be staying the night. We have excellent rooms."

"Then you misunderstood," Gill said. "I've just come to look round."

Aftershave raised a hand. "I'm not driving, I'll have a vodka martini … shaken not stirred."

Ling-Ling gave him an old-fashioned look but nodded at the waitress who scurried away to a well-stocked bar in one corner.

A door opened in the opposite corner and Derek Pierce came out. He saw Gill and hurried over, swerving round the pedestal, his arms out straight as if he was an impresario welcoming a famous diva. He took Gill by the shoulders and planted wet kisses on both her cheeks. "Gill, so glad you could make it. Has Ling-Ling been taking care of you?"

"Hello, Derek. Can I introduce a business friend of Rick's. She disengaged herself from Derek's hands and crooked a finger. "He's just arrived from Spain."

Aftershave held out a hand. "Tristan Roberts," he said using the false name from his false Colombian passport. "Nice place you got here."

Gill could see that Derek was miffed at her having a companion but he forced a smile as he took Aftershave's hand.

"Spain, eh. What do you do there Mister Roberts?"

"This an' that, whatever can make a few euros, you know. Anyway call me Tristan, everyone does."

"Well, Tristan, perhaps you'd like to try your luck on one of the tables while I show Gill around. What's your game?"

"Eh! Oh, blackjack, bit more skill involved wi' that."

"Ling-Ling will get you some chips. First fifty quid on the house."

Ling-ling was standing to one side, fingers pressed to the side of her head. She nodded and looked at Derek. "A word please, Mister Pierce."

Derek excused himself and went to her so close their heads almost touched. Gill saw a brief flash of concern cross Pierce's face as Ling-Ling whispered in his ear. She saw him grimace and nod. Ling-Ling turned away.

Pierce came back with a false smile. "Sorry about that, bit of business. Where were we?"

"About to give me fifty quid," Aftershave said.

"Oh yes. I'm afraid Ling-Ling has something else to take care of. Adele will sort you out," Derek said as the waitress came back with the drinks. He took Gill's Perrier and frowned. "We'll have to do better than this. Come into my office we have some Champagne cooking."

Gill nodded at Ling-Ling's back. "Hope there isn't a problem."

Derek shrugged. "Nothing she can't handle. She's my head of security, not much gets past Ling-

Ling." He put a proprietary arm around Gill's waist and pulled her along with him.

Gill halted as they reached the glass-topped pedestal. "What's this?"

Derek grinned. "It's why the casino is called the Golden Nugget. It's a real nugget, pure solid twenty-four carat gold and worth about ten grand." He slid his hand around her waist again and edged her towards his office door. "Now, how about that glass of champagne?" She forced a smile and then her mobile vibrated in her pocket. She stopped again and pulled the phone out to read the display. "It's Rick," she said, "I have to take this." She turned away from Pierce and put the phone to her ear. "Yes, sweetie?"

Lacey sounded breathless. "I've just made a connection between the mine and Chinese special forces. They're armed and dangerous. I think Pierce is in it up to his neck. Whatever you do, be very careful."

"Always, Sweetie." She was pleased he sounded concerned. She broke the connection, put the phone away and turned back to Pierce.

"Everything okay?" he asked. "I thought Rick might be here too."

"Rick's busy, he always has someone else to do." She shrugged, "there's always another woman in the background."

Pierce grinned an unattractive leer. "Maybe you'd like to get your own back."

Gill shrugged again. "Maybe, but Rick's not a man to cross, he could make life very unpleasant. I

184

have to know I'm not jumping from the frying pan into the fire."

"I get the picture," Pierce said.

"As long as we understand each other, Derek. I'm not an easy lay and I'm not cheap. These things always come with a price tag attached."

She allowed him to slide his hand around her waist but this time his fingers edged up to brush her breast. She doubted it was accidental. It seemed that Derek was prepared to pay the price.

32

Lacey was half-way back to the Discovery when the sound of a racing engine forced him to take cover in the bushes. With headlights blazing the black Range Rover careered up the narrow track heading towards the quarry. In the backwash from the lights, Lacey caught a glimpse of Bill's face in the driving seat through an open window as it raced past. Something had brought him at breakneck speed and it was probable that the guards had missed calling in at a specified time.

He stepped back on the track and loped to the Discovery where he called Gill. It was necessary to warn her as soon as possible that she could be walking into her proverbial hornet's nest.

He was about to pull out of his parking spot when a second vehicle raced past heading after the Range Rover. Something had rattled their cages, that was certain. On the way back to Kingswear he phoned a report on his findings to Ben Reid's office answering service. It was too late for the brigadier to still be working but he knew the answering machine was checked every few minutes by the duty officer who would file the messages in order of urgency for Ben to see as soon as he arrived back at his desk. As his was just a routine report, Lacey thought it would be low down on the list of priorities.

Back on the boat he fired up his laptop and searched for information about gold on Dartmoor.

What he found surprised him. Gold in minute quantities had been discovered for hundreds of years, although none of any significance, until now, it seemed.

The search engine also threw up information on gold finds in the west of Scotland at Cononish near Tyndrum, which were very recent, and historical mining in Wales at the Gwynfynydd Mine which started in 1860 and continued until 1988. Exclusive exploration rights had been granted as late as 2020 for a mining company to continue searching for gold at the Welsh site. Lacey thought it was possible that a seam ran down the whole of the west side of the British Isles.

He sat back and scratched his head. It appeared that gold mining in the quarry was genuine but the find had not been registered with the Crown Estate, even if so, it was unlikely they'd give permission for it to be taken away as it was deemed to be Mines Royal, especially unlikely if it was panned gold.

It was no wonder the mine was so well protected as it was an illegal enterprise but it still left the question of why were the Chinese involved? It wasn't a connection that came readily to mind. Lacey knew the Chinese weren't short of gold, they produced over thirteen percent of the world's supply, overtaking South Africa as the world's largest producer back in the early part of the 21st century.

His chain of thought was interrupted when the satellite phone burred. He snatched it off its cradle. "Yes?"

There was a few seconds of hollow silence then a quiet voice. "Rick, it's Andee."

"Andee, thank god. Where are you?"

"Mozambique. The SEA Team found us. They brought supplies and we were able to charge the sat phone batteries."

"How are you? Are you okay? You sound stressed."

"I'm all right. There's lots to do here, people have been shot and injured in other ways. There's still a lot of the Covid-19 Delta variant around too. We're doing our best but it's not easy."

"Are you getting enough sleep?"

She laughed and it again sounded hollow. "Never get enough sleep, we're working eighteen hour days, at least we are now that we have fuel for the generators, there's such a backlog of cases to get through."

"I've been worried about you."

"You needn't. It was a bit hairy security-wise to begin with but the SEA Team leader says they are under orders from Ben to stay on as security until things settle down."

"That's a weight off my mind. Any idea when you'll be coming back?"

There was a long silence. "Andee?"

"I've been thinking a lot," she said.

"That sounds ominous."

"I won't be coming back."

He felt his stomach lurch. "Oh?"

"This is difficult, I don't know how to say this."

"Try."

"There's no one else. It's just that you and I seem to want different things. You're happy to bury yourself in that house in Chichester and potter around on the boat but I need more. I've always been an adrenaline junkie, you know that, and you were always so adventurous up until you retired from the ISPA. When we first met at that hospital in London, I felt attracted to your innate violence, you were a force of nature, radiating danger, and I couldn't get you out of my system. Then you saved me from the IRA ..."

"I'll never forget it was my fault you became a target. I'll also never forget you saved my life twice, the second time on that mountain on Andros."

He thought he could hear her smile but it was a sad sound of apology.

"After that we got married," she said. "I've enjoyed almost every minute but I can't see any future for us. My life is here with Médicin, here where I can do some good for people who have nothing. I shall always be away for most of the year and it's not fair on you."

"Do you want a divorce?"

"I don't want anything other than to be myself, the woman you married and not a shadow of someone I can't ever be."

"That last night we spent together, you were saying goodbye then."

"I suppose in a way I was. But it wasn't until I got here that I finally realised how claustrophobic our lives had become. The occasional dinner at the yacht club didn't hack it in the excitement stakes."

"I'm sorry, Andee, to disappoint you."

"Don't apologise, Rick, you have nothing to apologise for. I'm being inordinately selfish in one respect, wanting it all my own way but also I want you to have a life too, a life without wondering where your wandering wife might be and not have to worry about her."

"I'll always worry about you, Andee. It comes with the territory. If you want time to think about this …?"

"No, I've had all the time I need. The decision is made, I hope you understand."

"I do, more than you realise. I guess I've seen the writing on the wall for a while now. It's your life Andee, you must do what you must but I'm going to miss you."

"You're making this too easy for me, Rick."

"I know that's not the case, it will never be easy … for either of us … but I'll not stand in your way. I'll get the papers drawn up for you to sign the next time you're back in the UK. I'll make the house at Crystal Palace over to you, somewhere for you to live whenever you're between assignments. There will be money if you need it."

"I don't need money, Rick, I have enough."

"Well, if there's anything …"

"I know, I only have to ask. There is one thing … I want you to be … to live a life of your own … no ties, no regrets." She paused. "Can you do that for me?"

"I can try."

"I have to go now, I'm due in theatre in a few minutes."

"Keep safe, Andee."

"You too, Rick. Bye." There was a hiss of static and she was gone.

Lacey put the phone down and sat heavily. He knew she was right. He had let the fear of Al Qaeda discovering his new identity rule his life; the fear that Andee would also be a target. Once he was out of the protective cocoon of the ISPA he had hibernated, rusticating himself in the country. He could not have been much fun to live with over the past years. Andee was a brilliant surgeon who was wasted doing routine surgery at a NHS hospital. She was doing what she was born to do, chasing her own star, but their trajectories had diverged. Now he had to come to terms with finding his true self. Any reservations he had about tackling this operation had blown away with the fight at the mine. Any fear that he had that he being a target would again endanger Andee's life was lessened. How ironic that she should make her decision now that he was on active service. The old David Troy was coming back and the enemy was in a dangerous place.

33

Pierce led Gill into his office. It was large and spacious with a view over the bay and must have once been a superior suite when the hotel was running. There was a desk and three leather couches arranged around a low glass-topped coffee table complete with ice bucket, a bottle of cheap champagne and two glass flutes. There was a bar in one corner with an array of optics and another door which, Gill assumed, led into a bedroom.

Gill pointed at the two flutes. "No Shelley?"

Pierce shrugged out of his jacket and flung it across the back of one of the couches. "Might as well be comfortable. Shell's gone to visit her mum for a couple of days; place is all ours," he said with a leer that passed as a smile. He held up a flute. "Drink?"

"As I told Ling-Ling, I'm driving."

"Just one won't hurt. Then again, maybe you'll change your mind and stay over."

"Rick's expecting me back."

Pierce pretended to look at his watch. "We've got a good couple of hours to get better acquainted." He poured some champagne into the flute and cursed as it overflowed the rim and ran down his hand. He sucked the moisture. "Never could get the hang o' that."

Gill picked up the empty flute and took the bottle from him. She tilted the glass and slowly poured the champagne turning the flute upright as she did so. She pushed the bottle back at him. "Not rocket science, Derek. Trick is to take your time and not rush things. The best things in life are those that can be savoured." She took the drink and moved to the furthest couch, sitting and crossing her legs.

His eyes ran up her legs from the ankle to the thighs. "You're a great looking woman, Gill, you've kept yourself in shape, I like that."

Gill gave him a bored look as if she'd heard it all before. "And what do you have to offer, Derek?"

He sat opposite her, legs akimbo, and raised his glass. "More than you might think. Cheers."

"But is it enough? Rick's not the sort to take things lying down, he's likely to throw a fit and it won't be pretty. I need to know I'll be well looked after."

"You don't have to worry about him. I'll take care of him."

Gill raised her eyebrows. "How?"

He rose and sat beside her, putting a hand on her thigh. "Never you mind. All you need to know is that money talks and I have plenty of it … and friends who ain't afraid to get their hands dirty when it's needed."

"Talk is cheap, Derek, but I told you, I'm not." She picked up his hand and moved it.

"I tell you I can look after you. Woman like you could be worth it." He put his hand back on her thigh and ran it up towards her crotch.

193

Gill shook him off and stood. "You get nothing for free, Derek. A glass of cheap plonk doesn't give you a licence to grope the goods."

Pierce sneered. "How much then?"

Gill drew herself up to her full height and gave him a withering look. "What do you take me for, a hooker? You talk a good fight but I know Rick, he's no pushover. He's American, he has friends in New York, the type that invented concrete overcoats. It's not money I want, it's out, but out with someone who can take care of me to make sure I don't end up floating in the river like that other poor sucker."

Gill thought she saw a flicker of concern flash across Pierce's face at the mention of Forrestal. It was brief and she wasn't certain but Pierce bit on it as she hoped he would.

"Yeah, that's a point, why's Rick so interested in that?"

"He's a friend of the family. He got a phone call from the States asking if he could gee-up the police down here, to try and get a result on the enquiry. I was packed to go to St. Tropez and he drags me down here. Trouble with Rick is once he gets his teeth into something he's like a Rottweiler, he won't let go."

"And has he … got his teeth into something?"

Pierce sounded casual but Gill had a thrill of confirmation. Pierce was worried. She shrugged and went to stand by the window. It was beginning to get dark and lights were coming on at the marina and on the anchored ships in the bay.

"Well?" Pierce was getting impatient.

Gill turned. "Well what?"

"Has Rick found out anything?"

"I don't know, he keeps his own counsel but he's had meetings with the police and with the navy people from the college. He got a bit excited about something but he kept whatever it was to himself. I wish he'd give it up, I'm bored."

Pierce stood and walked behind her running a hand around her waist and kissing the nape of her neck. "I could help you with that." His hand slipped up towards her breast and she stood back putting a heel onto his toes. He yelped and let go. Hopping on one foot, his face puce. "Why'd you do that, you silly bitch?"

Gill took two strides and hit him in the chest with the flat of her hand sending him reeling back onto a couch. She knelt beside him and twisted his bowtie in her fist.

"You need to learn something if we are going to get on, Derek. I'm not sure of the type of woman you're used to, although knowing Shelley I can guess, but you're now playing in a different league. I'll let you know when you can take liberties and it's not yet. Not until you show me that you're not just a bag of hot air." She stood and smoothed down her dress. "Call me a bitch again and I'll cut your balls off. Am I clear?"

She didn't wait for a reply but walked into the casino. Aftershave had half an eye on the door and nodded as she came out.

He threw his cards on the table. "I'll cash out now," he said to the dealer.

The woman gave him a wide smile as she raked in his cards. "Cashier's on the ground floor, sir."

Aftershave picked up his chips and tossed her one worth twenty pounds. "Ta, darlin'. Next time, eh?"

Gill looked at the stack of chips in his hand. "Good night?"

"Coupla, hundred," he said as they walked to the lift.

Gill pressed the call button. "See anything interesting?"

Aftershave nodded. "Those two tables, the blokes in the penguin suits. They're droppin' a lot o' cash tonight. Not one of 'em has won a hand the whole time I've been watchin'."

"Bad poker players?"

Aftershave grimaced. "No one's that bad."

The security guard was still standing by the lift doors when they came out.

Aftershave gave him a wide grin and showed him the stack of chips. "Where's the cashier, mate?"

The man said nothing but hooked a thumb at the far corner where a woman sat behind a metal grille. Aftershave grinned again and sauntered past. As they waited for the money Aftershave gave Gill a questioning look. "How'd you get on?"

Gill grunted. "More hands than a watch factory. I'll fill you in later."

He pushed the roll of twenty pound notes the woman handed him into a pocket. He waved at the security guard as they left but the man was on his mobile and didn't respond other than to scowl into the handset.

Gill's car was parked on the far side of the car park and they strolled across to it. "We're being followed," Gill whispered.

"Yeah, I know, bloke was hangin' around in the shadows." There was a sound of running feet and they turned. The man had a mask, one left over from the pandemic, and looked comical. Not so funny was the long serrated blade he held in his hand. He pushed it towards Aftershave's face.

"Give me your fuckin' money."

Aftershave sighed. "You've got to be kiddin'."

"*Now!*"

Aftershave spread his hands wide then moved faster than the eye could follow as the knife was twisted out of the thief's hand and he was sent sprawling onto the gravel, his middle two fingers broken. He whimpered, pushed his ruined hand into his jacket and scrambled backwards the way he had come before jumping to his feet and running off.

"Amateur night," Aftershave said and threw the knife into the shrubbery. "Funny thing though, that bloke stank of fish."

34

Lacey was alone with his thoughts as Gill and Aftershave returned. He was sitting in the dark on the stern looking across at the lights and activity on the Dartmouth side, which at nearly midnight was still in full holiday mode. He had a glass of malt by his side but had barely touched it. He had found long ago that drowning his sorrows never worked, just left him with a hangover; more pain than he needed.

He looked over at the two as they came through the small transom door. "Help yourselves to a drink and come back out. We need to talk and now's as good a time as any."

Gill gave him a searching look. "Everything okay?"

She had concern etched in her voice and he nodded. "We'll talk when you're ready."

Aftershave had gone ahead and he came back out as Gill was loitering, with a half-full glass in either hand. "C'mon, Petal, after the night we've had we need this."

Gill took the glass and sniffed the contents. "Single malt."

"Yeah, Ard Beg, a good one. Found it at the back of the cupboard."

"Locker," Lacey corrected. "Did you run into some trouble at the Golden Nugget?"

Gill took a seat at right angles to him and shuffled along to make room for Aftershave then fixed her gaze on Lacey. "After you. Seems to me that you have something on your mind."

Lacey picked up his tumbler and took a sip, taking the time to get his thoughts in order. He then told them of his experiences at the quarry, leaving nothing out and finishing with his puzzlement over Chinese involvement.

Gill and Aftershave had stayed silent throughout the tale but now looked at each other. Gill spoke first. "Some things are now beginning to make sense. Pierce has a solid gold nugget in a glass case on display at the casino, that's why the place is named the way it is. He didn't say how he came by it."

"Did you find out anything useful, any leads to the murder or the reason for it?"

"His security chief is Chinese," Aftershave said.

"Yes, and she took a call which rattled Pierce," Gill added. "Probably news of your doings at the mine. She disappeared soon after."

"Anything more concrete?"

Gill pursed her lips. "Most of this is conjecture but I had the distinct feeling that Pierce knows something about Forrestal's murder. I baited a hook and he bit good and hard. Whatever the reason, he was concerned about the subject and for an instant he let it show."

"I'll tell you what is concrete," Aftershave said. "Pierce is crooked. That casino is a front for something else, it's not kosher. I watched twelve men playing poker and all they did was lose, every one of them, all the time. That's not natural, it was a payoff, a big time payoff."

"For what, though?" Lacey said.

Aftershave shrugged. "Search me but it was definitely fishy, bit like the smell of the bloke who tried to mug me for my winnin's."

Lacey raised his eyebrows and Gill explained. "Maybe Pierce doesn't like to lose," she said. "The security man was on his mobile when we left. He knew that Aftershave had won a couple of hundred and had notes in his pocket."

"Coincidence?" Lacey asked.

Gill frowned. "Unlikely, I don't believe in that sort of coincidence. That was enemy action. Easy enough to explain to the police if anyone complained that muggers would be attracted to the car park of a casino and hard to prove otherwise. I reckon genuine big winning punters wouldn't get to keep their winnings for long."

"Maybe it was the security man's little scam," Aftershave said. "I didn't take to him and he didn't take to me. Maybe it was his bit of revenge for his hurt pride."

Gill shrugged and sighed. "You could be right but I'm willing to bet that fingers Pierce would have his hand out for a cut."

"You really don't like him, do you?" Lacey said.

"Dislike is too mild a word. Loathe is closer. The man's a snake. It takes me all my self-control not to smack him in the mouth every time he opens it."

"He tried it on," Aftershave said. "Hands everywhere." He waggled his fingers.

Gill snorted. "Not funny."

She fell silent as Lacey watched her and waited. He knew there was more to come.

She sipped her malt and held the tumbler in both hands her shoulders hunched as if she was cold. "I have a confession."

Lacey said nothing just tilted his head to one side.

"Go on, then," Aftershave said.

Gill shot him a barbed glance. "I stirred the mud big time, Rick. I led Pierce on, told him the only way he could get his way with me was to take care of you. I set you up, deliberately, to try and break the logjam we're in. He boasted he had friends who didn't mind getting their hands dirty and I thought it might bring Forrestal's killer out of the woodwork. I'm sorry, I've put your life on the line."

Lacey uncrossed his legs and sat up. He wasn't sure of Gill's motives but he would probably have done the same in her position. She was right, they had been getting nowhere fast. It was plain that Pierce and the Chinese were hand-in-glove if the reason for their partnership was still clouded. That the Chinese were killers was beyond doubt but what were they doing here and why was it so important that they would risk murder to cover up their activities? They needed someone to ask and Gill's ploy might provide the method. He could see she was waiting for his reaction and decided to put her out of her misery.

"Good thinking, Gill. We've been on the back foot for too long. It's about time we became proactive. We'll see if Pierce is just hot air. If nothing happens in the next day or so, we'll go pay him another visit."

He saw Gill puff out her cheeks in relief. "Thanks for taking it so well, Rick. I thought I might have overstepped the mark."

Lacey gave her a level look. "You did but if things work out it may prove to be the break we need." He turned to Aftershave. "It's best if you stay aboard for tonight. Use the third cabin, you know where that is. There's another Sig 226 in the armoury, I'll sort it out for you."

He rose and went below.

Aftershave put his hand on Gill's arm. "Don't kick yourself over it, Petal."

"I don't know what I was thinking. I just wanted to get away from that slimy lech. At the time I thought he was just spinning me a line about his killer friends, trying to get his leg over. Now I know differently and I've put Lacey's head on the block."

"Operational necessity, Petal."

"Was it?"

Aftershave sniffed. "Anyone else and you might not be so bothered."

Gill gave him another sharp look. "What's that supposed to mean?"

"You can't fool your Uncle Aftershave, Petal. You've developed a soft spot for him."

"Don't be stupid."

"I've seen that look in your eyes before. The sooner you admit it to yourself the better you can come to terms with it. I don't want you freezing up when the shit hits the fan."

35

Gill was awakened the next morning by the rumbling of the twin diesels and a slight vibration running through the cabin. It had been a restless night for her as the truth of Aftershave's observations began to sink in. She had to admit to herself that she had feelings for Lacey, feelings that she hadn't felt for another man since Ricky's death. The few affairs that she'd had had been brief and unsatisfactory, no one measured even half way up to Ricky … until now. She couldn't put her finger on exactly why Lacey was different but he was. The pity of it was that he was married and it could go nowhere other than the depths of heartache.

She climbed out of bed, ran a brush through her hair and climbed into jeans and a T-shirt to find out what was happening.

Lacey was on the flybridge checking dials and Aftershave was leaning on the starboard side grinning at her like the famous Cheshire Cat. She ambled over to him.

"What's the SP?"

Aftershave glanced up at Lacey's back. "Skipper's decided to take a cruise out to Torbay, to test the water, so to speak. Not sure exactly what he's got in mind, you'd better ask 'im that yourself."

Gill nodded and climbed the steps to join Lacey. She made sure she stayed out of touching distance, she no longer trusted herself to stay grounded.

Lacey glanced around at her and smiled. She felt her stomach muscles tighten and wished Aftershave had kept his mouth shut. In her case ignorance had been bliss.

"What's the plan, Rick?"

"We're going to have a nose around the bay. Forrestal had picked up that Narcosub signal near to where the *Norfolk* was anchored and then it disappeared, according to his notes. Subs don't just disappear, especially not when they're being tracked by the most sophisticated sonar on the market. There has to be an answer and it's somewhere out there." He turned his head seaward and raised his chin.

"It's a bit of a long shot," Gill said.

"I know." Lacey pushed the twin throttles forward in neutral and the engine noise increased. He checked the dials and gave a satisfied nod. "We're all set. We'll need to tank up at the fuel barge but otherwise we have all we need. If you and Aftershave could manage the lines we'll get underway."

"What do I have to do?"

"Just unhook them from the cleats and throw the lines onto the pontoon, I'll do the rest."

She and Aftershave did as they were asked and Lacey eased the big boat away from the pontoon using the bow and stern thrusters. He steered using the twin throttles and spun the boat in its own length to point seaward before nudging it alongside the fuel barge and holding it there against the incoming tide. It took fifteen minutes to fill both the big tanks. Lacey paid on the MI6 card and then nosed out past the Mew Stone turning to port when they were clear.

Gill climbed back up the stairs and sat on a comfortable bench behind the helm seat as Lacey put the boat up on the plane and they surged forward. He turned and beckoned her over. "Would you like to helm?"

She furrowed her brow. "I don't know how."

He eased out of the seat to make room for her. "It's not difficult. The helm is the same as a steering wheel on a car. Turn it right and the boat turns to starboard, the same with turning to port. The twin levers are the throttles pull them back and the boat will slow, pull them all the way back and the boat will stop as if it's hit a brick wall as the engines will be in reverse. The only other things you need to know is: one, pass to starboard of oncoming vessels, two, yachts have right of way." He pointed forward. "And three; see those small buoys? They are lobster pot markers left by the fishermen. Run over one and you could get a line tangled around a prop so steer clear of them. Otherwise it's a piece of cake." He turned to leave.

Gill had a sudden surge of panic. "Where are you going?" He grinned and she felt her stomach flip again.

"To get the coffee on. Looks like it's going to be another fine day weatherwise so you shouldn't have any problems."

She bit her lip. "Okay, but where are we going?"

"Keep heading due east. In a short while we'll be passing Berry Head and then we'll be into the bay. If I'm not back by then turn north-east and run towards the anchored ships."

"You'd trust me with this?"

"I'd trust you with almost anything, Gill."

"Really?"

He laughed. "Well …"

She bared her teeth. "Right this second, Rick Arnold, I think I hate you."

He was part way down the stairs and she heard him call back, "hate's good."

"Better than nothing at all," she whispered to herself. She began to concentrate on steering the boat. It really was as easy as he'd said. The boat was a thoroughbred and responded to the slightest touch. She checked the speed and found they were cruising at a comfortable fifteen knots. There were many other boats sailing around and she needed to keep alert, especially for the yachts which seemed to have rules of their own, and the frequent lobster pot markers which were often hidden in the slight swell and not seen until the last moment. After a few fraught minutes she relaxed and began to enjoy herself. The sun was warm and the wind slight. If it wasn't for the mission they were on ticking away at the back of her mind every waking second, it would have been a perfect day.

She was deep in thought and didn't hear Lacey climb back. He put a hand on her shoulder and she felt a shiver run down her spine. She jerked upright.

"God, you made me jump."

He passed her a mug of coffee. "You nervous?"

She gave a determined shake of her head. "I was concentrating, I didn't hear you."

"How'd you like it?"

"The boat?"

"What else?"

"There he was again answering a question with a question. "She's fine, great, really, a beauty."

He grinned. "Don't get me wrong when I say that makes the pair of you. You look good at the helm, almost as if you were born to it."

"I can see why you love it, Rick. It's exhilarating."

He sniffed the air. "Today the weather's good. Not so much fun in a Force 8. He inched closer beside her and she thought he was going to put his arm around her but he bent forward to study the dials. "Good job, Gill, right on course. We'll make a sailor of you yet."

They passed Berry Head and Torbay opened up in front of them. Lacey pointed. "Head for the cruise liners, we'll take a nose around before anchoring up."

"Are we looking for anything in particular?"

"Maybe we'll know it when we see it."

It took another twenty minutes to cross the bay and they circled the two huge liners and headed closer to the shoreline.

"The *Norfolk's* gone," Lacey said. "She was anchored up not far from that tanker. Budge over, Gill, I'm going to find a shallow spot to drop the hook." He used the depth sounder to find a sandbank and released the anchor running out six times the depth in chain. He cut the engines and the silence seemed almost eerie for a few seconds before the raucous calls of herring gulls intruded.

"This is near the spot where Forrestal got his readings," Lacey said. He looked seaward where the bulk of the tanker could be seen half a mile further out riding high in the water.

Lacey pointed. "She's unladen,"

Gill shrugged. "So?"

"They usually anchor up here fully loaded waiting for the price of oil to increase. It's unusual for a tanker to be sitting here empty."

"There's probably a good reason."

"Maybe, but seeing as she's in an area of concern, it might pay to check her out."

36

Lacey climbed back up to the flybridge with a notepad in his hand. Gill was stretched out on the sunbed with her designer sunglasses perched on her forehead and a pair of 10x42 Leica binoculars by her side. Lacey liked the view but kept the thought to himself.

"There's nothing much happening aboard that tanker," Gill said. "Not so much as a gull landing on the deck."

Lacey waved the pad. "I have some data here. The ship is called the *New Venture* and she's registered in Liberia under a flag of convenience to a company in Colombia which has offices in Hong Kong."

Gill sat up and dropped her feet to the deck. "West Africa, South America and China, quite a mixture."

Aftershave followed Lacey with coffee mugs in his hands. He offered them round and sat heavily on the space vacated by Gill's legs and puffed. "Hot, ennit?"

"I thought you'd be used to the heat by now," Gill said.

"Air conditioning, Petal, that's what makes the Spanish summers bearable."

Gill hooked a thumb at Lacey. "Rick's got some interesting data."

Aftershave nodded. "I know, I was down there when he was digging it up on the laptop. All sorts of stuff I don' understand."

Lacey took his mug and the notebook to the helm seat and swivelled to face them both. "There's a system that all ships over three-hundred gross tonnage and most fishing boats have to have fitted. It's called AIS, the Automatic Identification System which is monitored by both ground stations and satellite. It's mainly for calling in air-sea rescue but the ships use it for anti-collision technology as it shows all other vessels in their area with range and bearing. It's a useful piece of kit for surveillance too. I was able to log onto the website and get tracking data for the ship." He flipped a page on the notebook. "She was pinpointed unloading at the Barrancabermejer refinery at Santander in Colombia two months ago and then sailed directly here without picking up a cargo. Her skipper is on record as reporting engine trouble and the ship is awaiting spares to be delivered, hence the long stay in Torbay."

"Makes sense," Aftershave said.

Gill nodded. "It would explain the delay in leaving and the fact they are unladen."

"It's also very convenient," Lacey said.

Gill tipped her mug at him. "You're adding up the Colombian and Chinese connections, the possible sighting of a Narcosub here in the bay, Chinese Special Forces, an idle ship that came directly from the cocaine capital of the world and coming up with a cause and effect."

Lacey smiled his slow smile and it crinkled his eyes. "That's about the size of it. All theory of course. I may be adding two and two and making five. And still no nearer knowing how Forrestal ended up getting himself shot."

"Inspector Craddock was banging on about the increase in drug usage in this area. More drug users means a bigger supply. Maybe the cocaine is coming from that ship," Gill said.

"Not our problem," Aftershave butted into the conversation. "Not unless Chinese SF have started running the drug trade 'ere. Much as I'd like to think they're capable of anything underhand, I can't see it meself."

"The biggest users are rich kids and city traders down here for the summer, bringing their urban bad habits with them," Lacey said. "*I* can't see what the Chinese could gain from hooking a few hundred spoilt brats. It's more than likely something to do with that gold mine, that's why they're guarding it."

Gill frowned. "We're going round in circles and in danger of disappearing up our own prop shafts. We need to decide some priorities and get some hard and fast facts. It may be we've been splitting our attentions and need to narrow the focus. Aftershave's right, the drug business is not our problem but in order to take it out of the equation we need to check it out first."

Lacey held up a hand. "You're forgetting Derek Pierce. He's tied to the mine and to the Chinese connection. He's not tied up with drugs that we know of."

Gill looked disgusted. "It wouldn't surprise me, he has a history with drugs, I wouldn't put any perversion past that greasy bastard. You're right, let's concentrate our firepower on Pierce."

Lacey nodded. "Fine how do you suggest we do that?"

"Drugs must be ferried ashore by that Narcosub. It has to surface somewhere."

Lacey let out a humourless laugh. "There's miles of coastline, countless bays and dozens of beaches. We can't watch them all. It's pointless watching that tanker from here too. If they're using a sub they'll launch it from underwater."

Aftershave grinned. "Like one of them James Bond films. A big hatch in the hull."

"That's fiction," Gill snorted.

"It would explain why it disappeared from Forrestal's sonar," Lacey said. "There was always an element of scientific fact in the Bond movies."

Gill spread her hands. "So, what do you suggest?"

"It's unlikely they'll bring anything ashore on this stretch of coast, it's too busy with holidaymakers. I reckon they'll head out into the bay and maybe head for a quiet cove somewhere. We'll up anchor and put ourselves seaward of the *New Venture*."

Gill gave an exasperated sigh. "What good is that going to do if we can't see anything?"

"I'll switch on the fish finder. It's sonar but far less powerful than the kit they have on the *Norfolk* and less sophisticated. The deeper the water the wider the cone the sonar throws out and the more chance we have of picking up a big echo. Here," he waved both of them over to the instrument panel and pointed to a screen. "This is it. There's a repeater on the main helm position below so we can keep an eye on it wherever we are." He switched the instrument on and waited while it warmed up. "It shows the bottom, whether it's hard or soft. Fish show up as arcs, the bigger the arc, the bigger the fish. The deeper it goes the less chance of surface interference. All in all we should head for the deeper water seaward and keep our fingers crossed. I have a fishing rod aboard. We can throw a line over the stern and troll back and forth all day if necessary at a slow speed." He grinned. "We may even catch dinner."

Aftershave rubbed his hands together. "Ooh, cod'n chips, lovely."

Lacey grinned. "No cod around here. More likely a slack handful of mackerel if we hit a school. They're not bad eating, if you don't mind the bones."

Aftershave grimaced. "Oh well, beggars can't be an' all that." He shrugged. "Give us those mugs, I'll go and wash up."

Gill sidled up to Lacey as Aftershave left. "What are the chances, Rick?"

He looked at her sideways as he started the engines. "Close to nil, I'd guess."

214

"But worth a shot?"

"It won't hurt to spend a few hours out here. It'll give Pierce time to get his tough friends organised, if that's what he wants to do. There's worse ways to spend a day." He began to winch up the anchor. "And worse people to spend it with."

She put a hand on his arm. "Are you okay, Rick?"

"Why d'you ask?"

"You just seem different. I can't put my finger on it but I can't help feeling something's changed."

"It's nothing for you to worry about. I'm fine." He had to hold back the temptation to blurt out about Andee's decision. He didn't need sympathy and he wasn't about to ask for it. He could feel the old strength of character and determination growing in his psyche. His mind was hardening and his combat readiness with it. The gunfight in the mine had proved he still had the capability. If there was going to be violence he was ready.

37

It was beginning to get dark. The sun had dropped below the headland and Lacey said it was time to pack up. Gill was taking her turn at the helm, trolling slowly west towards Berry Head. They had been at it most of the day with nothing to show for it except half a dozen mackerel that Aftershave had caught. She was feeling tired. The fresh air and sunshine, together with the constant alertness needed to helm and keep an eye on the fish finder had worn her down. The tiredness wasn't a bad feeling but the disappointment of not getting a result rankled. Lacey had been right, there was little chance of pinging the Narcosub but it had been worth a try.

Lacey came topside to stand beside her. "Head for home, Gill. It'll be dark in an hour and I want to be moored up by then."

She gave him a navy salute. "Aye, aye, skipper, hard a port it is."

Lacey leaned over the rail and called down to Aftershave. "Reel it in now, we're finished for the day."

Aftershave waved an acknowledgement and began to wind hard on the reel. The rod viciously bowed and it was torn from Aftershave's hands as the fish finder pinged.

"Contact," Gill yelled, "a big one and it's gone right underneath us."

Lacey spun around. "Try to keep a contact on it. Which way was it heading?"

"Hard to tell," Gill said. "South I think. The sonar cone just caught the edge of it, whatever it is."

Aftershave bustled up the stairs to join them. "Sorry about your rod, Rick. It was yanked right out of my hands. Look, there it is on the surface going at a rate of knots." He pointed ahead at the reel and butt of the rod creaming through the waves and getting further away.

Lacey grabbed the binoculars and focused on the tiny furrow the rod was making. "The water gets deeper out there, if it is the sub and not a basking shark, and it dives, we'll lose it. There's only fifty yards of line on that reel, the rod will be pulled right under." He handed the glasses to Aftershave. "Keep an eye on it," then he turned to Gill. "Open her up let's get as close as we can without spooking them. They'll be used to pleasure craft criss-crossing above them but might take fright if we stick too close to their heels."

Aftershave dropped the glasses from his eyes. "Too late, Rick. It's just gone under."

Lacey pointed to the horizon. "Anything out there?"

Aftershave nodded. "Several motor boats headin' this way at speed. You can see the bow waves, a couple of yachts also headin' in and a fishing boat out there."

"The pleasure boats will be heading in to Torquay Marina for the night," Lacey said.

"What do you want me to do?" Gill asked.

Lacey grimaced. "Let's go back to plan A. Head for Dartmouth. We've lost whatever it was and it's unlikely we'll get it back."

Gill eased the twin throttles forward and the powerful boat rose up on the plane. Lacey leaned across and adjusted the trim tabs to bring the bow down and increase speed. He nodded ahead. "Keep well to port of the fishing boat as you round the Head. Give him plenty of room, he may have nets out."

Gill saluted again. "Aye, aye, skipper. Any more orders?"

Lacey grinned but it lacked his usual humour. "Just don't hit anything."

Gill gave him a sharp look. It sounded as if Lacey had had a bad day but she knew that wasn't the case. The day had been good apart from losing the contact. Lacey gave out an aura of having a weight suddenly land on his shoulders from a great height.

He turned to leave before she could ask any questions. "I'll be below if you need me," he said.

Aftershave watched him go and shrugged. "What's up wi' Rick, Petal?"

She raised her eyebrows. "You've noticed it too?"

"Yeah. Not sure what the cause is though. Whatever it is, he'll get over it. I get the feelin' that the colonel is tougher than he looks."

Gill grinned at him. "So, you've noticed *that* too."

"Velvet glove, iron fist, Petal. I don't mind sayin' that little scrap we had got me thinkin'. He's no pushover."

Gill paraphrased a Johnny Cash song. "*I've fought tougher men but I really can't remember when.*"

Aftershave nodded. "That about sums it up, Petal." They were approaching the fishing boat and he put the binoculars up to his eyes. "No nets by the looks of it, one of 'em is pulling up a lobster pot." He stiffened and bent forward, bracing himself against the sunbed. "Well I'll be buggered."

Gill frowned. "What is it?"

"That bloke hauling on the line."

"What about him?"

"He's got his right hand all strapped up. Looks like he's havin' trouble pullin' on that rope."

"Our fishy-smelling friend from last night?" Gill said.

Aftershave gave her a wry grin. "Odds on."

"What's the name of the boat?"

"Wait till we get around the stern. And stop rocking so much, it's hard to keep a picture."

"It's the tide around the head. It'll settle down once we straighten up."

Aftershave grunted and refocused the binoculars. "That's it, hold it steady. Got it … I think. Looks like *Shelley P.*"

Lacey had come topside without them noticing. "What's so interesting?"

Gill glanced over her shoulder at him. "Aftershave thinks the crewman on that fishing boat was the one who tried to mug him last night. Bandaged right hand and he smelled of fish."

"I broke a couple of his fingers when I took the knife off him," Aftershave said with a hint of satisfaction.

"What was the name of the boat?" Lacey said. "I didn't catch it."

"*Shelley P,*" Gill said. "No false modesty with the Pierces. I bet that's one of theirs."

"Better than evens," Aftershave said and laughed.

"You'll get no argument from me on that score," Lacey said. "Budge over, Gill, I'll take her from here. If you and Aftershave will handle the lines when we get to the pontoon it'll save having to call out the marina hands."

Dusk was falling as he nudged the boat onto the pontoon and held her there while Gill and Aftershave hopped off and looped the lines over the cleats. He shut down the engines and sat on the helm seat with a sigh.

Gill climbed up and picked up the binoculars from where Aftershave had left them. She glanced over at the Marina office and along the Quay where two large refrigerated pantechnicons were parked backed on to the water with their tail doors wide open ready to receive the day's catch when the boats came in. She raised the binoculars and stared. Almost hidden in the gloaming behind the trucks was a black Range Rover.

38

Gill nudged Lacey and handed him the binoculars. She nodded towards the fish quay. "You see what I see?"

Lacey frowned, took the glasses and looked himself. "Well, well, another turn up. Last time I saw that vehicle Bill was driving it. I wonder what he's doing there?"

"We could find out," Gill said and gave Lacey a smile.

He nodded. "We'll have to be careful not to spook him. There's not many places to set up an OP there."

Gill smiled again and he could see the light of battle in her eyes; she had a plan.

"There are some boats chocked up on the hard standing along from the fish quay having repairs done. It's late, there'll be no one working on them now. We can climb up on one and use it as an observation post. We're unlikely to be seen from below."

Lacey panned the binoculars along the short line of boats. "There's a cabin cruiser halfway along which has its stern overlooking the fish quay. If we can get in that we can see everything we need to and keep out of sight."

"So we're agreed," Gill said.

It was a statement not a question and Lacey nodded, he liked the idea. It wouldn't be a long stake-out as the Range Rover would wait only until the fishing boats came in. There was no other reason for it to be there. "I'll take the first watch, you and Aftershave take a break and relieve me in an hour. I don't expect it will be a long night."

"You sure you wouldn't want Aftershave to go with you? He's a dab hand at picking locks."

Lacey gave her a rueful grin. "Yes, I know, he made short work of getting aboard here, but you needn't worry, I did the course, I'll figure it out." Lock-picking lessons had been part of his training and he was good at it. The type of lock that was fitted to the average boat would only take a few seconds to open.

He rattled down the stairs with Gill in his wake. Aftershave was spread out on the couch with a cold beer in his hand. He waved it at them. "Drink, I think we've earned it."

"*Day ain't over yet*," Gill said with a mock American accent and a frown.

Lacey turned and gave her an enquiring look.

She laughed. "It's a line from the film *City Slickers*. It stuck with me and seemed appropriate. It was when one of the characters was asked if he'd killed anyone that day." She shrugged. "Quoting lines is a habit I picked up from my father. He's always spouting something; usually moral and uplifting. I tend to aim lower in the morality stakes."

Lacey gave a slow shake of his head, pulled his Sig from a drawer and clipped the holster inside his belt. "Let's hope you haven't been gazing into your crystal ball, ma'am." He rummaged in another drawer and pulled out a roll of tinfoil, tearing off a piece and folding it into a pocket. He put the strap of the binoculars around his neck and pushed his mobile phone into another pocket. He checked his watch. "21.45 hours. If anything happens in the meantime I'll call, otherwise I'll see you at 22.45 or thereabouts."

Aftershave looked from one to the other. "What's up?"

Lacey hooked a thumb as he was halfway out. "Fill Aftershave in."

There was enough glow from the street lamps to light the way and he didn't need to use his phone as a torch. The boat he had selected was a Beneteau Antares, a thirty-footer with an open rear deck and large cabin windows. It was up on chocks ready for anti-fouling with a short climb onto the rear deck. As he suspected, the lock was easy to open. He had brought the tinfoil in case the door was alarmed but he needn't have worried. He settled himself inside with a good clear view over the fish quay. The two truck drivers were talking together, leaning on the front wing of one of the trucks and smoking. The lettering on the side was in Spanish and he caught the occasional lisp of Castilian drifting over. The Range Rover was parked rear-end on to him but at a slight angle and he could see the driver's elbow sticking out of the front offside window.

He stacked cushions to sit on, one on another, so that he didn't have to crane his neck, put his mobile on the table, watched and waited.

His hour was almost up when there was a slight thump from the deck and Gill slid in beside him. "Budge up, Rick," she whispered, mimicking his phrase.

He felt her warm leg press against his through his thin slacks and her warm breath on his cheek.

"Anything happening," she whispered again in his ear.

He felt a shiver run down his spine and barely controlled it. Her perfume was rich and musky. He took a breath. "Nothing yet. The two truck drivers stood around yakking in Spanish for a while but both are now sleeping in their cabs. Nobody's moved from the Range Rover but the driver's fingers have been drumming on the door so I guess he's getting bored."

"Let me see."

He handed her the binoculars and she stared through the optics for some seconds. "There must be some action soon. They surely can't have expected to wait too long."

"That was my assessment," Lacey said. He thought he should move his leg away but didn't. He was enjoying her warmth and nearness. Her perfume was playing havoc with his olfactory senses. He wanted to compliment her, tell her how good she smelt. It might give her the wrong impression but he had to say something.

"That perfume you're wearing."

"Yes?"

"It's very nice but … you know when we were jungle fighting we couldn't even clean our teeth in case the enemy would smell the toothpaste."

She turned her face to him in the gloom. "Can I sense a lecture coming?"

"It's just that perfume tends to linger. When the owner turns up tomorrow he'll know someone's been here and we won't be able to use it as an OP again if we need to."

"I haven't had time to shower. I've been in the sun all day and didn't want to think you had a wet poodle sitting next to you."

"I appreciate the thought and under normal circumstances I wouldn't complain."

"All right, Rick, I take your point and it won't happen again."

"It is a very nice perfume …"

"Quit while you're ahead, Rick," Gill interrupted.

He coughed a chuckle. "Now you've got me thinking what I must smell like."

"Coming up roses," Gill murmured then stiffened and put the binoculars to her eyes. "Heads up, there's a boat coming in."

Two came in together, one was a large trawler which soon had crates of ice-packed fish loading into the two trucks. The second was the *Shelley P.* with two baskets full of lobsters. One of the crewmen carried them across to the two Spaniards and began to barter. While they were occupied another crewman, the one with the bandaged hand, hefted a large plastic-wrapped box across to the Range Rover. The car door opened and Bill stepped out. He walked to the rear of the car and raised the tailgate with a foot under the bumper. The man struggled to push the box inside and Bill heaved him away to finish the job himself.

Lacey had his phone out taking pictures. Bill dropped the tailgate, stopped at the corner of the Range Rover and looked all around before resuming his seat behind the wheel. The car's brake lights came on, the engine started and he pulled away.

Lacey grunted and checked the images he'd taken. He had good full face and side view shots. He emailed them straight to Ben at ISPA headquarters. Maybe Bill had a record.

Gill stood and stretched, arching her back. She turned to Lacey. "What did you make of that?"

"Lacy grinned. "Some sense at last."

39

It had been well past midnight when they got to bed, Aftershave gonking down in the third cabin again for convenience. Gill had spent time composing and sending the state of play to Blake. Lacey had dictated most of the content and she was happy for him to do so. She added her own comments later in the privacy of her cabin.

There was a good indication that drugs were being brought ashore by the *Shelley P* after rendezvousing with the sub at the lobster pot at the tip of Berry Head. Lacey thought it likely that a frogman had left the sub to attach the package to the lobster pot line to avoid having to surface. It made sense and was similar to the way the men of the Special Boat Service were transported to their various targets by submarine.

It would tie Derek and Bill to the drugs trade that was plaguing Craddock if it could be proved that the package delivered to Bill held drugs. There was little doubt in her mind but finding that proof could be problematic. Aftershave had chipped in the reminder that losing at the gaming tables in the casino was a crafty way for dealers to pay for their merchandise. The cash would just be counted as winnings and wouldn't raise a single eyebrow. It was all beginning to fit. Their suspicions had been sent to Blake and they were awaiting a response. Gill had no doubt that Lacey had sent a similar message to Ben Reid.

Again the bugbear was they were no nearer finding out why Forrestal had been murdered. Catching drug dealers was not part of their remit, not unless it was the catalyst for Forrestal's death. Had he discovered it together with the China connection, or was there something else behind it all? Lacey hadn't allowed her to mention the gold mine as he wanted nothing to link them to the two dead guards. Even using their secure communications wasn't sufficient guarantee that word wouldn't leak out. Lacey had little trust in MI6's ability to keep such things secret; there had been too many leaks in the past. It was something she could identify with, she didn't trust them either. Blake to a point but there were always too many fingers in the pie for her peace of mind.

Thinking of Lacey brought up the question of her feelings. She was struggling with the idea that she was falling for him. Yet when he touched her, or when she touched him, she felt something, a strange buzz throughout her body and she liked it. He had given her a mild bollocking about her perfume but in such a cack-handed way it sounded like a compliment. Was he complimenting her or just trying to take the edge off the reprimand? She rubbed her hand along her leg where it had rested against his, remembering the warmth and the delicious tingle. He hadn't moved his leg away but maybe he hadn't felt it the way she had. He was difficult to read sometimes; his mind on the work in hand and no time for distractions. She wondered what it was like inside his head.

She knew he could be a little paranoid about some things. As they were trolling across Torbay he had spent the time fitting tiny cube cameras in the main saloon and beneath the overhanging flybridge. They were so tiny, barely three centimetres across, they were almost invisible unless you knew what to look for and where to look. They sent constant digital images directly to his mobile phone. He said he'd had them for some time but hadn't got around to fitting them until Aftershave had reminded him by breaking in undetected. She had to admit to feeling safer in her bed that early morning.

She yawned and stretched. The excitement of the evening had kept her adrenaline flowing but now tiredness was creeping up on her. She switched off the overhead lights and settled down on the wide bed. It was too warm for the duvet so she just lay on top as her mind began to drift.

She was almost asleep when a soft tap on the door snapped her awake. "Wha ... what?"

"It's Rick, he hissed."

A sudden surge of excitement clenched her stomach. "What is it?"

"Open the door."

She hadn't locked the door since that first night. "It's open."

He eased through it. Light filtering in from the distant street lamps outlined his body. He was wearing shorts and a T-shirt. She felt her heart thump against her ribs. "This is a bit sudden."

He snorted. "We've got company, grab your pistol."

"Oh!" She felt oddly deflated but slid off the bed, put on her silk dressing gown and pulled the P7 from her shoulder bag.

He reached across and showed her the live images on his phone. "Two men just rowed up in a dinghy. They're on the stern deck trying to figure out how to get in without waking us."

Gill had a sudden thought. "What about Aftershave?"

She saw the glint of his teeth as he grinned. "He's ready." He took the phone back and stared at it, the screen lighting his face with a demonic glow. "One of them has a jemmy, he'll bust the lock."

Gill wriggled round and leant on his shoulder, her breasts brushing his back sent a thrill through her. She dragged her thoughts back on an even keel and pointed. "I know that one, he's a security guard at the casino."

Lacey grunted. "Maybe your boyfriend is living up to his word and sending in the heavy mob to work me over." As he spoke the two men rolled ski masks over their faces. There was a pop and the sliding door inched open.

"They're in," Lacey breathed.

"What's the plan?"

Lacey looked over his shoulder. "We'll take them in the passageway. Aftershave will cut off their retreat. I'd like to have a word with them before we send them on their way." He opened the door a crack and peered through. Two dark shapes were edging down the companionway, their shoulders touching either wall as the boat gently rocked on the falling tide. He waited until they had passed the third cabin without checking it. He switched the phone to torch mode, stepped out, turned on the dazzling beam and raised his Sig so that they could see it. "That's far enough, gents."

They both turned in unison but Aftershave had stepped out of his cabin and hit the first man in the throat with the web of his hand. The man choked and staggered back onto his mate. They both fell to the floor.

"Just keep still, there folks," Lacey said. "This here is a Sig 226 and I'm not afraid to use it. Now I want you both to drop whatever you're holding and push it to one side. Mister Roberts there will make sure you don't get any funny ideas."

The first man was still choking and holding his throat. Aftershave put his foot on his free hand and took the jemmy from his fist. The other man pushed a sawn-off shotgun reluctantly towards the bulkhead but only took his hand off it as Aftershave raised his own pistol. "Uh, huh, mate. I'd have both your eyes out before your brain cells could send a signal, so don't be a silly boy."

"Both of you roll over on your faces," Lacey ordered.

They bound both men with their own bootlaces, pulled them to their feet and took them into the main cabin where they were pushed onto one of the benches. Lacey lit the helm position lights and pulled the masks off both men. "To what do we owe the pleasure, guys?" Neither said anything but stared sullenly at the carpet. He looked at Aftershave. "Keep them quiet." He turned and passed Gill who was leaning on the bulkhead with her arms folded across her breasts. "I'll be back in a few seconds, honey."

He was as good as his word as less than a minute later he climbed back up the companionway screwing a black muffler onto the Sig's muzzle.

"I'm not in the mood for games, guys, so one more time, why are you here?"

Gill put a hand out to him. "You're not going to shoot them, are you, Rick?"

"Give me a good reason why not?"

She hesitated. "I can't."

He raised the pistol and pointed it at the big security guard. "Time's up."

40

"Hang on, Rick, I recognise that bloke," Aftershave said. "He's the mouthy git who works security at the casino."

Lacey slid his eyes across to look at him. "The point being?"

"I'd like to do the business. Got my back up, he did."

Lacey thought for a second then nodded. "Okay but not here, I don't want to mess up my boat. We'll take them out into the Channel, top them with their own shotgun and tip them over the side." He warmed to his theme. "We'll take the dinghy they rowed up in and leave it drifting out at sea. If the bodies ever get found people will think they had a little argument, topped each other and fell overboard."

Aftershave grinned. "Sounds good, boss. Let the fishes have some dinner and nothing to tie us to it. Nice. Just like that pair we did away with in Spain," he added with a wink.

"Now wait a minute." It was the smaller of the two, the one who Aftershave hit in the throat. His voice was still croaky and it made his nervousness all the more apparent. "I didn't sign up for this. There's no need. We only came to rough you up a bit, mister."

"Shut up, you dildo, they ain't gonna do nothin'. They're bluffin'," the guard said.

Lacey grinned at the unintentional rhyme and it made his face look harder. "Let's call it poetic justice, shall we." He turned to Gill. "I don't want you involved with this, honey. Go take a break and sit in the car. We shouldn't be more than a couple of hours."

The second man shot the first a nervous glance then spoke again. "God's truth mister. We never meant no 'arm."

Lacey turned his laser beam glare on him. "Then why bring the shotgun?"

"Just for frighteners, we weren't gonna use it, honest. Were we Dwayne?"

"I said shut your cakehole, Ron."

Lacey grimaced and his voice hardened. "Just another body floating in the river, huh?"

Dwayne's head shot up from studying the carpet. "That weren't nothin' to do with us. Look I heard you was askin' after who did that Yank navy bloke but you can't pin that on us."

Gill, who hadn't moved until that point, pushed herself off the bulkhead. "I don't know, it seems there are some similarities. The man was shot and dumped in the river here."

"Now look, missus," Dwayne said. "We just got told to rough up your old man so that you knew Mister Pierce was serious, like. He's got the hots for you and he wanted you to know he could take care of the business, know what I mean?"

"Is that what happened to Commander Forrestal?" Lacey asked

Dwayne shook his head. No, nothin' like that. He was after Ling-Ling. Seemed like he had it really bad for her, he did, but you could tell she wasn't interested."

"She scares the shit outta me," Ron said and shivered. "I wouldn't like to get on her bad side, hard as nails she is. Good looker though, makes you wonder don' it?"

"Wonder what, Ron?" Lacey asked.

"Why she turned out that way. Good looking girl like her could have done anythin', been someone, a film star maybe."

"Perhaps the sugar and spice got mixed up with the snips and snails," Gill said.

"Eh?" It was obvious Ron didn't get the inference.

Lacey took Gill by the elbow and spoke so that the two men wouldn't hear. "Go to the car and give Blake a call, get him out of bed. His obbo team will still be staying close by, get them to pick up these two and take them somewhere safe. I think we've got as much out of them as we can, maybe his people can get more. I doubt if these two idiots killed Forrestal but you never know. Some heavy questioning might shake something else loose."

Gill frowned. "You want the obbo team to come here?"

"No, we'll RV around the point at Blackpool Sands; there's a car park there. We'll anchor up in the cove and wait for them to arrive then we'll take these two ashore in the dinghy. It won't hurt them to think we're going to carry out our threat for a while. It also won't hurt to get Pierce nervous when his bully boys fail to turn up tomorrow."

Gill grinned and nudged him. "I told him you were a hard case. Now he'll believe it." She turned away. "Two minutes to pull on jeans and a sweater."

When she returned Aftershave had bound the two men even tighter, tied their legs together with their own belts and gagged them both with Lacey's tea towels. He showed every sign that he was enjoying himself. He waved as she went past. Lacey was on the stern tying the men's dinghy's painter to a cleat. He looked up as she passed. "The sooner they get to Blackpool Sands the sooner we'll be back." He watched her as she walked up the finger and admired her poise. He clamped down on the thought, it was leading somewhere he was reluctant to go."

With Aftershave working the lines he had the big boat out of the mouth of the Dart, past Stoke Fleming and anchored off Blackpool Sands in less than twenty minutes. The two men had squealed, coughed and grunted the whole way, looking with round frightened eyes every time Aftershave went near them to check their bonds.

Lacey switched off the engines and sudden peace descended. He checked the time. It was almost three in the morning with another star-spangled sky overhead. The weather had held beautifully for the past few days but he knew it would not last for much longer; it never did.

He lounged back in the helm seat and thought about the information Dwayne had given out. He did not think the man was a good enough liar to deceive him and the thought of being landed with the blame for Forrestal's death had obviously unnerved him. It was too obvious a fear to be an act. It had surprised him that Forrestal had a thing for Ling-Ling. Maybe it shouldn't have, by all accounts she was a beautiful woman but it was interesting to get Ron's take on her character. Neither Gill nor Aftershave had drawn any conclusions about Ling-Ling, other than she was Chinese and the head of security which begged the question of how and where had she been trained for the role. It had been something he had pushed to the back of his mind but now it had taken on a greater significance. She too needed to be checked out.

He turned in his seat. The two men had gone quiet but for their laboured breathing. Aftershave was sitting opposite them with his feet up and Andee's rolling pin in his hand. The inference was obvious and the two men seemed to have got the message.

Headlights split the darkness and two vehicles drove into the car park and stopped with their beams shining across the beach. One set flashed three times.

Lacey stirred out of his seat. "They're here," he said to Aftershave. "Time for these guys to go." He went onto the aft deck and pulled the wooden dinghy close to the swim platform. Aftershave, who was far stronger than his size indicated, picked Ron up in a firefighter's lift and carried him out squealing and squirming.

"Stop wriggling, you maggot, or you're gonna get wet," he said and dumped Ron into the dinghy. He went back for Dwayne who was bigger and heavier but still managed to carry him out. He dropped him on the swim platform. "Roll into that boat under your own steam, mate, otherwise it might capsize."

Dwayne did as he was told and sat staring up at Aftershave wondering what was going to come next.

Lacey untied the dinghy's painter and handed it to Aftershave. "Walk it around the side while I get the tender ready. He dropped the tender onto the water, went below for the outboard and had it fitted in minutes. With Aftershave holding the painter he towed the dinghy to the beach. Figures were standing at the water's edge with torches. Lacey swung the tender around and told Aftershave to release the painter. The dinghy carried on and grounded on the sand.

Lacey put the outboard on idle and called across. "They're all yours. Take good care of them."

One of them waved. It was the woman. "We need to talk," she yelled.

Lacey ignored her and gunned the outboard. He had a lot to think about and he needed to speak to Ben. He had the feeling that things were coming to a head.

41

Gill couldn't sleep. She had tossed and turned for a while but gave up, pulled her dressing gown around her more tightly and went up to the saloon. Lacey was sitting with his feet up and a mug of fresh coffee in his fist. He was looking at his laptop screen and glanced up as she came over.

He nodded towards the galley. "There's a pot brewing. Help yourself. Cowboy coffee I'm afraid, hot and strong."

She grimaced. "As if I needed keeping awake." She poured herself a mug and settled opposite him, tucking her long legs beneath her. She held the mug in both hands and sipped. She pulled a face. "Jeez, you weren't kidding. It is strong."

"You could water it down. It's the way I learned to take it in the States. I wasn't expecting company this early."

"What time is it?"

Lacey glanced at his wrist. "Zero-five-thirty."

Gill's eyes widened and she shivered. She put the mug down and pulled the dressing gown tighter. "It's chilly."

"Always is on the water at this hour. It'll warm up soon but there's a blow forecast for tomorrow. You might want to dig out your warm underwear."

She gave him a mischievous grin. "What makes you think I have any?"

He screwed up his eyes as if assessing her. "I'd guess you're the kind of woman who would be ready for anything. Victoria's Secret one day and M&S winceyette when it's called for. The kind of woman who carries a P7 in her purse, just in case."

"Your kind of woman?" She was sorry she had said it as soon as the words passed her lips but he didn't blink.

"My kind of partner for sure."

His reply could be interpreted in different ways and she mentally kicked herself for letting down her guard. Too tired, too early, and the strong coffee hadn't yet kicked her brain cells into life. She tried to cover her embarrassment by changing the subject. "Have you had any sleep?"

He shook his head, leaned forward and turned the laptop screen towards her. "I've been kinda busy. This will interest you."

She stood and walked over, went to her knees and angled the screen so that the light didn't reflect off it. "What is this?"

"A reply I got from Ben. I'm not sure how to take it."

She scanned through the text. "It says here that he has informed the local police about the drug angle but they can't do anything due to lack of evidence. They can't work on theories alone and if we aren't able to come up with anything tangible they can't ask for a search warrant to be issued for the casino. Too many can'ts for my liking."

Lacey stood up and refreshed his coffee. "Which puts the ball back in our court, I guess. Anyway,

I'd be surprised if Pierce was stupid enough to keep the drugs at the casino, he'd have a distribution network set up and a patsy to carry the can."

"Someone like Bill?"

Lacey strode over, sat and hit a couple of keys. "Let me show you something else. This is Bill, or Jovan Bilic to give him his proper name." He hooked a thumb at the screen where a much younger man dressed in paramilitary uniform and carrying an AK47 was grinning at the camera.

Gill looked at Lacey. "Serb?"

"Seems he was some sort of paramilitary commander with Arkan's Tigers. The Serbian War Crimes Prosecutor's Office has a file on him but it's unlikely he will ever be brought to justice for any crime, not many of them have been. It seems that the Tigers were something of a hot potato with the Serb authorities and a lot was simply brushed under the carpet to save some red faces."

"And now he's here," Gill said.

Lacey hit another key. "And married to Kate, nee Copley, sister of well-known London hood, Johnny, who the ISPA came across when the Russian mob tried to take over his territory a few years back. Copley was into all sorts of criminal activities then but retired to Spain when the Russians got too close and sliced his face. The cops have been trying to pin stuff on him ever since but without success. Due to the ISPA's involvement the Russians never managed to move in and no one knows who took over Copley's illicit businesses."

"Until now?" Gill queried.

Lacey shook his head. "There's no way of knowing. Maybe his sister and Bilic took over; Bilic sure has the credentials for rough stuff. He doesn't speak very good English, that's why Kate speaks up for him; they're as close as a worm to a rotten apple. According to the Met Police, they met while Bilic was working as a bouncer at one of Copley's dives. A real hard case by all accounts."

Gill spread her hands to him. "Where does that leave us?"

"A little wiser but no closer." Lacey scratched his head. "We still have diddly squat on Forrestal's demise."

Gill got off her knees and went to sit beside him. "Okay, we know that the Chinese are involved, they have a mini sub operating in our waters from a ship registered in Liberia. It came here from Colombia and we are assuming they are supplying hard drugs to the Pierce-Bilic combine. We know that Forrestal knew about the sub and was worried enough by it to keep the note of the one movement he detected in his wallet. We know he was killed by a Chinese Special Forces pistol and you had a fight with two Chinese guards at Bilic's mine. Pierce and the Chinese are inextricably linked, that we know for certain. We also know for certain that he, Shelley and the Bilics have dodgy backgrounds and ties to serious criminals. It's beginning to look likely that Forrestal was doing his own sleuthing and, if Dwayne is to be believed, was cosying up to Ling-Ling, possibly looking for leads and maybe that's what got him murdered. How am I doing so far?"

Lacey smiled. "Pretty much spot on. We can't yet guess why the Chinese are so interested in Pierce's gold mine. Interested enough to post two armed SF soldiers to guard it. One can only assume that he's paying them in gold dust rather than cash, which would make some sort of sense as it keeps everything financial way below the radar."

The thought had occurred to Gill that the Chinese were protecting their investment and Lacey's theory backed that up. "Way I see it, we need proof, hard conclusive evidence."

"I was coming to that," Lacey said. "I need to get aboard that ship."

"Don't you mean we?" Gill was determined not to be left out of the loop.

"You don't know what I have in mind. There's only one way to board that ship unseen and it isn't from the sea. One way only ... and it's damned risky."

42

Gill gave Lacey a tart look. "Since when has being risky been a reason not to do something in our business?"

"You don't know what I have in mind."

"Does it matter? We're both in this together and I won't be treated as if I can't make my own decisions on whether something is risky or not. I may be a woman but that has never stopped me."

"Whoa, hold it there. Don't get on your feminist high horse Miz Arnold. For starters that wasn't my intention to belittle your capabilities. For what I have in mind I need someone here who can handle the boat and from what I've seen you fit that bill."

"Okay, smartarse, what's this plan then?"

"A HALO drop from ten-thousand feet onto the boat's deck. It's a big enough target to hit, over three-hundred metres stem to stern and fifty metres wide. With the kit we have it should work but if I miss I need this boat standing by to fish me out."

Gill snorted. "I'm HALO trained. I dropped into Afghanistan a few years back, behind Taliban lines. Why can't *I* drop onto the ship and you stand by with the boat? You're a far better sailor than I'll ever be."

Lacey gave a heavy sigh and stood. "Come with me." He crooked a finger. She stood and followed. He went to the back cabin and opened one of the deck-to-ceiling lockers. Inside was a metal container that was as tall as Lacey was with a keypad code box. He punched in the code and the door sprang open.

Gill took a step back. "What the hell is that?"

Lacey put a hand inside and pulled the item out. "It's a fighting suit. It's made from Kevlar and ceramic plates which are interspaced with thin sheets of Magnesium Alloy and Boron Steel. It's armour that is much lighter than fitted to the current mark four vests but extremely bullet resistant. It's also coated with a compound called Starlight which was developed by a chemist called Maurice Ward and makes the suit totally fireproof. High velocity rounds can penetrate where the layers are thinnest at the sides of the breast plate and sides of the thighs but it will stop most slugs. There's a neoprene lining which helps cushion the impact of hits." He pulled out the helmet from where it was plugged into a charger. Gill's jaw dropped at the sight. It was shaped like an ant's head with an angled gold coloured visor and protrusions at the top and side.

Lacey held it up. "This is a work of art. It's based on jet fighter technology. It has night vision and infra-red capability. It has a built in range-finder and compass. When it's sealed it acts like a gas mask. There's a cylinder attached to the suit which gives seven minutes of oxygen. The visor is armour plate and shaped to deflect all but direct hits on the apex." He pointed to two of the bumps on the brow of the helmet. "There's a digital video camera and microphone. It can record to a chip at the back of the helmet or transmit live to a control centre."

Gill sucked in her cheeks and Lacey could see she was impressed.

"And?" she said.

"They are made to measure and this one is made for me. I can get aboard and video everything we need, hopefully without getting seen, but if I am seen I can fight my way out."

"How do you plan to get off?"

"I'll be wearing a life vest, I'll jump over the side and you can pick me up."

Lacey saw disbelief cross her face.

"You've got to be kidding. That's a hare-brained idea. There's no way I'd let you go in there alone. It's bound to be seething with Chinese SF and god knows what else. You need back-up."

Lacey was irritated. "Haven't you listened to a word I've said?"

"Oh, sure, the Starship Trooper kit, I understand but someone has to have your back."

"I need you aboard the boat to hook me out."

"Then you'll have to rethink it. It's crazy leaping off that ship. It must be sixty feet to the water from the deck, you could break your back or shatter that dodgy leg. There's acceptable risk and there's unacceptable risk. This falls into the latter category."

"It's a risk I'm prepared to take," Lacey said. He'd done some training at the American Naval Academy at Annapolis where they had a high diving board in Lejeune Hall that simulated jumping from the deck of an aircraft carrier but that was only thirty-three feet. The extra twenty-seven feet would make a great difference especially as he would be in full kit and carrying weapons. He hated to admit it but Gill had a point; it was crazy but right then he could see no alternative if they were to get aboard the tanker. They? He'd thought it. She was right again it was a job for more than one but there was no way he'd let her accompany him without similar protection. A Kevlar vest wouldn't be enough to save her life if the insertion went hot.

He needed to protect those he cared for and had failed in the past. His first wife, who was sucked into his undercover world unwittingly and paid the price, Andee who was taken by PIRA and tortured. Now Gill. She was a trained soldier and he had no right to treat her any differently from a male squaddie; she wouldn't thank him for it but he couldn't help a feeling of helplessness creep over him.

He gave a nod of resignation. "All right. Let's see what can be done." He put the suit back in its coffin and with Gill following went back to the saloon. It was still too early to call Ben so he typed up an email. He looked at Gill. "What are your measurements?"

"What?"

"Your vital statistics … for the suit."

"Oh! 35-24-34."

"Your cup size?"

"Do you really need to know that?"

"Yes."

"B. You're enjoying this aren't you?"

"Shoe size?"

"Seven and a half."

He typed the figures into the email. "I guess you're around five-eight."

"Spot on."

"I've asked if they can adapt a suit for you ready for tonight. There'll be a Skyvan waiting at Exeter Airport with it and the chutes. It's going to be touch and go with the timing though."

"Must it be tonight?"

"The forecast isn't good for tomorrow. The wind is expected to reach Force 8 for a couple of days. We can't HALO in those winds and expect to land with any degree of accuracy. Low Altitude Low Opening is out of the question as any aircraft flying close overhead will attract attention and we don't know what radar set-up they have aboard."

"You're serious about this, aren't you?"

"I just have to work on a Plan B to get us off. It would be great if Ben could get us the shipyard construction drawings for that tanker. I don't like working blind. How are your close-quarter battle skills?"

"My CQBs are rusty. It's been a while since I've had to use them," Gill admitted.

"We'll need to work on actions-on, hand signals and such. We don't want to go in half-cocked."

Aftershave came up the companionway yawning and scratching. "What time is it?"

"Early," Gill said.

He sniffed. "Can I smell coffee?"

Gill waved a hand. "Some in the galley."

Aftershave looked from one to the other, his eyes crinkled in suspicion. "Have I missed anything?"

Gill laughed. "Only plans for the stupidest thing I've done in years."

Aftershave's face brightened. "Great, count me in."

"I have another job for you," Lacey said. "I need you to go back to the casino. I want a close-target reconnaissance, details of the layout, fire exits, ways of getting in ... or out in a hurry, positions of security cameras and where the security office is located; you'll know what's needed. Once Gill and I have finished tonight, we'll be paying them a call."

43

It was a busy day. Gill watched with something approaching awe as Lacey went about setting up the insertion with emails, and phone calls. She was renowned for her organisational abilities but Lacey was a notch above, evidence of his five years driving a desk at the ISPA. He got the plan approved in principle and set about putting the details together.

He asked Gill to keep Blake in the loop.

When she called him Blake seemed unsure but agreed it could be useful to find out if the tanker was acting as a mother ship to the narcosub. There was a period of silence. "Are you sure this HALO thing is a good idea?" he then said in his lazy drawl.

"Not one of my better ones," Gill replied, "but I'm damned if I going to let Mister Arnold out of my sight. We've come so far, we've learned a lot but we're still lacking hard proof. I want to make sure I'm there when we get it."

"I admire your tenacity but then again it's what I've come to expect of you, my dear. It's why we wanted you in on this."

Gill winced. "Don't patronise me, Blake. You needed a patsy so that the Firm's grubby fingerprints won't be all over any fallout."

"Oh my, you have grown so cynical over the years. I shall pass your proposals along the usual channels but I don't see that there will be a problem with approvals despite my misgivings."

"I do hope not. If you don't keep your end up it could be goodbye forever."

"Oh, don't be so melodramatic. I'm sure it won't come to that."

"It's not your arse on the line, Blake."

"Perhaps not but I do have a certain amount of affection for you. I'd hate to have to be present at your funeral so perhaps you would cut me a little slack."

Gill smiled, although Blake couldn't see it. She loved winding up the stuffed shirts at Vauxhall Cross. Blake was more laid back and had helped her on previous occasions, when it had been in the Firm's interests, so she tended to make life a little easier for him but this was so important the gloves were off.

"Don't let us down, Blake, or, if I survive, I'll never forget it."

"Do I detect a veiled threat?"

"Take it any way you want but I mean what I say."

Blake sniffed down the line. "I never doubted that, not for an instant."

"As long as we understand each other," Gill said. "I have to go, there's a myriad things to do."

"I understand," Blake replied. "Just one more thing. What should we do with the two rapscallions you presented us with?"

"Hang on to them. You could question them but it's pretty clear they're low-level muscle and don't have a clue what their bosses are up to. We don't need them back in play until this is over though."

"You know we don't have the authority to detain them," Blake said. "There's nothing we can charge them with that will get the Little Sisters over the river at Thames House excited."

Gill tutted. "You'll think of something. Just keep them out of our hair for a few days and make sure they keep their mouths shut afterwards." She broke the connection and turned to see Lacey watching her.

"All okay?"

She grimaced. "I wish the people at Riverside were as cooperative as yours. How far have you got?"

Lacey grinned. "Ben's come up trumps on the tanker. He's emailed the drawings. Not for the *New Venture* but for a sister ship, the *New Horizon*. There may be some small differences but basically they'll be the same general layout. It's a mid-deck tanker which has tanks on two levels designed to limit spillages. It means there's no double hull which makes it easier for an underwater sub bay to be fitted into one of the tanks." He turned his laptop so that she could see the marine architect's drawings.

Gill whistled. "They've thought of everything."

Lacey grinned again. "Let's hope not everything. We need to study those drawings to get the layout fixed in our minds. It's a big ship, easy to get lost if we don't know what we're doing."

"I'll say, it's like a labyrinth."

Lacey's smile eased a little. "Yeah. Plenty of places to stash drugs but I'd guess they'd stow them someplace near to the sub pen."

Gill grimaced. Looking at the plans had brought home to her the enormity of their task. The Chinese weren't about to put up a sign saying 'drugs here' with a pointy arrow, not that she could read Chinese anyway. She glanced up at Lacey. "Seems the best bet. We just have to find our way down there."

Lacey's grin widened again. "Piece of cake."

Gill couldn't help returning the smile. "I just love your optimism. Now, anything else?"

Lacey sobered. "They're having some trouble getting a suit altered to fit your measurements but they figure it'll be ready before the Skyvan takes off from Northolt. We have a couple in hangars there for convenience as it's close to our headquarters. We're not talking comfort, there are no seats other than for the pilots but we're not going to be aboard for long. They'll bring any extra kit with the chutes."

"Extra kit?"

"Yeah, a few bits and pieces that may come in handy."

"I hesitate to ask."

"I've ordered a couple of Heckler and Koch MP5SDs. I take it you're familiar with them."

"That's the silenced version. I've trained on the MP5 but without the muffler."

"They work the same except we use low velocity ammo. There's little recoil and it's barrel heavy by comparison with the straight MP5. The downside is that we lose some penetration with the nine mil rounds so we have to work close in. That shouldn't be a problem in the confines of the ship. If it comes to a firefight, aim for the killing-T to make sure they go down and stay down. That's across the eyes and down through the centre of the body as far as the chest. A round anywhere there is a certain kill."

"I know about the killing-T. I spent hours on the ranges in the killing house at Credenhill when I was training for the Det."

"Doesn't hurt to remind you. Especially as your CQB currency has lapsed."

Gill looked for something to throw. She knew it was a wind-up by the look on Lacey's face. He could barely suppress a grin.

"Bastard," she said but she smiled to take the sting out of it. "There'll be a price to pay for that … when you least expect it."

He held out a hand to haul her to her feet. "Sounds like a promise. Come on, let's get some lunch at the yacht club and make like everything is normal."

His fingers closed around hers, firm and dry and she felt a shiver run up her spine. She really would have to watch that. "Give me ten minutes to clean up."

He let go of her hand. "Sure, no rush."

He walked out to the stern deck where Aftershave was sitting watching the boats ply to and fro. He looked up at Lacey. "Everything sorted, boss?"

Lacey shrugged and sat beside him. "Almost. Fancy some lunch at the club?"

Aftershave shook his head. "No, you two go alone, I don't want to play gooseberry."

"It's business."

Aftershave screwed up his small face until it looked comical. "Yeah, sure. Don't worry, I'll cook those fish I caught. That yacht club's a bit too posh for me."

"Okay, if you're sure."

"Yeah. You two have things to talk about." He paused for a few seconds. "Look, I'm Gill's biggest fan. I came here to keep her safe and I'm worried I won't be able to do that tonight."

Lacey put a hand on his arm. "Do you love her?"

Aftershave gave him a sharp look then shook his head. "No, not love. I have a lot of time and respect for 'er. She treated me like a human being right from the start. You see this mush o' mine. Most women wouldn't give me a second look, treated me like I didn't exist but not her. I'd be lyin' if I said I didn't fancy 'er, she's special, but I think you know that. I wouldn't want anythin' to 'appen to 'er."

"I'll try but you know what this business is like, I can't promise."

"But you'll do your best, yeah?"

255

"Better than my best, everything I can."

Aftershave nodded. There was a glint of tears in his eyes. "Then that's the next best thing to me bein' there."

44

Aftershave watched them walk down the pontoon side by side, not exactly arm in arm but their shoulders were almost touching. Gill and Rick. He had a flashback to his time in Spain working close protection with Ricky Keane's team, minding Gill on her dangerous undercover assignment infiltrating an ETA commando outfit that was detonating bombs but Gill's intervention put an early stop to the carnage. That was why she was awarded an MBE although she never spoke about it.

His mind came back to the present and the current situation. He could see what was happening. Gill, although she tried not to show it, was forming an attachment to Rick. He didn't think it would end well.

His own life hadn't been a bed of roses. The eldest son of an Irish labourer and a Welsh Jamaican mother, his early life had been one of constant trauma. He was small, far from attractive and bore the brunt of lewd and racial comments. His dad had died early from sclerosis of the liver and his mum had struggled to keep the family clothed and fed. That was why he had decided to enlist and it had been the making of him. He was fit, extremely strong for his size and had built an indomitable spirit that refused to be beaten. He joined the SAS, passing the selection process where most others failed. He excelled at gymnastics and the dirty unarmed combat style that the SAS disparagingly called Jap-Slapping in a dig at the Japanese martial arts culture. He became the Regiment's top bare hand fighter and taught others his skills. He taught Gill the rudiments in her apartment in Spain and she had picked up the basics quickly, learning enough in a few afternoons to be able to hold her own in a Saturday night brawl at a Tyneside pub.

Lacey was a different proposition. In the few seconds that they had fought it was obvious that the man was a well-trained and hardened fighter. Aftershave wasn't sure whether he liked him or not, not yet, but maybe that was a leftover from knowing Ricky Keane so well. He had been one of the group which had pulled Ricky and Gill out of a fierce firefight in Afghanistan, where Ricky got hit, a wound that eventually led to his death and Gill's untimely widowhood.

The thought brought Loxl to mind; another rare woman who could see past his features and into his heart. He had loved her from the first moment he had laid eyes on her. A pocket Venus, with a voluptuous figure and a mane of jet black hair that she tousled constantly, irritating for some but endearing to him. She had helped him build his business in the Basque region. When his time with the army was up he had taken his lump sum and invested it in a bar in Vitoria, building a small empire of six bars over the years with the patronage of Loxl's friends. Aftershave felt uncomfortable at times when the subject of his cover story, of coming from a feuding family in Colombia, was raised but it had yet to be questioned. It excused his accented Spanish and gave him a reason to disappear from time to time to sort out 'family affairs', when he was working as a K for MI6. That was under duress and again to mind Gill as she penetrated a PIRA Active Service Unit.

Loxl did not know he was a British soldier who had helped to destroy ETA's commando and he fervently hoped it would stay that way. She had taken up again with ETA's political wing, Herri Batasuna, when the businesses started to fail during the pandemic and he saw less and less of her until she was arrested by the Basque police. His one remaining bar was still losing money and he could see the writing on the wall for his life in Spain.

This brief break back in the UK gave him time to consider his options and he had welcomed the call from Stu. The three of them, he, Stu and Gill, had been close friends for years and he knew he could rely on them if ever he needed any help.

He shuffled into a more comfortable position. Cloud was thickening from the west and beginning to blot out the sun although it was still warm enough to sit out. He was very worried about the plans that Lacey had laid for the night. Worried for Gill's sake.

He had spent time with Air Troop and knew the problems involved with a High Altitude Low Opening jump. It meant free-falling for eight-thousand feet until the chute opened automatically and they could steer it onto the Drop Zone, in this case the deck of a ship. It was anchored which improved the chances of hitting the target but was still a risky operation. He could see why Lacey had opted for HALO, they would spend less time in the air than the alternative High Opening technique where they could be more easily blown off course by a freshening breeze despite the chutes' advanced manoeuvrability. It was the least worst option as the Low Altitude technique was out of the question due to the suspected presence of Chinese SF soldiers who could be alerted by a low flying aircraft right over the ship.

That thought opened up another can of worms. What would they find once aboard? Chinese Special Forces would be no pushover if they were forced into a firefight. The ship was huge and there was no guarantee they could find any evidence of drugs before they themselves were discovered. The longer they spent on the ship the greater the chances they would never get off. Which raised the next question of how they would manage that should they survive to need an exit strategy. He could understand the desire to find a smoking gun but was this the only solution? The problem was he couldn't think of another.

Lacey's assurance only partially allayed his fears for Gill. It was his job to safeguard her and he was being side-lined. He had to accept it but if anything happened to her he would hold Lacey responsible. As illogical as that was it would make him feel better to assign blame and to take it out on the man who had led her to disaster.

He shook his head, he was beginning to feel sorry for himself and it wasn't something he had time for. There was work to do to plan his own operation. A normal close-target recon would not require him to enter a property openly but here he would, he needed to count and place cameras, find the security office where the monitors would be watched by security staff and identify any bolt holes. He could locate any exits from the outside by doing a circuit around the building, again watching out for cameras. It was normal for a casino to be thoroughly monitored but he did not want to be caught unawares by hidden lenses. It was a responsible job that needed to be done well or any subsequent action could prove fatal. Lacey had already come into hot contact with the Chinese and their possible presence at the casino, together with the delightful Ling-Ling, was not something he'd take lightly.

His cover was intact. He'd play the punter again with the money he'd won burning a hole in his pocket. It would be interesting to know how Pierce was coping with the disappearance of his two thugs and whether Tristan Roberts's association with the Arnolds would have him seriously scrutinised.

He went back inside the saloon to find the Sig that Lacey had given him. He took it down to Lacey's armoury and set about cleaning and reloading the pistol. He wiped fingerprints off each round as he slotted them in place in the magazine and tested the pistol's trigger weight by dry-firing. He was impressed; someone had worked on the trigger to make it light and crisp. Come trouble tonight he'd be ready.

45

Aftershave drove them in the Discovery and dropped Gill and Lacey at the P2 car park at Exeter airport where they found their way to the executive lounge in the Executive Jet Centre. They carried soft holdalls and looked like a couple of rich people off on holiday to somewhere exotic. It was late, the airport hadn't yet fully recovered from the downturn in public flying and they were the only two people there apart from a bored hostess who asked if they wanted a drink which they both declined. They settled down to await the Skyvan's arrival which was scheduled for 01.00 hours. Lacey stretched out on two seats and dozed off, his long day and lack of sleep finally catching up with him.

Tired as she was, Gill couldn't sleep with the thought of what was to come and went to chat to the hostess; idle conversation that passed the time until the aircraft arrived. It wasn't hard to lie to the woman, to tell her they were on a business trip and the plane they were expecting belonged to her husband's company, which was partly true if not entirely honest. Obfuscation came easily to her and she lumped in some technical jargon to confuse the poor girl.

With a roar of twin props the Skyvan rolled up to the Jet Centre. The night went quiet as the pilot cut the engines. The hostess nodded at the window. "I think that's your plane."

Gill smiled her thanks and went to wake Lacey but he was already climbing to his feet. He grabbed both the bags. "Ready?"

"As I'll ever be," Gill said.

The pilot was standing by the aircraft's nose as they walked out. He held out his hand. "Colonel Lacey, sir, it's a pleasure."

Lacey dropped a bag and shook. "What's our ETD?"

"It's quiet so I can call up the tower anytime you're ready to leave."

"Did you pack the kit?"

The pilot put a thumb over his shoulder, "In the back. Hope we haven't forgotten anything."

"Brought the return tickets?" Gill said.

The pilot laughed. "Must have missed those."

The rear door was open and they stepped up into the box-like fuselage. It was as bare as Lacey had described except there was a man seated at a communications console with two wide screen monitors.

He stood as they entered. "I'm Jack, your control and jumpmaster, sir. We'll test the comms kit when you're ready."

Lacey dropped the bags. "We've already met, haven't we, Jack? You are the brigadier's driver."

Jack beamed a wide smile. "The brig thought it better to keep involved personnel to a minimum, sir. Need to know an' all that."

Lacey nodded. "Sounds sensible. Now, if you wouldn't mind giving us some privacy we'll get into the suits. I have mine here," he hefted a holdall, "where's the other?"

Jack turned and pointed to the coffin-like box on the deck behind him. "All the kit's there, sir. Call when you're ready." He left to join the pilot outside.

Gill looked at Lacey and arched an eyebrow. "Aren't you going to give me some privacy while I get mine on?"

Lacey shook his head. "You'll need help. It's your first time and you'll struggle otherwise." He reached over, popped the lid on the coffin and pulled out Gill's suit. He held it up. "Okay ma'am. Strip down to your underwear, we'll see what kind of a job they've made of this."

Gill squinted at him to see if he was joking but soon realised he was serious. She shrugged out of her top and slacks. "You're lucky it's Victoria's Secret today," she said. It wasn't, it was La Perla, but Lacey seemed disinterested in her choice of underwear and helped her pull on the ultra tight-fitting suit that clung to her every curve. It was fastened with Velcro and nylon clips, had a personal role radio transmitter fitted behind her left shoulder and a holster for a pistol moulded on both thighs. There was also a fighting knife strapped to her right calf with a blade made from a non-magnetic element that wouldn't set off metal detectors. Lacey explained all this as he was fastening the suit tight.

"Not bad," he said, "for a rush job. Can you breathe?"

"Just about."

"Good enough." He pulled his own suit out of one of the holdalls, peeled off his own clothes down to tight-fitting briefs.

Gill saw the scars of past battles on his body. She traced the shape of one with a finger in the air. "You've been through the mill a bit."

He turned his head to look at her as he put his feet into the suit's legs. "Old times."

"Not worth mentioning then," she said.

He pulled the suit up to his shoulders. "Get the clips for me, would you."

She did as he asked and snapped the clips closed. He pulled his helmet from the second bag and latched it in place. Now he really did look like an alien with the helmet and ceramic armoured plates on his chest, back, shoulders and limbs distorting his body shape. He picked her helmet out of its box and dropped it over her head. He flipped a switch and the displays lit up in front of her eyes. The dimly lit cabin suddenly grew bright and sharp in shades of grey and green. As she turned her head the compass bearing changed with the range distances varying within a few feet. They went to zero as Lacey stood in front of her. He reached over her shoulder .

"Can you hear me now?" His voice seemed to fill her head, quiet but distinct.

"Yes, I can hear you."

She heard him chuckle. "So can Jack and the boys back at headquarters who will be monitoring us through a satellite link so mind your language."

266

"*In this space someone can hear you scream,*" she said. "That's paraphrasing the puff line from *Alien,* in case you didn't know."

"I know. Jack can you hear us?"

"Aye, sir, loud and clear." He came back into the aircraft and stood beside his desk unit.

"Ben, are you tuned in?"

"Yes, Rick, we're with you. Can we have visual?"

Gill felt a hand on the back of her head and then watched as Jack clicked a button on the side of Lacey's helmet. She watched him walk to his console and switch on the monitors. "I have visual on both screens, Brigadier. Are you picking up the signals?"

"Yes we have it, thanks. Everything is A-OK at this end."

Lacey was rummaging in the box and came up holding two sports parachutes and handed one to Jack.

"Let me help you on with this, miss," Jack murmured inside her head. "I hear you know how to use one of these so I won't get technical. The altimeter is set for two-thousand feet. Check the one I'll strap on your wrist to be sure. If the chute doesn't deploy automatically you'll have to do it manually."

"I know the drill," Gill said. She was feeling mildly annoyed that these men were treating her as a novice.

Lacey appeared in front of her and held out a pistol. "Glock 17." He pushed the pistol into the holster on her right thigh, secured it, then reached for her left arm and pulled up two elastic straps that she hadn't noticed. He snapped a fully loaded magazine into both. "Thirty-two extra rounds for the Glock."

Jack's grinning face swam into view and he handed her the Heckler and Koch SD machine pistol. He pointed to the optical sight. "Moulded to fit your visor, zeroed at twenty metres. Where the red dot lands, that's where the bullet will hit. Any questions?"

"Spare mags?" She felt a hand on her left thigh and saw Lacey's hand pushing two curved magazines into elasticated loops.

"Another sixty rounds," he whispered in her ears. "Let's hope we don't need them." He bent down and picked another small bundle off the deck. "Hold your arms out."

Again, she did as she was asked with no comment as Lacey strapped a self-inflating life jacket around her. It was small and shaped like an upside down horseshoe that fitted around her neck. "Just in case," he said.

She noticed that he had also put on a harness with several grenades hanging from it. The colours were indistinct but could have been, smoke, stun, or even fragmentation grenades. The extra kit he had mentioned.

Gill felt the deck tremble as the pilot started the engines. The rear door closed and the small aircraft lurched forward. She staggered and put a hand out to the fuselage to steady herself but she needn't have bothered as Lacey's arm came around her waist and held her tight. "Best to sit on the deck until we're ready to jump," he said. He bumped his helmet against hers. He had switched off his mike and she could just hear the hollow sound of his words through the Kevlar. "Whatever happens, stick with me, honey. Good luck."

She felt his arm tighten in a hug but she could not feel his body through the armour plate. She was disappointed and then thought, as unsatisfactory as it was, it might be the last embrace she'd ever have.

46

After leaving Gill and Lacey at the airport Aftershave drove down to Torquay. It was late but he had no doubt that the place would be in full swing. He parked on the far side of the car park overlooking the bay and checked around before leaving the Discovery. He pushed his hands in his pockets and sauntered along a footpath which edged the car park as if he was admiring the view and taking a breath of air. There were plenty of shrubs and trees to use for cover and he made his way first to the left of the building and then to the right. The rear was shielded by a high brick wall but there was an alley that ran between the wall and the rear of the casino, used for deliveries and collections. There were security cameras placed along the alleyway, high up on the wall. There was no way he could reach the back of the casino without showing himself to watching security men. He guessed there would be double-width doors for groceries and laundry to pass through and he decided to try to get a look from the inside.

The set-up hadn't changed from the first time he had visited, except the security guard was a new man. It was busier with most of the slot machines in use and the blackjack tables now lined with punters but with a few seats still vacant. He picked one. The croupier was the woman to whom he'd given the twenty-pound tip. She recognised him and smiled as she dealt the next hand of cards to the players.

"You want to sit in, sir?" she asked.

"I'll just watch for now, see how the cards are fallin' tonight. That all right?"

She smiled again and nodded. "Decks are due to change anyway so it won't be a problem." She spoke without stopping the deal and he waited while the hand was played out as if he was really interested but noting that there was a camera above every table, black domes secured to the ceiling. There was a cluster in the centre of the ceiling above the slot machines watching the play for any signs of malpractice. It was nothing unusual, he had been in casinos before and this one was no different. He waited as the next hand was dealt. It was obvious that the players didn't have much clue on how to properly play the game and it was rare for one to win. He caught the croupier's eye and pulled a face. He mouthed I'll be back and sidled away towards a bar where the barely clad waitresses were standing leaning on the counter waiting for someone to order a drink. They raised themselves as he approached but dropped back into their original positions with disinterested looks in his direction as he took a seat on a bar stool.

The bartender walked over and raised his chin in the universal what do you want gesture.

"Got any San Miguel?"

The barman nodded.

"I'll have one but make sure it's cold. I hate warm beer."

The man nodded again, went away and was back in a minute with a bottle and a frosted glass on a tray with a receipt slip. Aftershave picked it up and winced. He waved it at the barman. "Oi, I only wanted a bottle o' beer not to buy the whole bloody casino. Eight quid, you're havin' a laugh."

The man shrugged. "That's the price, sir." He pointed to a list tacked to a wall. "That's what it says there."

"If I had my binoculars I might be able to read it," Aftershave grumbled. He fished in his pocket and put the exact amount on the tray. If the bloke thought he was getting a tip he had another think coming. He picked up the bottle and swigged from the neck as he looked around. The cashier's cage was to his right with a door behind it which looked solid enough to front a prison cell. There was another behind the bar which led to a storeroom where the liquor was kept. It must have had a connecting door to the cellars and kitchens below but there was no way he could reach it without being seen by the barman and waitresses. On the far side, beyond the lift and security guard was a double-width door operated by keypad and kept locked. As he watched the door opened and another security guard came out and relieved the first man. Aftershave glanced at his watch. It was midnight. Maybe they changed the detail every two hours.

The small group around the blackjack table drifted away and the croupier was left alone, clearing away the cards and chips. He slid off the stool and walked over.

"Hello again."

She smiled. "Hello, sir, come back for more have you?"

Aftershave grinned. "Came back to see you, you're my lucky charm." He craned his neck to read her name tag. "Fern, that's a nice name."

She leaned forward and whispered. "It's not my real name. They make us have fancy names here. "I'm Sally, really."

"Even better," he said and winked. "Worked here long, Sally?"

"'Bout, two years. I was on the cruise ships till the bottom fell out of the cruise business. It's a job but as soon as I can I'm out of here. Look, sir, you'll have to play or I'll get it in the neck if I'm not working."

Aftershave pulled out his roll of winnings. "Okay but there's no rule that says we can't chat while we play, is there?"

She shrugged. "S'pose not. You know the table limits, don't you?"

"Yeah, give me a hundred quid's worth o' chips."

She took the notes and pushed them down a slot at the back of the table before counting out twenty chips. "What d'you want to chat about?"

"Anything. I'm a stranger here. I live in Spain but I came over to see some friends. They've nipped off for the night an' left me on my lonesome. I just need someone to talk to … to help pass the time."

She dealt them two cards each. Aftershave picked his up. "Sounds as if you don't like workin' here much." He tossed two chips onto the table. "Hit me."

She lowered her voice to just above a whisper barely audible over the pinging of the slot machines. "The boss is a bit of a groper and his wife, bloody hell, if you get on her bad side you know all about it, bit of a tartar she is."

Aftershave laid his three cards down. "Pay nineteen."

Sally flipped her two cards over. A king and a jack. "Sorry." She scooped the cards and the chips away and dealt four more cards.

"D'you live here?" he asked.

"Saucy. Why'd you want to know that?"

"Just interested. It used to be a hotel, didn't it?"

"Yeah. There's some rooms but they're reserved for paying customers. I live in Torquay in a pokey bedsit which I share with my partner. She's over there at the bar, one of the waitresses."

Aftershave got the picture. He was being put on notice. "Nice, lucky you. Must be a drag though havin' to travel here every day. They must put you through it security wise."

"Not anything I'm not used to. Swipe cards to get in and all that but once they know your face it ain't so bad. Are you playing or what?"

Aftershave picked up his cards. An ace and eight of clubs. He pushed the remainder of his chips forward. "Hit me."

Sally flipped over the eight of spades. Table rules said he couldn't stick on seventeen. "Hit me again." The next card was the ace of spades. Black aces and eights, a dead man's hand. Aftershave felt a small shiver run down his spine and wondered whether it was an omen.

Sally was looking at him, head tilted to one side. "Are you sticking?"

The rule was to get the croupier to beat you. He was on the verge of a five-card trick but what were the odds of getting a three or below? Too long. He flipped over the two face-down cards. "Pay nineteen again."

Sally turned her two cards over. A king and a seven. She flipped the next card. A nine. Bust. "Looks like your luck's in again tonight, sir."

Aftershave nodded but the superstition bothered him. "Let's hope it lasts."

47

The little aircraft was noisy and draughty as it ground its way up to ten-thousand feet. Lacey was used to it but the vibration still rattled his backbone as he sat on the deck next to Gill. The pilot had informed him they had five tenths cloud at five-thousand feet and they would have to drop through it before they would see their DZ. The ship's superstructure was lit up with its riding lights on the bow and stern but the deck itself was illuminated by two floodlights, one pointing fore and one aft. To land unseen they would need to drop outside the twin cones of light.

"Colonel Lacey, sir." It was the pilot.

"Yes."

"Nearly time, sir. Wind's up a bit but we'll drop you at the right spot."

Then it's up to us, Lacey thought. The man was a well-trained Special Forces pilot who knew his stuff or he wouldn't be working with the ISPA; they only hired the best. Any mistakes would be down to himself ... or just bad luck.

Jack's voice sounded inside his helmet. "Your call sign is Sunray, sir. The lady is Sunset. If you and she wouldn't mind standing up, sir, we'll do the final checks."

Lacey unlatched his safety belt and helped Gill to her feet. She had hardly spoken since take-off and he wondered if the tension was getting to her. Jack was hovering around checking webbing and harnesses before he gave a thumbs-up. He crushed two Cyalume glow sticks and stuck them on the back of each of their helmets.

He was wearing a long safety belt and went to drop the hydraulic ramp at the rear of the aircraft that the ISPA versions had fitted as standard. Cold air rushed in as the red light above the door flickered on.

Jack held up three fingers. Three minutes. The aircraft lurched and all three of them staggered together.

"Shit." Lacey heard Gill's muffled oath and had to grin.

"Sorry," the pilot said, "air pocket. There may be others, hang on to something."

Lacey picked up a safety belt and wrapped it round his hand.

Gill grabbed his free arm. "I think I'll hang on to you. If we go out we'll go out together."

Jack held up one finger. "Standby, standby."

It was a long sixty seconds but the green light eventually flicked on. "Go!" Jack shouted.

Lacey dropped the belt and strode forward, Gill right alongside. He took a deep breath and plunged into the night. He could hear Gill's rapid breathing as they hurtled downwards headfirst, picking up speed. Lacey flared into the stable position and waited until he could see the glow of Gill's Cyalume just below him then he steered beside her.

"Cloud cover coming up, we may lose sight of each other for a few seconds," he said, "but keep steady." He glanced at the spinning numbers on his altimeter. Six-thousand and dropping rapidly. The first wisps of murk flashed past and then visibility went altogether. Lacey switched on his infra-red receiver and kept Gill's glowing shape in view. The act had caused his descent to slow and he was now over a hundred feet above Gill. He dipped his head and arrowed down until he was once again alongside her.

"You okay?"

She laughed. "I'd forgotten how exhilarating this could be."

"This is the fun part," Lacey replied.

They broke through the cloud cover. Lacey spun around trying to orientate himself and find the ship amongst the lights below. There were clusters of them from several ships anchored in the bay and it took him a few seconds to pick out the tanker.

"Follow me," he said and changed his bearing.

"Three thousand," Gill said. She sounded calm but there was an edge to her voice as the tension rose.

With a crack and a whistle the chute deployed and Lacey's headlong descent was brought to a halt with a vicious jerk that swung his legs down. He reached up and grabbed the steering toggles before looking around to find Gill.

"I'm above and to your right," she said in his helmet. I can see your glow stick."

"Good, follow me in."

"You've already said that."

"Thought you might have forgotten."

The chutes were good. Lacey slowed his descent and went to hover at around a thousand feet while he studied the ship. The twin spotlights shining on the deck helped him pick out a good spot for a landing. It was a small stretch of deck but he was sure he could hit it. He spilled air from the canopy and spiralled down slowing his rate of descent. He could feel the wind gusting from the west and adjusted his course. The wind would make it tricky once he'd entered his final approach. The ship was growing larger in his visor. He was still over the sea and needed to make sure he had enough altitude to clear the rail and turn in to the exact spot on the deck. He could feel the wind, stronger now, tugging at the canopy and rigging lines. He checked up looking for Gill but he could not see her, the black suit and black parachute blending with the night sky.

"You still with me?"

"Treading on your canopy."

"Wind's a bastard, be careful."

"Wilco."

Lacey turned in for the final approach. His boot soles brushed the rail and he pulled hard on the toggle to turn sharply along the length of the deck. His feet touched metal plate and he released the harness to collapse the chute and let the wind blow it clear over the side.

He turned to see Gill following in. She was too low and her legs caught the rail tipping her body forward until she was face down hovering over the deck. The wind caught her chute and it billowed over the side in the wake of Lacey's canopy. She started to slide back over the rail, the pressure of the wind towing her over the water.

He leapt to her and caught her arm, holding on for dear life as the strengthening wind pulled her further over the rail.

Lacey hooked his free arm through her lifejacket and held it in the crook of his elbow. The wind was pulling them both over the rail. He braced his feet against the metal side, reached down for his knife and began to saw through the bowstring-taut rigging lines. He felt the nylon straps of her lifejacket begin to slip through the buckle and become looser. Her upper body was dragged away by the wildly bucking parachute as the straps lengthened even more.

"Grab hold of me," he yelled.

"I'm trying," she screamed back. She clawed at his arm to take the weight off the lifejacket straps and gripped tight. "Don't let me go, Rick."

The para cord lines were tough but the knife's blade was razor sharp and he cut through the nylon. The lines flailed away and the pressure on Gill's body dropped. He heaved her over the rail and she landed in a heap at his feet.

"Fuck, that was fun," she said.

He squatted beside her and banged his helmet against hers. "Language, honey. Ben will be turning red."

"I've heard worse," Reid's voice crackled in their helmets. "Sit rep?"

"We're aboard," Lacey said. "Just."

He pulled Gill to her feet and they tossed what they didn't need over the ship's side. "Ready to go to work?"

He heard her exhale sharply. "I've nothing else to do." She paused. "Rick, thanks, you probably just saved my life."

"All part of the job, partner. But don't thank me too soon. From now on in it gets really hairy."

48

Aftershave glanced at his watch. Well past 02.00. If all went according to plan, Gill and Lacey should be on the deck of the tanker by now.

He had played a few more hands and was just about breaking even. The conversation with Sally had gradually dried up as she became suspicious of his questions and his reasons for asking them. It had seemed like chat-up to her to begin with but he realised he may have gone too far with questions about the casino. Her face had hardened and she became noncommittal before clamming up completely other than to play the cards. He left the table, cashed in his chips and went to sit back at the bar. He watched as she edged over to the security man and whispered in his ear casting sly glances in his direction as she did so. The security man nodded and spoke into his cuff as they did in the movies when depicting Secret Service men. Aftershave always found it was better to clip a microphone to a lapel or wear a throat mike that way it kept both hands free and you could speak without making it obvious. He smiled as he remembered a time in Washington when a big Secret Service man had come out of a building and stood posing on the steps with '*Secret Service*' emblazoned across his chest. He couldn't help asking what part of '*secret*' didn't the man understand? He got a stony stare in reply which had amused him even more.

Aftershave knew all about secrets and how to keep them; that was why he never had the Regiment's winged dagger badge tattooed on his arm like some had. There was too much in his life he didn't want people to know about to advertise the fact.

He finished a second San Miguel and reluctantly paid another eight pounds for the privilege. He thought he had enough now to help Gill and Lacey plan their operation should all go well on the ship. He had a sudden twinge of concern at the thought; what if it didn't go well?

He slid off the stool and made for the exit. He almost reached it when Ling-Ling cut across and stopped him. He gave her an artless smile.

"Wotcha, come to say goodbye, 'ave you?"

She smiled back but it was the look of a striking cobra, all fangs and hooded eyes. "Mister Pierce, he wants to say hello."

Aftershave pointedly looked at his watch. "It's gettin' late. Give my regrets to Mister Pierce and tell him we'll meet another time. I'll look forward to it."

Ling-Ling moved closer. "He says now. You come, yes?"

Aftershave turned his head and saw the security man close by watching with his hands clasped together over his groin. The look on his face was not friendly. They weren't planning on taking no for an answer. He knew he could insist on leaving and they would have a hard time stopping him but a public brawl wasn't a good option. There were too many people milling around and the scrap would more than likely end up on the front page of the *Express and Echo* with accompanying mobile phone pictures. He didn't need the publicity. He smiled at Ling-Ling again.

"Right, how can I refuse?"

She moved to him and took his elbow. It looked friendly but he felt her thumb dig into the ulnar nerve and the back of her hand brush against the Sig's butt. Clever girl, she knew her business.

They walked across the casino floor with the security guard in close attendance. They drew a few speculative glances, as if people were deciding if he'd been caught cheating. A couple of wry grins too; better luck next time, mate. It wouldn't do the casino's security reputation any harm.

This time the lift went to the second floor and opened onto a hall with doors spaced along one wall just like a regular hotel corridor. Ling-Ling led him to a door and opened it with a swipe card. She didn't release her grip on his elbow as she did so, and the guard stayed hovering close behind. Aftershave could almost feel his hot breath on the top of his close-cropped head. Someone should tell him not to stand so close.

Aftershave allowed Ling-Ling to push him through the door but as she did so she expertly flipped up his jacket and pulled the Sig from its holster. He shot her a quick admiring look then turned his head to view the room. It was several rooms knocked into one and turned into a palatial office with thick carpets, leather seats and a wide curved rosewood desk with three large monitors on one side. Bilic was reclining on a leather couch behind a stainless steel and glass coffee table, one leg crossed over the other, ankle on knee. Pierce was sitting behind the desk in a revolving chair that looked as if it would swallow him. He had a glass in his hand which he held up in salute.

"Glad you could join us, Mister Roberts." He looked over Aftershave's shoulder at Ling-Ling.

"He was armed, Mister Pierce." She held up the Sig.

Pierce waved a finger. "Naughty, naughty."

Aftershave turned his head. Ling-Ling was standing out of reach and the security man was behind her and to one side. He thought that Pierce was probably no good in a fight but he knew Bilic could look after himself. Good as he was, three to one wasn't great odds when at least two of them were well-trained in the black arts of unarmed combat. From what he'd seen of Ling-Ling, she could handle herself. The guard was a question mark but he seemed to be just muscle without much clue. He decided to relax and see where his invitation was leading. He smiled at Pierce. "What is it you wanted to see me about?"

"Couple of things but first I'd like to know why you come to my place with a shooter in your pocket?"

"Old habits," Aftershave said. "I feel naked without one, goes with the job I s'pose."

"What job would that be?"

Aftershave had already decided on his cover story. "I'm Missus A's minder. I'm paid to look after 'er."

"I suppose you have a licence for that." He pointed to the weapon that Ling-Ling was still holding up.

"Course, concealed carry licence. Got it when I worked in Ulster, mindin' a politician." He wondered if Pierce knew that was all bollocks but hoped he wouldn't be clued up on the niceties of firearms legislation. He knew if you told a lie with enough conviction people would take it as gospel. Concealed carry was allowed in Ulster for those at risk of terrorist attack but not on the British mainland. "Now, what else did you want to know?"

"You've been asking a lot of questions about this place. I'd like to know why."

Aftershave looked from Pierce to Bilic as if coming to a difficult decision. "Not sure I ought to tell you, it's confidential like."

Pierce raised his eyebrows and sat forward resting his elbows on the desk. It was an invitation to continue.

Aftershave hesitated again, running his tongue around inside his cheek in a nervous gesture. Then he shrugged. "All right but don't tell Mister Arnold I told you, he'd probably kill me."

Pierce was becoming impatient. "Well?"

"Missus Arnold liked this place, said she liked what she saw here. She asked Arnold if he would buy it for 'er. He sent me to suss the place out a bit before he makes an offer."

Pierce gave an explosive snort of laughter and sank back in his seat. "That's a good one." He raised an arm to Bilic. "Hear that, Bill? Yank thinks he can buy us out."

Bilic's grunt of a laugh held no humour that Aftershave could detect.

Pierce turned his gaze back to Aftershave. "Who does he think he is?"

"He's got friends, Mister Pierce, know what I mean. He usually gets what he wants." It was edging Gill's embroidery which made it seem all the more believable.

Pierce sneered. "He's not the only one with friends, he's biting off more than he can chew if he thinks he can take over here."

Aftershave shrugged again. "Fair warnin' Mister Pierce. He don't take kindly to people steppin' on his toes or standin' in his way." He paused and looked around again. "Look, I've said enough. If that's it I ought to be goin', I'm expected back."

Pierce shifted in his seat. "Just one more thing. I sent Arnold a message the other night but I haven't had a reply. The messengers haven't come back."

Aftershave made a big 'O' with his mouth. "What?"

"Mister Arnold took his boat out late the other night but I didn't know why. Maybe ...?

"He wouldn't be that stupid."

"He's nobody's fool. I doubt if they'll ever be found."

"Well that makes my mind up for me. Tit for tat. Ling-Ling."

Aftershave was fast but Ling-Ling was a shade faster. The Sig landed on the side of his head with stunning force and the lights went out.

49

Lacey pressed the switch on the side of his helmet and told Gill to do the same with hers. After a few seconds Jack's voice sounded coming through via satellite link as the small aircraft continued on its flight towards St. Helier. "I have video streaming from you and the ship's schematics on my other monitor. I'm recording."

"We're on the starboard side looking back towards the superstructure," Lacey said.

"I've got you. Go aft. There should be a hatch in the bulkhead on your right beneath the overhanging flybridge."

"I remember," Lacey said.

"It leads onto a stairwell that goes up to the sleeping quarters, the galley, mess hall and then to the bridge. The other way it goes down to a covered gantry that runs between the two layers of tanks the length of the ship. There's a similar one on the port side."

Lacey looked along the deck. They had cover from the layers of pipes that ran along the deck but had to pass through the beams from the spotlights. Gill watched as he scurried forward bent double. She followed a pace behind. He stopped as they reached the edge of the pool of light.

"Keep low and move as fast as you can until we're out of the light," he said, his voice distinct inside her helmet. "Ready?"

"Yes."

"Go."

They reached the next patch of shadow without an alarm being raised. Gill had always kept herself fit but was breathing hard by the time they reached the hatch set into the base of the superstructure. She had been expecting a small square opening but this was a full size door that was dogged shut but unlocked. Lacey eased it open. It was dark inside but the night vision systems kicked in automatically once away from the lights on the deck. Lacey had told her they worked on the same basis as self-dipping car headlights to prevent them from flaring out and blinding their wearers.

The ship was quiet, apart from an occasional metallic clang and the distant drone of generators deep in the engine room. They found the steps leading down and went to the lower level. The gantry that Jack had mentioned was more like a corridor painted in a light colour with emergency lighting every fifty feet. At the very end there appeared to be a door that was closed and halfway down a junction which led across the width of the ship to the port gantry.

Lacey pointed upwards with a thumb. "Tanks above." He pointed down with a finger. "Tanks below. I can't see anything along here to interest us. We'll try the port side."

"What do you think is behind the door ahead?" Gill asked.

"Probably the chain locker for the anchors and maybe a workshop for the engineers. We'll take a look if nothing else grabs us."

They turned left into the connecting corridor. The port gantry was identical to the starboard one and they edged their way forward towards the bow. "Looks as if we're wasting our time here," Lacey said. "We'll try opening the hatch at the end."

Gill shivered although it was warm in the suit with perspiration beginning to trickle down her neck. "I don't like the idea of getting caught in this area, Rick, we'd be sitting ducks. No way to get out other than the way we came in."

"Agreed. Let's try that hatch."

It was another large door dogged closed but with a metal bar for a handle encased in rubber. Lacey pushed it up and the door swung outwards towards them. A distant hum sounded from inside and they stepped over the coaming, closing the door behind them. The room was dimly lit but seemed to be another corridor running the width of the ship. It had doors leading off it on the bow side and a skeletal ladder that went downwards through the deck plating. The hum was coming from below. Lacey went down it first. Gill followed and couldn't believe her eyes. It was as if they had entered a hangar. The lower bow port tank had been converted into a wide space with open water taking up a quarter of the width. The miniature submarine was floating in it. A bulkhead had been built halfway along and she could see a wide corridor beyond it, well-lit and looking more as if it belonged on a cruise liner than below decks on a tanker.

"Impressive," Lacey said. "Jack, are you getting this?"

Jack's voice came back garbled. "You're … breaking … up … Colonel."

"Too much metal around us," Lacey said. "I'll switch to back-up recording." He moved left and tried a door. It was open and he poked his head in. "Store room." He walked in and hefted some boxes and cans. "Just sailor stuff far as I can see."

Gill tried the next door. It was a small cabin with a desk, radio console and computer monitor. "Probably submarine control," she said.

Lacey was about to walk past when a door opened further along and a loud voice speaking Mandarin echoed down the corridor.

Gill reached out a hand and pulled Lacey into the cabin so hard he collided with her. She started to fall but he snaked out his arm and caught her around the waist.

"She gasped and took a breath. "This is getting to be a habit, Colonel."

She couldn't see his expression through the gold visor but she hoped he was smiling.

Two sets of footsteps receded and Lacey poked his head out. "Clear."

The next doors opened onto empty cabins with wet suits hanging on hooks but the fourth, the one the men had left, had a light showing through a circular glass port set at head height in the door's face. Lacey sneaked a peek. "There's another door inside. It looks like some sort of vestibule with lockers and a room beyond. The far door is solid steel and has a wheel lock, like on a submarine's hatch. Couple of hefty bolts too."

"Could be interesting." Gill said in a whisper. She was not sure why she whispered, her voice could not be heard outside the confines of the helmet but with her rising excitement came an increase in nervous tension and a whisper had been an automatic response. "Might be something in there they don't want people to see."

"Let's go take a look," Lacey said and pulled the cabin door open. They stepped over the coaming and Lacey closed the door behind them before easing across to the second door. The bolts were slid open with their padlocks hanging on a hook beside the door. He pointed. "Careless … unless they're coming back soon."

"Better be quick then," Gill said.

Lacey put a gloved hand on the door's metal face. "It's vibrating, not much but enough to feel it." He slung his MP5 so that it dangled behind his right hip and used both hands on the wheel. It turned easily, evidence of frequent use. It opened inwards with a hiss and a whoosh of air as the rubber seals around its edge were released. Lacey paused with the door open an inch. Strong white light threw a beam around the seal that sliced across the deck like a laser.

Gill heard Lacey grunt. "That's odd."
"What is?"
"It's some sort of air lock."
"*'Curiouser and curiouser, said Alice'*," Gill murmured.

Lacey pushed the door open another few inches and the beam widened as he did so. He pushed his head around the jamb. "Bloody hell!"

Gill nudged him. "What is it?"

He stepped back. "Take a look."

She pushed forward and copied his actions to push her head into a place where she could see into the area beyond the door. Immediately to their front was a glass wall with an air lock set into it. Beyond that was a well-lit laboratory with benches, microscopes and other scientific paraphernalia. The lab was empty but various lights flashed on serious looking kit and there was a whirr of electronic equipment. The entire lab was completely enclosed in a glass shell. She pulled her head back. "What the hell?"

"I don't know but I don't like it," Lacey said and he sounded ruffled. "Maybe they're cooking heroin. I've got the video. Let's get out and see what the experts make of it."

They turned back just as the outer door opened and two men came through. They stopped dead, mouths open with surprise and fear, then one screamed and launched himself across the room to hit a red button on the wall. Lights flashed on and an ear-splitting klaxon rent the silence.

50

The second man tripped over the coaming and fell on his back in the corridor. Gill leapt after him and swung the butt of her MP5 against his head. Lacey dealt with the other in the same way and bundled himself out after Gill. He looked left as doors clanged open and men spilled out in a variety of dress, some in T-shirts, shorts and flip-flops, others in khaki drill and carrying weapons. Someone shouted and pointed. A weapon cracked and a bullet careened off the side of Lacey's helmet. It made his ears ring.

"Gloves off, Gill, they want a firefight."

He dropped to one knee and sent two-round bursts at the crowd filling the corridor, dropping two soldiers and sending the others scurrying for cover. "Make for the ladder. We need to get to the stern and we can't get past that lot. Move, I'll cover." He pulled a smoke grenade from his harness, pulled the pin and sent it rolling. He switched to Infra-red and picked out another target through the orange fog that was beginning to rise from the spluttering grenade. He turned his head to see Gill's feet disappear through the hatch and ran to the ladder. Bullets were pinging and whining off the walls, un-aimed shots but no less dangerous. He hauled himself up the ladder in double-time.

Gill was waiting for him, covering the door. "Now what?"

"Take the starboard gantry and head back the way we came."

She ran the width of the ship and pulled open the connecting hatch. "Clear."

Lacey was right behind her. "Go!"

They ran fast and reached the lateral gantry that joined the port and starboard corridors when the hatch at the end burst open and several men in grey combat suits came through. Lacey dived into the opening and pulled Gill in with him. "Check port."

She did at a run and poked her head out. "More this side."

"Figured as much. We'll take our chances with these boys. Are you ready?"

"Say the word."

Lacey dropped to one knee and peered around the corner. Bullets chipped paint from the wall above his head. He unhooked two more grenades and one by one pulled the pins. He leaned out and tossed both at the advancing soldiers. A bullet smacked into his armour plating but he barely felt it. The grenades exploded with brilliant white flashes and sharp multiple detonations that made his head ring even inside the helmet. He looked out again and the bulk of the men were on their knees holding their ears and moaning.

Lacey stood. "Let's go." They ran through the groaning bodies. One less affected raised his suppressed sub-machine gun. Lacey put two rounds through his chest and kicked the weapon aside. "Keep going," he snapped at Gill.

She ran to the hatch just as another two soldiers shouldered it open and poked the muzzles of their assault rifles through. She leapt at the door and hit it with her full weight, slamming it against the men's arms. She heard a shriek of pain, pulled the hatch open and put rounds into both of them.

Lacey rushed past her, skipping over the twitching bodies and made for the staircase. Heavy footsteps sounded from above. Gill joined him.

"We're going down. You first, I'll cover."

"I don't like stairs," Gill said.

"Who does? You know the drill, just do it."

She held out a hand and Lacey dropped a grenade into her palm. "Frag."

She nodded, pulled the pin and dropped the grenade down the well, it bounced hollowly twice before detonating with a sharp crack. Gill raced down behind it keeping her back against the wall as she ran. "Clear."

The noisy feet were on the landing above. He could hear a cacophony of voices all shouting together, then one louder, issuing orders. The noise stopped but he could now see ankles edging down the steps above. He fired several short bursts to discourage them and followed Gill down, leaping the steps three at a time, ignoring the twinges of pain from his leg.

Gill banged her helmet against his. "Where now?"

They were on a metal landing with a single hatch set into the inner bulkhead. Lacey scanned his memory for the plans of the ship. "Down one more level."

They turned to run when a grenade bounced down the stairs and landed between them.

"Frag," Lacey screamed, kicked the bomb into a corner, dragged Gill to the ground and rolled on top of her. The grenade exploded with a loud sharp crack sending dozens of tiny fragments flashing out, some ricocheted off the walls scouring paint and sharp splinters from the metal. They hit Lacey's suit like grains of sand blown by a tornado. The worst of the blast was directed upwards by the metal plate floor and had gone over their prone bodies.

He rolled to one side and climbed to his feet, pulling Gill up with him. "Get going."

Feet were pounding on the steps as well-trained soldiers followed their grenade. He waited at the corner of the stairwell until he had targets and put men down with aimed bursts. It was a grim thought but he was glad the Chinese generals did not approve of body armour for their troops. The concentrated fire sent the remainder back up the flight. Another grenade wasn't likely as it would finish off the wounded but he would put nothing past the Chinese army.

He scampered down in Gill's wake. Lights were now off in the stairwell and the night vision equipment kicked in. He found her in a corner, her MP5 aimed up the stairs.

"Looks like this is the end of the line, there's nowhere else to go," she said.

He let his MP5 dangle on its sling and ran a hand over the hull. There should be a hatch here somewhere. It's where the pilots get on and off the ship."

"And that's gonna help us how?"

He grinned although she couldn't see it. "There are ways." He tried his radio. "Jack, Ben, are you receiving, over?"

Nothing but mush came back at him. He tried again with the same result as he walked the length of the platform they were on. He found the flanges of the hatch and the dogging locks. He spoke to Gill. "I've got it. Keep the bastards busy while I get it open."

"Hurry, I can hear them moving the bodies off the landing above, it won't take them long to put in an assault. More grenades first, I guess."

Lacey hustled past her. "Then I'd better give them something else to think about." He unhooked one of his last two grenades. He pulled the pin, ran half way up the flight and lobbed it onto the landing. It fizzed rather than exploded and a hail of bullets cracked and whined around him, one scarring his visor and jolting his neck.

"What was that," Gill asked as he slid down beside her.

"CS Gas. It should sort them out for a bit and give us a breathing space. Speaking of which it'll start to drain down here. You've got seven minutes supply of oxygen if you need it. Valve's on your belt."

He turned back to the hatch and began to work the latches to get it open. He called Reid again but there was no reply. He needed to get through or they were as good as dead.

51

Gill felt a sudden vibration through the soles of her boots. "What's that?"

Lacey turned his head from struggling with the latches. "They've started the ship's engines, they're getting out."

"Taking us with them," Gill replied.

"That's their plan. They think they can keep us down here until they're out to sea, then the sky will cave in on us. God knows what weaponry they have up there but I've already seen one or two armed with Type 85s. They're 7.62mm. Catch one of those in the wrong place and we'll know about it. Suppressed or not, they can still penetrate Kevlar, or, at the very least bust a bone or two."

"I just love your little rays of sunshine, Rick."

He yanked harder on the dogging clamp. "Don't you have a quote for that?" he said.

"Only one that comes to mind is Monty Python's *'Always look on the bright side of life'*."

"Sounds sensible, if not entirely practical given our current situation."

Gill moved so that she could see partly up the metal stairs. "They seem to have moved away from the gas."

"They'll be back. I don't doubt they have gas masks stowed somewhere on board," Lacey said. "We've given them a bloody nose, downed some of their men, they'll be back looking for retribution if nothing else. They know we can't go anywhere, they've got us bottled." He gave another heave on the clamp and it moved with a squeal of rusted metal.

Gill turned to him. "Are you planning on getting us wet?" There was a deep rumbling from forward. "Is that the anchor being raised?"

"Yes to the second part," Lacey replied. He heaved on the clamp again and gasped with the effort. "And no to the first part unless we can get this hatch opened.

Gill slung her MP5 and walked to him. She gripped the metal bar with both her hands between his. "Why didn't you ask for my help?"

"I needed you to guard the stairs. But now we have a breathing space and I'd be happy for some assistance."

She smiled. "Which way do I pull?"

"Towards the deck." Lacey grunted and heaved downwards.

Gill swung on it, lifting both her feet off the deck to add her whole weight to the effort. It worked, the latch squealed again and the bar turned dumping her on her bottom."

Lacey reached down to help her up. "Good, only one more to go."

"I don't want to hear a word said about me landing on my bum when we get out, Rick, *comprende*?"

"Our secret."

She couldn't see his face but heard the chuckle in his voice. "So glad you could see the funny side." She gripped the second clamp. "C'mon, let's get this done."

The second latch opened far more easily and Lacey pulled the wide door inwards and back. Fresh air rushed in and they could hear the slap of water on the hull as the ship began to move slowly forward hauling in its anchor chain as it did so.

Lacey tried the radio again. "Jack, Ben, receiving, over?"

There was a burst of static and Jack's voice came back. "Got you, sir. Where are you?"

"Still aboard but we have some serious company. Ben, are you there?"

"Here. Sit-rep."

"Down by the starboard pilot's hatch, just above the waterline at the stern."

"I've got it," Jack cut in.

"We've managed to get some video recorded on chip which looks interesting but our hosts have taken umbrage. It's getting a little sticky here."

Gill listened to the exchange. A little sticky was putting it mildly. "Hello, sir, what the colonel means is our hosts have us at a severe disadvantage. We only have one way out and that's over the side and into the water. The bugbear there is that the ship has weighed anchor and is beginning to move. We jump in and we could get sucked into the propeller vortex."

"Why didn't I think of that?" Lacey said and she could hear a note of sarcasm seeping out. It annoyed her. "You have a better idea?"

Lacey didn't answer her but spoke to Reid. "Did you get what I asked for, Ben?"

"Took a bit of arm twisting, but yes."

"Call sign?"

"Bravo, November, Charlie, two."

"Thanks, patch me through."

"You're through, it's all yours, good luck, out."

Lacey repeated the call sign three times, this is Sunray, are you receiving, over?"

"Hello Sunray, this is Bravo, November, Charlie, Two.

"This is Sunray, what's your position, over?"

"Two hundred metres off the stern, running without lights."

"Can you take us off the starboard pilot's boarding platform?"

"It's blowing a bit of a Hooley but we'll do our best."

Gill nudged Lacey "What the hell's going on?"

"The cavalry is on its way."

There was a clatter from the companionway steps and a grenade hopped part way down before it exploded with a deafening crack. Red hot shards lashed into the hull above their heads.

"Let's hope the cavalry get here in time," Gill yelled. "The natives are getting restless again."

"I hoped I wouldn't have to do this," Lacey said and unhooked his last grenade. "Cover me."

Gill eyed the odd shaped canister. "Is that what I think it is?"

"White phosphorous. Keep their heads down."

Lacey took the steps two at a time as Gill hosed rounds towards shadowy figures on the stairway above. Another grenade came skipping down and she kicked it into the well where they had been standing. It bounced twice and fell out of the open hatch into the water where it exploded with a dull thump.

"Sunray, what the hell was that?"

The voice crackled in Gill's helmet and she replied. "This is Sunset, we have a minor problem but we're sorting it. Keep coming."

Lacey had reached the landing where a body lay spread-eagled on the metal plating. Others were massing above ready for an assault. Calm voices were issuing orders and excited ones replying. He pulled the pin on the WP grenade and looped it up onto the next level.

"Go," he snapped at Gill.

She had no idea how much damage a WP grenade would do in an enclosed space but it would not be pretty. It burned at 3000 degrees Celsius and blew white hot phosphorous in a billowing arc that stank of garlic. She hoped that Lacey knew what he was doing, fire on an oil tanker could be devastating.

He dragged her to the hatch just as a motor cutter pulled up alongside, rocking in the heavy swell. He heaved her across the gap that narrowed suddenly so that the launch crashed into the tanker's hull and bounced away just as Lacey jumped. He missed his footing but clung on to a guard rail, feet dangling over the side as the cutter pulled away.

A thick white cloud billowed out of the hatch and licked the paintwork off the cutter's hull. Shrieks and exploding ammunition could be heard as the cutter accelerated away.

Lacey was still dangling over the side and Gill reached out a hand to pull him over the rail and onto the narrow side deck where they both collapsed in a heap.

"I reckon we're even," Gill gasped.

"What the fu…?" Lieutenant Tarrant appeared from the cabin. "What the hell are you?"

Lacey pulled himself to his feet. "I'm Sunray and this is Sunset." His accent was now Home Counties.

"Bloody hell, that get-up …"

"Official secrets, Lieutenant. Need to know and you don't."

Tarrant took off his cap and scratched his head. "Right, look, whoever you are, I don't get any of this."

"You did a great job. Thanks for saving our butts."

The helmsman poked his head out of the cabin. "Tanker's in a bit of a mess, sir. Channel 16 has lit up like a Christmas tree with skippers calling in. It's all over the net."

"Shit," Lacey said and brushed past Tarrant to get to the VHF set. The helmsman's jaw dropped when he saw him.

Lacey picked up the Mike and pressed the send button. "Mayday, Mayday, Mayday, this is the tanker *New Venture*, we are under attack by pirates. Shots have been fired. Mayday, Mayday, Mayday …" he turned to the helmsman, "position?" The figures were given to him and he read them out over the air. He finished with, "please send help."

52

Tarrant pulled angrily at Lacey's arm. "What on earth are you doing?"

Lacey turned his ant-like head to him, and spoke still with a distinct English accent. "Two things, Lieutenant, one is making sure that ship doesn't get away and the second is providing a cover story for what went on tonight. Sunset and I were never here and you were just out on a night navigation exercise. That clear."

"Official secrets?"

"If you haven't already signed it there will be a copy waiting for you when you get back to the college, that I can guarantee. Same goes for the crew of this cutter."

"What about my blistered bloody paintwork," the helmsman said out the corner of his mouth. The VHF burst into life and a tinny foreign voice blurted out.

"This is the captain of the *New Venture*, we are not under attack I say again we are not under attack, it is a hoax." The message was repeated twice more and then the radio went dead. Nobody used Channel 16 once a Mayday had been called until the Coastguard had given the all clear.

The helmsman gave a cynical grin. "Good luck with that, mate, nobody's gonna believe you don't have a gun to your head." He turned to Tarrant. "Where we bound, sir?"

Tarrant looked at his own reflection in Lacey's visor. "Well?"

"I'll let you know." He dropped his voice and spoke on the radio to Gill. "Did you get all that?"

She shrugged. "Most of it. Where *are* we going to land by the way? We can't exactly walk the streets wearing this gear and I'm damned if I'm going to wander around in my underwear."

Lacey shrugged in turn. "Hadn't gotten around to thinking about that."

"You do surprise me. Maybe if I'd been in on the navy coming to our rescue I could have given it some consideration."

"Yeah, sorry. Was only meant to be a Plan B."

"I hesitate to ask what Plan A was," Gill said.

Lacey could hear the annoyance in her voice and couldn't blame her. He turned to Tarrant. "Do you have a dinghy or life raft aboard?"

"Certainly, we wouldn't set sail without one."

He turned away again and spoke quietly to Reid. "Ben, are you still with us?"

"All the way, soldier."

"Could you get on to Six and have their people meet us at the same place we dumped the two crooks, that's Blackpool Sands, in about two hours? We'll need some clothing, coats, sweaters, anything to cover these suits and two boxes to take the helmets."

"Wilco. It makes my night to get Blake out of bed. You've set the cat amongst the pigeons by the way. There's a full scale operation on the blocks.

309

SBS, the works, they're planning to assault the ship. Choppers will be on their way by daybreak."

"Can you tip them the wink that there are some nasty dudes aboard who tend to shoot first and ask questions later. We thinned some out but not all."

"Thanks for the heads-up. I'm sure the boys will be grateful," Reid said.

"There's something odd about that ship, very odd. I'll send over the video as soon as we get back to the boat. Get the experts to check it out."

"How's Sunset holding up?"

"I'm fine, Brigadier," Gill said. "Just a little in the dark."

Reid chuckled. "Par for the course. Given time you'll get used to it."

"Maybe I don't want to get used to it, sir."

"It's your call. Now I have things to do so I'll leave you in Jack's capables if you need anything."

"Listening in," Jack's cheery voice cut in. "We'll do a touch and go at St. Helier and come right back to Exeter. Got to keep the Air Traffic Control records straight."

"Thanks Jack," Lacey said. "Probably won't need you again but keep a listening watch just in case."

"Wilco, sir, Jack out."

Tarrant was still waiting for a reply to his question. He hadn't been able to hear the muted radio chatter and was becoming impatient. "Well, sir?" he repeated. "Where are we bound for?"

"Sorry, Lieutenant. Make for Blackpool Sands. If you could ferry us ashore we'll be met there."

"Aye, aye, sir, Blackpool Sands," the helmsman said. "Take us a while in this sea; it'll rough up more round Berry Head. Should get there just before dawn though."

"Oh, god, I'm feeling queasy already," Gill whispered in Lacey's ears.

"Don't throw up in the helmet if you can help it."

"You're all heart, Rick."

Lacey pulled on Tarrant's sleeve. "D'you have a heads aboard this tub?"

"Sea toilet, not much but all we've got. Down below, starboard side."

"Thanks." Lacey took Gill's elbow. "There's a loo down below. I'll help you off with your helmet but you'll have to put it back on again, we can't let these guys see who we are."

Gill swallowed hard. "Can we make it quick?"

Lacey helped her down as the boat bucked and twisted on the waves. He shut the door behind them and unlatched her helmet. She blinked in the darkness and ran her fingers through her matted hair. "I must look a fright."

Lacey pulled off his own helmet. "You look a little green around the gills."

She nodded and put a hand over her mouth. "I'm aptly named then. Fair weather sailor, that's me." She stood, pulled open the door to the heads and vomited.

Lacey held her steady on the bucking deck while she vomited again and sank into a sitting position with a groan. "God, I feel awful."

Lacey wiped her mouth with a paper towel, gently and carefully. He sat opposite her, leaning against the door to keep anyone else out. "You'll get over it. I was seasick before I got my sea legs."

"Right now I feel as if I never want to set foot on a boat again."

Lacey grinned. "Are you glad you came?"

Gill threw a balled up paper towel at him. "Right this minute I hate you, Rick Arnold."

He gave her a thoughtful look. "You've said that before but I guess that's better than no feelings at all."

They were paddled ashore just as the first tinges of dawn was lighting the sky. They were met by the same woman who had been warned and wasn't surprised by their appearance. She had brought some old anoraks and a couple of cardboard baked bean boxes for the helmets. She asked no questions and was silent all the way back to the marina, leaving them on the road outside the car park to walk the final leg to the boat. It was still early and no one was around, the weather keeping any early risers safely inside.

Gill flopped onto the couch as soon as they entered the saloon. "I need a shower and a day's sleep but I expect both will have to wait until we get squared away. She looked at the time on the ship's clock. "I'll get Aftershave up, he can make us some coffee while we get out of these suits and clean weapons."

She levered herself to her feet as Lacey fired up his laptop and pushed in the video chip. He looked dog-tired, Gill thought, but as they sang, *'when the going gets tough …'*

She rapped on Aftershave's cabin door. "Drop your cock and grab your socks. We need you topside." She grinned as she waited for a ripe reply but got nothing but silence. She frowned and pushed open the door.

She rushed back to the saloon. "Rick, we have a problem."

He looked away from the screen and gave her a tired grin. "Don't tell me, *Apollo 13*."

"That's not a quote. Aftershave's not aboard, he hasn't returned from the casino, something bad must have happened to him."

53

The sound of a raised voice brought Aftershave back to consciousness. It was loud but he couldn't understand the shrill words. He blinked his eyes to try to get them back in focus but his right eye stayed obstinately glued shut.

He twisted his head around, pain lanced up the side of his head and he groaned. He tried again, carefully, and had a view beneath the stainless steel legs of a couch. He was face down on a carpet against a wall. He tried to move his arms and couldn't, ditto for his legs which were clamped together and bent back at the knee where his heels almost touched his fists. It was cramped and painful.

He blinked again and tried to clear his monocular vision and bring his mouse-eye view into focus. His head ached viciously and he could barely work his jaw on the right side. It came back to him in a flood and he groaned again, not so much in pain but at the memory of being caught off-guard by Ling-Ling. He was losing his edge, he should have seen it coming.

He tried to wriggle into a more comfortable position and failed. Whoever had tied him up was a professional and it would take him hours to work his way free, provided he was given the opportunity to do so, which he doubted. The voice was still screeching but he could now recognise a Chinese dialect, whether Cantonese, Wuhan,

Mandarin, or any of the other forty-one recognised dialects he couldn't tell. Whoever was speaking, a woman, probably Ling-Ling, was unhappy about something and giving earache to whomever was on the other end of the line. He was happy she was unhappy, he owed her something far worse than hurt feelings.

He tried to open his right eye again but it was firmly glued shut. Judging by the pain in his head on that side he thought it was probably dried blood that had run into his eye from the head wound and congealed.

The phone was slammed down on its charger.

"What's the problem?"

It was a male voice, English; Pierce. Aftershave concentrated harder.

"The ship has been infiltrated and is leaving," Ling-Ling said. Her English accent had improved from earlier when she had cut him off at the door. Home grown, he thought, or maybe the product of a Special Forces language school.

"They still have my goods." Pierce in a huff. "They're bought and paid for."

"There will be a delay, Derek. It is far more important that the ship is taken to safety."

"What'll I tell my customers? I promised delivery by the end of this week."

A note of contempt sounded in Ling-Ling's voice. "They will have to be told there will be a delay, a wrinkle in the supply chain. It will be overcome and they must be patient."

"I don't think the Exeter dealer is the patient kind."

"Then you must tell him, one moment of patience may ward off a great disaster, one moment of impatience may ruin a whole life."

"I don't think he'll appreciate your fortune cookie proverbs and he may take it as a threat."

Ling-Ling's voice hardened. "Then he would be a wise man indeed."

"No worry, I take care of him." Another voice, heavily accented, eastern European.

"Not too much rough stuff, Bill," Pierce pleaded. "He's worth a few thou a month to us. If he kicks up just have a gentle word with him, eh."

The couch above Aftershave's head groaned and squeaked as its occupant moved. He saw a pair of large booted feet walk into his eye line.

"He cut up rough, I take Exeter, no worries."

Pierce grunted a laugh. "That'll go down like a lead balloon with the rest of the dealers. They won't like lookin' over their shoulders waitin' to see if their turn is next. They won't like the idea of a London mob movin' into their territory."

"They will have little choice but to be patient," Ling-Ling said. "We hold the key to their market, they will not easily replace our goods from another source, they will have to bend the knee and be grateful that we are still willing to meet their demand. A week perhaps, perhaps two, then we should have re-routed the supply chain."

"Okay, I take your point," Pierce said. "We'll leave it for now until things settle down. Bill can field any grumbles and take care of anything heavier. Look, I gotta go, it's getting late." He paused and Aftershave could hear him picking up items from his desk. Then he cleared his throat as if about to voice something unpleasant.

"What are we gonna do about our friend over there? We can't have him floatin' in the Dart like that other bloke."

"That was a mistake, we should have taken the body immediately not left it to be washed away on the tide. Don't worry, we'll think of something interesting for Mister Roberts," Ling-Ling said.

"Well, okay, as long as it don't wash up outside my door. I've got enough problems with his Yank mate sniffing around and threatening trouble.

"Shelley's back from visitin' her mum tomorrow and I want him out of here sharpish."

Bill gave a nasty laugh. "You should keep dick in pants, Derek, you make trouble for yourself with woman."

"Yeah, but that one's top-notch merchandise, worth the risk."

"Not if Shelley catch you with pants down."

"That's my problem, mate, I can deal with it. It's the husband I'm more concerned with. He sounds like a real hard case."

"Then we take care of him too; Ling-Ling and me."

There was a few seconds of silence then a door opened and closed as Pierce left.

Ling-Ling's stiletto heels came and stood next to Bill's boots. "What have you got in mind for our friend here?" She leaned her weight on the seat back and her shadow loomed over Aftershaves head. "He's still out. I may have fractured his skull."

"Then it make it easy. I will take him to mine. He will be buried where no one find him, with your two damn guards who shoot each other."

"And Arnold and his wife?"

"Maybe accident at sea, far away from here. Maybe I give her to Derek to play with then sell her. There is still market for blonde her age in Middle East. "

"Just be careful. Derek may be weak but he was right about one thing, we do not want any more bodies on our doorstep, it will look bad. Nothing else must come back to bite us."

Bilic grunted and changed the subject. "What was problem with ship?"

Ling-Ling sighed and sat heavily on the couch. "The message was garbled. From what I could understand, they were boarded and attacked, they think by just two people who escaped and whose motives are unknown. There was a fire on board that was doused quickly but the captain was in a panic and almost incoherent. He was rushing to get outside British waters before they could be boarded again. The ship holds too many secrets. It is a big disgrace that he allowed his ship to be attacked and for those responsible to escape."

"What of our special consignment?"

"Don't worry. You already have all you need. Remember, handle it with care, we don't want any unpleasant consequences ... not yet."

54

Lacey put down the cover on his laptop and stood. He could not help a spasm of pain cross his face. Gill saw it.

"You all right?" She looked at him closely in the growing light. "You're bleeding."

Lacey put a hand to his side and it came away red. "Just a scratch I guess. A splinter from a grenade cut through the Kevlar. I'll deal with it later. Are you sure Aftershave hasn't decided to get some sleep at the hotel?"

Gill picked up her mobile and rang the hotel reception desk. She shook her head at the reply. "No, they haven't seen him for two days."

Lacey grimaced. "Then we have to get to that casino. No time to get out of these suits and into a shower, we have to get moving." He disappeared below and came back a minute later with boxes of 9mm ammunition. "Pick up the helmets. I'll reload the mags on the way."

Gill found the keys to her Mercedes and they rushed to the car park. The drive to Torquay was manic as Lacey wiped rounds clean with gloved hands and thumbed them into empty MP5 magazines.

He glanced across at her, seeing worry and concentration etched in the fine lines around her eyes. He held up one stubby round. "These are full load 2Z but the mufflers will cope, you'll hardly notice the difference except the point of impact will be higher. If you're going for a head shot, aim for the mouth."

She shot him a glance. "Are you expecting another firefight?"

"I expect the worst but hope for the best. Sod's Law generally applies and I prefer to be ready for anything."

"*The first casualty in any battle is the plan for it,*" Gill quoted and grimaced.

Traffic was beginning to build up as they entered the outskirts of Paignton on the A3022. They came up against the rear of a delivery lorry which slowed them down until a clear stretch of road allowed Gill to slalom around it to take the A379 into Torquay. Lacey could see that Gill was becoming more and more agitated at each delay, taking risks overtaking that bordered on the suicidal but she was a brilliant driver.

"I see you've done the course," Lacey said.

Gill shot a glance at him. "One-up in Belfast … unless I was nursemaiding a new operator." She pulled her eyes back to the road and passed a lorry on the wrong side of a traffic island.

"One-up. I'm impressed," Lacey said. "It's not everyone the Det let's out on their own in bandit country."

"And you'd know that, how?" Gill said.

Lacey grinned. "I hear things."

Gill shot him another glance and slowed to pull into the casino's almost deserted car park.

They crept in and stopped just inside the entrance. Lacey undid his seat belt and climbed out. He walked a few paces then came back and knelt by Gill's door. "The Discovery is in the car park. He's still here."

She pushed the door open and hurried to the boot to put in their borrowed anoraks and take out the helmets. She handed one to Lacey. "He may still be here but in what condition? I know he's a big boy and can look after himself but it would take something serious to keep him here."

"Maybe he's having a fling with Ling-Ling," Lacey said in an effort to calm her down.

She shot him a baleful glare. "Is that you looking on the bright side, Rick? If so, I'd prefer to get the SP before I jump to any conclusions."

"Okay, point taken but we have to keep our cool. We're going in cold. Apart from your visit we have no idea of security or layout. We may be walking into your proverbial hornet's nest or a champagne party in full swing."

"Softly-softly, I get it." She jammed the helmet on her head. "Latch me up."

Lacey latched on his own helmet then helped her with hers. "Just so you're aware. The infra-red has drained the batteries. We're on short-range audio intercom only, no video, no night vision, no Jack or Ben, just mark-one eyeball."

"Okay, got it. Also no witnesses, no video evidence, no liberal lawyers screaming for our balls if this turns bad. Anything else?"

"Just take a couple of deep breaths. I know he's your friend and I know you're worried about him but the best way we can help is to keep our own professionalism and not go rushing in at half-cock. *Comprendes*?"

He saw some of the tension go out of her shoulders and heard her cough a small chuckle.

"Your accent is awful but I get the message, boss."

"Right. It seems the punters have left. Lights are out but there are cameras high up on the wall to this side and along the front over the door. Not sure if their security will still be monitoring the screens but if so we'll have to be careful or we'll lose the element of surprise. We'll take out two of the cameras and create a blind spot. Maybe they'll think it's a malfunction. I'll take the one over the door if you take the one on the wall. Ready?"

"As I'll ever be."

They manoeuvred themselves into position where they could both get clean shots at the cameras but still remain in cover. Lacey counted down and they fired two two-round bursts. Both cameras shattered.

Lacey ran to the doors and pushed a shoulder against them. "Locked. Stand back." Another short burst smashed the lock and he heaved one side open.

"Door to the left of the lift," Gill said. "I think that leads to the security office."

They ran through the darkened slot machines to the door. "Keypad entry," Lacey said.

Gill pointed upwards. "There's enough cameras, if they're awake they have seen us by now.

Lacey nodded, stood back and crashed a foot against the door, It rattled but held. He kicked it again and this time the latch gave and the door swung inwards onto a staircase leading upward.

"Not stairs again," Gill breathed but Lacey heard her.

"The quicker we get up them the better."

They reached the next floor before they heard heavy footsteps running in the corridor beyond the fire door. The door burst open and three men shouldered their way through, all waving silenced pistols. They stopped dead, eyes wide, mouths agape, as they saw the two ant-like figures. The surprise was brief and they swung their pistols to fire.

Lacey double-tapped one and Gill another. The third got off a shot that slammed into Gill's chest sending her staggering back. Lacey double-tapped him, turned his head to see that Gill was still standing and went through the door into the corridor.

"That hurt," she grumbled.

He didn't reply but raced up to a partially open door. It led into the security room filled with monitors and two men seated in front of them speaking rapidly into microphones. Both turned in surprise and both froze for an instant before leaping to their feet and reaching for weapons. Lacey butt stroked the first, twisted and slammed the barrel of his MP5 into the face of the second. Both went down without a sound. He kicked their weapons away, tore wiring from the consoles and quickly bound both men to the legs of the steel benches that held their equipment. He found the recordings and ripped them out of the machines.

Gill went ahead into the big gambling room with the gold nugget in its glass case at the centre. On impulse she undid the cover, a quick twist to the left, and took the nugget, pushing it into one of the empty elastic straps on her wrist. She ran for the door to Pierce's office and tried the handle. It opened easily and she slipped inside.

"Where are you?" Lacey's voice whispered in her helmet.

"Along the corridor. Keep left and you'll reach a room with poker tables. There's a door right ahead. I'm in there."

"Wait for me."

"Sure," Gill said but she had no intention of waiting. The office was empty but she could hear noises coming from the other room, the one she assumed was Pierce's bedroom. She edged her way to it and turned the door knob. Again it was unlocked and she eased through it. She was right, it was a bedroom with clothing spread over the bed in an untidy heap. Water was running in the en-suite shower room and she could hear off-tune singing. She marched in. Pierce had his back to her lathering himself with shower gel. She pulled open the door, reached in and grabbed a handful of his hair, pulling him backwards out of the cubicle to sprawl legs akimbo on the tiled floor.

She jammed the MP5 into his naked groin. She kept her voice low and gravelly. "Where's Roberts?"

Pierce squealed, his eyes wide with fear. He made a grab for the muzzle but she jabbed harder and he squealed again. "No! Please."

"Where?"

"I don't know."

She flipped the muzzle and put a round into the tiles, creasing the fleshy part of his shoulder, before pushing the hot barrel back into his groin. "Next one takes your balls off. *Where?*"

Pierce was sobbing, holding his shoulder as blood oozed between his fingers.

"Last chance."

"Next floor. The office suite, that's where he was last I saw him."

Gill slammed the MP5's butt into the side of Pierce's head.

"Office suite, next floor up," she said to Lacey.

"Thought I asked you to wait."

"You can spank me later. Take the stairs, I'm right behind you."

55

They raced up to the next floor, pausing just long enough for Lacey to duck his head through the fire door to check the corridor was clear.

The found the door marked *'Office, Private'* and stood one on either side. Lacey counted down on his fingers and shouldered the door open. They burst in checking all around. The room was empty.

Gill went to the far side where one of the leather couches was pulled away from the wall. She knelt down and ran her hand over a dark red patch on the carpet. It was still wet. "There's blood here, a big pool of it."

Lacey grunted an acknowledgement and walked behind Pierce's desk where one of the monitors was live showing a view of the corridor.

"They must have seen us coming and legged it," he said.

Gill turned her head and pointed. "That door. There's a blood trail."

Lacey was at her shoulder in seconds. He crashed his foot against the jamb and the lock gave, splintering the thin wood. Another room with a desk and monitor but again empty. Gill slipped past Lacey and pulled open a door leading back to the corridor. Blood drips had pooled next to the threshold. "They waited here for us to pass. They can't be that far ahead."

"Hope that's not wishful thinking," Lacey muttered but the blood was very fresh, the small droplets hadn't dried at the edges.

Gill was already out the door and scanning for more sign. "This way." She ran towards the fire exit taking a left at a dogleg in the corridor. She hadn't taken another two paces when Ling-Ling popped out from an alcove at the far end and blasted two rounds from Aftershave's Sig at her. One round caromed off her helmet and the other smacked into her ceramic epaulette and sent her spinning.

Lacey fired over her falling body but Ling-Ling had dodged back into cover and the bullets smacked into the wall where her head had been a split second earlier.

Lacey dropped to one knee and snapped a glance at Gill. In that split second Ling-Ling appeared again and hit Lacey twice in the chest. He rocked back on his heels and by the time he had regained his balance Ling-Ling had turned and fled through another fire door.

He grabbed Gill's arm. "You okay?"

"My head's ringing and my arm feels as if it's been chopped off at the shoulder. I think the muscle's strained."

"That was a Sig she was using. All that noise might have woken the neighbours."

Gill lurched to her feet. "C'mon, she's getting away."

"I bet that leads down to the service entrance. If we go back we can cut her off. There's one hell of a high brick wall at the back and I guess the only way out is down the service alley at the side of this place."

"She must have someone else with her, from what I could see, she wasn't bleeding," Gill said.

"Yeah, another one at least. Look, I hate splitting forces but maybe you should follow her and I'll make it around the side. If they want to continue this shootout, we can catch them in a crossfire."

Gill nodded. "What are you still doing here? Go!"

Lacey went, sprinting to the staircase and leaping down a flight at a time, hurdling the three muscular Chinese men they had killed and raced through the slot machine filled lobby. He ran along the front of the building and stopped by the corner of the service alley.

"In position."

"Roger that," Gill's slightly breathless voice replied.

"Do you have eyeball?"

"No, but I've found another pool of blood. I guess whoever is bleeding must have needed a rest. Shit!"

Lacey heard the sharp crack. "You hit?"

"No but I've caught up with them. It's Bilic, he's carrying Aftershave but I can't get a shot. Ling-Ling is covering from behind the rubbish bins. They're heading for the Range Rover."

"On my way," Lacey snapped and sprinted the length of the alley to the far corner, it took less than five seconds but in that time the scenario had

329

changed. Bilic had dropped Aftershave in a crumpled heap on the concrete and Ling-Ling was standing over him with the pistol pointed at Aftershave's head. He could just hear her voice. "Stay back or he dies."

Gill was advancing slowly, her MP5 in the aim. She stopped and partly lowered the weapon.

Bilic had scrambled into the Range Rover's driver's seat and started the engine. He leaned over and pushed open the front passenger door before moving the big car up close behind Ling-Ling.

Lacey had a shot and said so.

"Hold fire," Gill said, "in case Ling-Ling's nervous reaction twitches her finger and takes Aftershave's head off."

Ling-Ling took a step back and pulled the passenger door across her body. As she did so she hitched her backside onto the seat, swung her legs up and pulled the Sig's trigger. It was all done so slickly that Gill had no time to react before the car door slammed closed and Bilic accelerated away straight at Lacey.

Gill fired short bursts at the car's rear but did little damage.

Lacey leapt clear onto a pile of black bin bags as the car swept past. He managed two bursts at a rear tyre, one-handed. He knew he'd hit it but the tyre didn't deflate.

He gave a despairing grunt. "Run flats."

"Rick, it's Aftershave, he's been shot."

Lacey levered himself off the bags which had split and spilled rotting kitchen waste over him. He shook it off and went to help.

Gill was on her knees holding both hands over a wound to try to stem the bleeding. Lacey tore the field dressing off his harness and pushed it over the gaping wound. He leaned over and pulled Gill's out too. He pushed that over the first. "Hold that. Is he breathing?"

"Yes, I think so."

"I'm still here," Aftershave croaked. "Can't … get rid of me … that easy."

"We have to get him to hospital." Gill said.

"That you, Petal? Can't see … too well."

Gill was half-laughing, half-crying. "Yes. Just as well, you wouldn't know me in this kit."

"The Discovery is in the car park but I don't have the keys," Lacey said.

"Jacket pocket," Aftershave said.

Lacey fished them out. "One minute."

He dashed to the car and within the time had it parked with engine running and doors open. He tossed his harness and weapons into the back then leant down so that Aftershave could hear him. "I'm going to lift you now and it's going to hurt. Ready?"

There was no reply, he had passed out.

Lacey grunted. "That's a blessing, he won't feel a thing."

With Gill's help he bundled the wounded man into the back of the Discovery. Gill had untied his bonds and his legs flopped to one side.

"The bastards," she said and sniffed.

Lacey unlatched her helmet and pulled off his own. He paused as he saw her tear-stained cheeks. "We'll have to drop him at accident and emergency and then run for it. We can't stay around to field any questions."

Gill pointed to herself. "These suits …?"

"Can't be helped. Let's hope the medics will be too busy to wonder. Leave all the mags and weapons in the car and maybe we'll look like we're from a Star Wars convention."

Gill climbed into the back with Aftershave and pulled his head onto her lap. "Oh, god, look at his face. You know where this hospital is?"

"Unless they've moved it it's on Newton Road. I went there once after I had a fall rock-climbing with the school." He punched the information into the satnav. "Yep, same place. Got it. Hang on."

"Hurry, Rick, he's not breathing too well. I'm afraid he's not going to make it."

56

After they dropped Aftershave into the tender care of the NHS, Lacey drove straight back to the casino to pick up Gill's Mercedes. There was no sign of police activity, the place looked deserted. No one had reported hearing gunshots, the nearest buildings were too far away for the reports to carry. Pierce, if he had regained consciousness, wasn't going to be in any hurry to call the police.

Once in her car Gill called Blake. There was some clearing up to do at the hospital. Any security footage of her and Lacey had to be erased or removed and a cover story invented. The medics would have informed the police, they were bound to with a gunshot wound. The police would need to be told it was a Special Forces operation that was to be kept quiet. Coming from MI6 they were more likely to believe it although they would probably kick up rough over not being informed about an operation on their turf.

Blake agreed to organise it and send his team to Torbay Hospital to deal with the video recordings before the police got their hands on them. He wanted a full report on his desk by close of play in return.

Lacey smelt like a pig sty and she had seen him off with the old anorak that had been left in the car covering the top part of his suit. She drove down to the seafront and parked overlooking the bay while she let the emotion of the morning wash over her.

Her adrenaline had long ceased to pump and the tears flowed for Aftershave. She had got him into this, it was her responsibility. She knew he would not blame her, it was all part of the game but that did not make it any easier to bear. She had his blood on her hands ... literally. She held her fingers up and inspected the brown stains before angrily pushing them into her pockets where she could not see them.

If he died, how would she be able to face Loxl with the news? She mentally kicked herself. She was already burying the little man but he was a fighter who never knew when to give up. He would survive if anyone could.

Her thoughts turned to Lacey. She was holding it together with him but only just. She tried to be detached and not to give her feelings away by being hard-nosed and off-hand. Maybe it was working on him but she was kidding herself. The man was special, she knew, and he had proved it time and again over the past days. A one man army. No wonder the ISPA had brought him out of retirement. He'd be the first *she'd* call in a crisis. A man who, for an American, knew much more about British Special Forces practices than he should. And that English accent on the boat; it had come so easily, so perfectly Home Counties. An enigma.

She let her mind roll back over the hours. The free-fall para drop onto the ship where Lacey had saved her from going over the side, its strange layout with its secret corridors and laboratory. She was a scientist, a chemical engineer, but she had never seen a lab quite like that one. Totally sealed against outside contamination? Or sealed to prevent whatever chemicals they were working with leaking into the ship's air-con system? Maybe they'd never know.

Blake had told her that a full anti-pirate maritime interdiction operation was proposed to retake the ship with the Special Boat Service already working on a plan, complicated by the fact that the ship was heading at full speed out of the English Channel and would reach international waters before they had time to mount an operation. It would not stop the operation but it would mean that prosecuting any offenders would be impossible under British law. Gill had a grim smile at that, there were no pirates to prosecute, only those in Lacey's imagination. Privately, Gill hoped that when the SBS stopped the ship a more thorough search might persuade the government to impound it. It would not end the West Country drug problem but it sure would slow it down for a long time to come.

The legality of the situation bothered her. It didn't appear to worry Lacey and maybe that was the ISPA's modus operandi, get the job done quickly and effectively and let someone else take the credit … or the blame. Any evidence of their part in the morning's events was being systematically removed with a hint of Special Forces involvement which would keep curiosity at bay. Should word of it ever reach the press they could be fobbed off with need to know. Neither the SAS nor the SBS ever talked about operations and would neither admit nor deny taking part. That thought eased her mind a little; it was less likely she would be thrown to the wolves if expediency required a tethered goat.

She started the engine and tested her shoulder by turning the steering wheel. It hurt but she could drive without embarrassing herself. She checked the dash clock and was amazed that it wasn't yet ten-o-clock. The morning had seemed to last forever with time elasticising. Less than eight hours since they had parachuted onto the *New Venture's* deck. It seemed like a lifetime.

The drive back was more sedate, there was more traffic to contend with and a shoulder that made turning the wheel too quickly a painful experience that kept her within the speed limits, although she was aching to get out of the stifling suit and into a hot shower.

The wind was still blowing hard, bringing with it squally showers that lashed the windscreen for a few minutes before dying away. She parked in the marina car park and waited for another vigorous squall to send people running for cover before she attempted the walk to the *Andrea Two*, hoping that no one would notice the odd ceramic greaves below the hem of her anorak.

She climbed aboard and dumped the dripping anorak on the aft deck before shuffling into the saloon and collapsing on a bench seat. She took a deep breath and sat upright. She was dog-tired and needed help to peel her out of the suit. "Rick?" she called.

"Below."

She levered herself to her feet and went to find him. "Where?"

"My cabin."

She pushed open the door. He was standing inside the en-suite shower cubicle with his suit half off, sleeves and body dangling from his waist. He had a cloth in his hand and was trying to sponge blood off his side that had run in rivulets down to his beltline.

She sucked in a breath and pulled the cloth from his hand. She dabbed some of the blood away but it was still seeping from a small hole. She gave it a closer look. "I think there's a piece of metal still in there."

"Wondered why it stung," he said. "Can you get it out?"

She poked the swelling with a finger and he drew in a sharp breath. "Painful?"

"Just get it out. There's a first aid box in the locker."

"It'll hurt."

"It already hurts."

"It'll hurt more. You sure you don't need a hospital?"

"I'll cope."

Gill pulled a wry face. "Okay, if you're sure." She pulled out the medical kit and found a pair of tweezers, a scalpel handle and blades in tin foil. She fitted a blade. "You'd better sit down."

The splinter had penetrated a muscle and she could just see one end of it. Lacey wasn't heavily muscled but he was in good condition and the flesh was firm although creased with old scar tissue. She pressed on either side of the wound as gently as she could to open it. "Stand by, sport. You want something to bite on?"

He held up his right hand with its stunted little finger. "I've had worse."

"I can see. Hold that cloth beneath the wound to stem the blood." She dug with the scalpel which increased the blood flow and made him grunt. It was enough for her to get a grip with the tweezers and the piece came out at the second attempt. She held it up with a triumphant grin. "Got it."

Sweat was running down Lacey's upper body and his teeth were clenched tight. He tried a deep breath but stopped halfway. He released it slowly. "There's some antiseptic powder in there and some wound dressings. Would you mind doing the honours?"

"You probably need a couple of stitches in that," Gill said as she found the items she needed. "Might be a while before it stops bleeding."

"I'll live with it."

She pushed the pressure pad against the wound and stood close to him as she wound the bandage around his ribs. "Phew, and you need a bloody shower, you still stink."

"Thanks for reminding me. You don't smell of Yves Saint Laurent either."

She laughed and tied off the knot. "Can you help me out of this suit, it seems to be stuck to me?" She raised her arms and grimaced as her shoulder twinged. "Ouch! I'll have to remember to be careful."

He pointed. "What's that under your wrist band?"

She paused and thought. "Oh, I'd forgotten about that. It's the gold nugget from Pierce's display case." She flipped it out with a thumb and held it up to the light. "He says it's worth ten grand." She frowned and took a closer look. "I'm no geologist but I'd be surprised if this was worth ten pence. Judging by the colour, I think it's iron pyrite, fool's gold."

57

Lacey took the nugget and tossed it in his palm. "I'm no geologist either but I read somewhere that pyrite looks more like brass with streaks of greeny-black. This does match that description. Who's the fool, I wonder?"

"I'm not sure but I'm wondering how long I have to stay sucked into this suit," Gill said.

She turned her back, Lacey leaned across and pulled the Velcro tabs apart. He peeled back the material around her neck as far down as her shoulder blades. "You should be okay now to manage the rest."

She turned her head and gave him an arch smile. "Don't be shy, Rick, you've seen me in my underwear already. My shoulder hurts like blazes and I still need a hand."

"You're sure?"

"C'mon, we're both grown-ups."

"That's what worries me," Lacey muttered. He knelt and unlaced her boots, gingerly pulling one off at a time. Then he stood. "You'd better stand up too with your back to me."

Gill did as she was asked and he slowly peeled the suit down over her torso and both her arms. It came free with a sucking sound and she was left with a sheen of perspiration on her body.

"They sure make these things a tight fit," she said as he eased the suit over her hips and down her thighs.

He put her in a sitting position and knelt again to work the material down her calves and ankles. "It was a rush job. They made it a little too snug for you, maybe you were underestimating your measurements." He wanted to make a joke of it, he was feeling uncomfortable. He shouldn't have but he was finding her more and more attractive and it was disturbing him. He rolled the heavy suit into a ball and stood. Gill was frowning at him.

"Are you saying I'm putting on weight?"

"Oh, I wouldn't dare, ma'am. You look pretty good to me." He said it before he could stop himself and immediately wished he hadn't. Her bra strap had slipped off one shoulder and showed a thin puckered scar. He nodded at it desperate to hide his faux-pas. "Looks as though you've had a set-to with a bullet."

She turned her head and touched the scar with her chin. "Got caught in a crossfire. I didn't have the benefit of one of those suits." Her face tightened. "Lost a friend that day." She pulled the strap back in place to cover it. "I could have plastic surgery but I keep it as a reminder not to get careless in future." She nodded at him. "What about you, you have your fair share of mementos?"

He held up his hand again and waved it at his bandaged side. "Both AK47. I lost some good friends then too. The leg was a bomb; one time I got a little careless." He had a sudden flashback to when his cottage in Wales was booby-trapped by a former Stasi assassin. It had nearly killed him. If it hadn't been for Andee who was quickly on the

341

scene, he'd have died in the ditch where the explosion had thrown him.

Gill leaned forward and gripped his arm. "You all right?"

He shook his head to clear the images. "Yeah, sure." He put his free hand over hers. "Go get your shower and get dressed, ma'am. We still have work to do."

She leaned into him and kissed him on the cheek. "Yes, boss."

Gill was again the Vogue model-like Missus Gill Arnold when she found Lacey in the saloon watching his laptop screen with an intense expression on his face. He angled the screen so that they could both see it. "This is live drone footage," he said.

She sat beside him and watched as two Merlin and two Wildcat helicopters circled the *New Venture.* The *Norfolk,* stood off to one side recalled from sea training in nearby coastal waters. Two of the *Norfolk's* inflatable ribs were braving the lumpy seas alongside the tanker's hull.

Gill unconsciously put a hand on Lacey's thigh. "What's happening?"

Lacey hardly noticed the intimate touch, he was too engrossed in the action. "The SBS are about to board the ship. They'll have to fast-rope out of the Merlins, there's no way the guys in the ribs can get a line up on that deck. The ship is still on full speed and whatever they do it's going to be hairy."

"Where are these pictures coming from?"

Lacey gave her a swift glance before riveting his eyes back on the screen. "Your pal at MI6 patched me into the loop. Thought we'd like to know what was happening."

"That was good of him," Gill said. "Blake's not all bad."

Lacey nodded at the screen as the camera zoomed in on one of the Merlins. "They're trying an approach. The two Wildcats will run interference."

Gill pointed. "Look, there are men on the tanker's deck."

Lacey squinted, trying to focus on the vibrating image. Then he frowned. "Hell, two of those guys are carrying a MANPAD; looks like an FN6. Those bastards mean business."

Gill frowned in turn. "MANPAD?"

"Yeah, Man Portable Air defence. It's an anti-aircraft missile works with infra-red. If they target those choppers at least one will go down. They're setting up."

The circling drone's camera zoomed out to take in a wider view. The second Merlin was hammering in from the port side, turning to give the door gunner a view of the deck. Red tracer lashed down like a mini-Guy Fawkes display as rounds ricocheted off the metal decking and pipes. The two man missile team went down, pieces flying from their bodies as the heavy 7.62mm rounds tore them apart. Other men on the deck opened up with rifles and machine guns at the passing helicopter and it quickly pulled away trailing a thin streak of smoke.

Gill tightened her fingers on Lacey's thigh. "The chopper's been hit."

They watched as the damaged Merlin circled towards the *Norfolk* to land heavily on its helipad.

The second Merlin and snipers in the two Wildcats put down heavy accurate and concentrated fire on the tankers deck and drove the gunman into the shelter of the superstructure where they were pinned down and then driven back inside.

The Merlin swooped in to hover over the foredeck. Two ropes were dropped and men could be seen sitting in the doors on either side when the aircraft suddenly jerked up and veered off rapidly. The two ribs that had been keeping pace with the tanker pulled away too.

The tanker appeared to shudder and white water gushed up in plumes along its length. It slowed quickly and began to go bow down into the sea.

"They've blown the bottom out of her," Lacey said. "They've no intention of being boarded."

Gill's fingers tightened even more on his thigh.

Lacey put his hand over hers. "This isn't great for my blood pressure ... nor my circulation."

Gill seemed genuinely surprised and allowed him to lift her hand away. She folded it into her lap and nodded at the screen. "What about the crew?"

"If they get into the water the ribs will pick them up but I've a feeling there won't be many survivors."

"Suicide mission?"

He closed the laptop with a snap. "Wouldn't lay odds against it. They are making sure there's no evidence and no one to talk. All we've got is the video we shot and the Chinese could claim it was nothing to do with them. The ship is registered in Liberia and there will be no paper trail giving proof of Chinese ownership. The finger will be pointed at the Colombian cartels. Anyway, we'll have nothing to link the ship to the drugs trade, nothing that can be used without us standing up on our hind legs which we won't be allowed to do; not even if the trial was held in camera. I guess we've blown it."

Gill shook her head. "Not entirely. There's Pierce, Bilic and Ling-Ling to deal with." She stood and grabbed her handbag with the P7 in it. "I'm going to pay Pierce another call. Coming?"

58

Lacey couldn't decide when the relationship had turned Gill from junior assistant to equal partner but he liked it. He knew Gill was capable and he was happy for her to take the lead. He had known many strong and capable women, that was the way he liked them, and Gill was proving to be up there amongst the best. She had the bit between her teeth and wasn't about to spit it out.

There was one more test she had to pass. It was nothing to do with her being a woman, it was the same test he expected all the people he fought alongside to pass before he was completely at ease with them. He was a hard taskmaster, he admitted it openly. His soldiers had called him Spartan behind his back because he was hard on them but even harder on himself; that and the fact they probably couldn't differentiate between Troy and Sparta. The thought made him smile and Gill caught it.

"What's funny?"

"Just an idle thought."

"What was that?"

"Maybe we ought to get some sleep before we go."

Gill grimaced. "We can sleep when we're dead. Have a cup of your cowboy coffee, it'll spark up your brain cells."

Lacey pulled a wry face. "Why the rush?"

"Pierce is reeling. He's had his place turned over, his security men killed and his gold nugget taken. He'll be on a downer and now's the time to catch him before he has time to pull himself together."

Lacey grinned. "Fair enough." He opened a drawer, took out his Sig in its IWB holster and pushed it inside his belt. The muffler he put into a jacket pocket so that he had some weight to swing the jacket wide if he needed to reach the pistol quickly. He buttoned the jacket on the central button and nodded. *"Lay on MacDuff."*

Gill raised an eyebrow. "You're quoting Macbeth at *me* now?"

"Seems to fit the mood."

"You like Shakespeare?"

"Some. I like the comedies, not so keen on the tragedies. I need to be taken out of myself sometimes and maybe the tragedies remind me too much of who I am."

Gill smiled and it softened the battle mask that was beginning to form on her face. "I can identify with that." The mask slipped back in place as quickly as it lifted. "Let's go, before we miss the boat."

For the second time that day they drove the route into Torquay and parked in the casino car park. It was no longer empty. A locksmith's truck was parked near to the double entrance doors and there was a red Jaguar sideways on across three bays.

The locksmith and his mate paid them no attention as they sidled past a hastily written sign which said closed for repairs. There was no one on security and Gill pressed the lift call button to reach the first floor.

They found Pierce in his office with Shelley tying a rough bandage around his head. His arm was in a makeshift sling.

Gill feigned surprise. "Whoa! Looks as if you've been in the wars, Derek."

Shelley gave her a sullen stare. "What do you want?"

"We were passing and thought we'd drop in for a chat."

"I don't want to talk to you," Piece said. "Your blokes did this, didn't they?"

Gill spread her arms in mute denial. "I don't know what you're talking about, Derek."

Pierce jerked his chin at Lacey. "Maybe you don't but I bet he does."

Lacey raised his eyebrows and sat on the arm of a settee. "Don't have a clue."

The denial passed right over Pierce's head. "You tryin' to scare me out, or somethin'? Well it ain't workin'."

"Scare you out? Why would I want to do that?" Lacey said and smiled the kind of smile that had icicles hanging from it.

"Your mate Roberts. He said you wanted to buy me out."

"Did he now. I wonder what gave him that idea."

"Don't play the innocent with me. I know your game, you and your New York mates. Well I've got friends too, see."

"You're playing out of your league, Derek," Lacey said.

Gill put her arm out towards him. "Take it easy, Rick, you know what you're like when you lose your temper."

Shelley was looking from one to the other with a worried frown. "What's this about buying the place … Derek?"

"It's what I heard from his mate. He's eyeing it up."

"Speaking of Mister Roberts, what have you done with him," Gill asked.

Pierce jerked as if stung. "Nothin'."

"He came here last night but didn't come home."

"Nothin' to do with me. Maybe he found a bird to shack up with."

"Tristan's not what you'd call photogenic, is he, Rick? Not the sort to have an easy time of it with the ladies."

Lacey gave her a humourless grin. "Back end of the Staten Island ferry. Never known him get laid easy."

"I don't know, do I? What am I, his keeper?" Pierce said.

"What about your two friends, Derek? Bill and Ling-Ling. Would they have a clue?" Gill asked as if the idea had only just occurred to her.

Pierce shifted uncomfortably in his seat but an ugly gleam had come into his eye. "Maybe. They was here last night. They was talking to him for a while. Why don't you go and ask them?"

"Where can we find them?" Lacey asked.

"Bill's probably workin' at the quarry out near Buckfastleigh. Ling-Ling has a room here but I ain't seen her since last night. Don't know where she is."

"Okay, Derek. We'll find the place." He stood. "Let's go, Gill." He turned and walked out the door.

Gill gave Shelley a leer, leaned over the desk and whispered. "Don't forget our little business arrangement, Derek." She sauntered towards the door but stopped at the threshold. "Oh, I notice your little gold nugget is missing. Did you lose it?"

Shelley was looking daggers but Gill ignored her and stared at Derek with an expectant look.

"Somebody took it, it's gone missin'."

"Oh! What a shame but I expect you can get another one. Where did that one come from?"

"Not that it's any business of yours but it was Bill's. He's gonna hit the fuckin' roof when he finds out it's been taken."

"Well, good luck with that," Gill said and blew him a kiss. "Ciao, baby."

She part closed the door and stood outside to hear Shelley snap at him. "What was that about a business arrangement with that tart?"

"Not now, babe. I've gotta ring Bill, let him know those two are on their way. He's gonna be ready for 'em and no mistake."

Gill pulled a grim face, delved into her shoulder bag and pulled out the second burner phone. Lacey gave her an enquiring look but she ignored him. She punched 999 into the handset as they walked to the lift.

"Hello, I need the police," her voice sounded shaky. "Hello, is that the police. I've heard screams and something that sounded like shots as I was walking past the Golden Nugget, the casino … yes the new one in Torquay, hurry they sound as if they're killing each other … no … got to run … I think they've seen me." She cut the connection with a satisfied smile. The lift doors opened and she led Lacey in. "Leaf out of your book. I don't think they've had time to move the bodies. Our Derek and Shelley are in for a fine time explaining all that away. I don't think he'll be dealing drugs from here for a long time to come."

She wiped the burner phone, crushed the sim card and dumped the bits in a bin at a layby on the way back to Kingswear.

59

"I said he'd lose it." Gill was in the passenger seat of the Discovery. She looked across at Lacey and saw the slight smile on his face. "What's amusing you now?"

"The way you dropped him in it with Shelley and the police. He'll have a hard time talking his way out of all that."

She smiled in turn, remembering the look on Shelley's face. "If looks could kill. Just a little payback for Derek, although I'm not sure who Shelley blames the most, me or her shit of a husband."

"Don't mince your words, Gill, tell it like it is."

Gill laughed. She liked the way he was relaxing with her, enough to crack a joke. "Maybe we can see some light now."

He screwed up his eyes as if contemplating a disappointing reply. "I'm not sure how much light we can see yet. It's pretty obvious that whatever happened to Forrestal was at the hands of those who run the casino but we don't yet know why for sure, or who pulled the trigger. Those three guards at the casino were all armed with the same type of pistol, the same calibre, as the one that killed the commander, the QSW-06, 5.8 mm."

"You seem to know a lot about Chinese military kit, Rick."

"Like you, one of my jobs as a desk jockey for the ISPA was to keep up-to-date on hand-held, shoulder-mounted, arms development, just in case our people came up against them. It could have been boring but I enjoyed the research."

Gill gave him a long shrewd look. "There's something else ...?"

He screwed up his face again and this time ran a hand through his greying hair. "It's that piece of pyrite that's bothering me. They seem to have a working gold mine out at Buckfastleigh so why give Pierce a piece of fool's gold and pretend it's the real thing. Why the deception?"

Gill gave it some thought and came up with an obvious conclusion. "Maybe Bilic is ripping Pierce off."

"I wouldn't put it past him, he's a nasty piece of work, but there's got to be more to it otherwise it doesn't make sense. If the mine is producing gold I can understand the security they've got. But if all they're digging out is pyrite there's got to be another reason for armed guards and electrified fences. It's been nagging me for a while but this morning's revelation has brought it to a head. I did some research on gold prospecting on Dartmoor and found that there's never been that much to it. A few ounces of dust over the centuries but not enough in recent years to make it worthwhile mining for it. The recent finds in Scotland and Wales kind of made me think it was possible to find gold in commercial quantities down here but history tends to say otherwise."

Gill leaned back in her seat and studied his face. "You think it's a cover operation?"

"I'm beginning to think so."

"Then let's go and take another look."

Lacey turned his face towards her. "Listen, ma'am, I'm just about bushed and so must you be. We'll get back to the boat and take some rest. I've put my suit on charge and I'll do the same for yours. We'll go in tonight, when it's nice and dark. They'll be expecting us, we know that, but they won't know when and they won't know how. If we can surprise them it will make our job easier. Extreme prejudice. We know what we can expect from them."

She knew Lacey was right. Tiredness had crept up on her and the soporific hum of the tyres had made her eyes droop. The thought of getting back at the people who had injured Aftershave was pushing her hard but a few hours rest made sense. It would give her time to catch up on the promised report to Blake, check with the hospital and get some sleep. The last bit sounded good. She closed her eyes but was jerked awake when the Bluetooth car phone rang.

Lacey answered it.

"It's Jack, sir."

"Yes, Jack, what is it?"

"That query you put in hand about the woman called Ling-Ling."

"Go ahead."

"Sorry it's taken so long but we couldn't find anything on her. No documentation at all, no National Insurance number, no NHS number, no tax returns, no immigration status … nothing. Then the brigadier had an idea to look further afield. We found an entry on an MI6 file which could fit the bill. There's a captain in the Chinese Peoples' Liberation Army that's a possibility. It's unusual for China to allow its women soldiers into front-line roles but it's becoming more common. From what we could find this woman is one of the first to join an elite Special Forces unit called *Oriental Sword*. She's a skilled linguist and has trained in Qigong, the martial arts they teach them. According to one report, she can shoot the balls off a fly at a hundred metres. She's also quite a stunner to look at and is an ace at gymnastic dancing. That sound like your Ling-Ling?"

Gill remembered the double-taps that had hit her, the two snap shots that hit Lacey's chest and the smooth lissom way Ling-Ling had slinked into the Range Rover.

"Jack, this is Sunset. I'd say that sums up our Ling-Ling to a 'T'."

"Glad to be of help. Seems like you'll have your hands full with that one. Good luck."

Lacey cut the call. "That answers some questions and raises some more."

"Like why are the Chinese sending one of their top people here," Gill said.

Lacey nodded. "That's one of them."

They left the car in the marina car park and walked the pontoons to the boat.

"I'll put the kettle on," Gill said and kicked off her shoes.

Lacey disappeared below but was up just as the kettle boiled.

Gill held up a teapot. "Found this in the locker. You'll have a proper British brew today."

Lacey smiled but it was a tired one. "Sure, why not." He was about to sit when the Sat Phone warbled its distinctive call. He reached for it and listened.

Gill saw his face tighten and his jaw clench. He closed his eyes and said. "Yes, thanks for letting me know."

She poured the tea and handed him a mug.

He put the mug on the chart table and stood silently staring out over the river.

"Bad news?"

He turned to her and she could see his eyes misting. "It's my wife, Andee, she's gone missing."

"Missing from where?"

"Mozambique. The Médicin Sans Frontières' camp was raided by rebels. They took her. We lost two men in the firefight."

Gill leaned forward and gripped his hand. "I'm so sorry. What are you going to do?"

"I'm not much for religion ... but ... pray, I guess. That was the general on the phone, he's sending two teams to Mozambique as soon as they can get them on a plane but it will be days before they arrive. The rebels could disappear in that time and I'm not sure what good they can do when they get there."

She pulled on his hand. "Come and sit down, drink your tea while it's hot. Old English custom when things go bad."

He nodded but she could see his thoughts were elsewhere. She guessed what was going through his mind. "No use blaming yourself, Rick."

He looked up and a spark of life returned to his eyes. "No, you're right. I couldn't have made her stay even if I'd tried, which I didn't. She would have gone anyway no matter what I said. She's like that, driven by a need to be the best damn gunshot wound surgeon ever."

"Speaking of gunshot wounds," Gill said. "I need to check on Aftershave. I have to call the hospital."

Lacey nodded and waved a hand.

She googled the number and rang. "Hello, I think you have my brother in your hospital … his name? His name is Señor Tristan Roberts." She waited whilst the receptionist scrolled through her list and then replied. "Oh, yes. You're his sister you say?"

"Si, yes, his sister. He is on holiday from Colombia."

"I'll put you through to the ward."

The phone rang and was answered by a breezy voice. "Ward sister."

"I am ringing about my brother, Señor Roberts."

"Mister Roberts … the one who was brought in early this morning?"

"Si, yes, so I believe. I must know how he is."

"Well … I'm very sorry … he's taken a turn for the worse and he's been rushed into surgery. You'd best prepare yourself for some bad news. The surgeon isn't very hopeful I'm afraid."

60

Gill broke the connection and turned to Lacey. "He's in surgery. No more than a 50-50 chance." She choked back a sob. "All my fault, I should never have asked him to come."

Lacey held out an arm and she went to lay her head on his shoulder. "They say Misery makes company, don't they?"

"You told me not to blame myself," Lacey whispered into her hair, "now I'm saying the same to you. It's not your fault." He tightened his arm around her shoulders and she gripped the front of his shirt in a tight fist as her body spasmed in little convulsions.

They sat like that for several minutes. He could feel her warm tears soaking through his shirt and he held her tight until she stopped shaking.

She turned her eyes up to him. "Rick, take me to bed. I don't want to be alone, not tonight."

If he had been stronger, if things had been different, he might have refused but the past days crowded in on him, his sense of loss and the emptiness of his life. He could not, would not, refuse her cry for comfort, he needed it as badly as she did. He had nearly lost Andee all those years ago by refusing to let go of the past and he would not make the same mistake again. But however he dressed it up, it did not alter the fact that he found Gill so attractive, so alluring, that he finally admitted to himself her plea had pre-empted what he was already thinking.

He took out his mobile phone and set the alarm to 23.00 hours. He held out his hand to Gill and led her down to her cabin with its king size bed.

The alarm woke her. Lacey had gone and the huge bed was empty. She stretched and yawned, then smiled as memories returned.

The cabin door opened and Lacey came in with two mugs of coffee held in one hand. He sat on the edge of the bed and handed her one. She looked at him over the rim as she sipped.

"No regrets?"

He smiled and shook his head. "Never."

She crinkled her nose. "Me neither." She sat up and let the duvet slide off her breasts.

He grinned. "I think you're wrong about your cup size," he said.

She snorted a laugh and tried to hit him with a pillow without spilling the drink but it was a half-hearted attempt that missed.

He stood and glanced at his watch. "Fifteen minutes and I'll come back to help you on with the suit."

"Rick?"

"Yes, ma'am?"

"Thanks ... for the coffee."

"Sure. Fifteen minutes, okay?"

He left to take Gill's suit off the charger where the batteries for the electronic systems had been topped up. The infra-red system was greedy and it was used sparingly to save the batteries. He put on his own suit before checking his watch. His laptop pinged an incoming email. He frowned and opened the cover. The message made him shiver.

He went below and knocked on Gill's cabin door.

"Come in, Rick." She was standing by the shower room in her La Perla underwear. Her hair was damp and she was towelling it, careless of her semi-nakedness. She had a natural poise and grace that was entrancing. He held his breath as he watched her, just for a second reliving their lovemaking.

She dropped the towel on the wet floor and smiled. "Time to get into this version of the Iron Maiden?"

He held up the suit. "More like the Maid of Orleans putting on her armour."

"Let's hope not, I'd hate to end up like her."

"Not in this suit. It's totally flameproof and heatproof. As long as there are no gaps at your wrists and ankles between the gloves and the boots you could walk into a blast furnace and not feel a thing."

"You're joking."

"No, I'm not. I was buried under white phosphorous and came out without a singed hair."

Gill pulled an incredulous face. "Seems you've led an exciting life."

He helped her on with the suit and she wriggled as he closed it up.

"Seems less snug." She turned and grinned at him over her shoulder. "Maybe that exercise earlier did even more good than I thought."

"The neoprene lining tends to give a little with wearing. It's normal."

She wrinkled her nose. "At least you could agree with me."

He gave her a half smile but it soon faded. "I'm in work mode. Come up, I've got something to show you."

He could tell Gill was about to make another wisecrack but she seemed to think better of it as the underlying seriousness in his voice hit home and her face sobered. He led her up to the saloon where his laptop was open and lit up. He pointed "Read that."

Gill sat and ran her eyes over the email.

Dear Brigadier Reid,

We have taken a look at the video footage that you emailed to us and the scientists here are of the firm opinion that the laboratory in question is of a type used in the manufacture, development and study of chemical and biological agents. The containment precautions are such that they would, in normal circumstances, prevent any accidental release of contaminants and are similar to those we employ here.

We hope this information is useful. If we can be of any further assistance please do not hesitate to contact us.

Porton Down Biological and Chemical Threats Laboratory.

Gill turned her head and stared at Lacey. "What does this mean?"

"That the ship was a floating biological and chemical weapons development unit. It was no wonder they sank her rather than let her be boarded. After Covid-19 was suspected of leaking out of the lab in Wuhan it would make sense for the Chinese to move their labs into isolated places, then if anything was to leak out it could be contained, for instance, to a ship's company. A ship could also be sunk if the contagion got out of hand."

Gill bit her lip. "Nasty. I thought the World Health Organisation had given the Chinese the all-clear."

"They did but they waited too long to go in and the report was overseen by the Chinese government themselves. The jury's still out on the verdict that the virus was manufactured at the lab in Wuhan. If it was, I believe it was accidentally released. Even so the Chinese will move heaven and earth to keep the fact they are engineering such viruses covered up."

"But what the hell was that ship doing here?"

"There's an answer to that but I don't much like it," Lacey said.

It was as if Gill read his mind again. "What if they were bringing more ashore than just Pierce's drugs?"

"Collected by Bilic in his Range Rover," Lacey continued.

"And taken to his well-protected quarry on Dartmoor," Gill finished.

To do what with and when? Lacey thought. The previous pandemic had caused the world huge problems. Viruses were like dirty bombs only far more effective. Weapons of mass disruption they were termed. If another pandemic was to happen with a newly engineered virus, upon which the existing vaccines would be ineffective, the country and probably a large swathe of the developed world would suffer tens of thousands more deaths, be bankrupted, left financially, possibly literally, defenceless and ripe for takeover. It was too awful a thought to contemplate but he could see the logic only too plainly; the lesson not lost on the calculations of military strategists.

He pulled on his gloves, picked up the heavy holdalls containing their weapons, helmets and change of clothes. He tilted his head at the distant car park. "Time we went to find out for ourselves just what Bilic had in that package."

61

They left the Discovery in the same place that Lacey had parked it previously, hidden up a side track that appeared not to have been used for months. He called up Jack, sitting in the belly of the Skyvan, to check he was recording. If the man was put out by being called from his bed in the middle of the night he gave no indication.

Lacey led the way to the gap beneath the fence. He had come prepared this time with a thick branch to prop up the lower strands of wire for their now much bulkier bodies to squeeze under.

Gill dropped onto her back, fish-tailed under the wire and took up a defensive position as Lacey followed. With night vision on she did not need the light from the lamp above the Portacabins, she could see well enough.

Lacey squirmed up to her elbow.

"Clear," she said.

He grunted an acknowledgement, climbed to his feet and ran to the edge of the quarry workings beneath a towering mound of spoil. She watched as he took up a fire position.

"Go," he said inside her helmet. She moved to take up another position closer to the temporary buildings. The old infantry mantra of one foot on the ground springing into her mind like the memory of a long-lost friend. Lacey covered her as she moved as she had covered him. How relevant it was in these suits, impervious to all but the heaviest and highest velocity rounds, escaped her but Lacey had insisted they take every care, briefing her minutely during the journey on what to expect and how they would deal with every scenario that his imagination and experience could provide. She smiled at the thought, she could feel the adrenaline coursing through her bloodstream and was both excited and a little apprehensive.

Bilic had been forewarned. He was an experienced field commander and knew the score. There would be surprises; hopefully more for Bilic and Ling-Ling than for them. She scanned the immediate area through the MP5's optic sight and saw nothing but the flit of moths caught in the glare of the lamp.

"Clear," she said to Lacey.

He started to move forward. She saw his foot kick against something. He stopped, crouched down and gripped whatever it was holding it in front of his visor.

Jack was on the radio immediately. "It's a SID," he said. "Seismic Intruder Detector. They know you're there."

As he spoke a flash lit up the sky from the rim of the quarry three hundred metres away and a rocket propelled grenade ploughed into the spoil above Lacey's head sending shale and metal fragments flying. A second missile seared over Gill's position and exploded in an airburst which rattled shrapnel off the back of her helmet.

"Get to the buildings," Lacey snapped.

Gill pushed herself to her feet and sprinted into the cover of the Portacabins. She thought it unlikely the RPG operators would demolish their own quarters but who knew?

A third missile airburst above where she had been and then Lacey skidded in beside her in a shower of gravel.

"They want to play rough," he said.

She had to smile at that. Their weapons did not have the range to take on the RPG teams, they would have to grin and bear it.

The Portacabin door burst open and a man stepped out screaming into his headset. He saw the pair of them squatting in the lee of the building and swung his weapon down. Gill and Lacey fired together and the man toppled off the short flight of steps into the dirt.

Lacey was carrying a webbing haversack over his shoulders. He had picked it out of a holdall with the weapons but had not confided its contents to her. He dragged it round in front of him and undid both buckles.

He nodded at the Portacabin's door. "Don't let whoever's in there get out."

As Gill stood guard he crawled under the cabins, where the drainage pipes fed down into a septic tank buried in the ground. Gill could not see what he was doing but it took him a minute to complete. He crawled out beside her.

"When I say go, run like hell towards the mine entrance over there. It's about fifty metres and you need to cover it in five seconds."

Gill was about to say you've got to be kidding, when he shouted "*GO!*" She launched herself forward, running as fast as she could in the heavy armour. A missile whooshed over her head and she felt a shove in the back as it exploded. Then Lacey ran alongside and grabbed her elbow, propelling her headfirst into the mine entrance. She landed face down with Lacey on top of her. She turned her head to see the Portacabin seem to shrink then expand before huge pieces flew skyward. The noise of the explosion, when it came, hit her at the same time as the shock wave. Debris blew in through the mine entrance and covered them both in dust and pieces of plastic and insulation.

Lacey rolled off her and she twisted to face him. "What the fuck was that?"

"PE4," he said. "Thought it might come in handy."

"Full of surprises, aren't you?"

"Just a precaution. You never know when you're going to need a few demolition charges. It's taken care of their control centre, it's going to be a guessing game for them now." He swivelled to his feet, shouldered his MP5 and began the Special Forces shuffle along the mine tunnel, taking small steps, bent forward into the weapon, eyes focused on the optic sight. Gill kept tight behind him mimicking his actions. He called Jack but got no reply, the rock walls blocking the signal.

He stopped and two brass cartridge cases ejected from the slot on his MP5. "One down," he said and moved on.

Gill stepped over the still twitching body. The man was a European wearing hefty goggles that had been smashed by Lacey's bullets. "They have night vision."

"We have Streamlights," Lacey countered, tapping the powerful white light torch mounted beneath his barrel. "It'll flare out their goggles."

They rounded a bend in the tunnel and were met by a hail of automatic fire that chipped lumps off the tunnel walls and smacked into Lacey's helmet and chest plate. He fell back against Gill and wheezed. "Damn, that'll bruise."

He switched on the Streamlight and returned fire. Gill dropped to a knee beside him and added the weight of her firepower to the battle. Three men had taken up positions behind the sluice but they were too dazzled by the white beams to return accurate fire.

Lacey moved forward, firing as he went, double-tapping rounds into the fallen bodies on the far side of the sluice. One man stood upright and fired blindly in Lacey's direction.

Gill hit him four times but the man refused to drop. She remembered Lacey's advice and went for the slash of a mouth visible as a black line in her sights. The MP5 clicked open on an empty magazine. "Dry," she yelled.

The man was still firing as his sight adjusted, turning as he did so. Lacey vaulted the sluice, ducked, pulled his knife from its calf sheath, straightened and rammed the blade into the man's neck. The man swung the barrel of his carbine and

369

Lacey caught it under his left arm as he worked the knife through the man's vocal cords and out through his throat. He let the man fall, his legs drumming a tattoo as he clutched at his neck in a vain attempt to stem the blood.

Lacey pulled the carbine out of his fist and dropped it into the running water.

Gill replaced her magazine with one from her thigh strap. "Sorry, should have counted the rounds fired."

Lacey changed his own mag. "Learn and live. They're wearing body armour, our nine-mil won't penetrate." As he spoke he was running a gloved hand around the frame of the metal door. He tried opening it but it was firmly locked. "No padlock or keyhole, that's odd. It can only be opened or closed from the inside."

Gill's knee knocked against something that fell with a dull thud followed by the glug of liquid running free. "What's that?" She looked down at some five-gallon jerry cans that were stacked in a corner.

"I can smell gasoline," Lacey said. "Those cans weren't here the last time I came."

Gill held up a hand for silence. She had good hearing despite the muffling effect of the helmet and she could hear boots crunching on the gravel in the tunnel. The noise stopped around the bend where the boot wearers could not be seen. A voice called.

"You come out. You have nowhere to go. Come out and maybe I won't kill you like you kill my Tigers."

"Bilic?" How does he know?"

Lacey pointed at the camera high up in a corner. "Maybe you should come in and get us," he called.

Bilic chuckled but there was no humour in the sound, only menace. "You too chicken, eh? Well how you like be fried chicken?

Gill heard a scrape and a hissing sound. Light flickered in the tunnel. A boat flare was tossed hard into the cavern. It bounced off a wall and rolled towards the spreading pool of petrol.

62

"Oxygen on, get in the trough," Lacey screamed.

He grabbed Gill around the waist and hefted her bodily into the wooden sluice with its swift-flowing water. He fell in behind her as the rolling flare reached the petrol fumes. The fuel ignited and the flame shot along the stream until it reached the overturned can. It exploded, bouncing off the wall and spraying burning fuel in a great flaming arc that ignited the other cans in the stack. The explosion was not so much a bang as a dull roaring thud as liquid flame engulfed the cavern setting fire to every flammable item it touched and sucking air in through the open tunnel in a howling hurricane.

The water in the sluice began to bubble in the heat. The flow was cut off as the trestle carrying the sluice collapsed. Lacey rolled out of the broken trough and dragged Gill into a corner as close to the floor as they could get.

Gill's helmet banged against his. "Thought you said these suits were fireproof."

"They are but the ammo in the mags isn't. I didn't want it cooking off."

The fire was losing its intensity as the fuel burned away but still licked hungrily at the woodwork and pit props. "The roof might give way soon," Lacey said. "Time to get moving."

"Moving where? I've a feeling that Bilic will have the mine entrance covered with RPGs in case we somehow get out of this inferno. We can't take a direct hit from one of those and survive."

Lacey swung the sodden haversack to his front and pulled out a small block of plastic explosive. "Our key."

"Oh, shit, that *will* bring the roof down."

He didn't reply but moulded the golf ball sized explosive into the door frame. He pushed a detonator into the plastic and attached a length of thirty-second fuse. He used a burning ember to light it. "Get back in the corner and lay as flat as you can. This might hurt a bit."

The cavern floor was now running in water from the fractured sluice making steam rise in hissing clouds as it touched the burning woodwork. It flowed through a square cut hole in the cavern wall and disappeared. Lacey splashed to Gill's side and lay down with her.

The PE4 went with a sharp crack that brought dust and shale down from the roof, followed by larger stones and slabs of granite.

Lacey hauled Gill to her feet as rocks continued to fall and one of the pit props collapsed bringing part of the roof down with it.

Gill coughed. "I thought you were only going to blow the bloody door off."

Lacey laughed at the old joke; he liked her sense of humour in extremis. He put his shoulder to the twisted metal door and heaved it open. "Inside, quick, before the whole darn roof caves in on us."

They both fell through the door into a wide stope. This one had a metal cage around two humming industrial generators and a large petrol fuel tank. Cables ran from it in two directions, one set back into the cavern they had just left and the others through a sealed hole in the rock wall above a circular stainless steel hatch that looked as if it had been taken from a nuclear submarine. It had a wheel at its centre and a small round glazed porthole above that.

Lacey pushed the ruined door closed behind them and pointed at the heavy bolt that normally held it shut, now twisted out of its box by the power of the explosion. "They don't seem too keen on visitors."

There was a roar of falling granite and dust filtered through the twisted door frame.

"There's no way out for us now," Gill said.

Lacey grunted. "If we can't go back, we'll have to go forward." He moved to the circular hatch and peered through the porthole before turning the wheel. The hatch swung open with a hiss of compressed air. The cavern beyond was longer and wider than the previous stope with a bench running along one wall. Sacks of white powder were laid on its surface and there were digital scales, spoons, masks and other items dotted along its length. Drums of boric acid were piled in a corner.

Gill whistled. "This is where they cut the cocaine."

Lacey prodded his toe against a cardboard box full of plastic containers. "Ammonia Hydroxide. The bastards are making Crack too." He turned around and looked at a row of metal cabinets that lined a wide stope in the opposite wall below more cameras. Each cabinet had a keypad lock and were all closed except for one which was partially ajar. He hooked it open and stared inside. A light had come on as if it was a refrigerator and he could see rows of small glass vials each with a green cap. He pulled the door open further for Gill to see. "What do you make of this?"

The light reflected off her gold visor and he wished he could see her eyes.

"Refrigerated storage facility. At a guess those are vaccines."

Lacey took a vial, put it carefully into his haversack and moulded it into a slab of PE4. He pushed the door closed. "I wonder what's in the other cabinets."

"Probably more of the same. It's careless of them to leave the door open. They must have been in a hurry to leave."

"Which begs the question how? There has to be another exit." He searched around and found a spade leaning in a corner, a relic of another time, but the wooden shaft seemed solid. He jammed the blade into a join in the doorframe of the nearest cabinet and levered until the door sprang open. A klaxon alarm sounded and red lights flashed along the roof.

"Hell's bells," Gill said. "What have you done?"

Lacey pulled open the door. It was filled with similar vials but these had red caps. "Red's the

Chinese colour for good luck, isn't it?" He picked out one vial and did the same with it as the other.

As he was doing that Gill trotted off a few metres. "Looks like the shaft takes a dogleg to the right further down. It might be the exit."

"Only one way to find out," Lacey said.

They followed the tunnel as it turned right and then left. After a hundred metres they found another circular stainless steel hatch. Lacey unsealed it and they climbed through into a tunnel that dropped lower through the granite. Water dripped from the roof and ran in small rivulets down the slope.

"Not your executive's entrance," Gill said.

"It was probably dug as an adit to funnel out water from the pit when the mine was originally excavated," Lacey said. "I expect it will exit somewhere close to the stream."

Gill chuckled. "You're a mine of information."

"Funnee!" Lacey responded. "I don't suppose you have a quote for that."

"I can think of one which could be apposite by Stewart Udall. He said, '*mining is like a search and destroy mission*'."

Lacey ducked his head under an overhanging rock at the adit's end and looked out over the shrub lined stream bank and a stretch of the moor beyond. "Yeah, I can identify with that."

He poked his head out and had a careful look around. His night vision picked nothing out. He switched to infrared and detected a heat source amongst the shrubs along the river bank. There was a sudden bright flare of light. He was about to shout a warning when an RPG flashed through the narrow space between them and impacted on the granite wall.

The shock wave buffeted them both headfirst out of the adit's mouth like corks out of bottles and sent them sprawling down the muddy slope.

The whole of Lacey's body felt as if it had been hit with a sledgehammer. He came to rest in liquid mud at the base of the slope and groaned. He checked his limbs then tried his radio. "Gill, are you okay?"

He turned his head to see where she was stretched face down, too far away for him to reach out and touch. He tried the radio again. "Gill, answer me, dammit."

Jack's voice interrupted. "Lost video, audio breaking up."

Mud in everything Lacey thought. His peripheral vision picked out movement. People were walking towards them. He slid his hand down to the Glock on his thigh, moving at snail-like slowness. He moved his head an inch to get a better view. There were four of them. One carried an RPG launcher with rocket attached, the others carried QBZ-95 bullpup assault rifles. The 95s were 5.56mm calibre but the RPG was a real menace. He felt his hand on the Glock's butt and tightened his fingers around it. He took a breath.

"Gill if you can hear me lie still and play doggo. Four approaching from your front right, armed and exceedingly bloody dangerous."

63

Gill could hear a buzzing in her head like a swarm of agitated wasps. The blast had knocked the wind out of her and it was impossible to breathe. She fought hard to get her lungs working but could not drag air into her aching chest. She tried again but could not force air down her throat. Her head began to swim and her vision blurred. She thought she could hear a voice far off but the words were faint; she could make no sense of them. She tried again to pull vital oxygen into her lungs and the first twinge of panic clawed at her mind. Blast lung, she'd heard about it and it could be fatal.

She concentrated as hard as she could and opened her mouth as wide as she could to try to suck in as much air as she could. She was amused by the repetitive cadence of her thoughts. She didn't know why she was amused, she was dying from oxygen starvation; perhaps her lungs had collapsed and she was becoming delirious.

She was blacking out, she could feel her body closing down. One more time. She tried hard and the air lock in her throat dissolved. She sucked a long ragged breath that made her eyes bulge with the effort. Her chest heaved as if she had just run a marathon.

A voice filtered into her consciousness. Words that had no meaning, it was gibberish to her oxygen starved brain.

Her vision was clearing but she could still see nothing, her visor was buried in wet earth, her head was lower than her legs which were on the up slope. She tried to clear her mind, remember what had happened to send her face down in the dirt. It came back to her suddenly; the mine, the RPG warhead and the concussion that had hit her so hard. And Rick, where was Rick?

Then the words came back to her, jumbled like anagrams, Rick's voice. He was okay. One by one the words sorted themselves into a sentence and she froze. *'Doggo'.* She knew what that meant. Then the rest of the message *'armed and extremely bloody dangerous'.*

She took a deep breath, her throat felt as if it had been sandpapered. "Rick, it's me. I can't see a damn thing. You'll have to talk them in for me."

She heard a cough. "Welcome to the show, glad you could make it."

"It's all right for you, my head's buried in crap."

"Do you have a weapon to hand?"

Gill grunted and felt beneath her body. "I'm on top of my MP5 and still have hold of the pistol grip."

"Okay. There's four of them about twenty metres out approaching at a slow walk. When I give the word roll over and give them the good news."

"I can't see through the sight to aim."

"Don't worry, you won't need to aim, just point and shoot."

Gill was silent for a second. "Rick, what are you up to?"

"One of them has an RPG. It arms after five metres so I'm going to let them get in real close. They'll be almost standing on your head."

"Rick Arnold, right this second I hate you," Gill breathed.

She heard him chuckle. "So you keep saying. Stay still now, they're almost here."

Gill was still breathing deeply but was trying to control the rise and fall of her chest. Her adrenaline rush had hit overload and that didn't help. She thought she could hear the swish of boots through grass and clenched her teeth. *Come on, Rick, they're getting too damn close.*

Her thumb found the change lever on the side of the MP5 and pushed it down off safe. She couldn't tell if it had gone down one click or two, from double-taps to full auto but hoped it was the latter.

"On three," Rick whispered in her ears. "One, two, *three!*"

She rolled onto her back in one swift seal-like movement and brought the MP5 up onto her chest. She squeezed the trigger and raked the barrel left and right until the magazine emptied. She heard several sharp cracks, so close together they melded into one, and a scream. She rolled back on her front and felt for another magazine, her last full one. She rolled yet again, pulled out the old mag and fitted the new as she climbed onto her knees. More sharp cracks and she was punched in the chest by a hard thud that rocked her back on her heels. Mud had slid down her visor and she could see a vague shape crouching in the grass not two metres from her. She let go half the magazine, punching the figure over. She lurched to her feet and strode forward two paces to put rounds through the man's head. She swivelled to her right and wiped a soggy glove across her visor. Another target, blurred but climbing to its feet. She swung into the aim.

"Whoa, it's me," Lacey said.

She dropped the muzzle.

Lacey picked up a handful of wet grass and wiped her visor. "Better?"

"Much, thanks"

She looked around at the four bodies as Lacey picked up the fallen RPG. "We got them all?" She nodded at the RPG. "Thinking of tank-busting?"

"I want to deny them its use. It's too dangerous to leave lying around. These four, two Serbs, two Chinese by the look of them," Lacey said. "The Chinese are wearing lab coats under those combat jackets.

"How many did I hit?"

She could hear the amusement in Lacey's reply. "Just the one. You really put the wind up them though, took their minds off me long enough to sort them out."

Gill took in a deep breath ignoring the hurt in her chest. "Bastard, you used me as a diversion. I could have been killed."

Lacey shook his head. "Not much chance of that once I'd taken down the guy with the RPG. Those 5.56mm rounds just bounce right off."

"They bloody hurt."

"Oh, yeah, I was forgetting that."

"It's not funny, Rick, I'll have a bruise tomorrow right between my C cups." It was the post combat release of tension that brought out her sense of humour. She put a hand on his arm. "All right, maybe it is funny."

His voice became serious. "We need to get these two vials to Blake. God knows what's in them but I've got a bad feeling about it."

Gill hooked a thumb at the mouth of the adit. "We can't go back the way we came, we'll have to walk around the quarry."

Lacey looked up at the sky. "The clouds are clearing, I can see Orion's Belt. Looks like a good night for a tab." He looked at his watch. "It will be getting light in an hour or so, we don't have much time." He hoisted the RPG onto a shoulder. "Come on then."

They started off walking over the tussocky grass but within a hundred metres found a gravelled track that wound its way around the hill into which the quarry scarred deep.

Gill was at Lacey's shoulder and kept stride with him as he went into a jog trot. "Do you think all this noise we've been making might have disturbed the natives?" she said between breaths.

"Maybe there'll be complaints in the local press about night blasting at the quarry keeping people awake but I doubt if anyone would think anything else. I guess that's the beauty of using a quarry as cover you can get away with murder; things that go thump in the night won't raise too many eyebrows." He paused and slowed his pace as a thought came. "Why … do you think it may be a problem?"

"It's just those headlights heading our way. Maybe someone's called the fuzz."

Lacey looked where she was pointing and saw the vague splashes of light that announced a vehicle approaching at speed, the driver hitting a few potholes in his haste.

It was still out of sight around the edge of the quarry workings and coming from the direction of the fenced-in stockade but now Gill could hear the muted roar of a powerful engine. "I think we'd better get off the track."

64

Cover was sparse. They hid themselves in a fold in the ground and waited as the headlight brightness increased and the volume of engine noise reached a dull roar. Night vision snapped off and they were left with just the illumination from the fast approaching vehicle.

With a hiss of air brakes an eight-wheel tipper truck rounded the edge of the quarry throwing full beam across their prone bodies.

Lacey doubted if they had been spotted by the men clustered in the open back, one with a Type 67 machine gun precariously resting on the cab roof pointing forwards over the driver's screen. Two more were holding RPGs, pointing skyward.

"Do you believe in karma?" he whispered to Gill.

"I believe in getting out of here with our skins intact," Gill murmured in reply. "Only it's looking less and less as if we're going to make it."

The tipper slowed down to a fast walking pace and trundled towards the adit mouth. The driver braked suddenly pitching the men in the back forward.

"I think he's seen the bodies," Lacey said. He didn't want the men to debus. Once they had feet on the ground they'd be far more difficult to deal with.

He rose to his knees and lined up the RPG on the truck's fuel tank. He squeezed the trigger and the primary charge jetted the missile out for eleven metres before the propellant ignited. The fiery trail rocketed across the hundred metres and impacted on the fuel tank exploding the diesel in a huge expanding fireball that engulfed the whole vehicle. Men, their clothing ablaze, jumped clear to roll in the dirt to douse the flames. Ammunition heated and exploded sending tracer flying into the night sky.

Lacey dropped the launcher tube. "Time to go, while they're still sorting themselves out of that mess."

"Is that what you mean by karma?" Gill said. She sounded shocked.

"Reap what you sow," Lacey said and moved away from the glare of the flames. Gill followed hard on his heels. They hadn't gone far when another set of headlights fanned their beams across the track and the black Range Rover careered into sight. The driver slammed on the brakes when he saw the burning wreck and both front doors were flung open. Bilic leapt out of the driver's seat and Ling-Ling slipped smoothly from the passenger side. They both stepped forward a few paces to stand side-by-side against the car's grille, staring open-mouthed at the pyre.

"*Ling-Ling,*" Gill said.

Lacey could hear the suppressed fury in her voice and put out an arm to stop her but it was too late, she was already running towards the car, her MP5 shouldered in the aim. Ordering her to stop was pointless. He started off after her.

They reached the edge of the flickering cone of light together. Ling-Ling must have sensed something or detected movement with her peripheral vision and she turned. She screeched a warning to Bilic and pulled Aftershave's Sig from her belt. She was fast and she was accurate. Hollow-point rounds smacked into Gill's chest plate and she staggered to a stop. Ling-Ling slipped around the bonnet to the driver's side. Lacey returned fire with his Glock until he too was punched over by the power of the hits against his armour. He rolled into a prone position. Another round whined off his helmet and made his head ring.

Gill was on her knees pumping the last of her magazine load towards the car but the lack of penetration was making little impression on its bodywork.

Bilic climbed into the driver's seat and slammed the gear lever into reverse. Ling-Ling climbed up on the running board but lost her grip as Bilic accelerated viciously backwards. She was tossed into the thick grass at the track's edge.

Lacey took a shot at Bilic but all he achieved was a starred windscreen as the bullet ricocheted off. Bilic swung the car back the way he had come and the night got blacker without the headlights as the fire had died to a red hot glow of tortured metal.

"They've gone, the bastards have got away," Gill said.

Lacey checked his kit. The night vision had not come back on. The battery had flattened. "How's your helmet working?" he asked.

"Not good. I seem to have lost everything except PR radio."

"That has its own power supply but it won't last forever. We've lost Jack too, no satellite uplink."

"Just like the good old days," Gill said and laughed but it sounded bitter. "All this kit and we still can't finish that bitch Ling-Ling."

"Another time, maybe. We need to get these samples to our people, we can't be going off half-cocked on a revenge crusade." He pointed to the wrecked truck. "Some of those men are getting their act together. They're probably in no condition to continue the fight but let's not hang around to find out." He changed the magazine in the Glock and shoved the pistol into its holster. "Last sixteen rounds, let's hope I won't need them." He looked up at the sky. "Dawn's not far off. I guess it would be better to take a circular route across the moor back to the Discovery. I don't think we should risk going through the quarry with Bilic and Ling-Ling on the loose, no knowing what else they have up their sleeves. The RPGs are bad enough but that machine gun on the truck was really bad news. We wouldn't come off best if hit with one of those."

"A hike across the moor, how lovely," Gill said as they moved off.

Lacey smiled to himself. "No worries, ma'am, the moor is my country, we won't get lost."

"That wasn't why I was whinging," Gill retorted. "How do you pee in these suits?"

Lacey did laugh now. "You don't, not unless you want to create a new meaning for fill your boots. We sweat it out for the short time we usually wear these things. Hang in there. We'll find you a nice rock to go behind once I've peeled you out."

"You're all heart, Mister Arnold."

"You'd better believe it."

Lacey struck off north into the moor proper. He had the route planned in his mind, a wide loop away from habitation towards Ryders Hill and then a turn west and south to circle back towards the outskirts of Deancombe where the Discovery was parked. They could do the whole circuit in less than two hours without meeting another soul in the rough country. It was two hours he didn't want to lose but safety was now the overriding factor. They had to deliver the vials to Jack at Exeter Airport and he could not afford to have them broken. God alone knew what was inside them and how dangerous it was.

Neither of them looked back as they climbed the rising ground away from the quarry and neither of them saw the dark shape of Ling-Ling rise from the grass to follow them.

65

The sky began to lighten to their right as Lacey led them north and with it a gauzy mist rose from the damp close-cropped sward. The mist was thicker in the hollows, sometimes thick enough to obscure Lacey's back for a few paces. Gill wanted the sun to rise to warm up the dank chill and suck up the moisture. Her visor was beginning to mist up with droplets condensing on its shiny surface and she continually wiped them away. She concentrated on walking, avoiding the patches of heather and rock, to keep her mind off the pain in her bladder. She wished she didn't drink so much coffee but now knew why the suits had no Camelbak hydration packs included with the kit.

She caught up to Lacey's elbow. "I don't mean to whinge but I'm getting desperate."

He nodded. "Not much further. There's a place I know up ahead. Another five minutes should do it."

"I hope it's not any longer. I thought I could hack pain but this is getting silly."

"Yeah, I've been there, I know." Lacey said and she thought she could detect a note of sympathy in his voice.

The mist swirled as a light breeze sprang up and Lacey pointed. "There. A small outcropping of granite. Ladies on the far side."

They stopped in a natural hollow at the front of the rock where Lacey unlatched her helmet and undid the clips and straps on the back of her suit. He pulled the top half down over her shoulders.

"I won't be long," she said and walked around the far side of the rocks out of view.

Lacey unlatched his own helmet and took it off. He undid the mike and headset from its clips and fitted them to his head, the small thin transparent microphone and ear plugs hardly visible against his skin.

The sun cracked the horizon and sent shafts of orange light through the mist. He sat on a small rock and opened the haversack to check on its contents. The two glass vials were still in one piece, the wads of plastic explosive giving them protection from accidental bumps. He checked them again before re-securing the buckles.

A pebble rattled behind him but he did not turn. "That was quick."

A cold muzzle was pushed into the back of his neck.

"Stay very still."

"You must be Ling-Ling."

"Where is the other?"

"Gone ahead. Left a few minutes ago."

The pistol was jammed hard against the small vertebrae at the base of his skull. "You have something of mine."

"Can't imagine what that could be." Lacey was assessing the odds and they weren't good. He was sitting which reduced his options to zero for disarming her, she was a professional and the trigger on the Sig was lightened to just a four

390

pound pull. There was no way he could surprise her and survive.

"You set off the freezer cabinet alarms in the mine and you removed two items. She held up her phone. The cameras are very good, you cannot deny it."

"Must have been the other guy."

He heard her snort a humourless laugh. "With the bag that you hold in your hands? I want you to put it on the ground very slowly. Do not drop it or you will wish you had not."

Lacey slowly pushed the haversack out to the full extent of his arms. "What are these, Ling-Ling, these things that needed the cream of the People's Liberation Army to guard them?"

"Put the bag down carefully or you will regret it."

He felt the Sig's muzzle pressure release and saw a foot slide sideways around him then pain exploded at the side of his head. The blow wasn't hard enough to knock him out but temporarily daze him so that he saw stars.

Ling-Ling snapped out a hand and grabbed the haversack's strap that was hanging loose.

"Freeze!" Gill stepped around the large boulder that had sheltered her, with her Glock in the aim.

Ling-Ling pushed the Sig into Lacey's temple. "Drop your weapon or I shall kill him."

"Then you'll die too," Gill said.

"If this bag is dropped many people will die," Ling-Ling said. "Throw down your weapon, now."

Lacey's head was clearing and so was his vison. He saw Gill was undecided what to do; working out the consequences for each option. But there were no options bar one. "If you do, she'll kill us both, Gill. It's T-time, take the shot."

"But …"

"Do it."

Ling-Ling had worked out her options too. She spun, snapping the Sig into the aim. She was fast but Lacey held onto the bag which slowed her for the fraction of a second it took Gill to fire at the twisting target. The Sig bucked in Ling-Ling's hand as she fired back but the drag on the satchel's strap threw her aim off.

Gill's Glock was loaded with full power 2Z ammunition. The first round hit Ling-Ling in the shoulder, the second nicked her ear as she fell back alongside the rock that Lacey was sitting on. He twisted round as she fell and landed on her chest, the ceramic armour knocking the breath out of her. He let go of the satchel and grabbed for her gun arm, forcing the pistol out of her grip by twisting it inwards against her thumb. It fired again as her finger caught on the trigger and Lacey felt her body buck.

He rolled off as Gill ran up for the coup-de-grace. Lacey held up a hand. "Hold it."

Gill stepped back but kept Ling-Ling covered. "Is she dead?"

"No, not yet but it won't be long." He put an arm under Ling-Ling's shoulders and raised her head, ignoring the blood that was seeping out of her ruined ear and shoulder. "Ling-Ling, can you hear me?"

Ling-Ling opened her eyes. "Yes." She coughed and pink foam bubbled from her lips.

"What's in the vials?"

Ling-Ling coughed a laugh and brought up more blood. "You will find out soon enough."

Gill holstered the Glock and dropped to her knees beside Ling-Ling. "It's all over now," she said. "You've lost, whatever your plan was it's finished."

Ling-Ling's black eyes opened and rolled towards her; she had a smile on her face. "Ah, Missus Arnold. Do not be so sure." Her voice was weakening and Gill tried again. "What do you mean?"

Ling-Ling's smiled widened and then her eyes rolled up and she gasped out her last breath.

"She's gone," Lacey said.

"Gill looked at him and sat heavily on the grass. She let her breath out in a whoosh. "What do you make of that?"

Lacey laid Ling-Ling's head down and closed her eyes. "I think we'd better find Bilic and quickly."

66

"We're going back," Gill said.

Lacey nodded. "We have to, there's no choice now. Turn around."

Gill did and Lacey closed her suit. He held up a helmet and she shook her head. "Too claustrophobic and none of the electronics are working."

"Might save you from a bullet in the brain."

"I'll take my chances."

Lacey nodded and showed her how to remove the mike and earpiece from the helmet and use a chin strap to fix it to her belt. "Just in case you need it again. Radio check."

"I can hear you. The PRR's working." She pointed at Ling-Ling's body. "Are we just going to leave her here?"

"It's pretty remote up here and she's unlikely to get found anytime soon. Once we get back to the car we can call in your undertakers to clean up."

Gill looked thoughtful. "I'm not sure MI6 does that anymore."

"They'll know someone who does. C'mon, times a-wasting, we need to get back to find Bilic."

They checked weapons on the move. Both were short of ammunition for the MP5s, Lacey had a full magazine plus a few rounds for his Glock and Gill had around the same. One part of him was pleased; she had passed his final test and fired when ordered even though all her instincts would be against it. Then another thought crowded in. "We're in no shape for a full-on shooting war," he said as he jogged, "we'll need a low profile approach, what the old SAS hands call keeni-meeni."

Gill had to smile. "Giving your vintage away there."

He glanced across at her. "Just something I picked up somewhere. It's Swahili for the movement of a snake in grass."

Gill grunted. "That sums up Bilic too."

The sun was fully up over the horizon now and the day was getting warmer. The last vestiges of mist had been sucked up and there was little cover except for natural folds in the ground and the occasional outcropping of rock or small stand of gorse.

As they neared the quarry Lacey dropped flat and leopard crawled into a dip in the ground.

Gill crawled in beside him. "What now?"

Lacey nodded to where the adit vented onto the down slope. "The Range Rover is back."

Gill peered at the distant shape. "The bodies are still there. Obviously Bilic isn't a great one to respect his dead Tigers."

"They're no further use to him," Lacey said. He studied the burnt out truck wreckage. It was still smoking but there was no movement around it. He pointed. "They've left the bodies there too. The live ones have gone to get patched up."

Gill sucked in her breath. "There's Bilic."

The man had ducked out of the mouth of the adit with a black plastic crate in his hands. Another man followed with a similar box. Bilic opened the tailgate and pushed the box inside then turned and took the second box from the other man placing it carefully with the first. He waved his arm and both men scrambled back up the muddy slope to disappear into the adit's mouth.

Lacey pushed himself to his feet. "C'mon." He ran with Gill on his heels down the slope to the flat area, crossed that and came to a halt in the lee of the burnt truck. He checked again and then made a run for the Range Rover. He slid into a sitting position on the far side, invisible from anyone leaving the adit. Gill slithered in beside him.

He unbuckled the satchel and took out his last free slab of PE4, a detonator, a length of fuse and a cheap plastic lighter. He rammed the detonator into the plastic and attached the fuse to it, cutting the free end of the fuse at an angle with his knife. He handed the satchel gently to Gill. "Take care of that and cover me."

Before she could reply he was on his feet and running up the slope, slipping and sliding in the wet mud but finding enough purchase to get to the top without falling on his face.

Gill propped the satchel against a wheel and positioned herself at the rear of the Range Rover where she could get a shot into the adit's mouth, keeping Lacey's back out of her line of fire.

He disappeared into the opening, stepping over the chunks of rock blown down by the RPG. He found a wide crack in the surface and pushed the plastic into it, draping the fuse down the rock face. He held up the lighter and cranked the wheel. The flint sparked but the wick did not catch. He flicked again with the same result. Now he could hear voices coming from along the tunnel. He flicked the wheel for the third time and the wick caught. He held the flame to the fuse until it started to splutter and burn.

The voices were getting closer. He tucked the burning fuse into the crevice and turned to leave.

A voice screamed a warning.

He spun. Bilic was standing twenty feet away with another crate in his arms and his mouth open.

Lacey pulled his Glock and fired into the roof above Bilic's head sending chips of rock flying. Bilic jumped backwards into the man who was following him. He shouted words of Serbo-Croat and they both retreated around a bend.

Lacey turned to run. He reached the mouth of the adit and leapt down the slope, losing his footing and sliding on his back.

Bilic appeared in the opening with a pistol in his hand. Gill fired. The range was too great for accurate shooting but it made Bilic duck his head inside.

The second man risked a look and fired a burst at Lacey with a sub-machine gun, sending up fountains of earth. Lacey rolled into a ball covering his head with his arms as the rounds struck close.

Gill emptied her magazine at the man and nicked him. He stumbled back inside.

Lacey rolled to the bottom of the slope and made a dash for the cover of the Range Rover.

The explosion was loud and sharp. Dust and debris flew from the adit's mouth as granite crashed down sealing the hole. Rocks and stones cascaded over the car. Gill took shelter under the open tailgate as a rock starred the glass. Another crashed onto the metal roof and bounced over.

Lacey appeared at her side with the satchel in his hands and a grim look on his face. "Job done."

Gill hooked a thumb at the black crates. "I wonder what's in these."

Lacey shook his head. "I hate to think." He opened the driver's door. "Keys are in here. Looks as if we can ride out in style." He slid onto the seat and pressed the starter. The engine cranked into life. "Get in, Missus Arnold, let's get the hell out of here."

67

They swapped the crates into the Discovery, changed out of the suits into the clothing they had left in the car and headed back to Exeter. Lacey called Jack on the car phone with instructions to get them access airside so that they could load everything into the Skyvan.

Jack rang back within a few minutes with instructions on how to get direct tarmac access to the aircraft. They found the gate. Jack was waiting for them and they were waved through. He jumped on the running board and hung on as they crossed the apron to where the pilot had the Skyvan warmed up and ready to go.

The boxes were transferred quickly and Lacey handed the satchel to Jack. "Whatever you do, don't drop it. I'll call the brigadier to let him know that this has to go directly to his contacts at Porton Down for analysis. I don't know what's in those two crates but whatever they hold should be treated equally carefully, is that clear?"

Jack blinked and gripped the satchel tighter. "As crystal, sir."

The pilot sauntered over. "Cargo's squared away, Colonel. Flight plan is posted for Northolt and we're cleared to go."

"Don't let me hold you up."

The pilot grinned and saluted. "Yessir."

As they talked Gill climbed into the Discovery to use the phone. She rang Blake and for once was put straight through to him.

"Ah, I've been awaiting your call. It's good that I didn't hold my breath."

"We've been busy, Blake. This is the first chance I've had."

"Busy? Yes indeed. The cat is truly amongst the pigeons. The Devon and Cornwall Police are having conniptions."

Gill couldn't help a grin at the terminology. "Why so?"

"It seems that the Golden Nugget was raided and three men left dead. The owner, one Derek Pierce, with whom I believe you are acquainted, is in custody, suspected of doing away with his employees. His story, apparently, verges on the manic. At one time he blamed Mister Arnold and the New York Mafia, at another, a spaceman with one golden eye. He had taken a blow to the head and so the police are giving him time to sort his story out. They found three bodies in the waste bins at the rear of the casino and three pistols of Chinese manufacture, all of the same unusual 5.8 millimetre calibre that killed Forrestal. I fear Mister Pierce will be asked many questions he will feel unable to answer. Is there anything else you have not found the time to inform me about?"

"Hold on to your toupee, Blake. Full report will come later but you need to get a clean-up crew over to Buckfastleigh to the south of Dartmoor. There are a few more bodies dotted about in and around a quarry that's owned by Pierce and Bilic. Bit of a mess I'm afraid. I'll text you the coordinates."

"What on earth have you been up to?"

"Long story but you had better get moving on this before some innocent hiker gets the shock of their life."

Blake was silent for almost a minute as he appeared to digest this stark information, then he said, "with all this mayhem, are you any nearer to solving this Forrestal enigma?"

"I think so, Blake, but I don't think you and your masters are going to like it much."

"I'm already having palpitations."

"Then you'd better get your pills ready to pop."

"That bad?"

"There's something else … there's a mine … an old gold mine. There's been something evil going on in there. We've sealed both entrances but you will need to get your people to dig their way in. Biochem Hazmat suits. Tell them to take no chances."

"Right … I'll be sure to tell them."

Gill wasn't sure if Blake was really all that worried. "Rick's sent his people some stuff. We don't know what it is but it's going straight to Porton Down, he's that concerned about it."

Gill heard a slow exhale of breath at the end of the line.

"I see," Blake said after a few seconds of silence.

"You don't seem that bothered."

Blake grunted. "Nothing surprises me much anymore. I'll look forward to receiving your report and ... oh, don't forget those coordinates."

"Five minutes." She broke the connection and thumbed buttons sending the latitude and longitude references that she remembered from the information on the display in her helmet. She thumbed in instructions on where to find Ling-Ling's body. She had just finished when Lacey slid onto the driver's seat having waved off the Skyvan. He cocked an enquiring eye at her.

She held up the phone. "Texting Blake. He's getting a clean-up squad organised." She nibbled her lower lip. "Funny, I told him about the stuff we sent to Porton Down and he didn't seem that surprised."

Lacey started the engine. "I'm sure they had some idea what to expect otherwise they wouldn't have bothered getting us involved. They must have known whatever was going on down here wasn't going to be good news, especially with Chinese SF involvement. I'm not sure though if they knew just how bad it was going to get."

Gill nodded. "He was whinging about the strike on the casino. He's going to have to field that one eventually when the lab results start to come back. The police aren't daft, they'll connect Aftershave's injuries with the place once they analyse the blood samples from the car park and maybe your girlfriend, Detective Inspector Craddock, will be dropping in for a chat over a cup of coffee. Seems Pierce has dropped your name into the mix."

Lacey grinned and rammed the car into drive. "We still don't know exactly why Forrestal was killed and by whom. I'm not sure we can help her much with that … not yet."

"We may have buggered up Ling-Ling's and Bilic's plans but that is one thing that still irks me. I really would like to know about that," Gill said.

"If only for the family back in the States?"

"For them and my own peace of mind. I hate mysteries."

Lacey eased the car out onto the busy A30. "I'm not sure we're going to be given the time to find out. The proverbial has hit the fan big time. I can't imagine what repercussions are coming from on high. There is going to be a major diplomatic incident, it'll get blown kingsize if the press get a whiff of any of this. The powers-that-be will try to roll it up quietly. The cover story will have to be good as some details are bound to leak out, they always do."

"So it's adiós to the good life then," Gill said and smiled. "Somehow I'll miss it … and you."

"Maybe," he said and switched on the radio. It was tuned to Radio Devon. "Jack said to keep a listening watch on this station for the news."

Gill looked across at him. "Did he say why?"

Lacey nodded. "He said it was relevant."

Gill threw her head back and raised her eyes to the roof lining. "Rick, sometimes I think I hate you."

68

The news came on some twenty minutes later and Lacey upped the volume at the end of the jingle. It was an extended bulletin and the female newsreader spoke in solemn tones.

"The BBC has learned more about the loss of the tanker, New Venture, with all hands. The Ministry of Defence were unable to explain the catastrophe and said that their troops had not set foot on the ship's deck before it sank. With no survivors it appears that pirates had sunk the ship rather than being taken prisoner. A MoD spokesman has intimated that the pirates were heavily armed and a helicopter of 845 Naval Air Squadron had been damaged by gunfire from the deck of the ship. There were no casualties amongst the crew and the helicopter landed safely.

"The tanker was not carrying a cargo and immediate tests of the waters in the vicinity show no serious signs of pollution other than the gradual leaking of the ship's fuel oil. It is intended that divers would be sent down to organise drainage of the tanks.

"Eye witnesses from other vessels in Torbay reported loud explosions from the tanker before it left its anchorage which may have been an initial attempt to board the ship from surface craft that proved unsuccessful. The MoD have stated it is not its habit to comment on operations of this type but any such activity by service personnel is mere conjecture and cannot be confirmed or denied. They revealed that all personnel

involved in the abortive operation returned to their bases unharmed, which is welcome news for everyone concerned.

"To other events now. Local businessman Derek Pierce and his wife Shelley are still helping police with their enquiries into the deaths of three of their employees who worked at the recently opened Golden Nugget Casino in Torquay. A police spokesperson has said that the investigation is in its early stages and they cannot comment further with regard to ongoing enquiries. The police are appealing for witnesses, and ask for two men of oriental appearance who were seen leaving the premises to come forward so that they may be eliminated from their enquiries also that the woman who made the initial emergency call contact them in confidence, as soon as possible, as she may have vital information.

"Missus Sandra McGuinness of Yelverton is celebrating the birth of triplets at …"

Lacey turned off the radio. "Seems the local newshounds have been busy."

Gill grimaced. "The fourth estate, where would we be without them?"

"They'll keep digging but I can see that the fix is in already," Lacey said. "The MoD will eventually issue a statement that will be disingenuous but close enough to the truth to satisfy most people. The press will know they won't get any more out of them and it will all be forgotten in a week or so."

"Yuh think?"

"Gill, you watch too much television," Lacey said and grinned. "Watching all that American stuff ain't good for your pronunciation."

Gill laughed then sobered and reached a hand across to touch his arm. "Is all this really over, Rick?"

He was steering the car into the marina car park and he stopped by the barrier. He looked across at her. "My crystal ball's a little cloudy right now."

"The fat lady hasn't sung yet?"

He screwed up his eyes. "When the dust has settled, when the loose ends are tied, then, maybe, I'll be able to see more clearly."

"You're not just talking about this operation, are you?"

There was an impatient toot from behind. He grunted and drove the car into a parking spot without answering.

Gill nodded. "I'll ring the hospital; find out how Aftershave is."

"He's been on my mind too. Hope the little guy's okay."

Gill opened her door. "He's tough. I'll let you know."

"Thanks. You can call from the boat."

Gill held up her mobile. "No need." She jumped out and walked to a spot overlooking the river.

Lacey watched her for a while and then shrugged. He walked to the boat, dumped the holdalls with the suits and weapons into the crew cabin then plugged in the electric kettle. He needed

406

a brew. He had barely settled down to drink his coffee when a voice called from the pontoon.

"Hello. Can we come aboard?"

Lacey levered himself up and slid open the glass door. "Detective Inspector Craddock. Sure, come aboard." He looked at the burly man standing behind her and she made the introduction. "Sergeant Warner."

Lacey turned and led them into the saloon. "Would you like a drink?"

Both shook their heads and sat as Lacey indicated the seats.

"Have you come to tell me you've found Commander Forrestal's killer?"

Craddock pulled an apologetic face. "Sorry, we're no further forward with that. It's something else we're investigating and I'd like to ask you some questions, sir."

Lacey frowned. "Can't imagine what that could be."

"Your name came up in connection with an incident at the Golden Nugget Casino yesterday."

"Gee, I heard about that on the news today but I'm sure I'm not going to be any help there."

"Mister Pierce, the casino owner, seems to think that you may have something to do with the happenings there."

"Derek? I only met the man, what, twice. I can't think why he should implicate me."

"He seems to think that you want to buy the casino and it was an attempt to frighten him into selling. He says you have Mafia connections."

Lacey gave a heavy sigh and shook his head. "I really don't know how he got those crazy ideas. I've no intention of buying a casino, his or anyone else's. I have no connection whatever with the Mafia, in fact, I've only ever been to Italy twice and neither time did I visit Sicily."

"Not the Sicilian Mafia, sir, the New York variety," Craddock said.

"Whatever, the answer's the same."

"So you're saying that there's absolutely no truth in his accusations."

"You can check all you want, my life's an open book."

"Why do you think he would want to implicate you?"

Lacey shrugged. "Could be several reasons. I know the guy had the hots for my wife but she's not the kind to go for a man like him and it rankled. Maybe he heard I was stirring things up about Commander Forrestal's killing and maybe he got nervous for some reason. Maybe he's just plain crazy or maybe he's just trying to move the blame to someone else's shoulders. I don't know, Inspector, but it's your job to find the answers not mine."

"We'll do our best to do that, sir. Now, in the meantime, can you tell me where you were in the small hours of yesterday?"

Lacey smiled. "With my wife, where else?"

"And she will corroborate that?"

Lacey angled his head and nodded.

"Thank you sir, that will be all for now but I'd rather you didn't take this nice boat and sail off into the sunset until I say. Is that clear?"

69

Gill came back a few minutes after Craddock and Warner had left. She showed Lacey the phone in her hand. She looked happier than she had done since Aftershave's shooting.

"It seems he's pulling through. The op was a success and the surgeon is fairly hopeful he will make a full recovery. He's not out of the woods yet but things are looking up. They said I can visit him tomorrow if he continues to improve."

Lacey smiled and puffed out his cheeks. "That's good news. I can see that's made you feel better."

"He's a good friend, I'd hate to lose him … especially as …"

Lacey reached out and took her hand. "We've had this conversation before. It's not your fault. Ling-Ling shot him, it's down to her."

Gill tightened her grip on his fingers. "I know that but I can't help but feel responsible. If it wasn't for me he wouldn't be here."

Lacey pulled her gently to a seat and sat her down. "Look, Gill, consider this. You have a date with your boyfriend and arrange to meet him by the bus stop. As he's standing there the bus driver loses control and runs him over. He was there because you asked him to be there but was it your fault that the bus driver lost control?"

Gill frowned. "If you put it that way it makes more sense."

"Then maybe you'll feel a little better about yourself. We're in a rotten business, people die before their time and the rest of us have to learn to live with it. This time, Aftershave seems to have hit lucky. Next time, if there is a next time, it could be you in that hospital bed and him beating himself up because he hadn't taken better care of you. We have to learn to fold up those emotions and tuck them away for future reference so that maybe we can learn from the experience."

Gill chewed her lip. "Maybe I should have let you take the shot there behind the casino, maybe Ling-Ling wouldn't have shot Aftershave."

"And maybe she would have hit him in the killing T instead. You can't second guess these things and you can't live your life counting maybes."

Gill gave him a tired smile. "You'd make a good shrink, Rick?"

He returned the smile. "Just a little good old homespun common-sense. I've been there too many times not to understand the way you feel and what it takes to get over it without torturing yourself."

"Well, I feel better, thank you, doctor."

Lacey stood and picked up his coffee mug. He tilted it to study the congealing cold mess inside. "I didn't get to finish my coffee. As you predicted I had a visit from Inspector Craddock and sidekick. I'll make some more. Want some?"

Gill nodded. "Ah, the cute Craddock. I overheard them talking about you in the car park.

411

They didn't see me but I was close enough to get the gist of the conversation before they reached their car."

Lacey was arranging the mugs and boiling the kettle afresh. He looked across at her. "And?"

"I think Craddock has a bit of a soft spot for you. She seemed to think you were telling the truth. Your body language spoke for you. Her sidekick …"

"Sergeant Warner."

"… whatever … wasn't so sure. He thought you were way too smooth and way too sure of yourself. Craddock ended up by saying the scene of crime evidence would probably clinch it when it came through."

Lacey pushed a mug into her hand. "Wish her luck with that. We left absolutely no trace, another thing the suits are good for. In the meantime, I've been ordered not to leave the area and she'll want to check our alibis and speak with you at some point. I didn't lie, I said I was with you but I didn't say where. I guess she just assumed we were in bed together."

"Nice thought," Gill said.

Lacey checked his watch and sighed. "What say we get our reports written and sent off and then have dinner at the yacht club. It's been a long day."

Gill batted her eyelashes. "Perhaps we could have an early night and catch up on some sleep."

Lacey just smiled and opened up his laptop. "I reckon this will take me about two hours. Can you be ready by eighteen-hundred?"

Gill was dressed to stun and as they walked she linked her arm through his. He had a whiff of her expensive perfume and it raised the hair on the back of his neck.

"Are we going to be friends tonight, Mister Arnold," she asked.

"Wouldn't have it any other way," Lacey replied.

It was midweek and the club was only half full. They found a table and ordered. Fish again for Gill, buttered dabs, but Lacey wanted a medium rare fillet steak.

Gill looked across the table at him. "Would you like red wine with that?"

Lacey shook his head. "I'm no wine snob, I'll drink anything with anything. I think we'll have another bottle of that Sancerre."

Gill smiled. "Good choice." She reached across and took his hand. "Thanks." She looked up. "We have company."

Alan and Lillian Drew walked across to them.

"Hello you two," Lillian said. "Enjoying yourselves?"

Gill gave her a dazzling smile. "Never more so. It's lovely here."

"Pull up some seats and have a drink," Lacey said. "We've time before the food arrives."

"No, thank you, we really can't play gooseberry tonight, we can see that you two would like to be alone," Lillian said.

"Just checking that you have everything you need," Alan said. "By the way, was that Inspector Craddock any help?"

"Not much," Lacey said and crossed his fingers, "but who knows, something might turn up."

Alan rubbed his jaw. "I thought I saw her on your pontoon earlier. Came to give you the latest, I daresay."

"Something like that," Lacey said.

Lilian put her hand on Alan's shoulder in conspiratorial fashion. "Speaking of the police, have you heard about that man Derek Pierce and his wife. It was all over the news."

Gill smiled again. "Yes, we heard. Bad business."

"Bad for the club's reputation," Alan said. "Let's hope his membership doesn't leak to the papers we can do without the publicity that would bring." He turned and looked over his shoulder and his face momentarily froze. Then he forced a smile. "Anyway, nice to see you enjoying yourselves. We'll leave you to your dinner." The pair hurried away and Lacey gave Gill an enquiring look.

She raised her chin. "You'll never guess who the cat just dragged in."

"Don't keep me in suspense"

"The frowsy Missus Kate Bilic. She's not happy and she's looking daggers at us. She's not a member and without Pierce here to sign her in I think the Drews are about to show her the door."

Kate Bilic turned to go but as she went she made a gun with her fingers and pointed it at Lacey's head. Her thumb went down like a hammer and she gave an icy smile as she blew smoke from the imaginary barrel.

70

Lacey made scrambled eggs and toast and carried it to Gill's cabin on a tray. She was in bed propped up against the headboard and looked surprised as he knocked and opened the door.

"What's this?"

He smiled. "I won't make a habit of it but it seems we're at a loose end right now until the reports come back so I thought maybe we could treat today as a vacation, god knows we could do with one."

Gill shuffled into a more comfortable position as he put the tray across her knees. "Good idea, Rick. I could do with a break but I must get to see Aftershave sometime today."

He nodded. "I'll run you in."

She took a forkful of egg. "Hmm, good." She waved the fork. "I need to go into Exeter city centre first. I need some make-up and other girl stuff."

"That's no problem. I could do with a few things myself. A little retail therapy can't do any harm."

Gill waved the fork again. "What did you make of Kate's little mime show last night?"

Lacey shrugged. "I guess she was letting off some steam. We can't know how much Bilic kept her in the picture or how closely involved she was in their business. We know she has a gangster past so we can't just shrug it off as bravado. My guess is that the Pierce situation and the fact that her husband is missing has got her worried. Anyway, we'll be careful, we always are."

Gill rang the hospital and got the go-ahead to visit Aftershave in the ICU at fourteen-hundred hours. They left in the Discovery and it was then that Lacey found that he'd forgotten to charge his mobile.

"Sorry, Gill, we'll be out of touch until I can get this thing hooked up again."

Gill patted her shoulder bag, "Don't worry, I'm carrying all the protection I need."

Lacey found a place to park in Southernhay West and they walked through to the High Street.

Gill found a department store that had remained open after the pandemic had done its worst and bought the items she needed. She went to the ladies and left Lacey kicking his heels in the men's department before she re-emerged.

He didn't recognise her at first then did a comical double-take. Gill had changed her facial appearance with make-up, a head scarf and designer sunglasses. She laughed as she saw his surprise.

"I'm supposed to be Aftershave's sister from Colombia, I need to look the part."

He nodded. "It's worked, I hardly recognised you."

"Something else I learned when working with the Det in Ulster. You had to blend in or you'd get pinged. I also didn't want to take the chance that someone would recognise me from when we dropped Aftershave off … which reminds me, it's not a good idea for you to take me there in the Discovery … the car might get pinged. I'll grab a taxi and meet you back at the boat later."

Gill was shown into the Intensive Care Unit and stopped as she entered. She had never seen anyone with so many tubes and wires attached to them; not even Ricky after he was shot had so many machines hooked up to him. The nurse told her she had just fifteen minutes, less if she tired him too much.

There was one chair and she pulled it close to the bed and took Aftershave's hand.

He started a slow smile. "Hello Petal. I'd know that perfume anywhere."

Gill grinned in turn. "You haven't lost your sense of smell then."

He opened his eyes and turned his head towards her. "Buenos tardes, señora, como esta?" His voice was weak but his words were coherent.

"We'll keep it in English, less strain on the brain, but I'm fine, better than fine seeing you grinning that toothy smile at me."

He eyed her for a long few seconds. "You got yourself laid."

Gill's eyebrows went up. "How would you know that?"

His grin broadened. "Your Uncle Aftershave knows you too well, Petal. I remember that look; you had it in Spain."

Gill blushed beneath the make-up. "I'd rather not be reminded of that." She shuddered. "To think I was screwing a murdering terrorist."

"You weren't to know, Petal, not at the time."

"Well it seems your memory hasn't been affected either."

"Is the colonel the lucky man?"

"I've come to talk about you."

"What you see is what you get, Petal. I've got tubes in every orifice an' I'm stitched up like Frankenstein's monster. On the plus side I've got a couple of pretty nurses an' the doc says I'm on the mend. They'll be movin' me to a general ward in a day or so."

"I'm sorry about this ..."

He gripped her fingers tighter. "No need for you to be sorry; all part o' the game. My own fault, I should o' seen Ling-Ling comin'. It was her that clobbered me in the first place."

"That's not like you to get caught like that."

"Gettin' old, Petal. Just a bit too slow. Anyway, while they thought I was out I heard 'em talkin'. Seems it was them that did for Forrestal. That bloke Bilic and Ling-Ling was sayin' they should've moved the body before the tide took it."

"They're both dead now but that seems to solve that mystery. I'll let Rick know."

"Careful with him, Petal. I don't want you to get hurt, you know what I mean."

"I know and I've got my eyes wide open. It's ships in the night, nothing serious. You don't have to worry about me."

"But I do, Petal, I do. Always have … always … will." His grip on her fingers slackened as his voice tailed off.

The door opened and a nurse poked her head in. "It's time to go, miss. He needs to rest."

Gill patted Aftershave's hand and stood. "Si, gracias."

"You can come back tomorrow if you wish. But please call first as the police want to interview him about the shooting and we'll need to work around them. Just routine, I'm sure."

Gill gave her a vague nod as if she really didn't understand. But the thought occurred that if the police had matched his DNA with the blood and spattered flesh found in the casino's alley … they would want answers.

71

Lacey knew he had a problem as soon as he approached the boat. Two heavily built men stepped up behind him and followed him to the end of the pontoon, waiting as he climbed aboard with their arms folded across their broad chests. Once inside he could see why, Kate Bilic was reclining on one of his seats while another gorilla lounged against the helm seat with his right hand tucked behind his back. He mentally kicked himself for letting his phone die or the cameras would have forewarned him.

He smiled and nodded. "I was wondering if you'd turn up, Kate, pity you couldn't wait for an invitation."

She gave him the same icy smile of the night before then turned and picked his fighting helmet off the deck. "This yours?"

Lacey feigned surprise. "Now where did you get that?"

"Interesting little room you have at the stern. All sorts of things the police might be interested in, if I was the kind that went running to the fuzz when I needed a problem sorted."

"You have a problem? Sorry to hear that."

Kate's smile changed to a sneer. "Don't get smart with me, Arnold … if that's your name. "Where's my Bill?"

"I'm sorry, you've lost Bill?"

Kate sat up straight. "I said not to be a smart arse or Pete here will have to rearrange your face. I got a call from Bill last night. He said he was having problems with two men dressed in spacesuits with golden eyes. The same two he saw at the casino." She swung the helmet and threw it at him.

Lacey caught it and held it to his chest.

"That was the last I heard from Bill," Kate continued. "Pete's been to the quarry this morning and the place has been cordoned off, Navy Ordnance, or something, the bloke on the gate said there'd been an explosion and it was dangerous, wouldn't let Pete in, but he could see the place was a mess, everything blown to hell and I know now that's down to you. That helmet proves it."

Lacey sidled across the deck to sit on the opposite side of the saloon. The gorilla, Pete, turned with him, a disfiguring sneer on his face and his hand still held behind his back.

Lacey looked Kate in the eye. "I don't know where Bill is."

Kate grunted. "Something tells me you're a lying bastard but it don't matter, it'll come out in the wash and I'll know soon enough. It won't make any difference for you though. Bill had plans for you and that woman of yours and I'm going to make sure they happen. Where is she?"

"Visiting a friend. She won't be back today."

Kate grunted again. "Now why don't I believe that either. Every time you open your mouth a lie comes out. I'm not going to bother asking who you really are, I'm not that interested in your cover story, or whatever it is you call it, and I don't want to waste time having Pete beat it out of you. So we're all going for a little boat ride. Get this thing started."

"And if I don't?"

Kate inclined her head. "Pete."

The big man pushed himself upright and stepped across the deck, left hand outstretched and right hand drawing a double-edged combat knife from its sheath.

Lacey stood, swung the helmet hard against the knife hand using the momentum to turn into Pete's body to ram his elbow into a soft gut. Air wheezed out of Pete's lungs and he doubled over. Lacey's clenched knuckles smashed the bridge of his nose in a reverse fist strike. He fell backwards hitting his head on the helm seat on the way down. Lacey spun again and raised the helmet to finish him off.

"No!" Kate shouted.

He shot her a glance. She had a pistol held in both hands pointed at his head. It looked as if she knew how to use it. The pistol had a muffler attached.

"I can kill you now but I rather not take the risk unless you force me to it," she said. "Get the fuckin' engines started before I lose my temper."

"And forget you're a lady," Lacey said.

"Don't push it."

Lacey held up his hands and then placed the helmet carefully on the chart table, its golden eye reflecting Kate's face. "Your wish is my command." He looked down at the hunched form of Pete holding his hand to his flattened nose. "Tell your ape not to bleed on my deck."

"That's the least of your troubles but it's a point. Pete, go and bleed over the side and get Mick the Mugger to come aboard instead of you. I need someone who can handle himself. You can help take off the ropes."

"Cast off the lines," Lacey said, "to be correct."

"You really like pushing your luck, don't you, Arnold."

Lacey put the throttles in neutral and started both engines. "What's life for if not to be lived on the edge?"

"I'll remind you of that in a little while," Kate said. She glanced aft and saw the other man take Pete's place. He signalled the lines were off.

Kate nodded. "You can take us out now, nice and steady."

"Where to?"

"Doesn't matter, just keep going straight ahead."

"You know it's all over, don't you Kate," Lacey said. "The drugs, the tie in with the Chinese, we know all about it."

"We?"

"You don't think I came here off my own bat, do you?" It was a mistake to kill Forrestal."

"He couldn't keep his nose out of our business."

"Not after he'd spotted your Narcosub."

She pulled a pained face. "That was another problem. We ran the sub into the Dart on a high

424

tide all the way to that Mill Creek where it got too shallow and it had to surface. We unloaded on one of the pontoons opposite the Noss boatyard. It was dark, we thought we wouldn't be seen, but that Yank was watching from that navy college. He must have had binoculars and he must have seen Ling-Ling because when he recognised her at the casino he made a beeline for her, like he was smitten but he was trying to suss her out. He must have followed her the next time we tried running the sub up the Dart for a delivery but we saw him and that was that. Moved his car back to Dartmouth and cleaned it up so there'd be no tie in with the boatyard. We changed to picking up at sea after that."

"So Bill killed him … or was it Ling-Ling?"

Kate laughed but it was harsh and humourless. "No, that was me. I stood to lose too much and I like to keep my hand in. Let's the men know they can't screw with me just because I'm a woman." She waved the pistol. "Shot him with this. It's going overboard when I'm done with you."

72

Lacey steered the big boat out through the mouth of the Dart and headed due south at a slow twelve knots; he wasn't in any hurry to get wherever they were going and Kate appeared to be in a chatty mood. It was obvious she wasn't about to let him live to tell the tale. He wanted to keep her talking, once she stopped it would get serious. He glanced over his shoulder and saw the new gorilla sitting on the aft deck with a Czech made Skorpion sub machine gun on his lap. Behind them rode a twenty-foot rib with Pete and another man in it. Kate wasn't taking any chances.

He took a look at her. "You're full of surprises."

"I like to keep people guessing."

"What's with the Chinese tie-up?"

"Wondered when you'd get around to asking that. They put the money up for the casino. There was a hole in that market after the pandemic closed the others down and it was a good way for the dealers to pay for the goods without anyone batting an eye. It was my Bill who pulled it off. He had an association with them dealing for weapons during the Bosnian war. He was kicked out of Serbia, after the Brits and the Yanks bombed them out, but he kept in touch with his contacts. He was only too happy to help them after they'd helped him and he hated you Yanks and the Brits, always looking for the chance to get his own back."

"So he opted to get people hooked on drugs."

"You've got a small mind, Arnold. You're only seeing the small picture. It wasn't just heroin and cocaine we were peddling. When the signal came we were going to dose up the drugs with something else."

"You were going to start another pandemic."

"Oh, caught on at last have we? That's right, all those smart young things who thought they were safe from Covid-19, busy sniffing stuff up their noses for fun were going to get more than they bargained for. This time it was specially engineered for the younger set, the ones of working age who travel, set to blow the economy of the west well and truly apart this time. This variant is contagious after three days but takes four weeks for the symptoms to show. Imagine how fast that would spread."

"And what were you getting out of it?"

"Bill was getting his revenge in spades. Me, I was plenty in pocket with the prospect of my businesses going through the roof. Sex, you've no idea what those twenty-something girls will do for a few quid to finance their habits, drugs, black market deals, food shortages, supply and demand. I was set to make a fortune before you turned up. I had the only vaccines in Europe. I could sell them to the rich wankers for twenty grand a pop."

"Don't you think the police will get your connection to all this. Why make it worse for yourself?"

"Oh, do grow up, Arnold. I wasn't born yesterday. My fingerprints are nowhere near any of this. Pierce and that tart of a wife of his will go down for it. I get the feeling Bill isn't in any position to worry about his part in it and my boys here have kept a low profile, let the Serbs do all the dirty work and drive the trucks with the drug deliveries. My boys kept it clean. We'll go back to London and let the dust settle. Me, I was just an innocent housewife with no idea what the hubby was up to."

"They won't believe you."

"Course they won't, not Johnny Copley's sister, but they won't have no proof and I can afford a good lawyer."

"Got it all planned out, haven't you?"

"Yes, dear, I have." She stood and looked behind the boat at the distant and disappearing coastline. "This is far enough." She turned and called. "Oi, Mick, get your arse in here." She turned back to Lacey. "Stop the boat."

He put the throttles in neutral and the boat gradually drifted to a stop.

Kate waved the pistol. "Right, up top."

Lacey raised his eyebrows and she gave him her now familiar icy smile.

"I don't want no evidence, no bullet holes in the walls, no blood on the carpets. That's why I didn't want Pete bleeding all over the place. This boat is going to be like that Marie Celeste, found drifting and empty. We'll clean up after you've gone, no prints, no DNA, apart from yours. We know what we're doing.

428

"No funny stuff, Mick's no pushover like Pete and despite what I've just said, he'll make a sieve of you if you cut up rough." She jerked her thumb upwards and Lacey followed her up the steps to the flybridge with the gorilla following just out of reach with his Skorpion pointed at his back.

She stood aside and let him pass so that he was on the starboard side behind the helm position. She leant the back of her thighs on the low port side screen as Mick came to stand beside her. She levelled the pistol at Lacey's head. He dived for the helm as she fired, smashed the port throttle full ahead and pulled down hard on the wheel.

The powerful boat leapt forward and heeled hard to starboard throwing Mick over the side and into the sea. Kate lost her balance and fell on the deck, the pistol flying from her grip. The sharp acceleration pinned her to the side as the boat careered in a circle but she clawed her way to where the pistol was lodged against the coaming.

Lacey flipped his jacket wide and his fingers found the butt of his hidden Sig. "Leave it, Kate."

She ignored him and picked up the pistol. She levered herself to her feet and braced against the screen, an insane look on her face.

"Don't," Lacey said and pushed out his left arm.

She did not stop, swinging the pistol muzzle towards his head.

He had no choice. He snapped up the Sig and fired twice, so fast the two shots sounded as one. The hollow point bullets punched into her chest and tossed her over the side to follow Mick into the water.

He pulled back the throttle and straightened the helm. The following rib was tossing on the ravaged water like a kid in a bouncy castle as the two men tried to pull the hefty and waterlogged Mick over its rubber side. Lacey steered back to hailing distance.

"It's over boys. Go back to London. Go find yourselves another employer, this one's cashed in her chips."

He accelerated away. He doubted whether the three men would disagree with him. There was no pay day in it. He wondered whether they'd bother to look for Kate's body and thought it unlikely. They would cut and run.

He set course back to the marina and went down to make himself a coffee. He had just filled his mug when the sat phone came to life. He snatched it from its cradle. "Yes?"

"It's Mark."

"Yes, General?"

"More news from Mozambique, from the surviving SEA lads."

"And?"

"It's not good. They followed the rebels for a while but lost them. They were headed north, back towards their stronghold in Tanzania. They've taken Andee with them. They're not sure of her condition but it can't be good, they're never gentle with women."

"Right, thanks for letting me know. When are the teams due to leave for Mozambique?"

"Soon. It's taken a while to get organised."

"I understand. I think we're more or less done here. The fat lady's sung her last song."

"I've seen the report you posted yesterday. Ben will be getting back to you." Sparrow paused then said, "sorry to be the bearer of bad news."

"We don't shoot the messengers anymore. Thanks, Mark." He cut the connection.

73

Gill was surprised to see Lacey's Discovery missing from the car park when she returned from the hospital. She walked to the boat and noticed a few small blood spots on the normally pristine deck by the port rail. Frowning she eased open the glass sliding door with its still broken lock and stepped into the saloon. She called but got no reply then she noticed the helmet on the chart table. She dropped her bag on a seat and picked up the helmet. It was unlike Lacey to keep his kit on show. She turned the helmet over and saw a light blinking inside the visor, the low battery warning LED.

Gill frowned again and turned the helmet upright. She noticed that the video recording button was depressed and switched it off. Lacey had been running the video recorder and she wondered why. She found the slot where the micro data card was housed and eased it out with her nails. Lacey's laptop was still on the table. She had been given the password as part of her briefing; in case Lacey didn't make it.

She plugged the card into the laptop's slot and ran the video. Her jaw dropped and she watched open-mouthed as Kate spilled the beans. Never in her wildest nightmares had she imagined that Kate was Forrestal's killer. She watched with mounting concern as Lacey was led up the steps to the flybridge. The boat began spinning at a fantastic rate with the horizon whirling past. Then she saw a body drop past the side window too fast to recognise who it was. Two rapid bangs sounded, another body toppled past the window and she drew in a sharp breath. The spinning stopped and the sound of a racing engine ebbed away, a sound she had not noticed until it was gone. She waited with her breath held and a hand to her throat until Lacey appeared and she let it out in one long relieved gasp. He disappeared from view and then came back in shot with a mug in his hand just as a phone jangled. She only heard his side of the conversation but she could tell by his voice it was not good news.

He disappeared again up the steps and the rest of the video was a long view of the sea through the window and the buildings on the Kingswear side as the boat was moored back at the marina. The last shot before the screen went black was of Lacey walking up the finger pontoon towards the marina office.

She waited an hour for Lacey to return but he hadn't shown up. Gill guessed where he might be and went to her car. She knew she had been right when she nosed her Mercedes alongside the Discovery in the car park at Haytor Rocks.

She looked up and saw a lone figure sitting on top of the rock. She climbed up and sat beside him. "Thought I'd find you here. King of all you survey."

He didn't look at her when he replied, his eyes fixed across the moor. "I don't feel much like a king. I don't like killing women. Now I've killed two in two days."

"You had no choice. It was an accident the first time and I saw the video of Kate waving a pistol at you and confessing all. Quite a turn up."

He did look at her now, the ghost of a smile crinkling his eyes. "Clever of you to find it."

She pulled her knees up to her chin and circled them with her arms. "Clever of you to think of recording it with the helmet."

He squeezed his eyes shut. "I didn't expect to walk away from that one. I had to leave something for the boys back at HQ to get their teeth into."

She lifted her chin from her knees. "What's going to happen now, Rick?"

"I guess you and I are redundant. We did what we came to do."

"Was it just a one-night stand, you and me?"

"I have to go away, Gill. I have to go to Mozambique."

"That call you took?"

"Yes. It was from General Sparrow. Not good news about Andee; they've lost her trail. I have to go with the search teams. We may no longer be in a relationship but I owe Andee a lot and I just can't stand by and leave her to her fate without trying my damnedest to find her."

Gill's heart lurched at the surprise revelation that his marriage was over and thought for a few seconds before replying. "Not down to me …?"

He shook his head. "No, it was already over, I've known for a while but just didn't want to face facts. But I still need to go ... for both our sakes."

"I'll be here when you get back."

He turned his head to gaze across the moor as if reaffirming a long-held friendship. "I know, I'm counting on it." He waited for a few seconds to let his words sink in then continued. "I've arranged to leave the boat here as a permanent berth holder as I don't know how long I'll be away and I don't have the time to sail her to Chichester. Can you drive me home once we get Blake to clear us with Inspector Craddock?"

She leaned into him. "Least I can do."

He reached across and took her hand. "Thanks. Maybe there's something I can do for you in the meantime."

"Oh?"

"How much do you need to keep your business running for a year?"

She sat upright, holding on to his fingers as if she never wanted him to slip away. "I don't know ... maybe a hundred and fifty... if it's not too much to ask."

"Dollars?"

She grinned. "No, a hundred and fifty-thousand pounds, you nutcase. If business doesn't pick up in a year I'll know it's time to call it a day." She chewed her lip and then blurted, "If it doesn't, I won't be able to repay you."

"It's not a loan ... or a gift. I'm buying fifty percent of the business."

"Forty-nine percent, I'm not giving up the majority vote. The rest we can sort when you get back."

He shook her fingers. "Deal."

"Rick … right this minute … I think I love you."

74

Epilogue

Blake eased himself into a more comfortable position as he faced Gill across her desk in Camberley. Stu came in and put a cup of tea on the corner of the desk, stood back and folded his arms across his chest as he waited.

Blake raised his eyebrows at Gill.

"Whatever you've come to say, Colonel, you can say in front of Stu. He's like a priest in the confessional, it won't go any further."

Blake nodded. "Very well, I know about Dalgleish. Get a chair, man, as this is likely to take some time."

Stu grinned and pulled a chair away from its usual place by the wall."

Gill rested on her elbows and leaned forward. "Let's have it then, sir."

Blake looked mildly surprised at her use of the honorific. "Well, where shall I begin? Let me see. The Chinese of course have denied all knowledge of their plot. Diplomatic channels have been burning up over the past week with accusation and counter accusation. The Chinese government declare it is all a western plot to blacken their good standing in the world and attribute the blame in retrospect for the Covid-19 outbreak of three years ago. Our masters have made it plain they will not tolerate any form of grey warfare but are batting on a sticky wicket as we have no absolute proof that the Chinese government was in any way to blame. There are elements within the communist party and the People's Liberation Army that work with a certain autonomy which insulates the actual government from any blame. The Chinese government says that if any Chinese national was involved in illegal activity then they are criminals out for their own ends used by British gangsters to feather their own nests. As an argument it has a sort of elegance to it, we really don't have enough proof and we as a nation cannot afford to alienate the Chinese in public. That is just as well as we do not wish to cause a panic in the markets that the thought of another more deadly pandemic would bring."

"So we are just going to let that sleeping dragon lie," Gill said.

Blake gave her a humourless smile. "Politics, my dear, and global trade which we desperately need to keep our economy afloat. We cannot allow any blips to appear on our financial radar."

"It stinks," Stu said.

Blake shrugged. "Of course it does, Mister Dalgleish. Geopolitics at play is never a fair game. However, the fact that they know that we know and if we know the Americans know, they pursued this particular grey policy, it will most likely deter them from trying it again anytime soon.

"Brigadier Reid had kindly sent me a copy of the Bilic woman's confession. Coupled with the report from Porton Down which more or less substantiates her claim as to the efficacy of the virus, it appears we have had a very close shave. The mine at Buckfastleigh was cleared and sealed with all the virus vials and the drugs in those black boxes destroyed ..."

"But not all the vaccines, I assume," Gill interrupted.

Blake gave her a cynical smile. "That would be counter-productive, wouldn't it? We have kept some for analysis so that our wonderful pharmaceutical companies can set up a rapid Cure-Vac production line if needed.

"The quarry is now closed and an unfortunate accident with the store of gelignite they use for blasting has been blamed. I doubt if anyone outside our immediate circle will be any the wiser.

"What about our part in this? Has it been squared with the local police?" Gill asked.

"The answer to that question comes in several parts. The admirable Detective Inspector Craddock has built an extensive file on the happenings at the Golden Nugget Casino. She has DNA, nine-millimetre bullet cases which belong to no weapons since discovered, a rough time line and a confused and varying story from Mister Pierce who, together with his wife, is to be charged with perverting the course of justice by moving and hiding the bodies of the deceased. That carries a life sentence.

There was no DNA or fingerprint evidence other than in Pierce's office and in the lift car where Missus Arnold has admitted her presence on two former occasions. None of the recovered cartridge cases held fingerprints which encourages the police to think that it was a professional hit team engaged by a rival criminal drug cartel. The two oriental men who were seen leaving the premises after the assumed time of the shooting have not been found which adds credence to that theory.

"The woman who made the emergency call has not come forward either and cannot be traced. The three victims all appear to be illegal immigrants of oriental origin who have no records of any sort; something else for which Mister Pierce may be called upon to answer.

"The Americans have been apprised of the commander's part in uncovering this sorry mess and his family told that he was something of a hero who did not die in vain although they will never know the full story. The commander was just navy, not navy intelligence as we conjectured but a man with a nose for the out of place; a nose which unfortunately got him killed.

"None of the firearms confiscated from the casino matched the bullets that killed the commander although they were of similar calibre. To compound the inspector's woes with regard to this case, the co-owner of the casino Jovan Bilic, and its head security officer are both missing, believed fled to parts unknown, possibly Eastern Europe. Bilic's wife has also disappeared and it appears to the police that they have run off together. They are suspected of travelling on false passports as there is no record of them having left the country. It is more difficult these days but

Europol has been invited to be on the lookout for them although cooperation is sadly declining now."

"There's nothing to tie Colonel Lacey and me to these occurrences then," Gill said.

"Nothing at all. Once the police were given all your details and you both appeared as white as snow, the accusations against Mister Arnold, a man of impeccable character, were dismissed as trouble-making by Pierce for reasons of his own.

"Which brings me to a rather sore point. "I was unaware at the beginning of Mister Murphy's role in all this. It was something of a shock to know that he was involved. The police questioned him with regard to his DNA being found inside the casino and in the alley behind the casino and asked about any involvement in the subsequent killings of which he was unaware. In the event we had already put a cover operation in place, that he was an off-duty Special Forces operator who had stumbled upon misdeeds and had paid the price for his public-spirited interference. His statement included references to illicit drugs payments and a recollection that he had overheard Bilic and the Chinese security officer admitting their part in Commander Forrestal's murder. The fact that drug dealing has declined significantly in Devon over recent days adds credence to the story.

"Mister Murphy, at your insistence, is now recovering in a private hospital in Surrey and will be troubled no further."

Stu smirked. "I said it was worth while keeping the private medical insurance going."

"As Mister Murphy is no longer on our books as a sub-contractor, his care falls outside our remit. Something for you to bear in mind for the future, Gill," Blake said.

Gill sat up and gave him an amazed look. "What future, Blake?"

"There's always room for a woman with your talent to work for her country. The powers-that-be are very grateful for your help with this matter. Who knows what tomorrow may bring."

"No way, Blake. I'm done, finished with all this. You just pay me the ten grand you owe me."

"Ah, yes." Blake pulled some sheets of A4 from an inner pocket and slowly unfolded them. He waved a hand over the pages. "These expenses seem rather outrageous. Clothes and shoes from some of the most expensive outlets in London." He spread his hands in a helpless gesture. "It's outside my area but I'm told the powers-that-be, despite their initial gratitude, cannot condone this sort of excess. I'm afraid we will have to deduct over four-thousand pounds from your fee to cover the cost ... unless ..."

"Unless what?"

Blake raised his eyebrows in unspoken answer.

"In your dreams, Blake," Gill said.

Blake smiled. "I know that Colonel Lacey has invested heavily in your little business but that largesse can't last forever. At some point you will need to remember who your friends are." He stood and picked his umbrella from where it hung on the arm of his chair, walked to the door and turned. *"Hasta que nos encontremos de nuevo,* Gill. Until we meet again."

The End.

Author's Notes

Now is the time to put matters into perspective. I've tried a little crystal ball gazing as to various outcomes two years in the future; only time will tell if my foresight is proven accurate.

It will come as no surprise that I have spent many happy years sailing Chichester Harbour, the Solent, the River Dart and the seaways along the Devon coast. I was a member of the Royal Dart Yacht Club for some years and must make it plain that the people we knew there were nothing like some of the characters I have portrayed in this story. Unceasingly polite and enthusiastic about their hobby, it was a pleasure to be with them.

The Chair of the Welcoming Committee is a fictitious position. What I can say with some certainty is that the restaurant and the food were extremely good the last time we visited.

I have spent much time in research. The details on gold mining in Devon are accurate and there was a very small quantity of gold found in the area around Buckfastleigh in the 19th century. It is also true to say that any gold found by panning belongs to the Crown and it is rare for permission to be granted for it to be removed from the site.

The Royal Navy strike cruiser *HMS Norfolk* is an invention. The last ship, the 6th to bear the name, was a Duke Class Type 23 frigate which was sold to the Chilean Navy in 2006. At the time of writing, there is no *HMS Norfolk* serving. Heavily armed, multi-role strike cruisers were first mooted by the United States Navy in the mid 1970s to counter the threat from similar Kirov class, nuclear-powered battle cruisers, being built by the USSR. Congress rejected the design in favour of shoehorning complex weapons systems into destroyers.

Narco submarines are frequently used by the Colombian drug cartels to import cocaine into the United States. A narco submarine (also called a drug sub) is a type of custom ocean-going self-propelled submersible or semi-submersible vessel built for smugglers. Some agencies have expressed concerns such vessels could potentially be used for purposes other than smuggling. The capabilities of these crafts is increasing, their operating areas are widening, and their numbers growing. It has recently been reported that a semi-submersible vessel has been found by the Spanish Policia Nacional in a warehouse in Malaga.

Newer submarines are fully submersible making them difficult to detect visually, by radar, or infrared systems.

The use of a mother ship to transport the submarines is my own invention.

Speaking of inventions, the ISPA fighting suit is loosely based on a combination of the 'Iron Man' suit under development by Raytheon which is expected to give the wearer extraordinary strength and speed of movement, the Tactical Assault Light Operator Suit (TALOS) programme which was discontinued in the USA in 2019 and a 'Future Soldier' vision, unveiled at one of the world's biggest defence shows in 2015, which was then in development by the MoD's Defence Science and Technology Laboratory. The downside to the Raytheon suit is the need for a power source which is beyond current portable battery technology and is the reason I have not given the suits in this story superhuman qualities. Fourth generation body armour, such as the Virtus body armour, currently in use with British forces, gives protection against high velocity 7.62mm ammunition as used in the AK47 when fitted with Enhanced Combat Body Armour (ECBA) plates.

After war broke out in the former Yugoslav republic of Croatia in the autumn of 1991 and in Bosnia in April 1992, Arkan and his units of Serb Volunteer Guards, also known as Arkan's Tigers, moved to attack different territories in these countries. In Croatia, the Tigers fought in various locales in Eastern Slavonia.

Allied bombing campaigns played a major part in ending the conflict.

Now on to a more contentious issue:

There has been much debate and speculation about the origins of the Covid-19 virus. However it is not beyond the bounds of possibility that an advanced scientific nation such as China or Russia, (which has a track record in using chemical and biological agents for its own ends) having noted the disruption that a virus can cause, would view the chance to gain ascendency in political, military and economic terms as an opportunity worth the risk.

Earlier this year (2021), a World Health Organisation-led mission to China said it was not looking further into the question of whether the virus escaped from a lab, which it considered highly unlikely.

However, in a later press briefing, director general Dr. Tedros Adhanom Ghebreyesus, head of the WHO, said: "Some questions have been raised as to whether some hypotheses have been discarded. The theory that Covid-19 originated from a laboratory in Wuhan has not been dismissed by investigators as has been suggested."

Further evidence that Beijing considered the military potential of SARS coronaviruses has come to light and has subsequently raised fresh fears over the cause of Covid-19. A dossier by Peoples Liberation Army scientists and Chinese health officials examined the manipulation of diseases to make weapons. Tom Tugendhat, Chairman of the foreign affairs committee, is on record as saying, "this document raises major concerns about the ambitions of some of those who advise the top Chinese Communist Party leadership".

Intelligence agencies suspect Covid-19 may be the result of an inadvertent Wuhan lab leak but there is, as yet, no evidence it was intentionally released. Tom Tugendhat continued, "even under the tightest controls these weapons are dangerous."

President Biden has since launched a 90 day enquiry into the relevance of such evidence which the Chinese government has labelled just a political gambit to discredit them.

About the Author

Whilst studying at the University of London Ed joined the Officers Training Corps and was commissioned into the Royal Regiment of Fusiliers before eventually joining The Parachute Regiment TA.

In civilian life, he founded a graphic design company where he honed his writing skills on marketing campaigns for national and multi-national companies.

Ed has personal experience with many of the weapon systems he writes about. He is the holder of three gold medals gained in national Sport Rifle competitions and has represented Lincolnshire over several years as a member of the County Lightweight Sport Rifle Team. He is an acknowledged marksman with both rifles and pistols.

He also is the holder of a Royal Yachting Association Yacht Master's Offshore Certificate and has a Maritime Radio Operator Certificate of Competence for VHF radio transmitters.

He took early-retirement which enabled him to devote more time to writing and lives in the Lincolnshire Wolds with his wife Barb.

'*The Grey Zone*' is his fifteenth novel.

Printed in Great Britain
by Amazon